## VELVET KISSES

"I'm sorry, she said. "I won't bother you now—"

He took her hand and drew her inside, closing the door behind her. "You're never a bother."

She took one look at the warmth in Leon's eyes and burst into tears.

"Allow me." He gently wiped Jurissa's wet cheeks as she closed her eyes. He dabbed her lids, and before she could open her eyes, she felt his warm lips caress them. His lips trailed down her cheek, finally settling over her mouth in a tender kiss that left her breathless. His arms urged her closer and she came willingly, remembering and needing the comforting feel of his body.

His lips parted against hers and she opened her lips to him, feeling the pleasing warmth he'd kindled inside her flare into sudden flame. She clung to him, knowing that nothing like this had ever happened to her, and she wanted the wonderful sensation to go on and on, to never end . . .

## ZEBRA'S GOT THE ROMANCE
## TO SET YOUR HEART AFIRE!

**RAGING DESIRE** (2242, $3.75)
by Colleen Faulkner

A wealthy gentleman and officer in General Washington's army, Devon Marsh wasn't meant for the likes of Cassie O'Flynn, an immigrant bond servant. But from the moment their lips first met, Cassie knew she could love no other . . . even if it meant marching into the flames of war to make him hers!

**TEXAS TWILIGHT** (2241, $3.75)
by Vivian Vaughan

When handsome Trace Garrett stepped onto the porch of the Santa Clara ranch, he wove a rapturous spell around Clara Ehler's heart. Though Clara planned to sell the spread and move back East, Trace was determined to keep her on the wild Western frontier where she belonged — to share with him the glory and the splendor of the passion-filled TEXAS TWILIGHT.

**RENEGADE HEART** (2244, $3.75)
by Marjorie Price

Strong-willed Hannah Hatch resented her imprisonment by Captain Jake Farnsworth, even after the daring Yankee had rescued her from bloodthirsty marauders. And though Jake's rock-hard physique made Hannah tremble with desire, the spirited beauty was nevertheless resolved to exploit her femininity to the fullest and gain her independence from the virile bluecoat.

**LOVING CHALLENGE** (2243, $3.75)
by Carol King

When the notorious Captain Dominic Warbrooke burst into Laurette Harker's eighteenth birthday ball, the accomplished beauty challenged the arrogant scoundrel to a duel. But when the captain named her innocence as his stakes, Laurette was terrified she'd not only lose the fight, but her heart as well!

*Available wherever paperbacks are sold, or order direct from the Publisher. Send cover price plus 50¢ per copy for mailing and handling to Zebra Books, Dept. 2466, 475 Park Avenue South, New York, N.Y. 10016. Residents of New York, New Jersey and Pennsylvania must include sales tax. DO NOT SEND CASH.*

# JANE TOOMBS
# Creole Betrayal

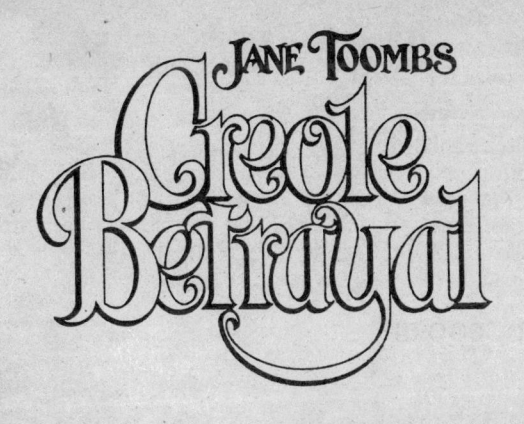

**ZEBRA BOOKS**
**KENSINGTON PUBLISHING CORP.**

ZEBRA BOOKS

are published by

Kensington Publishing Corp.
475 Park Avenue South
New York, NY 10016

Copyright © 1988 by Jane Toombs

All rights reserved. No part of this book may be reproduced in any form or by any means without the prior written consent of the Publisher, excepting brief quotes used in reviews.

First printing: September, 1988

Printed in the United States of America

## Chapter One

Jurissa Campbell Winterton stood at the rail of the three-master merchant ship *Yarmouth* and breathed deeply of the cool salt air, enjoying the feel of the ship plunging through the water — quite like riding a spirited horse, she thought. Turning her face up to the sun, she basked in its meager warmth, reflecting that this was her only glimpse of the sun in what seemed weeks.

The first days out of Boston had been like her wedding day: rainy and cold. Not a good omen for the marriage, her guardian, Arabel, would have said. Worse, the marriage took place on a Saturday. Arabel's rhyme ran through Jurissa's head again:

Monday for health,
Tuesday for wealth,
Wednesday the best day of all;
Thursday for losses,
Friday for crosses,
And Saturday no luck at all.

No luck at all. Perhaps that's why Philip had been confined to the cabin, seasick, since the voyage began. No, not exactly. The first night out he'd had too much to drink and the excess had made him ill. Afterward his mal de mer began. She sighed.

"It's far too pleasant a day to be sad," a male voice said from behind her, speaking in French.

Jurissa turned, unable to prevent her lips from curving into a pleased smile. "How nice to see you, Monsieur du Motier," she replied in the same language, wondering if, in her hurry to leave the cabin, she'd tied the ribbons of her bonnet into a decent bow. How awful to have him find her less than neat. She didn't understand why it was so important to her to appear attractive in his eyes, but she knew she tried her best.

"That's better. You have a lovely smile, Madam Winterton. You should never be sad; it's a shame to deprive the world of your smile."

He had a graceful way with words that charmed her, and his obvious admiration warmed her heart. Was it because Leon du Motier, though an American by birth, was of French descent? Was that the reason she found him so fascinating? Arabel's lover, Tanguay D'Artagnan, had been a Parisian aristocrat and oh, so romantic. Perhaps Frenchmen *were* more romantic than other men.

Jurissa flushed, turning her face from Leon. It was wrong of her to think this way. Not only was she a married woman but her husband, who was decidedly not French, lay ill in his bunk. Philip hadn't yet had a chance to show her how romantic he could be. She really shouldn't be speaking to Leon at all.

But, it would be so lonesome if she couldn't. She

hadn't met anyone aboard except Leon and though she tried to nurse Philip, his sickness made his temper short. She couldn't seem to do anything that suited him, and he kept ordering her out of their cabin.

"I can't stand that prissy smile of yours one second more," he'd told her only a few minutes ago. "For God's sake go up on deck and leave me alone. Yubah knows how to do for me better than you do, anyway."

That was another thing: Philip's slaves, Yubah and Silas. Arabel hadn't approved of slavery and she'd taught Jurissa it was an evil practice. But Philip was from Virginia where, he said, everyone owned slaves; as they did in New Orleans. He'd laughed at her protests, saying there was nothing wrong with slavery. What did that spinster who'd raised her know of the real world? Jurissa couldn't decide what to say or do — after all, Philip was the husband she'd agreed to honor and obey — and so far she'd just avoided Yubah and Silas as much as possible.

"We'll be entering the Gulf of Mexico soon." Leon du Motier waved a hand toward the rail where haze hanging over the water hid any sign of land. "The weather there will be warm and sunny. No more rain or gloom."

"March is always gloomy in Boston," she said, glancing at him under her eyelashes and thinking he looked very debonair lounging against the rail in his well-cut brown frock coat and tan trousers, his hat tipped casually to the left. Every time she saw him she found something new to admire.

"New Orleans in March will make you forget gloom and gray days. Ah, you'll love our city." Leon smiled, his teeth gleaming white against his dark mustache.

How handsome he was! Over six feet tall and slim,

with an elegant grace she secretly admired. He had black, curling hair, and brown eyes that were sometimes soft, but always deep. He was, he'd told her, twenty-six, eight years older than she. Philip was thirty-five and starting to put on weight—was it so disloyal to wish he didn't have a paunch?

"New Orleans will also love you," Leon added. "Beautiful green-eyed women with hair of flame are a rarity among us."

Jurissa smoothed the green silk of her gown. *Was* she beautiful? Philip had never said so. But then they scarcely knew one another, so he hadn't had much of a chance.

But Leon compliments you, an inner voice said, and you've known him a shorter time than Philip.

Why did she feel more excited standing next to Leon than standing next to Philip? When Leon offered his arm to guide her along the deck, as he had once or twice before, her heart had pounded until she'd thought it might burst from her breast when she touched him with her gloved fingers. Her breath came short, and she'd tingled all over. Exactly the way Arabel had always described her French lover's slightest touch.

"Ah, Tanguay was a prince among men," Arabel would say, tears in her eyes, a hand over her heart. "How dare that riffraff lay hands on him as they did? Condemn him? 'O liberty! O liberty! What crimes are committed in thy name!'

"The guillotine is a jealous mistress, Jurissa. She took my Tanguay from me forever. I shall never again feel the wonder of his lips on mine."

Philip had kissed her only once, Jurissa thought; a mere brush of lips after the wedding ceremony. She'd been so dazed at the time she couldn't clearly recall how she'd felt, but she was certain that wonder hadn't been a part of it. Nor tingling. Perhaps everything would change when Philip recovered his health.

"You frown," Leon murmured. "Is it you don't believe me when I tell you how you will enchant New Orleans? Once we arrive you'll find I've told nothing but the truth."

Jurissa decided it might be fun to be the toast of the town. He had to be exaggerating, but she couldn't help taking pleasure from his extravagant praise. He was so wonderfully unlike the few men she'd met in her life: staid and proper, and dull. Except for Philip, of course. She didn't yet know him well enough to decide what he was like.

"I've never been anywhere except Boston," she confessed. "My guardian was something of a recluse."

"Then, in comparison, you'll be entering paradise." Leon's voice was fervent. "Flowers instead of snow, rice and gumbo instead of baked beans, people who smile instead of frown, soft breezes off the Gulf instead of the cold Atlantic wind. And the coffee! Only in New Orleans do they know how to brew coffee."

"My guardian taught me the French way," Jurissa said, her eyes shining. How she'd enjoy making coffee for Leon!

"Ah, the way I like it." Leon shifted into French: "Black as the devil, hot as hell, pure as an angel, sweet as love."

He smiled. "I can't wait to taste your—" He paused, leaning toward her so his lips were bare inches from hers as he all but whispered the last word—"brew."

She was sure the bones in her legs had dissolved

completely, so weak did she feel. His breath was warm against her face and she smelled the rich odor of tobacco mixed with a faint aroma she knew was Leon's alone. The combination enticed her senses. She wanted more. She wanted—what did she want?

Whatever it was, it was wrong. Wrong to want anything from Leon. She was a married woman!

Jurissa stepped back. "Monsieur, if you please," she began, trying to bring coolness into a voice that persisted in shaking. "I don't think you ought to do such—"

"Then you will have to stop being so alluring," he broke in gently, "for I can't help myself when you gaze at me with your fathomless sea eyes. To probe their depths—ah!"

"You mustn't say such things."

"Don't you like to hear them?" He smiled slightly.

He was well aware of how he made her feel, Jurissa decided, eyeing that smile. It wasn't fair that he knew so much about the world and she so little. Arabel had confided a great deal to her, but always vaguely.

"True love is always romantic," Arabel would often say, sighing. "It is marvelous. Magnificent. Glorious. 'Love is the whole history of a woman's life, it is but an episode in a man's.' Madame de Stael wrote those words and she was one who knew. I was the most fortunate of women to have my Tanguay love me as deeply as I loved him."

But I'm not in love with Leon du Motier, Jurissa told herself. We've just met. Besides, I've already agreed to love Philip as well as honor and obey him.

Could love be summoned by order and promise?

"Love catches you unawares," Arabel had added. "It's a mischievous child who creeps up to startle you, then beguiles you instead."

She wasn't in love with him, but Jurissa had to admit she found Leon du Motier beguiling.

A seagull mewed overhead and, looking up at the sound, she noticed people on deck. A middle-aged couple, both wearing black, walked past them and she moved farther away from Leon. Until today, the bad weather had kept the few other passengers in their cabins, leaving the deck to the sailors and to her and Leon. The sun had lured people out today. Perhaps it was for the best. Without privacy Leon would have to behave. And so would she.

With a start she noticed the gigantic black man standing behind Leon. Silas. He was the biggest Negro Jurissa had ever seen; very dark, over six and a half feet tall, with arms as huge as tree trunks. She'd never seen him smile. He looked as though he could pick up two ordinary men, one in each ham-sized fist, and lift them into the air without even straining. He didn't frighten her exactly but he did make her nervous. Evidently Leon noticed her uneasiness because he turned to glance behind him.

Silas bowed his head slightly. "Missus," he said in his low, gravelly voice, "Yubah done sent me. Massa Philip, he want you."

Leon watched Jurissa Winterton walk away from him. She was tall for a woman and slender but delectably curved where it counted. As a man, he thoroughly approved of the empire style women were wearing these days. The short, fitted velvet jacket that ended just below her breasts revealed their high swell, and the straight skirt of her green silk gown didn't conceal the intriguing sway of her hips.

*Mon Dieu,* how that innocent air of hers excited him. Yet she was married, so no longer a true innocent. Leon grimaced. He'd seen her husband only once, their first night out at sea, disgustingly drunk. The man had to be mad to drink himself into oblivion with a desirable woman like Jurissa waiting in their cabin.

He glanced again toward the big Negro, belatedly wondering if the slave had been sent to spy on Jurissa. The black man had disappeared. Leon shrugged. He'd enjoyed the flirtation; he'd more than enjoy bedding the charming Madam Winterton, but perhaps a bit of discretion was in order. He had no taste for being challenged to a duel over a married woman. Certainly his father would never understand, much less approve.

Jurissa, like every other woman, would soon learn to mask what she felt, but how charming that she hadn't yet realized how those eyes of hers mirrored every feeling, every thought. He'd be willing to bet that, in some secluded, appropriate spot, he could have had her a few moments ago. He felt warmth in his loins as he remembered her sweet, elusive scent. Dismayed, he frowned.

It would be the height of folly to lose his head over this eighteen-year-old auburn-haired beauty, no matter how eager she seemed. No matter that she spoke exquisite French with a most fascinating accent. No matter that she hung on his every word, those soft, rose-petal lips slightly, enticingly open. No matter what it may lead to, Leon vowed recklessly, he was going to taste those lips at least once before they docked in New Orleans.

Jurissa arrived in the cabin to find her husband still in bed and Yubah cowering on the floor like a frightened child, one hand to her face. A thin trickle of blood ran across her light brown fingers.

"Oh, dear, have you hurt yourself?" Jurissa asked, staring at the young woman. For the first time she realized that, despite Yubah's lush curves, the slave couldn't be much older than she.

"No, missus." Yubah's voice was muffled by her hand.

Jurissa leaned toward her and Yubah shrank away as though she were afraid.

"Get out of here, slut!" Philip ordered, rising onto one elbow and glaring down at the Negro woman.

Yubah scrambled to her feet and hurried out the door.

"What on earth happened?" Jurissa asked.

"The only thing an uppity nigger understands is the whip. Since it's packed I had to use my fist."

Jurissa's eyes widened. "You mean you hit her? In the face?"

Philip's blue eyes darkened. "Would you have me ignore a slave who won't do as she's ordered?"

"But striking her in the face? She was actually bleeding."

"Those high yellows sometimes get to thinking they're as good as white folks. Maybe she's learned her lesson." His lips turned up and Jurissa recoiled from the malevolence in his smile. "If she needs another lesson, I can always unpack the whip."

She stared at her husband in undisguised horror. Was he actually threatening to lash Yubah with a whip? Why the girl was smaller than she was, a tiny thing, no more than an inch or two over five feet.

"No," she breathed.

"For God's sake wipe that stupid look off your face," Philip ordered. "She belongs to me and I have the right to do whatever I want with her. And you won't interfere. Is that clear?"

Jurissa swallowed. Honor and obey, yes, but she had to speak up against injustice. It was wrong to beat a woman, slave or not. She took a deep breath and opened her mouth just as Philip sank back against the pillows with a groan.

"I'll never climb aboard another boat," he muttered. "Don't just stand there gawking at me. Can't you see how ill I am?"

Jurissa decided to hold her tongue for the moment and wait until Philip felt better. She'd learned a great deal about nursing, having taken care of Arabel during her guardian's last six months before she died. But, though she tried her best to make Philip comfortable, nothing she did suited him.

"It's all Monty's fault," he complained. "Monty and that scheming shrew he married."

Jurissa couldn't understand how he could blame his seasickness on Montague and Hildegarde Evans.

He lifted himself onto an elbow again. "You can't be so dim-witted you haven't figured it out by now." When her face continued to mirror her bewilderment, he snorted with disgust and continued. "I thought they were my friends. 'Help us out, Phil, there's a good fellow,' Monty begs. 'Come along to Boston with us in case we have trouble.'"

Philip motioned to her to put another pillow under his head. When he'd arranged himself to his satisfaction he went on. "Don't you see how cleverly they trapped me? Involved me in a situation where I had to marry you or be labeled a cad? Once he had me where he wanted me, Monty promised me money after the estate was settled but I calculate my chances of seeing a cent of it are dim. Promises don't fill anyone's pocket."

He fixed his pale blue eyes on Jurissa. "You fell into their net just as easily as I did, the both of us two pigeons set upon by cats."

"Trapped?" she said. "Fell into a net?"

He rolled his eyes. "Didn't that old spinster teach you anything? How do you think I got into your bed that night?"

Blood rushed to her face and she looked away as she remembered what happened. She'd been roused from a terrible dream of being crushed by an evil darkness, to the equally monstrous reality of Philip's body lying across hers, and the shocked faces of Hildegarde and Montague Evans staring down at her while Arabel's maid, holding her lamp high, peered unbelievably over Hildegarde's shoulder. Try as she might, Jurissa couldn't comprehend what was going on. Her mind seemed full of spiderwebs whose sticky strands trapped every thought. She couldn't even summon up the will to shove away the snoring Philip. All she'd been able to do was gape in bewilderment at the disapproving faces.

"I assumed you came into my room without me hearing you," Jurissa said finally, forcing herself to look at her husband.

"And so I did. Because you were sleeping the sleep of the drugged. As I was. The drug must have been in the wine Hildegarde insisted we have for a nightcap. Once we were beyond awareness, they carried you up and got you into your nightie, then brought me to your bed."

Jurissa's hand rose to her mouth to stifle her shocked gasp. "Mr. and Mrs. Evans *arranged* to find you in my bed?"

"So you do have a glimmer of intelligence. I was beginning to wonder. Of course they did. Marriage was the quickest way to get rid of you, and it had the undeniable advantage of being completely legal. They didn't want you hanging around while the estate was settled. What if a clever lawyer decided he'd make a few dollars by trying to carve a slice of the plum cake for you, Arabel's ward? If nothing else, you nursed the old woman and should have been paid for that."

"I'd never take money for caring for Arabel!" she cried indignantly.

"Perhaps not, but you'd never get her nephew Monty to believe that."

She stared at him, her mind sorting the pieces and fitting them together to create a sordid picture. What a ninny she'd been, believing everything the Evanses had told her, letting them manipulate her like a puppet on a string. Manipulate her into a marriage with a stranger she now wasn't sure she even liked. To be fair, though, Philip had been their puppet, too.

"You really didn't want to marry me, did you?" she said slowly.

He shrugged. "I'd have preferred a woman with money. Not that I don't intend to hound Monty for what he promised me."

"And we actually didn't have to get married at all," she added.

"You think not? Hildegarde took care the servants saw us in bed together. What would you have done if dear Hildegarde allowed word to get around about your wanton behavior with a man you scarcely knew? Where would you have gone when she turned you out? I was in almost as tricky a spot because I was too dazed to recall exactly how I did get into your bed or what I might have done once I was in it. They took care to rush the wedding, calling the priest in the same day, before our heads cleared."

That explained having to get married in a white summer gown because she didn't own a more suitable white dress, and Hildegarde said there wasn't time to order one. It explained why Father Bennett had taken her aside and so earnestly asked her if she was certain she wished to marry Philip Winterton. In her confused state of mind she'd naturally told the old priest yes.

What conniving people the Evanses were! she thought. She should have suspected there might be something amiss about them from the many times Arabel refused to invite her nephew and his wife to visit when he wrote that they'd like to come. Jurissa sighed. It was too late for regrets. What's done was done. She and Philip Winterton were man and wife, whether either had desired it or not.

"So we're married." Philip's tone was cynical.

For better or worse. She wouldn't look back, wouldn't reflect on what she might have done if she'd known what the Evanses were up to. Jurissa raised her chin and stared him in the eye.

Philip was no Leon de Motier: handsome, debonair and charming. In fact, he was a far from prepossessing sight in his rumpled nightshirt, his blond hair lank and greasy, his face stubbled with several days' growth of beard. The cruelty he'd shown to Yubah repulsed her.

Still, he *was* her husband. She owed him loyalty. The least she could do was set aside her reservations and give him a chance.

"You have my promise that I intend to make the best of it," she announced firmly, doing her utmost to banish the beguiling Monsieur du Motier from her mind once and for all.

## Chapter Two

By late afternoon Philip had improved enough to call for Silas and order the slave to help him dress. Jurissa returned to the deck to wait until her husband was ready to join her and found a knot of excited male passengers gathered at the starboard rail, staring out to sea. She caught sight of white sails some distance away.

"What did the mate say her name was?" a man asked.

"*Colombe*," another responded.

"That's dove in French. What could be more innocent?"

"Lafitte's men have a grisly sense of humor," a familiar voice, Leon's voice, said, speaking in English. "They would find it amusing to name their ship after that most innocent of birds."

Jurissa located him in the group—the most handsome by far of the men. She longed to edge closer but being a lady, she didn't intrude.

"Whoever may captain her," Leon continued, "I do not think is interested in the *Yarmouth*. She appears to be heading away from us. If she's crewed by freeboot-

19

ers, they're looking for an easier prize." He motioned toward the cannon near the bow, one of four above deck. "We have little to fear from that dove, even if she is a pirate masquerading as the bird of peace."

He noticed Jurissa standing a few feet away. Nodding to the men he'd been speaking to, he left them and strode to her side. Her heart began to pound as he smiled at her, his brown eyes telling her how delighted he was to be with her.

"You told me only good things about the Gulf," she said, looking up at him and hoping he couldn't tell how breathless his nearness made her. "I don't believe you mentioned pirates."

"Ah, well, even in Eden there was a snake. Lafitte and his men are the snakes in our paradise. We tolerate them — why not? After all, they smuggle in excellent French brandy."

"You actually deal with pirates in New Orleans?"

Leon shrugged. "I don't in person. We all know, though, the merchants handle smuggled and stolen goods. Who can blame them when they can buy such goods cheaply? And, of course, they pass on their savings to us. Lafitte's company lives on the salt marsh islands at the mouth of the Mississippi River. Barataria, we call the region. No one knows how many men live there. Women and children, too. Families."

Jurissa stared in amazement. The pirates had families? It seemed unbelievable. "Does no one object to pirates living in this Barataria?"

"The *Americain* governor, Claiborne, offered a reward of five hundred dollars for Lafitte's capture." Leon smiled one-sidedly. "The only result was that Lafitte offered fifteen hundred dollars for the governor."

She shook her head. "Your paradise sounds lawless to me. What has happened to the poor governor?"

"Governor Claiborne is safe enough with us. No matter how we Creoles wish him gone, our eyes are open to the realities of life. Napoleon himself sold Louisiana to the United States, and we've accepted being a part of your country, like it or not."

She raised her eyebrows. "You call yourself a Creole, not an American?"

He smiled. "First and always a Creole. It means I am French and born in New Orleans, though some who are of Spanish blood also claim the title."

She'd never met anyone so different, so fascinating. His English was excellent, with an intriguing accent that she adored. His voice was gentle and rich and, when he spoke, the words seemed to settle into her bones, to become a part of her. She could listen to him forever, be it English or French.

"French, my dear, is the language of love," Arabel always insisted when she was teaching young Jurissa the language. "If you don't learn the words, how will you understand love?"

Now that she'd met Leon, Jurissa had a glimmering of what Arabel had been talking about. When he spoke French to her, Leon's voice all but caressed the words and she couldn't help but be warmed. If he whispered French love words into her ear she might very well melt like wax. Not that she'd let him do any such thing. She wouldn't listen if he tried. Philip was the only man who had the right to speak of love to her.

She moved a step back from Leon. "I'm waiting for my husband to join me," she said stiffly.

"He is better, then." There was no inflection in Leon's

voice.

"Yes."

"I'm happy to hear it."

He didn't sound happy and, to her shame, her heart rejoiced.

It was time to bow and leave the delectable Jurissa, Leon told himself. Leave her to that overweight blond sot of a man who didn't appreciate what he had. He reached for her hand, his eyes on hers.

Her hand was small and yet he felt its strength as her fingers tightened on his. Her breasts rose as she took a deep breath, and the cashmere shawl fell open. He caught his own breath.

She'd left off the velvet jacket. The neckline of the green gown she wore was modest enough but its high waist molded the silk against her round and firm breasts, and he saw her nipples were erect. For him. If he'd had any doubt of it, the flicker of desire in her eyes openly revealed her feelings. She wanted him as he wanted her.

*Bigre!* Didn't her oaf of a husband have enough sense to keep an enticing woman like this satisfied? Possibly it was due to a lack of manhood. Or the whiskey. Whatever the reason, there was bound to be trouble.

He still had her hand in his, nestled there as though wishing to stay forever. If he drew her into his arms he knew she would fit against him perfectly for she was exactly tall enough. The perfect size for him. Her breasts would be soft and yielding against his chest; his hands would fit neatly over her enticing bottom. His groin tightened and he dropped her hand abruptly. Never had a woman had such a profound effect on him. And in public!

"Missus," a woman's voice said gently. "Massa Philip, he be coming."

Startled, he glanced quickly at the the petite brown-skinned woman who'd come up to them so quietly he hadn't heard her approach.

"Thank you, Yubah," Jurissa said, seemingly as surprised as he.

The slave, having delivered her warning, slipped past them and away.

Leon's eyebrows rose. Was Jurissa so much less innocent than she looked? Was she so accomplished at flirting with men that her maid had orders to let her know when it was safe and when it wasn't?

"I can't get used to the idea of slaves," Jurissa said. "They make me uncomfortable."

He blinked. "I don't understand."

"I was taught it isn't right to buy and sell human beings. To own them as though they were animals. Like my husband owns Silas and Yubah."

"I was taught that if you own slaves, you must treat them fairly," he countered. "The du Motier motto is 'Family Honor, Fairness To All.' We would not be able to work our plantation without our slaves. Knowing this, we deal honestly and kindly with them."

She looked at him uncertainly, and he could see she wanted to be convinced but still had reservations. He'd noticed Boston inhabitants tended to have strange perceptions, and she'd been raised there. No doubt it would take some time for her to accept slavery as the necessity it was—if she ever did.

From the corner of his eye he saw her husband striding along the deck toward them. Leon told himself he should have gone when the Negro girl gave the warning. Now it would look as though he was trying to sneak off if he left before the man came up to them. Moments later Winterton stopped next to Jurissa.

"Mr. Winterton, this is Monsieur du Motier," she said. "Monsieur, my husband, Mr. Winterton."

Winterton nodded. "From New Orleans, are you?" he asked, cutting off Leon's greeting.

"I am," Leon acknowledged.

Winterton looked him up and down. "I'd hazard you live on a plantation."

"My father's, yes." Leon managed to ignore the discourtesy implicit in the man's tone of voice, but he knew he wouldn't be able to do so for any length of time. It would be best if he bowed out before he lost his temper. He nodded, first to Jurissa, then to Winterton. "It has been a pleasure to meet you, madam, and you, sir. If you'll excuse me?"

Philip waved his hand and Jurissa smiled.

Leon strode away along the deck. Even freshly shaven and sober, Philip Winterton was no prize, he thought. A man with no manners and, unless he had lost his judgement in such matters, a man with little money who was rapidly going to seed. Why had a beauty like Jurissa married him?

Philip grasped Jurissa's arm so tightly she gasped in pain.

"I won't have my wife flirting with men like a common slut," he snarled.

She glared at him, furious with him and with herself. Unless she lied, she could hardly deny she'd been flirting. Somehow, with Leon, she hadn't been able to stop herself. Of course it was wrong but, on the other hand, Philip had no cause to hurt her.

She wrenched her arm free. "I did nothing to demean myself or you," she said crisply.

"Don't let me catch you with him again." He gazed after Leon. "A Creole!" He spat out the word.

"I understood you to say you'd be going into business in New Orleans," Jurissa commented.

"I'm looking into the possibility, yes."

"If you do, won't you have to deal with Creoles?"

His glance was sharp. "What I do is none of your affair. You're my wife, not my business partner."

Jurissa swallowed, aware she ought to remain silent but was driven to go on. "I've heard the New Orleans merchants buy their goods from pirates. Surely you wouldn't want to be associated with—"

Philip slammed his hand on the rail. "Enough! Don't trot out any more of your morality tales. I'm no mealymouthed Boston spinster, dammit, I'm a man." His gaze dropped from her face to her breasts and his expression changed.

Suddenly aware of the opened shawl, Jurissa gathered it around her tightly, not wanting his eyes examining her body.

"I haven't had the chance to prove it to you, have I?" he said. "Never mind, tonight's the night." He smiled at her, his good humor restored, and offered his arm. "Shall we take a stroll around the deck until it's time to eat our evening meal? I find myself quite hungry."

Tonight, Jurissa thought, taking his arm but feeling none of the excitement she had when with Leon. Tonight Philip means to offer me the romance, the kisses, and the soft caresses Arabel so often spoke of. A husband's love.

She sighted, wondering if by tomorrow she would

have forgotten all about Leon du Motier and hoping the tender touch of her husband tonight would have exactly that effect. She wanted with all her heart to be a good wife, a proper wife to Philip, no matter why they'd married.

"They sighed a pirate ship to starboard," she ventured after a few minutes. "But she feared our cannon and veered away."

Philip scowled. "The British in the Atlantic and Lafitte's pirates in the Gulf. It's hardly safe to set foot on a ship these days. Once I'm off this one, I plan to stay off." He peered out over the blue-green water and her gaze followed his.

The lowering sun tinted the western sky, coloring the horizon clouds red and pink and gold. The *Yarmouth* was heading into that glorious flaming sunset, into a new territory. Into paradise, as Leon had insisted?

Jurissa set her lips firmly. She wouldn't think of Leon and she'd put everything he'd said from her mind. She was entering this new territory with her husband, and together she and Philip would make their life there as wonderful as possible.

Later when they had sat down to dinner, the man next to Philip, a Mr. Lansdown, someone with whom he'd evidently become acquainted, mentioned a game being arranged. Once the meal was over, Philip urged Jurissa to run along to the cabin.

"Get yourself ready. I'll be with you later," he said gently, putting an arm around her and squeezing her shoulders. "I haven't forgotten what I promised you."

Jurissa looked into his face hopefully but the avid glitter in his eyes appalled her. She turned away, trying to convince herself she enjoyed his embrace.

"I'll be waiting," she said, having to force the words out.

What was the matter with her? She was actually relieved Philip would be delayed.

Yubah was outside the cabin when she returned, and followed her in.

"I've told you I intend to dress and undress myself," Jurissa reminded her.

"I knows how to help good," Yubah said.

"I'm sure you do but I'm not used to being helped." She looked directly at Yubah as she spoke and couldn't miss seeing the girl's lip was split. She remembered with distaste that Philip had struck Yubah with his fist.

Jurissa's heart lurched with sudden fear. Philip could be violent. But Yubah was his slave. She was his wife. He would not treat Jurissa as he did Yubah. Not that he should hurt Yubah, either.

"How old are you?" she asked the girl.

"They tells me I seen sixteen summers."

"Why you're younger than I am!" Jurissa exclaimed.

"I be old enough to help you," Yubah said earnestly. "I be strong."

"Yes, I feel certain you are, but that's not the point."

"Don't send me off," Yubah pleaded. "Massa Philip say I got to dress you nice and fix your hair and all. I got to be your lady's maid. He get mad if you don't be liking what I do."

Oh dear, Jurissa thought. I certainly don't want Philip angry at this poor girl again.

"I suppose I can learn to be waited on," she said resignedly, then smiled at Yubah. "I'm afraid you'll have to teach me how, though."

Yubah stared at her for a moment, then giggled, her

hand over her mouth. She was quite pretty, really, with more delicate features than Silas.

"My husband tells me Silas is your brother," Jurissa said. "You two don't look much alike."

"We got the same mama, that be what."

"He's your half-brother, then."

"What you say, missus."

Jurissa grimaced. "I don't care for being called 'missus.' Let's think of something else. I don't suppose Philip would like it if you called me Jurissa. No, I'm sure he wouldn't."

"Back home, I say Miss Katherine to the lady I help and she be married. 'Course, I calls her Miss Katherine *afore* she get married."

"We could pretend you knew me before I got married. I like 'Miss Jurissa' much better than 'missus.' Maybe you could tell Silas to call me that, too?"

"I be telling him, Miss Jurissa." Yubah smiled at her.

Jurissa smiled back, the feeling growing in her that Yubah actually liked her. She decided she could become quite fond of the Negro woman — after all they were almost the same age. Maybe she'd found a friend. She'd never had a friend except for Arabel.

Arabel was fond of quoting the Frenchman, Delille: "Fate chooses our relatives, we choose our friends." Tears pricked her eyes. Arabel had chosen to raise her and love her when Jurissa's parents, Arabel's Scottish servants, perished with the cholera. She'd dearly loved her guardian. How she missed her!

"You be feeling poorly?" Yubah asked.

Jurissa sighed and shook her head, unwilling to discuss Arabel with Yubah. Not yet. Maybe there would come a time. She hoped so, because she didn't believe she could ever bring herself to talk about Arabel with Philip. She had the feeling he'd laugh at her confidences, and she couldn't bear to have Arabel ridiculed.

Once Jurissa was in her white batiste nightgown with the blue ribbons and the lace trim on the bodice and sleeves, it took Yubah some time arranging Jurissa's hair to her own satisfaction.

"You be so pretty, Massa Philip bound to be happy," Yubah said at last.

Jurissa, who'd been distracted by Yubah's talent as a hairdresser, was reminded of the reason she was being all gussied up and she stiffened. Her eyes met Yubah's dark ones in the mirror.

"I hope so," she said, embarrassed to find her voice quivering.

Yubah's lips parted as though she meant to say something, then she blinked and looked away.

Jurissa gathered her courage. After all, it was possible Yubah knew more about what was to come than she did. She'd miss her chance to learn if she didn't ask.

"Do you—that is, did anyone ever tell you what—I mean, at night—" Jurissa sighed and tried again. "I don't really know what's going to happen," she finished plaintively. "Do you?"

Yubah seemed surprised. "This be your first night with Massa Philip?" At Jurissa's nod she went on. "What my mama say to me, she say maybe the first time ain't gonna be the best but a girl can't be judging by it." She paused and, her eyes round and scared, added, "Just don't cross Massa Philip."

After Yubah left the cabin, her advice remained with Jurissa, going around and around in her head as she sat propped onto pillows in the bunk, waiting for Philip.

A husband was a wife's master. Philip was her master. What would he do that would make her *want* to cross him? Oh why hadn't Arabel been more explicit? Love was wonderful, she'd said. There were tender words, there were kisses and caresses. Was there more? If so, what was it? What happened between a man and a woman who loved one another? Or were husband and wife?

She didn't know Philip well enough to love him. Would she, after tonight? This waiting and wondering was making her more nervous by the minute. Why didn't he come back to the cabin and get it over with?

No, that wasn't the proper attitude for a wife. I ought to be looking forward to his embrace, she reminded herself. I must try to greet him with affection. I will try. More, I'll do it.

Time passed and he didn't return. The lamp burned low and Jurissa grew drowsy, sliding down until she lay supine, her auburn hair loose and spread over the pillows, her white gown fanned out about her. Her eyelids drooped shut.

He touched her with gentle fingers, drawing them slowly along her face, her neck, until he reached her breasts. Despite his gentleness, fire gathered under her skin where he caressed her and penetrated deep into the core of her being. She daringly reached her hands up to his dark curls, and they felt the way she knew they would: soft as the finest silk. How wonderful it felt to be touching him at last, as she'd longed to do.

Arabel had told the truth about the wonder of a lover's caress. Jurissa felt she was floating in a delicious sea of flame that tingled rather than burned.

Soon he would kiss her and she would know the taste

of him, a taste that would surely be more delectable than any dish ever prepared by the greatest chef in the world.

His mouth covered hers, hot and wet. He smelled of whiskey. The sour taste of it nauseated her. Jurissa's eyes flew open and she saw, by the lamp's feeble glow, Philip's blond hair. But he was supposed to be Leon!

Confused, she tried to wrench her mouth away. Had she been dreaming of Leon? But Philip was no dream, he was all too real. And frightening. His hands tore at the blue ribbons fastening the neck of her nightgown. He thrust a hand into the opening and grabbed one of her breasts, squeezing it until she cried out with the pain.

"Like that, do you?" His words slurred and she realized he was drunk.

"No!" she protested. "Don't."

He paid no attention. He shoved up her gown until she was naked to the waist. Folds of batiste covered her face, and she fought to push the material away. Even when her face was free she couldn't understand what he was doing. All she knew was she feared it. Where were the warm caresses, the love words?

He jammed a knee between her legs, spreading them, and fumbled at his pants. "Got a s'prise for you," he muttered. "Nice s'prise."

Jurissa raised her shoulders off the bed to stare at him, saw what he was easing out of his pants and gasped in shock. She'd never seen a man undressed before and what she saw horrified her. What did he mean to do with that? She must get away!

"Let me go!" she screamed, striking out at him with her fists.

He grabbed her wrists in one hand and held them over her head. With his other hand he began pushing the monstrous thing between her legs, hurting her.

Jurissa writhed and shrieked, mindless with panic.

"Shut your mouth!" he ordered.

Even if she'd wanted to obey, she was too terror-stricken. Philip stopped his probing between her legs and backhanded her across the face. Her head snapped to one side from the blow, and her screams died in her throat. Tears ran down her cheeks.

" 'S better," he mumbled. "Lie still or you'll get another."

Yubah's advice drifted across her dazed mind. "Just don't cross Massa Philip."

Yubah knew! She knew Philip meant to hurt his wife like this. Is that why he'd struck Yubah? Because she'd protested when he did the same awful thing to her?

The probing at her most secret part began again, and the pain drove Jurissa crazy, so that she scratched and bit like a cat in her desperate struggle to get away from the monster she'd married. She wrenched a leg free and rammed her knee into him. He cried out and doubled over, releasing her.

Jurissa scrambled from the bed and ran for the door to the cabin. As she opened it, she remembered she was wearing only a nightgown, so she grabbed her shawl from the chair and wrapped it around herself before diving through the open door and rushing through the passageway to reach the deck.

"Help!" she screamed. "Someone please help me!"

## Chapter Three

Leon stood by the rail staring into the darkness and listening to the swish of the bow cutting through the water blending with the creak of timbers. A quarter moon rode high among the stars and the night air, while cool, had taken on a southern softness. He could almost imagine he smelled the sweetness of Louisiana flora. Within a few days he'd be home. He wished he had better news for his father from Boston; the English blockade in the Atlantic was playing hell with shipping. Why didn't President Madison do more about the problem? It was fortunate cotton didn't rot readily and could be stored awaiting better conditions, but it also meant no money coming in.

Papa's health was far from good, and Leon hated to add another worry. On the other hand, maybe the lack of money would make his father stop urging him to set the date with Louise-Marie Rondelet. Unless, of course, Papa decided they had urgent need of her substantial dowry. He hoped not; he wasn't eager to marry and settle down.

Ah well, it would be good to be home again, no matter how bad the tidings he brought. How he'd missed New Orleans! And Louise-Marie? Leon smiled wryly. He'd have to admit he'd scarcely thought of her on this trip and not at all since meeting Jurissa Winterton. Louise-Marie might well prove to be a proper Creole wife, but she couldn't hold a candle to Jurissa.

He'd seen Winterton playing cards tonight, knocking back one glass of whiskey after another. Cards and drinking were fine if not carried to extremes. These *Americains* had no restraint. A Creole would rather die than be seen drunk in public. What a loss of honor! He couldn't understand why Winterton preferred cards and whiskey when he had a wife like Jurissa waiting. The man was mad.

How different Jurissa was from the belles he'd courted in New Orleans. Was that why she fascinated him? A lively intelligence lurked in those beautiful sea eyes of hers, as well as an eagerness to learn about the world she'd seen so little of. She was stunning with that thick auburn hair, translucent skin, and her tall and slim high-breasted body. A man might never want, much less need, another woman if he had Jurissa.

Leon shook his head. She had him under a spell as potent as any concocted by a *voodooienne*, a voodoo queen, from New Orleans.

The night watchman passed, carrying a lantern. "Anything wrong, sir?" he asked.

"I'm fine. Enjoying the night air for a few minutes before I turn in. Any further sign of that suspicious brig we sighted this morning?"

The sailor hesitated, then said, "She's trailing us, sir. Nothing to worry about. We're keeping a sharp eye peeled. Captain thinks she's trying to use us for cover, so to speak. To make it seem she's traveling with us, all innocent like. Mark my words, she's after game and game she'll find sooner or later. Not every merchantman carries the load of cannon we do."

Leon nodded and the watchman started to go on when a woman screamed. Both men froze.

"Help!" she called, her voice faint. Then stronger, closer: "Someone help me!"

The sailor held up the lantern and started for the passageway to the cabins, Leon on his heels.

A figure burst from the passageway onto the deck, sobbing. "Please, please help!" she cried.

Leon sprinted around the sailor and reached her side. *"Mon Dieu, qu'est-ce qui se passe?"* he demanded, lapsing into his native tongue in his urgency.

"He has attacked me!" she answered in French, her accent revealing to him her identity a moment before the sailor's lantern illuminated her face. Recognizing Leon, Jurissa threw her arms about him and clung to him, shuddering from head to foot.

"What's all this!" the sailor asked.

"She say's she's been attacked," Leon explained. "I know her, She's Mrs. Winterton."

"Shall I find your husband?" Leon asked her, noticing she was barefoot and had only a nightgown on under her shawl.

"No! He's the one!" She pulled away to stare into his face. "Oh, please protect me from Philip. He's a monster, a beast," she said again in French.

Leon thought quickly. Turning to the sailor, he said, "This seems to be a domestic upset of some kind. I'm acquainted with the couple and I fear Mr. Winterton had a bit too much to drink tonight. I'll take care of the matter so you won't be kept from your duties."

The watchman looked from Jurissa to Leon. "Does that suit you, ma'am?"

35

Jurissa clutched at Leon's arm. "Yes, yes."

The sailor started off along the deck, his lantern swinging. A door slammed in the passageway and Jurissa gasped.

"He's coming after me," she whispered to Leon, her voice quivering. "Oh, please don't let him touch me. I'm so afraid."

"I won't allow him to hurt you," Leon assured her, becoming acutely aware of her thinly clad body pressing against his.

"He's gone crazy," she insisted.

"You're safe with me. You'll always be safe with me." Leon stroked her hair as he spoke, his eyes fixed on the opening to the passageway. From somewhere inside a man cursed loudly.

She'd have to spend the rest of the night in his cabin, Leon thought, to give Winterton a chance to sober up. In order to get there, though, they'd have to enter the passageway. It was better if he waited to confront Winterton on the deck first. In his condition and in the darkness, with luck Winterton might not even realize his wife was there.

"Where's Yubah?" Leon asked Jurissa.

"I don't know. She's somewhere with Silas—I don't know where they sleep."

"Once I talk to your husband, I'll find her and see the both of you to my cabin."

"Your cabin?"

"Don't be upset. I won't compromise you. I'll stay on deck until it's safe for you to rejoin your husband."

She shivered. "Never!"

A figure lurched onto deck and she shrank away. Leon took her by the arms and put her behind him.

36

"Silas!" Philip Winterton shouted. "Where are you, you good-for-nothing black bastard?" He stumbled on toward Leon and Jurissa.

"Winterton." Leon spoke quietly.

"Who the hell are you?"

"I'm du Motier. We met earlier today."

Winterton muttered something that sounded like "Creole bastard," and Leon stiffened, then decided to ignore the slur. Winterton was too drunk to deal with. He'd let him go past, then escort Jurissa to safety before coming back on deck.

Instead of continuing on, Winterton stopped in front of Leon, a bulky silhouette in the dim glow of the lantern light slanting through the opening to the passageway.

"Saw her s'afternoon," Winterton accused. "Saw her with you. Little slut."

Leon held on to his temper with difficulty. "You're drunk, man," he said coldly. "Go back to your cabin and sleep it off."

"She came running to you, didn't she?" Winterton stumbled sideways as he reached unsuccessfully for Leon's arm. "Where's the bitch?"

Behind him, Jurissa muffled a shriek.

Winterton shoved Leon in the chest with the flat of his hand and he staggered back, knocking Jurissa to the deck. Her husband lunged at her and grabbed her by the hair. She screamed.

Leon regained his footing and, grasping the drunken man's arm, pried him loose from Jurissa, dragged him to the rail and pinned him against it. Winterton struggled but was no match for the furious Leon.

"If you were sober I'd consider challenging you," he

said, spitting the words from between his teeth. "I don't soil my honor by fighting with drunks." He grabbed the front of Winterton's shirt with both hands and, lifting him, flung him onto the deck so hard the man slid several feet on his back and lay stunned.

Leon strode to Jurissa who huddled against a bulkhead. He put an arm around her waist and led her into the passageway, then along it to his cabin where he unlocked the door and ushered her inside.

"You're safe here." He handed her the key. "Don't go out and don't open the door to anyone but me."

She clutched at him, her eyes dark with fear. "Don't leave me!"

*Le bon Dieu* knew he wanted to stay with her. To hold her in his arms until she stopped trembling, to quiet her fears with gentle caresses. To—Leon shook his head. "I can't stay. I'll find Yubah and bring her to you."

As he closed the door and heard her lock it behind him, Winterton's voice, shouting for Silas to bring him his pistols, echoed along the passageway. Leon took a deep breath and made his way back onto the deck. Drink truly scrambled a man's wits, and a witless man could be extremely dangerous.

Jurissa sat on Leon's bunk with her hands over her face, sobbing. More than anything she wished Arabel was still alive and she was back home in Boston, in the big, old brick house, the only home she could remember. When she lived there she was still a child with naught but childish problems. She was safe there. Would she ever be safe again? She feared not.

Leon had left her alone. She clutched at the key that he had dropped into her lap, terror drying her tears. What if Philip came for her? Could he break down the door in his fury? Leon would stop him! But Philip had been shouting for his pistols. What if he killed Leon?

She leaped to her feet and ran to the door, then stopped. No, Leon had told her to stay here. Besides, Philip might be lurking in the passageway. She shuddered and, retreating to the bunk, sat down again, her eyes fixed on the door, agonizing over what to do. She couldn't bear to think of Philip shooting Leon, but her fear of her husband was so paralyzing she couldn't make herself leave the cabin's safety.

The minutes dragged on. Jurissa hugged the shawl around her, listening with dread for the sound of a shot. She heard nothing but the frantic drumming of her own heart and the creaking of the ship. A long time later, a knock finally sounded on the door and she gasped in terror.

"It's Leon du Motier," he said in French, and she let out her pent-up breath.

When she unlocked the door and opened it, he pushed Yubah inside. "I'm afraid she's been hurt," he said. "Can you take care of her?"

Jurissa stared at the Negro woman. The left side of Yubah's face was grotesquely swollen, and she held her left arm with her right hand as she stumbled into the cabin.

"Yes. Yes, of course I will," Jurissa said. "What happened?"

His only answer was to point to a black case on the floor. "You'll find laudanum in a blue bottle inside the case. She'll need a dose. Lock the door after me." He disappeared.

Jurissa helped Yubah onto the bunk. Dark bruises showed on her light-brown arms, and her swollen face was rapidly discoloring. Jurissa poured water from the pitcher into the washbasin and soaked a cloth to lay over the left side of her face. She touched the girl's left arm and Yubah moaned. As gently as she could, Jurissa felt along the arm for broken bones and, not finding any, she finally narrowed the injured area to the left wrist.

"It must be a sprain," she said. "I'll fix you a sling."

After she'd done all she could for Yubah's injuries, Jurissa measured out ten drops of the poppy syrup into a glass and added water.

"This will let you rest," she assured the girl, helping her to sit up. "Drink it all." When Yubah was through, Jurissa eased her onto the pillow again. "What happened?" she asked, though she was afraid she knew. "Can you tell me?"

Yubah said nothing.

"I have to know," Jurissa cried. "Was it Philip? My husband, I mean. Mr. Winterton. Was he the one who hurt you like this?"

Yubah's, "yes'm," was more a groan than a word. Her eyes closed and she turned her face away from Jurissa.

Tears ran down Jurissa's cheeks as she covered the girl with a blanket. He'd hurt poor Yubah as he'd tried to hurt her, and her heart went out to the Negro woman. Oh, God, why had she ever married such a monster? What would happen to her?

Jurissa pulled the chair next to the bunk and wrapped herself in the remaining blanket. Though she meant to stay awake in case Yubah needed anything, the next thing she knew was that the lamp was out and someone was pounding on the door.

Jurissa leaped to her feet in the dark room, her heart

hammering against her ribs.

"Mrs. Winterton!" a man's voice, one she didn't recognize, called.

She swallowed twice before she could speak. "I'm here," she replied.

"This is Captain Fowler. May I come in, please?"

"How do I know you're who you say you are?" she asked.

"He is *le capitaine*," Leon's voice told her. "Let us in."

She drew her shawl close about her and unlocked the door. Dim daylight slanted along the passageway.

A short stocky man with graying hair stepped over the threshold, his eyes darting from her to the unmoving Yubah on the bunk and back. "Captain Fowler," he said curtly.

"My—my Negro maid has been hurt, Captain Fowler," Jurissa said.

"I've bad news, Mrs. Winterton," the captain said.

Jurissa's fingers twisted in the ends of the shawl she held clutched over her breasts. What could he tell her that would be worse than what had already happened?

"Your husband's missing," he went on. "We fear he's fallen overboard. We searched but there's no sign of him in the water."

Jurissa stared at him blankly, her mind refusing to accept what she'd heard. Fallen overboard? Philip? From the bunk came a low moan.

"I—I don't understand," Jurissa said. In her mind's eye she saw Philip stumbling from the passageway, saw him push Leon aside and reach for her. She could almost feel the pain when he caught her by the hair and she shuddered.

"Get a hold of yourself, madam," the captain urged.

Jurissa grasped the back of the chair to steady herself. "Philip's gone," she said aloud as if testing the idea.

Yubah moaned again.

"I understand he'd been drinking with some friends last night," Captain Fowler went on. "Is this true?"

Jurissa relived Philip's loose wet mouth covering hers, tasted the nauseating flavor of stale whiskey. She fought to retain her wits. "I — yes, he did smell strongly of whiskey," she managed to say.

"It may be why he had the accident." Captain Fowler's gray eyes fixed on her. "You wouldn't know of any other reason?"

Beyond words, Jurissa could only shake her head.

"The nigger gal — how did she get hurt?"

"A fall, as I told you, captain," Leon put in. "I gave up my cabin to Mrs. Winterton so she could care for the woman. She's quite attached to her maid."

Jurissa blinked. What was Leon saying? Yubah hadn't fallen; Philip had beaten her.

"I'm not overfond of accidents aboard my ship," Captain Fowler said, "but this appears to be straightforward enough. Your husband apparently fell overboard while incapacitated due to drink. You have my sympathy, Mrs. Winterton." He nodded his head to her, turned on his heel and left the cabin.

Leon eased the door shut and held out his arms to Jurissa who flung herself against him. "Is Philip really gone?" she asked, her voice muffled against his coat.

"I'm afraid so. There's certainly no sign of him aboard the ship." He patted her back soothingly.

After a moment Jurissa eased away from him, gathering herself into the folds of her shawl once more. "Is it so very awful to be relieved?" she asked in a low tone. "I

don't mean I wanted him to die because I didn't but—"
She sighed. "I never should have married him."

She wanted to nestle in Leon's arms and never leave them but she couldn't. It wasn't right, even with Philip gone. She must return to her cabin. Her gaze went to Yubah and she saw the Negro woman's eyes were open. Her right eye, rather; the left was only a slit because of the swelling.

Jurissa walked to the bunk. "How are you feeling?" she asked. "Can you sit up, do you think?"

"I be better, Miss Jurissa." Yubah's words were distorted by her injured mouth. She pushed herself to a sitting position with her right arm and swung her feet over the edge of the bunk, but didn't try to stand. "Ole head's dizzy," she explained.

"I'd like to take Yubah to my cabin," Jurissa said. "It's selfish of me to remain here and deprive you of yours."

"I'll carry her," Leon said.

Despite Yubah's protests, Leon swung her into his arms. Jurissa opened the door and stepped back, startled. Silas stood on the other side, looking blacker and more gigantic than ever.

"She be my sister, sir," Silas said to Leon. "I be toting her for Miss Jurissa."

Leon raised his eyebrows but slid Yubah into Silas's outstretched arms. Silas marched down the passageway and stopped outside Jurissa's cabin, waiting.

Leon reached the door and tried the latch, finding it unlocked. He pushed it open.

"Silas, please lay Yubah on the bunk," Jurissa ordered.

"Yes'm." Very gently he eased his half-sister down. "Please, Miss Jurissa, I take good care of her for you. I be used to tending sick folk." The huge black man's eyes pleaded with Jurissa.

After she watched how tenderly he dealt with Yubah, she realized that Silas didn't seem so threatening. After all, the man couldn't help his size or his dark color.

"I'll welcome your assistance," she said. "But not now. Later."

"Come, Silas," Leon ordered. "You can wait outside until Miss Jurissa calls you." Looking at Jurissa, he added, "If you need me I'll be on deck or in my cabin."

Once she and Yubah were alone, Jurissa slumped into the chair, staring at nothing. She could hardly believe Philip was dead, drowned. She hadn't wished him dead, never. But she couldn't deny she'd wanted him gone from her. Relief mixed with guilt churned inside her.

Poor Philip. He hadn't really wanted to marry her, she knew now. How unlucky for him he'd accompanied his friend Montague Evans to Boston.

"He be a devil man." Yubah's voice startled Jurissa. "Miss Jurissa, you better off with him dead."

How could she argue with Yubah? Certainly the way he'd treated his slave had made the Negro woman fear and hate him. Even she, his wife, had been terrified of him.

"I don't know what will happen next," Jurissa said slowly.

Yubah eased herself to a sitting position. "Ole head be getting better." She smiled, a grotesque parody because of her swollen face. "Don't you worry none, Miss Jurissa. Me and Silas take good care of you. That man who be from New Orleans, he sure do look like he gonna take good care of you, too."

Leon? Involuntarily Jurissa smiled at the thought of Leon "taking care" of her. How pleasant that would be. How exciting, as well. But she hardly knew him. A disquieting thought struck her. He might be married! She took a deep breath, surprised and dismayed by the pang that possibility caused her.

She had no right to expect anything from Leon, she told herself firmly. The only thing she'd ask from him would be advice about what to do once they reached New Orleans.

The next day, with Silas in the cabin looking after Yubah, Jurissa, wearing the black faille gown and black bonnet she'd had made for Arabel's funeral, ventured onto the deck. Whether it was proper for a widow to appear in public so soon, she didn't know, but she couldn't bear to stay cooped up one moment longer.

The other passengers eyed her furtively; no one spoke or nodded to her. When she'd walked around the deck twice and failed to find Leon, she admitted to herself that she wanted to see him, to be reassured by his smile and comforted by his caressing voice. Was it proper for her to knock on his cabin door? She sighed. Probably not but what else was she to do?

Leon took a moment to answer her knock. She saw he wore a dressing jacket and realized he must have been resting. No wonder—he'd been up all night because of her.

"I'm sorry," she said. "I won't bother you now—"

He took her hand and drew her inside, closing the door behind her.

"You're never a bother." His voice tingled pleasurably along her nerves.

There were so many questions to ask. Why had he

told the captain Yubah had fallen? Had he seen Philip again before the fall overboard? What on earth was she to do when the ship docked in New Orleans? To her utter amazement, she asked none of these. She took one look at the warmth in his brown eyes and burst into tears.

Leon's arm closed around her, holding her while he stroked her back, and he murmured soothing words. After a time she pulled back and retrieved a handkerchief that was tucked into the wrist of her glove. He plucked the black lace-edged square from her fingers, then untying her bonnet, he lifted it from her head and set it aside.

"Allow me," he said. As he began gently to wipe her wet cheeks with the handkerchief, she shut her eyes. He dabbed at her closed lids and, before she could open her eyes, she felt his warm lips caress one, then the other.

His lips trailed feather light down her cheek, finally settling over her mouth in a tender kiss that left her breathless. How velvet soft his mouth was, how wonderfully well it fit over hers. His scent beguiled her senses. His arms urged her closer and she came willingly, remembering and needing the comforting feel of his body.

His lips parted against hers, and the tip of his tongue touched her caressingly. She opened her lips to taste him, and his tongue slipped inside her mouth. At its touch the pleasing warmth he'd kindled inside her flared into sudden flame. She clung to him, obeying the urgent summons of her body to press against the hard length of his.

"You are so lovely; the most beautiful woman I've

ever met," he murmured against her lips in French, in the language of love. "I have never before felt such desire as I feel for you."

She wasn't certain what she felt. She only knew nothing even remotely approaching this had ever happened to her, and she wanted the wonderful sensations to go on and on, to never end.

## Chapter Four

As Jurissa clung to Leon she thought dreamily that New Orleans might mean paradise to him, but she'd found her own paradise here in his arms. Surely anything that brought such pleasure couldn't be wrong.

His lips warm on her throat, his hands sliding caressingly over the silk faille of her dress made her weak with desire. Though pressed close to him, she wanted to be even closer, wanted to merge with him until they were one. How this could be she had no notion, but Arabel had often spoken of the bliss of "becoming one" with her lover, and now Jurissa longed for it to happen to her.

When Leon grasped her arms and eased her away from him she moaned in protest, her eyes fluttering open. He cradled her in one arm and, taking her hands in his, one at a time, removed her gloves. Lifting her bared fingers to his lips he kissed each of them, slowly, sweetly, his mustache tickling her palms while the kisses burned through to her heart, setting it aflame.

"Oh," she gasped. "Oh, monsieur."

*"Non,"* he murmured, still speaking French. "Not monsieur. Tell me I am your Leon."

With his mouth hovering above hers, Jurissa could hardly breathe, much less talk.

"Say it," he urged, the tip of his tongue flicking

deliciously moist caresses along her upper lip.

"*Cher* Leon," she managed to whisper. He was more than dear to her, but she couldn't find the right words in French or English to tell him he was everything she'd always dreamed of in a man. And more, for despite Arabel's confidences, Jurissa had no idea a man could evoke such overwhelming sensations within her.

No wonder Arabel could never forget Count D'Artagnan. Like Arabel and her count, Jurissa would hold Leon forever in her heart. A quiver of dread shot along her spine at the thought they might someday be parted.

"Do not be afraid, my lovely one," Leon said gently. "I won't ever hurt you. I'd die rather than bring you harm."

Be afraid of Leon? Never! She snuggled into his embrace, her arms rising to go around his neck. This was no dream. Her hands were free to stroke through the exciting reality of his dark hair, the soft curls entwining about her fingers in welcome.

One of his hands held her firmly against him while the other slid along the side of her breast to cup it, bringing a bouquet of new and marvelous sensations to blossom inside her. His thumb moved back and forth across her nipple, and as it rose to press against the silk of the shift she wore under her gown, Jurissa moaned in delight.

His tongue coaxed her lips apart and dipped inside to bring pleasure to the secret crevices of her mouth. His taste was indescribably delicious. All the foods she enjoyed, even her greatest love, chocolate, were insipid in comparison. Nothing was like, could ever be like Leon.

"You are so beautiful," he told her, his voice oddly harsh as his warm breath teased her ear. "I want you, I need you for my own."

Jurissa murmured in assent. Didn't he know she was already his?

"Tell me," he insisted, "that you want me, too."

His breathing, she noted, was as erratic as her own and a frisson of delight seized her when she realized he, too, must be enthralled and shared these wondrous feelings.

"Oh, Leon," she whispered, "I do."

I do. The words seemed to echo forbiddingly in her mind. I do. The words she'd spoken in answer to Father Bennett's question of the marriage ceremony. Her marriage to Philip Winterton. Philip, who'd died so unexpectedly by falling overboard and drowning. Her husband, Philip. Never mind how she'd feared him—she *had* married him. Now, a widow of but a few hours, she was in the arms of another man. No matter how right it felt to be with Leon, it was wrong to dismiss Philip's death so lightly.

Jurissa forced herself to pull away from Leon. When he reached for her, she stepped back, shaking her head.

"I must not. It isn't proper. Not with Philip—" She bit her lip.

"Ah, but he is dead. What we do can't hurt him."

"It's wrong," she insisted, fighting her urge to nestle against him once more.

Leon frowned. "I did not understand you loved him."

"I didn't know Mr. Winterton well enough to love him." Even as she said the words, Jurissa knew they were a lie. No matter how many years passed, she'd never have come to love the man Philip had shown himself to be. Leon was a different matter. She'd met him scarcely a week ago and already loved him. For surely this emotion she felt for him was love. Otherwise, why would paradise lie in his arms?

Leon took a deep breath, doing his best to tamp

down his raging need for this green-eyed woman who'd so enchanted him. "I believe you did not wish your husband's death," he said, choosing his words carefully to convince her, "but you cannot deny you are relieved of your dread of him."

Jurissa smoothed her hair, as if by doing so she could brush away the feeling between them. Didn't she know his stamp was on her tempting lips, swollen with his kisses, that the flush of passion still stained her cheeks?

"I was afraid of him, yes." She wouldn't meet his gaze, looking everywhere but at him. "That doesn't excuse disrespect for his memory."

Despite his resolve not to upset her, Leon snorted. "I didn't suppose you to be a hypocrite."

Jurissa gasped, her green eyes clouding with anger as they met his. "You insult me, sir."

He shook his head. "You follow a custom but your heart isn't in it. It is, of course, de rigueur for widows to grieve but only last night you ran in terror from him, calling him a beast. I don't believe you mourn Winterton. Why pretend to me that you do?"

"I—I—" she sputtered, stiffening her spine. "I—it's wrong to simply dismiss him as though he never existed."

"Why not? Personally, I think you're well rid of the man. And with him gone you're free to do anything you choose."

"He didn't want to die. Who does?" Tears brightened her eyes. "Whatever his faults, he didn't deserve such an ending."

"Perhaps not." This was a concession to her feelings. Leon privately believed Winterton got exactly what such a man deserved, an undignified death, brought on by his own disgusting nature and habits.

Jurissa picked up her bonnet from the chest and

settled it onto her head. He reached out and plucked the ties from her hands.

"Permit me." As he slowly and carefully constructed the bow, he heard her catch her breath and saw the pulse in her neck throb wildly.

So, it was as he'd thought originally. She desired him as much as he wanted her but she was wary; she needed time. He was willing enough to play that game, providing she eventually became his.

"How is your maid?" he asked, stepping back.

Jurissa blinked. "Yubah? She's improving. Silas is with her now. I must get back." She turned toward the door.

Leon made no move to stop her. She would come to him when she was ready. It would be soon; there was no one else to turn to, no one else to comfort her. Not as he could. And she knew it.

At the door, Jurissa looked back. Did she know how her eyes gave her away? Hold me, her yearning gaze begged. Make me yours. His smile was one-sided. She'd chosen the rules, now it was her turn to obey them and she didn't like it. *Le bon Dieu* knew he'd like nothing better than to answer her plea by pulling her back into his arms, by stripping every garment from her and taking his pleasure from her magnificent body, and giving her the same pleasure in return.

He didn't think Winterton had truly aroused her, and he looked forward to showing her in their lovemaking that she was made for passion. The thought of it tightened his groin as his body rebelled against the delay in satisfaction.

"Au revoir," he murmured, bowing slightly. He'd made up his mind as to the course of this affair and would not be shifted. She must come to him, not the reverse.

When the door closed behind her, with the hint of a slam, he smiled. The smile broadened when he noticed what lay on the deck of his cabin. She'd forgotten her black gloves, giving her the perfect excuse to return—if she needed one.

I won't visit Leon's cabin again, Jurissa told herself firmly as she hurried along the passageway toward her own cabin. I'll greet him politely should we meet on deck.

How could he speak so brutally of Philip's death? How could he accuse her of hypocrisy? She'd not had time to grow accustomed to the idea of being married, but married she had been, and her husband had drowned. Was she supposed to ignore his death? She wasn't pretending to grieve but surely Philip's death deserved more than a quick dismissal in the arms of another man.

In her hurry to be with Leon she'd even neglected to pray for the repose of Philip's soul. That was inexcusable and must be remedied as soon as possible.

Inside the cabin, Silas knelt beside the bunk, spooning what appeared to be a thin gruel into his sister's mouth. He stopped when Jurissa entered and rose to his feet, dwarfing the cabin.

"She say she don't be hungry," he said, shaking his head. "I be feared for her, Miss Jurissa."

"I'll see she eats, Silas. You may go now." Jurissa knew she was being abrupt, but his presence continued to make her nervous.

"Yes'm. You want me, I be here." He shut the door quietly behind him.

She supposed she should have asked where he slept and how he found food, but she was too distraught to do anything about it at the moment. She crossed to the bunk and put a hand to Yubah's forehead.

Surprised at how hot the Negro woman was, Jurissa leaned closer and peered into Yubah's swollen face. "How do you feel?" she asked.

"Right poorly, Miss Jurissa." Yubah slurred the words together.

Jurissa stared at her. Obviously Yubah had a high fever. If only she'd thought to bring along the quinine she'd used when she'd nursed Arabel but, in the confused rush of the marriage, she'd left her medicines behind. She had nothing to ease Yubah's fever.

For the rest of the day and on into the evening, Jurissa did her best to help Yubah. She dribbled water between the woman's lips when Yubah refused to drink and bathed the fevered brown skin with cool cloths, paying little heed to her own mounting fatigue. As the night closed in, Yubah slipped into delirium, moaning in fright and struggling against something or someone only she could see. Jurissa panicked, afraid she couldn't save the Negro woman.

"Yubah must live," she whispered to herself, lightheaded with lack of sleep. "She mustn't die like Philip. I won't let her." In her weary mind the woman's illness was mixed with Philip's mistreatment of Yubah. It was as though he was somehow reaching from beyond, from the world of the dead to force his slave to join him. Jurissa was determined not to allow it. He'd done enough damage alive.

Leon, she knew, had medicines in the black case in his cabin and perhaps quinine was among them. Slipping a shawl over her shoulders, Jurissa opened the door. A huge dark form rose from the floor of the passageway to confront her and she retreated.

"Oh, Silas, how you startled me!" she cried. After

taking a moment to compose herself, she added, "It's as well you're here. I want you to stay with Yubah while I find medicine to help her fever."

He ducked his head to her and, with a mumbled, "yes'm," eased into the cabin and closed the door. Jurissa stumbled along the lantern-lit passageway. Outside Leon's cabin she paused and took a deep breath while she stared at the door she'd vowed never to knock on again. This was for Yubah's sake, not for herself.

Leon, fully dressed but looking half asleep, drew her inside his cabin.

"Quinine," she pleaded, noting he seemed taken aback. "You do have quinine, don't you? Say you do, please."

"Of course, I always carry quinine."

"Thank God! Will you give me some for Yubah?"

"Anything I have is yours, always," he told her reassuringly. "Your maid is worse, then?"

"She has a terrible fever. I fear for her life."

"Ah, *cherie*, you are trembling. Are you well, yourself?" He put an arm around her.

For the first time she realized her entire body was shaking so markedly she swayed on her feet. Jurissa leaned against Leon, drawing on his strength. A moment only to steady herself and she'd hurry back to Yubah. To her dismay, her legs gave way and she would have fallen if Leon's arms hadn't closed around her.

"You must rest." He lifted her and eased her onto his bunk.

"No, no, I have to help Yubah." She struggled to rise.

"I will bring the quinine to her," Leon said, picking up the black case, "and see that she takes it. Where is Silas?"

"With her. But—"

"I've talked to Silas and found him intelligent. He's

capable of nursing his sister and giving her the quinine when she needs it. You will accomplish nothing but make yourself as ill as Yubah if you persist in trying to take care of her." He held up a hand as she tried to protest. "No arguments. My mind is made up."

Before she could gather enough strength to rise from the bunk, Leon was gone with the case. I'll follow him in a minute or two, she thought dizzily, closing her eyes. As soon as this shakiness eases . . .

A gentle hand stroked her brow, pushing away strands of hair; Arabel's hand, Jurissa knew; a caring, loving hand; nothing to fear. Arabel had always been kind to her, even when she'd been a mischievous child. She was safe with Arabel, forever safe.

Poor Arabel who'd had the love of her life so cruelly taken from her. The count had told Arabel shortly before "the rabble" overran Paris that she had to sail for the English colonies in America and that he would join her as soon as he could.

Though Arabel pleaded with him to come with her, he couldn't leave his invalid wife and afflicted son, neither of whom were well enough to survive an ocean voyage. He was beheaded and Arabel never saw him again.

Jurissa became the child Arabel never had; Arabel became Jurissa's mother, replacing the lost parents the little girl barely recalled. She would never leave Arabel, not as long as she lived.

But Arabel became ill and, despite Jurissa's devoted care, had died. Now she was alone. But if she was alone, whose hand was on her forehead?

Jurissa's eyes flew open. A man sat on her bed, his hand caressing her hair. It took her long, confused moments before she realized she was not in her own room in Arabel's comfortable brick house but was lying on a bunk aboard the *Yarmouth*. A bunk that wasn't hers. Leon's bunk.

"Go back to sleep, *cherie*," he told her when she tried to sit up. "You are safe with me."

"Yubah? How is Yubah?"

"The quinine is taking effect. Silas tells me she's had such fevers before in Virginia and their former owner's wife cured Yubah with quinine. Silas has a remarkable quick mind, and he's most devoted to his sister."

"They don't look much alike," Jurissa said, sinking back into drowsiness, relieved by the good news.

"I suspect the master sired Yubah but not him, from what Silas told me. She certainly was a favored house servant until 'ole massa' passed on. The mistress then gave both Silas and Yubah to her dead husband's cousin, Philip Winterton."

" 'Ole missus mean to get shet of Yubah,' Silas said, "and she 'fraid I be trouble if she don't send me 'long.' I got the impression the widow gifted Winterton with the slaves to get rid of him as well."

Jurissa heard what he said through a haze of tiredness. She couldn't force her eyes to stay open no matter how hard she tried, so at last she gave up. Safe, Leon had said. She was safe with him.

Sometime later she was dimly aware of being moved and of a pleasant warmth next to her. She didn't rouse enough to be aware of what it was; she only knew the warmth comforted her.


Jurissa turned on her side away from Leon and snuggled her enticing bottom against him. Her woman's scent fueled his desire until he thought he'd go mad. He had to have her. Now. True, she slept, but if he began caressing her, as he longed to do, he knew she'd respond. Soon enough she'd be awake and eager for consummation. She'd be his and he'd be rid of this damnedable burning for her.

Gently he touched her hair, then eased his hand to her neck and down to the swell of her breast. She sighed. Ah, she was so soft, so delectable. He caught his breath at the thought of that softness, no longer concealed by clothes, pressing close against him. Because of her fair skin and auburn hair, the nipples of her high, proud breasts would be the rosy pink of a New Orleans dawn. Beautiful. Enough to drive any man out of his senses.

Yet he'd given her his assurance she'd be safe with him. Whatever had persuaded him to make such a promise? A Creole's honor forbade him to go against his word and take advantage of a sleeping woman. If anyone had told him he'd lie in bed next to a beautiful woman he desired beyond belief and not make love to her, he'd have laughed the man out of his sight.

His only consolation was that she had to wake up sometime. Until then, he had no choice but to do his best to relax and try to sleep. Sighing, Leon turned onto his back and crossed his hands on his chest.

Jurissa was an unusual woman. Though married, she retained the facade of innocence, almost making him believe each caress was the first she'd ever received from a man, and that no man except himself could evoke her passionate responses. It was most arousing.

She had an appealing naivete, despite her Bostonian views about the world. She didn't approve of owning slaves, yet now that she did, she wore herself out tending one of them. He had no doubt that if he hadn't reported Yubah was improving, Jurissa would have insisted on stumbling back to her cabin to help the sick woman, despite her own obvious need for rest. And there was her guilt over not grieving for the ignoble Winterton. He didn't agree but he admired her insistence that, no matter how she'd felt about her husband, the man's death deserved respect.

Unlike New Orleans belles, Jurissa wasn't a coquette. She was straightforward, showed her eagerness and even her need for him. He'd found it amusing at first, then increasingly exciting. And she wasn't afraid to let him know she had a mind as well as a body. Her frequent questions were to the point and she listened to his answers. She truly wanted to learn about the world, wanted to broaden her horizons. She was a woman who might well prove to be a man's companion as well as his love.

What would she do now that Winterton was dead? He hoped her husband had left her enough to live on comfortably but he feared it wasn't much. Winterton didn't impress him as a prosperous man. Still, she was young and very beautiful. Men would be attracted to her like bees to a fragrant flower. Even if she wasn't well off, she'd soon enough have marriage proposals.

An involuntary and violent pang of jealousy pierced Leon to the heart. She was his! No other man had the right to touch her. He'd challenge any who dared.

*Mon Dieu*, what was he thinking? He, who was formally betrothed to another woman. He was all Papa had left, and it would kill his father if he didn't marry Louise-Marie Rondelet as expected.

When Jurissa woke, the lamp, burning low, revealed the source of the warmth that had comforted her while she slept. Leon lay on the bunk next to her, his eyes closed, breathing deeply in sleep. Dark strands of hair curled onto his forehead, and she fought her impulse to brush them gently back. She shouldn't be here; she mustn't touch him.

He was so handsome; the most handsome man she'd ever seen. Arabel had said the same of Count D'Artagnan. Were men of French descent all good-looking? She couldn't believe any Frenchman surpassed Leon. How beautifully curved his lips were. A tingle sizzled through her as she relived his kisses. If she dared, she could lean over and press her lips gently to his. But what would happen?

Excitement rose, threatening to choke her as her breath caught in her throat. Leon, awake, would crush her to him; his lips, his hands would work the magic that transported her to another realm, an enchanted one that contained only the two of them.

It was safer to let him sleep, safer not to have those compelling brown eyes clouding her mind, dazing her with their passion until she was helpless to do anything but what he wished. She'd never before experienced anything like this terrible need she had: to touch him and to be touched by him. Was it wrong?

Arabel had taught that love transcended sin. If she was to be believed, and Jurissa had always taken Arabel's words as gospel, it wasn't wrong. Yet Philip's death haunted her; his shade came between Leon and herself.

Remembering how shocked and bewildered she'd been to awaken back in Boston and find Philip lying across her bed, Jurissa smiled sadly. The smile faded when she recalled how frightened and repulsed she'd been the next time he'd shared her bed. Leon would never hurt her in any way; he'd said so and she believed him. It seemed so natural to find Leon next to her. Natural and wonderful.

She closed her eyes and prayed soundlessly that Philip might be granted eternal rest and that she might learn to remember him without fear.

The moment of prayer had revealed to her that she must be content to wait, and Jurissa made up her mind what to do next. Opening her eyes, she gathered her will and eased carefully down to the end of the bunk and slowly, cautiously, climbed over Leon's feet to the floor. He shifted restlessly and she held her breath until he turned on his side, away from her. Picking up her shawl, she reached for the door.

When she stepped into the bright morning light slanting through the open door of the passageway, the middle-aged couple who always dressed in black came out of their cabin. Jurissa's face flushed but she raised her chin and, head held high, sailed past them to her own cabin, the woman's shocked "well!" echoing in her ears.

Yubah was sleeping, and Silas was curled on the floor beside her bunk. Hearing the door open, he pulled himself to his feet, blinking.

"Monsieur du Motier told me the quinine was helping Yubah." Jurissa knew she spoke sharply but couldn't help it. However she might feel, the world judged it wrong for a woman to spend the night with a man unless they were husband and wife. The middle-aged couple suspected what she'd done, and Silas certainly knew where she'd been.

"Yes'm, she be resting easy." His deep voice held an edge of joy. "I do what Massa Leon say and ole fever, he done be whupped."

"I'm glad." She tried to smile at him but couldn't quite manage it. "You've done a good job of nursing your sister, better than I."

"Miss Jurissa, you done save her with the medicine from Massa Leon. I be here to help is all. Ain't never gonna forget what you do." His black eyes sought hers earnestly. "Ain't never gonna forget."

At that moment her unease with Silas vanished. Though towering over her and everyone else, he proved to be a gentle and caring man. It was foolish to fear him because of his size and blackness. Jurissa touched his arm, startling him.

"You're a good man," she told him. "Together we'll soon have Yubah on her feet again, as good as new."

He looked at his sleeping sister, then back at Jurissa, and his broad grin clearly showed the joy in his heart. "Yes'm, we sure gonna do that."

When he'd left the cabin, Jurissa touched Yubah and, finding her forehead cool, nodded in satisfaction. She undressed to wash and put on clean undergarments. Examining her black gown she found the faille badly wrinkled from sleeping in it. She had no other mourning clothes, so she'd have to wear something else. No doubt the middle-aged couple would think the worse of her for that, too.


Leon woke with a start when the door closed. Jurissa wasn't beside him, and she was gone from the cabin. He slid his feet to the floor and stood up, running a hand over his stubbled face. What now?

If he had any sense he'd let her go and would make no attempt to see her again. It would be best for both of them. Other passengers would be quick to note his attentions to the new widow and think the worst. Jurissa's reputation would suffer.

On the other hand, she needed to be looked after, else she'd wear herself out nursing her maid. He'd clean up and go to her. It was no less than his duty to see that she ate and took a turn on the deck for the fresh air. If he was truthful he'd have to admit that, wise or not, he desperately needed to be at her side.

They had little enough time to be together; only the few days before the ship set anchor outside New Orleans. After that he wouldn't be his own master. He had Papa's precarious health to consider as well as Dindon, the du Motier plantation. And, of course, there was the matter of his betrothal to Louise-Marie. It would be impossible to explain Jurissa to his father or his fiancée.

He didn't want to have to explain her; he purely and simply wanted her. In his arms, in his bed. The way he felt about her might be unwise but he was caught in an obsession he was powerless to resist. It was as though she'd fed him one of the infamous voodoo love potions that bound a man forever to a woman.

## Chapter Five

Persuaded by Leon that she needed fresh air, Jurissa, in the soberest costume she had, a beige cashmere gown, plain except for three tiers of pleated silk ruffles at the hem, walked with him sedately up and down the deck. Over the gown she wore a tobacco brown spencer with long sleeves. Only her slippers and her bonnet were black. There was nothing she could do to remedy the situation, and she'd made up her mind to ignore any disapproving stares. She hadn't thought about words.

"And him scarcely dead," the middle-aged woman in black muttered to her husband in a voice plainly meant to reach Jurissa's ears. "Indecent, I call it."

She managed to pretend the woman's comment was beneath notice, but then she overheard two sailors swabbing the deck, their backs to Leon and Jurissa.

"What d'ye think—did the Creole help that poor bastard over the rail?" asked the first.

"For a redheaded gal the likes of her, I reckon I'd be tempted," his mate answered. "She's one of them there sirens from the—" He stopped abruptly, catching sight of Leon and Jurissa. Both sailors found urgent business elsewhere.

Jurissa felt as though her heart had ceased beating momentarily, as though the breath had been knocked out of her. She stopped, unable to move, the words echoing ominously in her head: "Did the Creole help that poor bastard over the rail?"

"Ignorant fools. Pay no heed." Leon's voice was tight with fury.

How could she obey him? What a terrible accusation! She turned to face him. "They don't really believe Philip's fall overboard wasn't an accident, do they?" Although she didn't intend to, she found herself whispering. "They can't possibly believe that you—" She stopped abruptly, remembering.

In her mind's eye a scene replayed: Philip in his drunken rage grabbing her by the hair; Leon forcing him away from her, forcing him up against the rail, then slamming him to the deck where Philip lay, stunned, while Leon helped her to his cabin. There Leon had left her and returned to the deck. He'd been furiously angry with Philip. Had they met again and, if so, what had happened?

Leon's eyes sought hers, his intent gaze inquiring. She bit her lip and looked away, her mind in a turmoil. *What had happened?* There was a long silence.

"Ah, Jurissa," Leon said at last. "Not you, too."

No, she wanted to cry, I trust you, I believe in you. You didn't push Philip. I know you didn't. You couldn't, wouldn't. At the same time, her mind, icy cold, showed her the way it might have happened: Silas bringing Philip his guns; Philip threatening Leon. Leon wouldn't intend to shove Philip overboard, no, never, it would be an accident.

"I'll escort you to your cabin, madame." Leon's voice was devoid of emotion, flat and formal. "And then I must bid you adieu."

Adieu, not au revoir. Farewell, not, till we meet again. Her heart heavy in her chest, her eyes stinging with tears that wouldn't fall, Jurissa walked with Leon in silence to her door. Even then she couldn't bring herself to speak and managed only a nod when he said good-bye.

Inside her cabin, the held-back tears burst forth. Jurissa dropped her face into her hands and sobbed. How could she have aligned herself with those who blamed Leon?

"Love is trust, love is faith in the beloved." How many times had Arabel said those words to her? "Without trust love withers and dies."

A hand on her arm startled her. Yubah, barefooted, stood next to her, concern in her eyes. "Something bad happen, Miss Jurissa?"

Making an effort to control her tears, Jurissa said, "You aren't well enough to be out of bed."

"Look to me like it be time I be helping you."

Staring at Yubah's bruised face, Jurissa was reminded of how cruel her husband had been. Leon, in contrast, was kind and thoughtful, not only to her but to Silas and Yubah. She didn't believe for one moment he deliberately threw Philip over the rail. No, not Leon. It wasn't in him to behave in such a cowardly fashion.

But accidentally, in a struggle with Philip? Accidents were beyond anyone's control. "Oh, Yubah," she wailed, "they're saying Philip — Mr. Winterton — was pushed into the sea."

Terror surfaced in Yubah's amber eyes. "No!" Her voice rose until she almost shrieked. "Don't you go believing lies. Massa Philip done fall on his ownsome, that's what. He drink all that whiskey and he fall."

Jurissa caught her by the shoulders. "How do you know? Did you see him fall? He hurt you. You must have been there."

Yubah hunched in on herself. "Didn't see nothing. I just knows."

Jurissa let her go. The girl had been frightened enough. She didn't want to scare her. "What happened between you and Mr. Winterton?" she asked, trying to keep her voice calm. "How did he hurt you?"

Yubah stared at her own bare feet. "Massa Philip, he be mad 'cause Silas don't come running with them guns. Massa Philip, he sees me, make to grab me and I be scared. I tries to run. Ole foot slip, make me fall."

"What happened then?"

"I don't be knowing." Yubah touched her swollen eye and glanced sideways at Jurissa. "Seem like I bang ole head on something. What go on, I don't be seeing, I don't be hearing 'cause I don't be there, me. Next thing, Massa Leon, he pick me up, tote me to where you be."

"You mean you knocked yourself out when you fell?"

"What you say."

"Where was Mr. Winterton when Monsieur du Motier picked you up?"

Yubah shrugged. "I purely don't know, Miss Jurissa. Seem like I be lost in a fog till you put me to bed."

Jurissa decided Yubah knew little more than she did. What she'd actually seen wasn't much and proved nothing one way or the other. "Where was Silas when all this was going on?" she asked.

Jurissa licked her cracked lips. "Didn't see Silas. I s'pect he be taking his time finding Massa Philip's guns so Massa Philip, he don't make no trouble."

Jurissa was moved to pity. Brother and sister must have tried to find ways of dealing with Philip to keep them from being beaten and to avoid trouble. It hadn't saved Yubah from Philip's fists but Leon's life might well have been saved by Silas's deliberate delay in bringing the guns to Philip. Evidently Philip never did get the guns, and without the guns he wouldn't have threatened to shoot Leon. So Leon wouldn't have had cause to defend himself.

Oh, why hadn't she simply accepted on faith that Leon couldn't possibly have been involved in Philip's accident? The sailor's accusation against Leon had shaken her, had shocked her until she couldn't think straight, and her addled thoughts led her astray. She should have followed her heart and believed in Leon, no matter what anyone said or did. Now it was too late; he'd never trust her again.

It was small consolation that at least she'd had the sense not to mention Leon's name to Yubah in connection with Philip's accident.

"Don't mean to take sick no more," Yubah told her.

With an effort, Jurissa brought her attention back to the Negro woman. "I don't blame you for being sick," she assured her. "The fever certainly wasn't your fault. I'm only happy the quinine cured you so quickly. I do think, though, you should rest until we can be sure you're completely well."

"I be fine. Don't need to stay in bed."

Yubah looked far from fine with her discolored, swollen face. She'd removed the sling but Jurissa knew her left wrist must be painful. Jurissa also was aware that no matter what she said, Yubah would insist she was able to resume her duties. The only way to get around that was with a direct order.

"I want you to stay in the cabin and sleep in the bunk you've been using," she announced. "I'll take the other one. I won't have you trying to work or wait on me until I give you permission. Do you understand?"

"Yes'm."

"Good."

If only she could solve all her problems as easily and directly, Jurissa thought. How could she have been so unthinking, so heartless as to have hurt Leon as she had? Was there any way to convince him that, deep down, she hadn't really doubted him? She couldn't think of one, and she had to stop fretting about it and try to go on.

God knows there was plenty to worry about. She was acquainted with no one in New Orleans. What was she to do when she arrived there? She'd need money for a place to stay. Was there money among Philip's belongings? She had no idea and no heart to search through his things to find out. Soon she'd have to, though.

As if reading her mind, Yubah said, "Don't be no work to neaten the cabin, Miss Jurissa."

Slowly Jurissa nodded. With Yubah helping her, she might manage to accomplish what was needed. It would be a relief to have Philip's belongings packed away, out of sight. He was gone and she must come to terms with that. She hadn't loved him, she hadn't even liked him, but she hadn't betrayed him, either. As best she could she'd tried to be his wife.

If it was her fault he staggered out onto the deck in

pursuit of her, it certainly wasn't her fault that he drank the whiskey. Perhaps if he hadn't been so dazed he wouldn't have hurt her. She'd try to believe that was true, try to think the best, rather than the worst of her dead husband.

Later, sitting on her bunk, Jurissa recounted the few gold coins she'd found in a leather pouch in a pocket of Philip's trunk. Though she knew nothing of the cost of staying in a hotel, she'd grown accustomed to paying the bills for Arabel after her guardian took ill, and she realized the coins wouldn't last very long. She badly needed advice and there was no one to ask. Except Leon.

His adieu had been final. He meant to have no more to do with her; he might even refuse to speak to her if she went to him with her problem. He was a gentleman and wouldn't close his door in her face, but what if he didn't bother to answer her knock at his door?

Leon smoothed the supple kid of Jurissa's black gloves between his fingers as he lay on his bunk staring into space. The fine leather was no softer or smoother than her skin. Her lovely translucent skin. The pillow under his head retained a tantalizing hint of her fragrance. Without realizing what he was doing, he turned his face into the scent, then swore at what he'd done. *Bigre!* Was he never to rid himself of her image?

Was it his heart that suffered or merely his pride? He'd never expected she would doubt him. Accept the word of a sailor against the honor of a Creole. Women. Who could trust them? He'd thought her different from other women he knew but he'd been proven wrong.

He must put her from his mind completely. Now. Before the ship lay at anchor off New Orleans. Jurissa Winterton had no place in his life once he left the *Yarmouth*. It was as well to end anything between them once and for all. Yes, the breach was inevitable, and because it had come about through her own doing, she'd have nothing to reproach him with. A simple matter, really, to avoid her for the rest of the journey, then there'd be no further problem.

His decision didn't improve his disposition. Why, he wondered, if his problem had been so easily solved, was he so melancholy? His life was in order, well planned, his future was not in doubt.

He would wed Louise-Marie. She would be a good wife to him in many ways. Papa would be happy. Louise-Marie's dowry would prop up Dindon until the bedamned English pigs tired of interfering with honest merchant ships. And the cotton and cured sugar could be shipped overseas in safety. Someday, *le bon Dieu* rest that it be later rather than sooner, he would be master of Dindon.

And would he be happy? Leon sighed. Louise-Marie had little fire. She wouldn't be a passionate wife. But if she failed, as he expected she would, to satisfy his needs, there were always the cottages of the rue des Ramparts and a quadroon girl for a *placee*; a mistress of color who'd provide what Louise-Marie could not. Louise-Marie would accept the necessity without mentioning that she knew, exactly as a proper Creole wife was expected to do. She'd be happy enough to be spared, for the most part, that part of marriage.

Leon twisted the gloves savagely and flung them away from him. *Mon Dieu*, how dull a life!

He sprang to his feet and began pacing back and forth in the tiny cabin. She was nothing to him, the Winterton woman. He'd wanted her, yes. What man wouldn't be tempted by that green-eyed witch? He'd longed to possess her but she'd have no place in his life once he made love to her. He would rid himself of that compulsion. The only reason she haunted him was simple enough: The affair had never been finished. He hadn't had her; they'd never made love. If they had, he'd be well on his way to forgetting her.

Yes, that was the answer. Leon stopped pacing and smiled one-sidedly. She might not trust him, might believe he'd pushed her husband over the rail, but he was willing to bet she'd still melt in his arms if he played his cards right. What Creole could resist gambling for such a prize?

Putting on his boots and collecting his hat, Leon started to leave his cabin, hesitated, turned back and plucked Jurissa's black gloves from the floor, then sauntered along the passageway.

Yubah opened the door to his knock. To his critical eye she'd improved but was far from well. She needed more rest. It didn't do to work a sick slave. Many died from this short-sighted policy. Not at Dindon, however. The du Motiers took care of their slaves. He opened his mouth to order the Negro woman back to bed, then clamped it shut. She belonged to Jurissa, and it was none of his business if Yubah's mistress had no concern for her maid.

Peering over Yubah's head, he saw Jurissa staring at him from inside the room. "Please tell your mistress I'm returning her gloves," he said to Yubah while keeping his gaze fixed on Jurissa.

Jurissa moved toward the door like a sleepwalker, her eyes wide and apprehensive. "I'll take the gloves, Yubah," she said. He thought she sounded a bit breathless.

He deliberately touched her fingers as he handed her the gloves, noting with amused dismay the slight contact affected him as much as it did her. Ah well, he'd soon be cured.

"I thought we might talk," he said crisply.

"Oh, yes! Yes, I'd like to talk to you. I need to." She glanced behind her as if considering the state of the cabin, then looked back at him.

Before she could invite him inside, he said, "If I'm not mistaken, your maid is far from well yet and needs to rest. I dislike having to turn her out of the cabin so we can speak privately. I'd prefer to go elsewhere."

He watched her ponder, knowing exactly what she was thinking. A turn on the deck risked more of the morning's unpleasantness.

"If you don't consider it too improper," he added quickly, "I suggest my cabin." He was well aware in daring to propose that she come to his cabin was not only highly improper but might, in some circles, be considered insulting.

Jurissa raised her eyebrows but made no pretense of being shocked, and he couldn't help but admire her honesty. She hesitated, catching her lower lip between small white teeth.

"Perhaps you are afraid," he challenged.

Her chin came up. "No, no, of course not. Why should I be?"

Leon shrugged, smiling coolly. "You gave me the impression you didn't trust me."

She shrank back as though he'd struck her, her eyes on her clasped hands. "I'm sorry. It was only —"

"I prefer to discuss the matter in privacy," he put in, cutting her off. "In my cabin."

She glanced up at him and, after a moment, nodded.

A frisson of excitement shot through him. The first obstacle — getting her to come to his cabin — had been the greatest, but he'd overcome it. He looked forward with eager anticipation to conquering whatever minor problems might surface once she was there. His reward would be worth any amount of effort.

Jurissa gave him a twisted smile. "I hardly think my reputation can become any more tarnished in the eyes of the passengers than it already is."

He frowned. For the first time since he'd formulated his plan, he was visited by a flicker of doubt. A Creole might engage in any amount of romantic intrigue, but he was always careful not to sully a lady's honor in public. Should he consider being more protective of hers?

"I wanted to come to see you," she went on, "because I badly needed to explain, or try to. But I wasn't sure you'd care to talk to me."

She'd intended to come to him? In that case he'd merely anticipated her visit by inviting her. No gentleman ever turned a lady away, certainly he would not.

"Shall we go, then?" he asked.

When he had Jurissa safely inside his cabin, the door shut, Leon found himself inexplicably nervous. Brandy hadn't been a part of his plan but he needed a drink. After seating her on the one chair, he brought out a leather case and extracted two of the four small stemmed silver goblets before lifting out a matching silver flask.

"French brandy," he explained, pouring a measure into each glass. "I'd like you to taste it."

She took the stemmed goblet he handed her and smiled up at him. "Smuggled by your Captain Lafitte, no doubt. Pirate goods."

He grinned in acknowledgment. "But none the worse for it."

Jurissa sniffed the liquor, swirled it daintily, then sipped and savored the taste before she swallowed. "Quite good."

His eyebrows shot up. "That's faint praise. You are a connoisseur, then?"

"Arabel—she was my guardian—taught me to appreciate fine wines and brandy. When she left Paris shortly before what she always called 'the unpleasantness,' she brought along enough to stock a creditable cellar in Boston."

"Ah, your guardian was French."

"No, she was Scottish, as I am. My maiden name was Campbell; hers was McLeod."

"Are you saying Madame McLeod fled the revolutionaries in Paris?"

"Mademoiselle McLeod, she never married." Jurissa warmed the silver goblet between her palms. "I miss her so very much."

Leon lifted the brandy bottle and poised it over her goblet but she shook her head. "Arabel also taught me to know how much I could drink without ceasing to become a lady."

"She sounds formidable, this spinster who raised you." Leon poured himself another tot of brandy, for some reason reluctant to begin on the seduction he'd so carefully planned. He found it enough for the moment to watch the varied expressions flit across Jurissa's face as she spoke of her past. This was a woman he wanted to learn more about.

"Don't call Arabel a spinster," Jurissa protested. "She may not have married but she did experience love."

His lips curled in amusement. "I have heard such stories before: The young girl whose fiancé dies tragically so she refuses all offers and clings to his memory the rest of her life. A waste. Only the very young and foolish believe love comes but once in a lifetime."

Jurissa set her goblet on the chest with a pronounced click and sat straighter in her chair. "Arabel lived happily with her lover for many years. He was a French aristocrat who was finally sacrificed to Madame Guillotine. Arabel would not have agreed with you about foolishness. True love, she often said, came but once and, if a woman or a man wished to know the greatest happiness to be had on earth, they must give up everything else and surrender to such a love."

Leon, somewhat taken aback, recovered enough to say, "And you—do you subscribe to your guardian's belief?"

A becoming pink crept up to flush Jurissa's cheeks, and she didn't immediately reply. "Have you invited me here to discuss my beliefs?" she asked at last.

His gaze roved to her breasts and on down to her fine-boned ankles showing below the ruffled hem of her gown before returning again to her face. "I find everything about you of interest."

Charmed by her deepening blush, he set down his goblet, reaching for her hand and drew her to her feet. Her fathomless green eyes held his. A man might drown while trying to plumb their depths. He drew a gentle finger along her flushed cheek to the corner of her mouth and brushed it across her full, enticing lower lip, If ever a mouth was made to be kissed, this one was. As he leaned closer he heard her catch her breath.

Would she protest now, placing a restraining palm against his chest and remind him she came here to talk? Not unless she'd changed remarkably in a few short hours. Unlike most women, Jurissa had never tried to hide her emotions from him. He was certain she waited eagerly for his kiss, and the knowledge made his pulses pound.

*Mon Dieu*, but her lips were sweet. She tasted of brandy and of herself, a headier brew than any concocted by a vintner. He never drank to excess but she could get him drunk with her kisses.

She'd removed her bonnet and gloves before sitting down, but not her short jacket. He unbuttoned the spencer without taking his lips from hers, the brush of his fingers against the softness of her breasts fueling his already flaming need for her. He slid the jacket from her shoulders and flung it aside, catching her to him.

His hands cupped the rounded thrust of her derriere and pressed her body against his hardness. He groaned with the agonizing thrill the feel of her brought. She clung to him, arms holding him close, the gasping rhythm of her breathing matching his own. She'd be no proper Creole wife. Passion flowed with the blood in her veins, and her mouth was hot and sweet with desire.

The buttons of her gown were at the back. One-handedly he fumbled them open while holding her to him. Easing her away from him, he slid the gown down until it fell to the floor. All that separated her loveliness from him was a sheer, low-necked chemise. Impatiently, he slid his hand inside it to her breast. Her moan, soft and eager, shivered through him.

"*Cherie*," he murmured, pushing aside the chemise so his lips could taste her breast, the nipple rising rosy pink as he'd known it would. She gasped in pleasure, her arms sliding down to his waist as her hips moved against him in a way that drove him wild with desire.

He tore the chemise from her and carried her to the bunk, easing her onto the coverlet, then yanking off his own clothes in a frenzy of need. Her eyes widened, clouding as he came to her naked. When he tried to take her into his arms again her pliant yielding had disappeared. She lay rigid to his touch.

"No," she whispered. "Don't hurt me." Fright quivered in her words.

He had no idea what was wrong but he certainly didn't mean to force her. On the other hand, he had no intention of stopping. Taking a deep breath, he pulled away from her and forced himself to control his desperate need. Not touching her otherwise, he leaned down to kiss her. At first her lips were cold and closed under his but gently, persistently, he eased them open with his tongue until finally Jurissa sighed and welcomed him into her mouth.

He trailed kisses down to her breasts and took one, then the other, into his mouth. His fingers, feather light, slid over the curve of her hip, stroking, caressing. She was so exquisite, so warm and soft as her body began to relax under his exploring hands that he felt about to burst with urgency but, somehow, he held back.

Jurissa gasped as his fingers slipped between her thighs, then moaned in little gasping breaths as he caressed her. Her arms fastened around his neck and she tried to press herself against him. "Leon," she breathed. "Oh, Leon."

He kissed her, long deep kisses, while his fingers pleasured her until she began to thrash her head back and forth, writhing her hips. Only then did he kneel between her spread thighs and ease himself inside her.

He got the shock of his life when his difficulty in entering made him realize she'd never known a man, that he was the first one for her. By then it was too late for him to stop; he could not. He could only plunge on. She cried out and he knew it was in pain. Making a supreme effort, he managed to stop moving, to give her time to recover.

"I didn't know," he murmured into her ear, feeling the words rasp in his throat. "I didn't mean to hurt you." He kissed her love-swollen lips. "I never want to hurt you."

Her lips were soft under his, answering his kiss. Her fingers caressed his nape, tangled in his hair. Slowly, carefully, he began to ease himself out, then in again. When she started moaning, he stopped, but her hands slid down to his hips and she arched to him. He knew then her moans were not from pain but from wanting him. Seized by a frenzy of delight, he loosened all restraint to enjoy her as she was meant to be enjoyed. To pleasure her as she was made to be pleasured.

In his own language he told her how lovely she was, how wonderful; the most beautiful, the most passionate woman in the world. His woman, meant for love, meant for him and no one else.

In his daze of passion he heard her words only dimly. "*Je t'aime*," she whispered in short sobbing gasps. "I love you. Only you. Forever."

When their lovemaking crested and receded, Leon had expected it to be the end. He reached his goal; she'd been made his in a way he'd never anticipated. He lay beside her, momentarily at peace with the world, feeling a victor's satisfaction.

Less than a half hour later, when new tendrils of desire rose in him and he reached for her again, he began to realize something was amiss. True, he'd set a subtle trap, a trap that had caught his quarry unawares, but he'd made one vital mistake. It had never once occurred to him he might be trapped along with her.

## Chapter Six

Jurissa, blushing, tucked the coverlet closer about herself as Leon, standing near the bunk, tantalized her by holding a wedge of cheese just out of her reach. She was starving but was too shy to uncover herself.

"If you would please hand me my shift," she said as loftily as she could manage. It was difficult to be dignified when you had no clothes on and the person you were speaking to was stark naked. Though she tried not to stare at Leon, his body fascinated her. How very differently men were fashioned!

"What are you afraid of?" he demanded.

"You know very well it's not proper to go about without clothes."

He laughed. "*Cherie*, it is far too late to worry about propriety."

He was certainly correct. Two times now he'd joined with her in the same strange, incredible manner, bringing such intense pleasure she'd half expected to die in rapture the second time. After such intimacy perhaps she ought not to feel embarrassed by her own nakedness or his — but she was.

Leon must have dressed and gone out for food while

she napped. She'd roused to find him peeling off his clothes, a tray of bread, cheese, and wine resting atop the chest. Now he teased her with the cheese. She didn't recall ever being so hungry but how could she let him see her without her clothes?

Of course, he already had, but she'd been so excited at those times she hadn't thought about nakedness.

"I swear your face grows as red as a broiled crayfish," he commented, setting down the cheese and advancing. "It makes me wonder if the rest of you has turned the same color."

"You wouldn't dare!" she cried, clutching at the covers.

"You think not?" He pounced on her and slipped his hands beneath the coverlet.

She squealed in dismay but as soon as his hands touched her bare skin her resistance melted like butter in the sun. He gathered her to him and his lips closed over hers. Through the blanket the part of him that had once frightened her pressed against her thigh, and she sighed in delicious anticipation.

"But I'm hungry," she protested when his mouth sought her breasts.

He lifted his head. "Shall I stop?"

She couldn't bear it if he did, and the wicked gleam in his eyes told her he was well aware of how she felt. "You're teasing me," she whispered into his ear.

"You hide yourself under the covers—don't you think that's teasing me?" Pulling away, he swept the coverlet completely from her and stared at her body. "Your breasts are more beautiful than the dawn," he said huskily. "And the rest of you—words can't express how exquisite you are."

Jurissa's embarrassment vanished in a surge of wild need that rushed through her as she listened to Leon and saw his own rising excitement.

"Take pride in these," he murmured, stroking her breasts with both hands, then trailing his fingers along her hips. "And these." She gasped in pleasure when he reached between her thighs and she scarcely heard his whispered, "And this."

She breathed his name, her eyes closing, her arms rising to embrace him. But he grasped her arms and held her away. She opened her eyes.

"You haven't told me what frightened you," he said. "I want to know so I'll never make you afraid again."

Jurissa gazed at him in dismay. How could she ever explain?

He bent to kiss her, nibbling at her lower lip. "Tell me," he urged, his breath hot and sweet against her mouth. "I want no secrets between us, ever."

"It was—it was you," she muttered, not looking at him.

"Me? What about me?"

"A—a part of you. I didn't know about men."

"How can I understand unless you show me what part you mean?" He kissed the tip of her nose.

"Oh, I couldn't!"

"*Cherie*, I assure you we'll both enjoy it."

She wouldn't touch him. He was teasing her again; he knew very well what she meant. Yet curiosity mixed with unsatisfied desire tingled through her and finally she sat up and laid a tentative hand on his crinkly dark chest hair and slowly, slowly, eased downward.

She heard Leon catch his breath and he closed his eyes when she neared her goal. He groaned when her fingers hesitantly felt along his throbbing hardness.

Tumbling her backward, he pulled her to him. "Ah, *cherie*, you drive me mad. I will never get enough of you."

His kisses and caresses drew her into another world, a magic world shared only by the two of them; a world where there was no separate Leon, no separate Jurissa; a world where they became one in love.

When she came to herself again, with Leon lying beside her, she thought of the scandal they must be causing aboard the ship. She smiled. What did it matter? She didn't care what others might whisper about her. She'd found her true love and they'd never be parted.

Later, she in her shift, he in his drawers, they sat eating bread and cheese and drinking wine.

"It puzzles me," Leon said. "You were married, yet as innocent as any maid. Did your husband never demand his rights?"

Jurissa felt her cheeks redden but did her best to ignore the blush. No secrets between them, Leon had said and she meant to keep it that way. "I didn't know what to expect. Arabel spoke only of love and kisses. She was vague about what else happened between a man and woman. And so when Philip—" She paused, wondering how she could bring herself to go on.

Leon scowled. "He tried to force you and he hurt and frightened you. Am I right?"

She nodded. "I'd never seen a man without his clothes. I had no notion of what he wanted. I didn't know—" She paused again, peering shyly at Leon from under her lashes. "Until you taught me in your own fashion, I didn't realize a man and a woman could take such pleasure in one another."

He leaned toward her. "With us, when you and I come together, it is wonderful." He flung out his hands, as if groping for the right words. "Not always does this—this—" He shook his head.

"You don't have to tell me. I know it couldn't be this way except with you." She smiled at him. "Love is what makes the difference."

Leon took a deep breath and refilled his wineglass. She waited but he retreated into silence.

If he hadn't told her he loved her, he *had* shown her, Jurissa assured herself. She must be content. She couldn't expect him to speak of marriage so soon after Philip's death. Why, she was scarcely a widow.

Something Arabel had told her popped into her mind: the sad story of a Boston woman whose husband captained a ship. When neither ship nor husband returned to port, they were presumed lost at sea. But there was no proof. When the woman, who considered herself a widow, wished to remarry after two years, she found it impossible without a complicated and lengthy court procedure.

Will something like that happen to me? Jurissa wondered apprehensively. I'm no longer a wife but legally I'm not yet a widow. I'm in limbo. I couldn't marry Leon even if he did ask me.

But she had faith in Leon. No matter what the difficulties, he'd find a way for them to be together.

"I remember you saying you lived on a plantation," she said, eager to learn all she could about him. "We don't have plantations in Boston."

Leon blinked, coming out of his reverie. "Plantations are but one of the amenities Boston lacks."

85

"Tell me about your home, please."

He leaned back and his eyes took on a faraway look. "Dindon is incomparably beautiful. My great grandfather was granted the land and began building what he called his chateau. Today his oak saplings have grown so their branches meet over the drive sweeping up from the river to the house. The oaks also circle to both sides, holding the house in a protective embrace. In the gardens flowers bloom all year, such flowers as Boston has never seen. The first du Motiers grew sugarcane. We still plant some acres of cane but cotton is our main crop."

"*Dindon*. Turkey-cock. Surely an odd name for a plantation?"

Leon smiled. "They tell me if I'd known my great-grandfather, I'd see the reason for the name. It seems he was king of the walk or knew the reason why."

"Your love for your home comes through in everything you tell me."

"Dindon is a heritage no du Motier has ever betrayed."

With each word he said about his New Orleans home he seemed farther and farther away from her. Suddenly feeling chilly in her shift, Jurissa shivered.

"I must dress," she said. "It's very late. Past time to return to my cabin. Poor Yubah must be worrying what's become of me. I didn't leave her food or the means to get any."

She thought Leon would protest, would make a move to keep her with him. Instead, he said, "I spoke to Silas when I collected the cheese and wine. He's taking care of his sister."

Shame crept over Jurissa. Though they were her

responsibility, she hadn't once thought, until this moment, of Yubah's welfare, much less Silas's. Leon had. He'd made certain the pair were all right. She must try to accustom herself to the notion that Yubah and Silas depended on her, for they did.

Expecting to find it awkward to don her garments with Leon watching, she discovered she was mistaken. He dressed himself at the same time, paying scant attention to what she was doing. At last, bonnet tied firmly onto her head, she pulled on her gloves, inexplicably fighting tears.

Leon opened the door and glanced into the passageway. "No one in sight," he announced, ushering her out. Her heart lifted as she saw he intended to escort her to her cabin. But, though he pressed her hand as he left her and murmured "au revoir," Jurissa felt his spirit wasn't with her but in New Orleans, at the plantation he loved.

More than he loved her? If he did love her. He hadn't said so. Surely a man and woman couldn't share what they had without love on both sides. Hadn't Arabel assured her of that? Inside her cabin, Jurissa leaned against the closed door and sighed. Somehow, Arabel's axioms about true love didn't comfort her as they once had.

Dreams plagued Leon's sleep, dreams of Jurissa as a mermaid who wept tears of pearl as she swam away from him forever. Dreams of Dindon in ruins and his father's voice from beyond the grave reproaching him for failing his sacred trust. The final dream was again of Jurissa, who slipped into his bed at Dindon to tantalize him with her caresses. He reached for her and woke alone and bereft.

He sat up and dropped his head into his hands. He was about as far from forgetting Jurissa as a man could be. Each time he touched her he wanted her more. And she, in her innocence, believed herself in love with him because of the passion she'd learned with him. What was he to do about her? And with himself? He shied from calling it love—what had love to do with desire? But he couldn't bear to think of another man holding her in his arms. She was his and he'd kill the man who touched her.

He couldn't possibly marry Louise-Marie, feeling as he did about Jurissa. On the other hand, how was he to explain Jurissa to his father? He frowned, considering. There must be a way. He'd find a way.

He lay back on the bunk, hands under his head, picturing Jurissa coming down the great curving staircase at Dindon in a sea-green gown to match her eyes, silken panels floating behind her as she gracefully descended. Smiling at him, coming to him, holding out her arms . . .

*Bigre!* A few hours without her and he ached as though he had yet to possess her. There was no hope of ending this before they reached New Orleans. The affair must go its way, must be allowed to burn itself out. And if it didn't? Ah, well, if it never ended he supposed he'd wind up marrying her. Papa would understand once he met Jurissa. She was so enchanting that if she met a hungry bull alligator in a swamp, the beast would take one look at her, roll over and let her tickle his belly. No mere male was a match for her charm.

Yet he didn't see how he could bring her to Dindon with him, not immediately. No, the proper approach would be to escort her to a hotel—the Orleans was the best choice—and see her safely established there. *Maman* would be easy enough to persuade. The slightest mention of a young widow all alone in the world would bring tears to her eyes. *Maman* would invite Jurissa to stay at the plantation the minute she heard of her plight. Papa was a different matter. Jurissa might well charm him but Dindon always came first with Papa. And now there was no one but Leon to take charge.

Leon shrugged. He'd worry about Papa later. In the meantime, he intended to do everything he could to keep Jurissa in his bed until the ship set anchor.

Jurissa retied her bonnet for the fourth time and smoothed her unwrinkled gloves. Yubah, her face almost back to normal, had everything packed and ready to be carried off the ship by Silas, who waited outside the cabin.

"Oh, I wish New Orleans was still halfway around the world," Jurissa cried. "Why did the journey have to end?"

"Seem like there got to be an end to most everything," Yubah said soothingly.

The words weren't what Jurissa wanted to hear. "I'm going on deck. I can't bear to wait inside the cabin," she said.

"Massa Leon say to stay here."

She absolutely could not, Jurissa decided. Let everyone aboard the *Yarmouth* cut her dead if they must, she didn't care. She'd suffocate if she didn't get outside and breathe fresh air. Above all she needed the reassurance of seeing Leon.

He'd explained why he had to take her to the Hotel Orleans—his father was far from well and his health had to be considered. Besides, Leon wished to have her meet his family properly, after his mother issued an invitation for Jurissa to visit Dindon. Her head understood why Leon wanted everything correct but her heart protested. She didn't want to be separated from him for even a day.

What was she to do with herself while she waited? And with Yubah and Silas, for that matter? The last thing in the world she wanted to be was a slave owner but, as Leon had pointed out, that's what she'd become.

"If I own them I have the right to free them, don't I?" she'd asked only yesterday. "Then that's what I'll do."

Leon shook his head. "You're responsible for your husband's slaves but, until Winterton is declared legally dead and the court rules on your inheritance of his property, they're still his, not yours. When you do own them unconditionally, you'd be foolish to free them. If Silas isn't of use, you might consider selling him when that becomes possible. He's strong and healthy and would fetch a good price. I'd buy him myself if he were available."

She couldn't bear to think about selling human beings; she'd never do it, and certainly she'd never separate Yubah and Silas. There was little to be gained in arguing with Leon, though, since he viewed slaves as possessions.

"So, although the court hasn't yet decided whether or not I own them," she said, "I must take the responsibility for Yubah and Silas."

He grinned at her. "It's no calamity. They'll come with you to Dindon when you visit. They'll fit in there and all will be well. You'll see. The trouble with you is you have no patience."

"*I* have no patience? What about *you?*" She'd gestured toward her clothes strewn over his cabin floor. "You won't even allow me the time to undress properly."

Jurissa smiled at the memory as she came out of the passageway onto the deck. Though she'd never dreamed it was possible, she loved Leon more every day.

The air was mild, even balmy, and the sun was warm. Such a variety of smells assailed her nostrils that she had trouble separating one from the other. Damp earth, she thought, and brine. A hint of fish, of strange and sweet blooms, and of something darker, unidentifiable, a bit frightening. New Orleans, a strange city in a strange land, now to be her home.

No one spoke to her but she hardly noticed as her eyes skipped past passengers and crewmen in a search for Leon. When he was with her, nothing was strange; nothing could ever frighten her.

"Do you ever do as you're asked?" His familiar voice spoke in French from behind her.

She whirled and saw him, handsome and debonair in a brown tail coat and fawn trousers. His frown couldn't conceal the gleam of laughter in his eyes.

"*Mai oui, monsieur,*" she replied demurely. "Depending on what I've been asked to do. And by whom."

"How is a man ever to know where you are if you refuse to stay put?" he demanded.

"You'll always know where I am," she promised, her

voice gentle.

He offered his arm and she put her gloved hand on it. Her anxieties fled now that she was with him. He found her a place next to him in the boat bringing them to the dock and made certain Yubah and Silas would follow in the next load.

She found it strange to walk on dry land once again with her legs still anticipating the sea's pitch and roll. The clamor and the flurry of dockside activity daunted her. Mule carts with shouting drivers clattered on cobbles, men called orders to laders, somewhere nearby church bells tolled.

Leon led her through this confusion and was assisting her into a hired carriage when she heard a man's voice, a Negro by the sound, calling his name.

"Francois!" Leon exclaimed and flung his arms around a tall, thin black man with a frizz of white hair. "Ah, it's good to see you. Have you come to meet me, then?"

"Seven days, now, I meet every ship, sir." Francois spoke French, as Leon did. "The master, he very low. Mistress worry, say find you, bring you quick."

Jurissa caught her breath at Leon's stricken expression. "How bad is Papa?" he asked Francois.

"You best hurry," Francois advised.

Leon turned to Jurissa. "I must go immediately to Dindon," he told her. "I planned to see you safely to your room in the hotel, but—"

She grasped his hand between hers. "I'm sorry your father is so ill. Of course you must hurry to his side."

"The driver will wait for Yubah and Silas, and your baggage, then drive you to the Hotel Orleans." He gazed at her, frowning.

"Don't worry about me. I'll be fine," she assured him, though inwardly she wasn't sure she'd ever be fine without Leon by her side.

"I don't know how long it will be before I can come to you."

She made herself smile. "I promise you'll be able to find me when you do."

He smiled in return and for a moment she thought he meant to kiss her in farewell. But, after a glance at Francois, Leon only pressed her hand. "Au revoir."

She watched him stride away with Francois, hoping he'd turn and wave. He did not and she chided herself for expecting him to when worry about his father had to be overwhelming him. Obviously, the elder du Motier was at the point of death if Madame du Motier had sent a servant to the docks to meet each incoming ship and look for Leon.

Quelling her own nervousness about being on her own, Jurissa told herself she'd manage very well and would wait patiently for Leon to come to her. Yubah and Silas might be her responsibility but Yubah, at least, was a companion of sorts. She wouldn't be all alone.

A week later, Jurissa, already upset because she hadn't had word from Leon, was forced to face the fact that the Hotel Orleans, though pleasant enough, was too expensive for her to stay on. Counting the two gold coins she had left, she worried that her money would run out before Leon was able to leave his father and come to her.

"I don't know what we're going to do," she confessed

to Yubah, whom she'd begun to consider as much a friend as a servant. "We can't stay at this hotel much longer. It costs too much."

"Seems like there be some other place to go for just a bitty bit of money," Yubah said. "You want me to look, I be going."

"I'll come with you," Jurissa offered.

"I do best by my ownsome. You be a lady. Don't be right for you to be talking 'bout money."

"But at least half the people in this city speak only French. You don't understand French. What about that?"

Yubah's eyes slid away from hers. "You don't be mad?"

Jurissa knew by now this was a prelude to Yubah admitting something she feared to tell. "I promise I won't be angry," she assured Yubah. "What is it?"

"Silas, he don't be knowing any French. I does. Ole Massa give me to Miss Katherine when we be bitty girls. Miss Katherine, she won't pay heed to her lessons lest I come along. They teach her French and I hears it. Pretty soon I knows the words just like Miss Katherine. Don't dare tell her. Don't be telling no one. Ole Missus say I uppity, whup me, sure."

"Oh, Yubah, you're full of surprises. Next you'll be telling me you can read."

Yubah cast her eyes down again and Jurissa began to laugh. "You can! You can read, can't you?"

"Bitty bit," Yubah admitted.

Impulsively, Jurissa hugged her. "I'm glad we're together. I don't know what I'd do without you."

Yubah beamed. "Never 'spect Massa Philip gonna marry a fine lady like you, Miss Jurissa. Silas and me, we be glad he dead and we be with you."

Jurissa couldn't chastise Yubah for her remark about Philip. If she were honest with herself, she'd admit she, too, found it a relief to be rid of Philip, though it made her feel guilty. Poor Philip. Did no one mourn for him?

"Why not take Silas with you?" she asked Yubah.

"He be looking for work."

Jurissa blinked. "Work? But how can he? I mean—" She paused, unsure exactly what she meant. She didn't want to be Silas's owner, but she was. If she owned him, how could he work for someone else?

"Silas and me, we knows you need money," Yubah said. "He gonna say his mistress send him out to work. That do happen. They gonna hire him 'cause he strong. He bring you what they be paying him."

"I don't know, Yubah. It doesn't seem fair."

Yubah shrugged. "You don't be needing Silas hanging round. You needs money."

It seemed logical when Yubah put it that way. To think I worried about assuming responsibility for them, Jurissa marveled. Instead, they're taking care of me.

Yubah returned triumphant with the news she'd found inexpensive quarters above a bakery run by a free woman of color, Tiana LeMoine.

"Miss Tiana, she born free," Yubah confided to Jurissa. "Her mama be a *placee*."

"I don't understand that word."

"*Placee* be pretty yellow Nigra woman, like that. Creole man, he buy her a little house; she be his."

"They get married, you mean?"

Yubah shook her head. "Creole man, he marry Creole lady, they live in fine big house. But he keep *placee* in her little house. He keep two women, wife and *placee*, that how it be in New Orleans."

Jurissa considered the matter. "Then our landlady's father was a Creole man?"

Yubah nodded. "He give Miss Tiana his name; she free."

Did Yubah's voice hold a touch of wistfulness? Jurissa sighed. She'd counted on Leon helping her establish her ownership of Yubah and Silas so she could set about freeing them. As it stood now, she was helpless to do anything.

"If you think the apartment above the bakery is suitable, I'm sure I will," she told Yubah. "It's certainly inexpensive."

"Ain't fancy but the rooms be big and clean and they be a bitty place in back for Silas to sleep. And Miss Tiana say she pay me a penny a day do I tote her goods to people. Silas, he gonna help a blacksmith. We gonna do just fine, no matter what. You wait and see, Miss Jurissa."

It sounded almost as though Yubah didn't believe Leon would come at all. Of course he would! Hadn't he said so? He didn't realize how little money she had or he'd have been here sooner. She knew he had to be missing her as desperately as she missed him. His father's illness must be grave, indeed, for she was certain nothing else would keep him from her.

Jurissa found the apartment exactly as Yubah had described: not fancy but suitable enough for someone who had to watch her pennies. After all, what difference did it make where she lived while she waited for Leon? As soon as he came for her she'd be leaving for Dindon anyway. Not knowing how to get in touch with him, she left a message at the hotel, giving him the location of her new quarters on the rue des Normandie.

Once she'd settled in, she found herself lonelier than ever since Yubah was busy delivering baked goods for Miss Tiana much of the time. She couldn't bear being alone with her increasing anxiety about Leon and, though she hadn't noticed young ladies walking unaccompanied in New Orleans, Jurissa felt she had to get out into the air.

In Boston, unmarried, she might have caused a raised eyebrow or two walking by herself but it wasn't truly improper. Customs were different here. Unmarried maidens were chaperoned at all times but she no longer fit into that category. Though she couldn't call herself either wife or widow at the moment, at least she'd been married.

Improper or not, she was determined to explore her new neighborhood, and she had no choice but to do so alone. Dressing carefully in an ivory silk ankle-length street dress, she donned her straw bonnet with the feather trim and, carrying a Chinese sunshade, set out along the banquettes, the wooden sidewalks built above the streets.

She was charmed by the two-story buildings of brick, some stuccoed over and painted in pale colors. All had what she called porches running along both stories—here the word used was galleries. The foliage, which she was able to glimpse through the doors shutting the courtyards away from the street, fascinated her. She'd never seen so many blooming shrubs with such gorgeous blossoms.

Tiny yellow birds flitted in and out of the shrubbery, and Negro women with *tignons*, brightly colored kerchiefs, on their heads, sloshed water along the planked floors of the galleries to clean them. Yubah had taken to wearing a *tignon*, made from a blue scarf Jurissa gave her, telling Jurissa it was the custom for women of color in New Orleans, be they slaves or free.

This city was so different from Boston—another world. Arabel might have felt more at home if she'd come to live here instead of Boston, Jurissa thought, remembering how her guardian had adored Paris. Arabel might not have found it a match for Paris, but, to Jurissa, New Orleans had a definite French flavor.

Unwilling to go back to her quarters so soon, Jurissa ventured out of the neighborhood, walking on until the banquettes ended and the two-story buildings gave way to smaller houses, cottages, really, with trees and bushes growing between them. The street, she noticed, was named rue des Ramparts. Wasn't that where Yubah had told her the *placees* lived? She was sure it was.

The one-story houses were modest but appeared comfortable and certainly well kept. A chestnut gelding was tethered outside one and, as she neared, a Creole gentleman appeared from inside the house and mounted the horse. Waving to the light-brown woman who was standing in the doorway watching him, he spurred the chestnut and rode off. Passing Jurissa, he stared down at her in evident surprise, belatedly raising his hat. The woman caught sight of Jurissa and stared, too. She scowled at Jurissa before ducking inside and slamming the door shut.

Jurissa hesitated, then turned to retrace her steps. New Orleans ladies, she decided, must not often, if ever, venture along the rue des Ramparts where, it seemed, they weren't welcome. Her curiosity had been satisfied; she'd have no need to come back again. In fact, the whole notion of *placage* turned her stomach. If she were married to a Creole, this would be one custom she couldn't accept. She didn't blame the *placees*. Like slaves, what choice did they have? No, it was the Creole men who were at fault. The men and the fact of slavery itself.

Would she and Leon ever marry? Jurissa sighed. Despite all she did to try to convince herself he'd soon be with her, her faith in him weakened more every day.

As she approached Miss Tiana's bakery, she noticed a sleek black stallion tied to the hitching post outside and her heart began to pound. Could it be? Leon's favorite mount, Tigre, was black, he'd told her.

But she wouldn't hurry to find out if he had come to her. If she didn't count on Leon being inside, she wouldn't be disappointed. And if he was there, it served him right to wait as he had made her wait. But it had been so long since she'd seen him, so very long. Unable to control her eagerness, Jurissa's pace increased until she was all but running. It had to be Leon.

If it wasn't, she'd die.

## Chapter Seven

Seeing a man inside the bakery, Jurissa stopped to peer into the window. His back was to her as he talked to Tiana LeMoine, but he was tall and dark-haired. Leon!

As Jurissa reached an eager hand to the door, he half turned and her arm fell to her side. He wasn't Leon. She stood for a long moment, so weighed down by disappointment she couldn't move.

Pull yourself together, she chided. The black horse didn't necessarily belong to the man in the bakery. Leon could very well be waiting in the courtyard. Hastening to the door, Jurissa slipped through, her eyes scanning the small enclosure.

He was not by the banana tree, nor in the shade of the hibiscus bushes by the tiny brick-lined pool. He was nowhere in the courtyard. Blinking back tears, she walked slowly toward the stairs leading up to her apartment. Perhaps Yubah was right; perhaps Leon would never come to her for all his sweet words and promises.

Instead of flying up the steps as she usually did, Jurissa gripped the white-painted iron railing to pull herself listlessly upward. Nothing waited for her there but loneliness and heartache. Without Leon, her life had no direction, no purpose.

Her fashionable heel-less slippers made small scuffling noises as she mounted the brick stairs, and she stared down at the pale tan leather, seeing how shabby this pair had begun to look. Perhaps, if they fit her, she would give them to Yubah, who had only one pair of stout work shoes. All her slippers were becoming scuffed; she needed new ones. Not that she could afford any. She didn't care. What did it matter?

A boot clicked on brick and she started, then relaxed. Silas, no doubt, looking for Yubah who was out delivering bakery goods. She glanced up, preparing to tell him and froze, her mouth agape. After her disappointment, she couldn't believe her eyes.

"*Cherie*," Leon exclaimed, dashing down the steps separating them.

She thought her heart would stop for sheer joy when he swept her into his arms and carried her back up the stairs, setting her down on the iron-balustraded gallery. She clung to him, half laughing, half crying.

"You weren't at the hotel," he murmured into her ear, "and when I came here you were gone. I thought I'd go mad when I couldn't find you."

She barely had breath enough to whisper his name.

He kissed her long and deeply, his body hard and demanding against hers. She pressed herself against him, afire from head to foot with the ravenous need his touch evoked. From him she'd learned the marvelous ways desire could be assuaged, none of them appropriate on a gallery, in full view of the street.

Reluctantly, she pulled away. "Won't you come into my apartment?"

She led him by the hand through the door, and he kicked it shut behind them. He flung his hat aside, then deftly untied her bonnet, tossed it on a table and began to remove her gloves. Remembering the first time he'd taken her gloves off, the time when he'd kissed each of her fingers, Jurissa felt her knees grow weak. She couldn't wait!

Taking her hand from him she yanked her gloves off and reached to undo the buttons of his coat. He smiled at her a smile that promised wonders in store, and made no move to stop what she was doing. By the time she'd progressed to his trouser fastenings, Leon's breathing held the rapid rasp of intense arousal. Her heart hammered so hard she felt it would burst through her chest.

"You'll have me taking you here on the floor," he muttered, scooping her up into his arms and stalking toward her bedroom.

In a wild rush, the rest of his clothes and all of hers scattered onto the floor as each strove to reach the hot and eager flesh of the other.

"You're truly here," she breathed, "truly with me."

"Where I belong." His words were almost as delicious as his kiss and she stored them to savor later. At the moment his lips and his body demanded all her attention.

Passion flowered quickly, violently between them, an urgent coming together that brought temporary surcease. Resting in the pleasant lull afterward, Jurissa knew with lazy anticipation desire would soon overwhelm them again.

"I missed you so," she said quietly.

Leon raised himself on one elbow to look down at her, his eyes gleaming with amusement. "Your greeting did give me such a notion, yes. As I recall, you tore my clothes off."

She felt her face redden.

He laughed, brushing a forefinger against her cheek. "Don't have regrets, my impatient *cherie*. I can't recall ever enjoying anything more."

She tugged gently at his mustache "You were gone so long I'd almost forgotten how this tickled."

His smile faded and he lay back. "I didn't stay away by choice."

"Oh, Leon, I know," she said hastily. "How is your father?"

Leon didn't answer immediately. Finally he sighed. "Papa's dying and there's nothing *Docteur* Marchand can do."

Jurissa put her hand on his arm. "I'm sorry. I know how you love him."

He turned on his side to face her. "Do you, *cherie*?"

"I loved Arabel very much. I would have done anything to keep her alive."

"You do understand, then. Papa's needs come first; I can't think of myself. I am the only one he can count on."

Smoothing an errant curl from his forehead, she said, "I only wish there was something I could do to help."

His mouth twitched into a half-smile. "Patience isn't easy for you, and I'm afraid I've that and more to ask of you."

Jurissa gazed questioningly at him and realized with a flick of alarm there was no humor in his smile, and sadness lurked in the depths of his brown eyes. Suddenly she didn't want to hear what he might say. She raised herself and leaned to him, bringing her lips close to his. "Can't it wait?"

He groaned and rolled onto his back, pulling her on top of him. "Make love to me, *cherie*," he whispered and touched the tip of his tongue to the convolutions of her ear.

A thrill shot through her and she threaded her hands into his hair, closing her mouth over his, tasting his man-flavor with her tongue. Her breasts rubbed against his chest until her nipples ached with need. His hands lifted her above his body so his lips could reach her breasts, soothing and inflaming her at the same time.

They must never be parted again. She was half alive without Leon. She couldn't bear to be without his embrace, to feel the wonder of his body next to hers. He knew, as she did, that they belonged together; she'd trust him to find a way to make it possible.

He would never give her up, Leon told himself, it was too much to ask. She was more beautiful than any other woman he'd known. Her shyness, mixed with eager passion, thrilled him as no other woman's lovemaking had ever done. Holding her like this was life itself. He'd be plunged into darkness without her.

Her fragrance, the taste of her, her softness—ah, he'd kill to keep her. Damn the problems! He meant to enjoy her while he could.

Lifting her hips, he guided her over and onto his throbbing need, sliding into the warm, scented have that was his alone. Her wordless murmur of satisfaction stoked his fire. Giving pleasure to her was as much bliss as enjoying what she offered him. She wriggled enticingly against him, and his surge of passion wiped away all thought until there was only the ancient rhythm of man and woman and love.

Leon treasured the moments of lying beside her afterward. With his blood temporarily cooled, he could take the time to appreciate her loveliness. It was a time of shared peace and, *mon Dieu*, how he hated to shatter it. He stared up at the ceiling and frowned.

"The plaster is cracking," he observed.

"What? Oh, the ceiling. It doesn't matter."

"You shouldn't be living in this place. It's not good enough for you."

Jurissa raised up to stare at him. "Why do you say that? There's nothing wrong with the apartment."

He sighed. "I suspected Winterton was short of funds but, like a fool, I neglected to ask you if you needed money. Obviously that's why you left the hotel."

She bristled. "I wouldn't accept money from you."

"That's ridiculous."

"No." Her mouth set stubbornly. "With Yubah and Silas to count on, I'm managing quite well, thank you."

"I meant to tell you, I've asked a *cousine* of mine, an attorney, to file the necessary papers to declare Winterton legally dead and to settle the estate. He'll be calling on you — Anton DuBois — and, like it or not, his bill will be settled by me."

For a moment he thought she meant to challenge this but she finally nodded. "I appreciate what you've done." Her voice was low, her tone reluctant.

He muttered a curse under his breath, shoved the pillow against the walnut headboard and propped himself up. "You can be most obstinate, *cherie*. I want to help you. Why is it so hard to accept that?"

"I do look to you for help, you know that."

"Apparently not if money's involved."

She didn't reply and he turned to her, lifting her chin with his forefinger so she had to look at him. "Why does it trouble you?"

Jurissa bit her lip. "I'm not certain. Perhaps money makes it seem as though there's a price on—" She waved a hand to include the two of them. "On this," she finished.

"Never!" He grasped her hand and brought it to his lips. "My foolish *cherie*."

She smiled slightly but her eyes held a tinge of apprehension. He sighed, knowing he had to tell her sooner or later and the longer he put it off, the more difficulty he'd have.

"Dindon means more to my father than anything else in life," he began. "More than my mother, more than me, more than—" He paused and added, "His own life."

Her eyes widened and he thought he saw fear flash briefly across them. "How can anyone love a place more than a person?"

"Papa does. And he's dying."

She pulled her hand from his and brought it to her own lips. He wondered if she'd truly wanted to place her hand across *his* mouth to prevent him from going on. If so, he could hardly blame her. How he wished there was another way out of this dilemma.

"Papa's far too ill to be told about you, about us, *cherie*," he said as gently as he could. "I can't bring you to Dindon as I'd hoped."

"I understand." She managed a small smile. "I'll manage as long as you come to see me when you can."

He plunged his head into his hands. *Dieu*, it was impossible to divulge the entire story; he couldn't do it.

The best he could do was to go halfway.

"Leon, what's wrong?" He felt her fingers tugging at his arm. "Please tell me."

He dropped his hands. "Dindon's in trouble because we can't sell our cotton. We need money and we need it now. But what I must do to find the money won't affect the two of us, *cherie*, I swear it won't." He smiled as best he could. "I've arranged a surprise for you."

She blinked and he sensed she'd relaxed. He didn't dare, not yet.

"Until Anton has Winterton declared legally dead," he said, "you aren't quite a widow—you do realize that."

"I know there's a legal problem because no one saw Philip fall overboard; no one saw him drown."

"Something of the sort, yes. Plus, as far as we know, he left no will. Eventually, of course, *Cousine* Anton will clear everything up. You'll like him, by the way. I tease him about his soberness but he's proved a true friend more than once. I'd trust him with my life."

"I'm sure I'll find your *cousine* everything you say. Is he, then, the surprise?"

"No. I only wish I'd been able to come to you sooner. I could have saved you the distress of having to move to such inappropriate quarters." He held up his hand when she seemed about to protest. "Wait. Hear me out. I'd completely forgotten the cottage Papa owns; a charming little place. It is, at present, conveniently empty. Ah, *cherie*, you'll enjoy living there and I'll visit as often as I can. It will truly be our place, yours and mine."

Jurissa reached for the quilt, pulling it up until her body was covered. "Where is this cottage?" Her voice was curiously flat.

"On a country lane so small it has no official name."

"Surely the lane must be near a named street."

What was bothering her? They had to be together. He knew she wanted that as much as he did. Didn't she understand what he was offering her? "If it matters," he said, "the closest street would be the rue des Ramparts."

She drew in her breath. He felt her stiffen.

"Now, *cherie*," he said quickly, "didn't you tell me yourself that your guardian, a woman you admired greatly, lived in Paris as the *amoureuse* of a French nobleman?"

"I accept that because I'm not legally a widow, we can't be married." Her voice was tight with some emotion he couldn't identify. "But I'm not Arabel, and this is not Paris."

Leon gestured in annoyed confusion. "We are together now, though not married. What is the difference if I come to you in the cottage, a place where I assure you is much superior to these rooms?"

"This apartment, at least, is not on the rue des Ramparts."

"Neither is the cottage. What—"

She cut off his words, anger quivering in her voice. "The cottage is near enough that street, by your account. Am I to be considered your *placee*; is that how you see me?"

*Bigre!* He should have realized, with her curiosity, she'd have knowledge of Creole customs by now. "*Cherie*, you wrong me. You are no quadroon to be bought for a man's pleasure. How could you believe I'd think that?"

"Yet you wish me to live in a cottage meant for

them."

"I swear the thought never crossed my mind. I only remembered the place was empty and hoped we might be together there."

"Can you tell me that no du Motier ever set up a *placee* in that cottage?" she demanded, sitting up in her anger so that the quilt fell away from her breasts.

Leon could make no such claim, aware his father had maintained a very beautiful quadroon there until her untimely death of Bronze John, yellow fever. In fact, he knew that was why the cottage remained empty over the years. Papa had loved the dead woman and never had the heart to replace her.

When he remained silent, Jurissa's eyes narrowed in accusation.

He caught her by the shoulders. "I can't be without you, don't you understand?"

"I only understand you believe you can buy my love the same way you buy slaves."

Anger thrust through his patience, scattering it beyond recall. He shook her. "Don't preach your Boston piety at me. You Easterners who never grew a crop of cane or cotton in your lives know nothing of our need for slaves here in New Orleans. Even if you did know what you were talking about, the slavery issue has nothing to do with what's between the two of us. You're speaking nonsense."

She tried to wrench free and he tightened his grip. "Let me go!" she cried, striking at him with her fists. He released her shoulders to grasp her wrists with one of his hands, too enraged to have any clear idea of what he meant to do.

Her breasts thrust against his chest in her struggle to

get away from him, and suddenly an overpowering desire mixed with his fury. Before he realized his intent, he had her pinned beneath him, her wrists held above her head, one of his knees forcing her legs apart.

"No," she cried, writhing futilely. "No, I don't want you."

"You damn well will before I'm through." He spit the words at her from between his teeth.

Shifting his weight so she couldn't move her legs and keeping her wrists above her head, he began teasing one of her nipples with his tongue until it peaked. He did the same with the other nipple, his free hand caressing her in the way he knew pleasured her the most.

Touching her, kissing her breasts increased his own desire, dissipating his anger like smoke in the wind, leaving only the need to make her want him as much as he wanted her.

"Ah, *cherie*," he murmured, releasing her wrists, "I don't mean to hurt you. Everything about you is so beautiful. I can't be with you without desiring you."

Furious as she was, Jurissa could have struggled against Leon forever, but his caresses and soft words of love undermined her rage. Her resistance faded and disappeared as she responded to his kiss, to his touch. Arching to him, she flung her head from side to side in helpless need. Now! her passion-inflamed body demanded. Now! Now! Only the tiny core of anger stubbornly embedded deep in her mind kept her from begging him to join with her.

She thought she'd die of her longing before he came into her in a tumultuous union, different from any other time they'd been together. As she reached a shattering fulfillment, sobs shook her and tears streamed from her eyes.

When it was over he still held her close. "Ah, *cherie*, don't cry," he begged. "I was out of my mind to hurt you."

"You—you didn't hurt me," she sobbed, trying to calm herself. She realized as she spoke it was half a lie. True, her body hadn't been harmed but the tears sprang from an invisible wound of the spirit.

"I can't help myself," he went on. "When I touch you I'm bewitched. I lose all reason. I never put any credence in stories of voodoo enchantment, but being with you makes me believe enchantment exists." He reached to brush tendrils of hair from her forehead. "Don't ever leave me, *cherie*."

As if she could! Didn't he know her love bound her to him for the rest of her days on earth? She'd never leave him. On the other hand, even for Leon, she'd never become a *placee*. Though nothing could change her love for him, the hurt had gone deep when he proposed such an arrangement.

"I don't know what voodoo is," she told him, "but I'll always be waiting for you to come to me. Someday, I hope—" She cut off her words. He must be the first to speak of marriage when the time came, not her.

He didn't ask what she'd been about to say, and sadness darkened his eyes again. Apprehension chilled her and she eased from his arms, preparing to rise and dress. She knew he'd held something back from her, and she feared hearing what it might be. If it made him so unhappy, what would such news do to her? At the moment, she couldn't bear any more.

"I haven't offered you food or drink," she said.

"Food is everywhere. I come to you for what no one

else can give me." But he, too, rose and began to dress. "I'll be back when it's possible," he told her at the door, kissing her. "You can't know how difficult it is to stay away."

From the gallery she watched him mount Tigre and ride off. Not once did he look back. Intent on Leon's departure, she didn't hear boots on the stairs and Silas's deep voice startled her.

"G'day, Mis Jurissa." He waited a moment, and when she didn't immediately answer, a frown of concern creased his forehead. "You be all right?"

"Yes, Silas, I'm fine." She didn't sound convincing, even to herself.

"Be something you want me to do, I do it."

She sighed. "If you could help, I'd ask you but there's nothing you can do."

He glanced along the street, his eyes following the route Leon had taken, and Jurissa realized Silas knew Leon had been with her. No doubt everyone who lived or worked in this block of the rue des Normandie did, too. Not that she cared. Nothing mattered to her except being with Leon.

"Yubah isn't here," she told Silas.

"Yes'm. Blacksmith, he give me ole wood. Gonna fix up where I sleep. Be all right with you?"

"If Miss Tiana agrees."

Silas nodded. "She be feeling poorly. Can't do no fixing. Her brother, he ain't handy. 'Sides, he work showing white folk 'bout fighting.

Jurissa realized from the puzzlement in Silas's voice that he didn't understand exactly what Tiana LeMoine's brother did. Because the landlady had told her, Jurissa did know.

"Men fight duels back in Virginia, don't they?" she asked.

"Yes'm, surely do. Ole massa, he get shot in his leg and he be limping after that."

"In New Orleans, the Creoles often fight duels with rapiers, pointed swords, instead of pistols. Nicolas LeMoine is a fencing master. He teaches fencing; how to use a rapier."

She wasn't sure Silas grasped this but he nodded. "Some things be different here, some be the same," he said.

Jurissa was not at all afraid of Silas now that she'd gotten to know what he was like. His gentleness extended beyond the care of his sister; to everyone and everything he dealt with. She'd seen how he bound up the broken leg of the landlady's cat and patiently encouraged the animal until it began to hobble around again. She found it hard to believe he'd ever hurt anyone, despite his gigantic size.

A word Leon had used stuck in her mind, something to do with a New Orleans custom, she was sure. Perhaps Silas knew what it meant. "Have you ever heard of voodoo?" she asked.

His face went blank, the dark brown eyes glazing over. He stood motionless and silent for so long she grew alarmed.

"Silas? Is something the matter?"

He blinked. "How come you ask me what you do, Miss Jurissa?"

"About voodoo? Because I never heard the word before today and I like to learn."

"Voodoo don't be for white folks." His dark eyes looked briefly into hers, then away.

She stared at him, having glimpsed something in his eyes that had nothing to do with gentleness; a flicker of pure savagery. Though not frightened, she was shaken. Silas had politely but very clearly warned her away from asking him any more about voodoo.

"I be going lest you want me for something," he said.

She gestured to him to go and he clattered heavily down the stairs. Yet she was aware he could move as silently as a cat stalking a bird if he chose to. Obviously she didn't know Silas as well as she thought. She smiled slightly as she entered her apartment. Silas didn't know her very well, either. Perhaps he thought he'd warned her away from the subject, but he didn't realize that the best way to fix her interest on something was to make a mystery of it.

While she waited for Leon to visit again, she'd keep from brooding about him by discovering all she could about voodoo so she could astound him by her knowledge when he returned.

He *would* return. He'd said so and this time she wouldn't allow herself to entertain doubts. Hadn't he sworn that whatever he had to do to raise the money for Dindon wouldn't keep them from being together?

It occurred to her to wonder how he would get the needed money, but she shrugged away the question. She knew nothing of business matters.

Feet pounded up the steps and Yubah burst into the room. "Miss Jurissa, come quick!" she cried.

"Come where? What's wrong?"

"Miss Tiana, she be on the floor and there be lots of blood. You got to help."

Following Yubah, Jurissa hurried down the stairs and into the back door of the bakery. She knelt beside her landlady's supine figure, noticing with dismay a pool of blood on the floor and red stains spattering Tiana LeMoine's white gown. The woman's brown eyes gazed fearfully up at her from a face turned gray instead of its usual brown.

"Am I dying?" Tiana asked.

Jurissa forced a smile she hoped was reassuring. "Of course not. What happened to you?"

Tiana raised a languid hand to clutch at her stomach. "I have had bad pain here a long time now. Today, blood comes up. I tried to crawl to my room but I'm so weak. Thank *le bon Dieu* Yubah found me."

"Get Silas in here to carry her to her bedroom," Jurissa ordered Yubah.

Before Yubah could so much as turn around, Silas edged through the back door. "I hears what you say, Miss Jurissa. I knows something wrong and I be waiting to help."

Once Silas had carried Tiana into her rooms on the other side of the courtyard, Jurissa sent him down to clean the floor of the bakery while she and Yubah helped Tiana into a nightgown.

"I'll send for your doctor if you'll give me his name," Jurissa said.

*"Docteur* won't do any good. He can't help what take hold in my stomach."

Jurissa heard Yubah's sharp intake of breath and glanced at her. Yubah was staring at Tiana, her eyes wide and frightened.

Tiana shook her head. "Don't be feared, child. You know what's meant for me won't hurt you."

Slowly Yubah nodded. Jurissa gazed from one to the other, realizing that, though they seemed to understand

115

one another perfectly, she didn't have the slightest idea what had passed between them.

"I think you should have a doctor," she insisted.

"No. What good are leeches taking more of my blood?"

Jurissa had to admit it was very likely that a doctor might use leeches. Thinking about it, she decided not to press the issue any further. "I learned a little about tisanes from my guardian," she ventured. "One I remember is for the stomach. If I can find what I need—"

"Won't do any good." Tiana's eyes seemed to sink into her head. She looked as though she might truly be near death. "A *voodooienne* bad-spells me to die. Who can save me?"

Sensing someone behind her, Jurissa looked around. Silas stood in the doorway, his dark eyes fixed on Tiana.

"Me, I can." His deep voice rang out like a bell.

## Chapter Eight

The sky had clouded over by the time Yubah and Jurissa left Tiana LeMoine's, and rain threatened as the two women climbed the stairs to the apartment. Once inside, Jurissa ordered Yubah to sit down at the table. Seating herself across from her, Jurissa looked sternly at Yubah.

"I did what was asked of me," she said. "I left Silas alone with Miss Tiana when she told me to, and I promised her I wouldn't interfere. I intend to keep my word but I also intend to discover what this is all about. From you."

Yubah looked down at her hands, clenched together. "I truly don't be knowing what Silas, he gonna do, Miss Jurissa." She shuddered. "Don't wanna know."

"It's voodoo, isn't it?"

Yubah shot her a fearful glance. "Don't like to be talking 'bout that."

"Why not? What frightens you?"

"Bad comes do you talk about voodoo."

"Nothing will happen to you. Tell me who or what is the *voodooienne* Miss Tiana spoke of."

"She be what Creoles call voodoo queen." Yubah's voice was sullen.

Jurissa touched her shoulder and Yubah jerked away.

"Stop acting like a goose, Yubah. I'm not going to hurt you and neither is anyone else. Just tell me what voodoo is."

Yubah took a deep breath and let it out slowly. "I be telling you, you don't ask me no more?"

"I can't promise but I'll try not to mention voodoo again to you."

"Always be voodoo, long as I know." Yubah hugged herself, her eyes meeting, then sliding away from Jurissa's. "Be ours, we don't be sharing it with white folks. Only way to get voodoo power, you got to be born with it. Not me, and I be glad. Silas, it be born in him so he got to use it. He tell me soon's we get here he feel voodoo be in New Orleans, just like home. I be scared so he say he don't mess with it here lest he has to."

"You tell me Silas has voodoo power yet you're not afraid of your brother."

"Silas, he do good! He help folk, not bad-spell them. He gonna take the spell off Miss Tiana, throw it back on the voodoo queen." Yubah huddled lower in her chair. "He gonna be in danger, Miss Jurissa. Queen, she got power, she fight Silas. She win, he die 'long with Miss Tiana. He win, he don't kill her 'cause Silas, he don't bad-spell. Queen, she don't die, she gonna come looking for him, gonna be bad trouble."

Jurissa stared at Yubah in amazement. She'd never heard such a fantastic tale in her life.

Yubah reached out and caught her hand. "I don't want Silas to die!"

Jurissa squeezed her hand and tried to find reassuring words. She didn't believe in this voodoo power, but certainly Yubah did and was terrified.

"Silas won't die," she said at last. "Your brother is

strong and he's working for good, not evil."

Yubah's amber eyes, brimming with tears, searched Jurissa's face. "I hope you be right, I surely do."

"In the end good will always defeat evil," Jurissa said firmly. That she *did* believe.

For whatever reason, Tiana LeMoine didn't die. Nor did she get worse. The next morning Jurissa sent Yubah to notify Nicolas LeMoine of his sister's illness, and he returned with Yubah.

Nicolas was slender where Tiana was gaunt, and the prominent nose and jutting chin that kept Tiana from being pretty made Nicolas a handsome man. He was also much younger than his middle-aged sister, perhaps twenty-five, and spoke excellent English.

"I thank you for taking care of my sister, Madame Winterton," he told Jurissa with obvious sincerity while Yubah gazed sidelong at him from under her long black lashes. "She tells me you saved her life."

Jurissa had no idea how much or little Tiana had revealed to her brother, but she thought it best to pretend she knew nothing at all. "I've told her I'll take over the baking until she's better. It will give me something to do."

He bowed to her as correctly as any Creole gentleman. "You're very kind."

"Miss Jurissa, she bakes good," Yubah put in. "She bakes French."

The comment startled Nicolas and cracked his all-too-proper armor. He grinned at Yubah. "What do you know about French cooking, girl?"

"More than you think," she said in French, giving him a saucy smile.

Jurissa smiled herself, pleased to see Yubah flirting

with the handsome Nicolas and enjoying his confusion over how to behave with her pretty maid.

"He be born free like Miss Tiana," Yubah confided to Jurissa later. "When he be a bitty boy, his papa send him 'cross the ocean to learn 'bout fencing. To France. He say he like me to come see what fencing be 'bout sometime. You maybe let me."

"Of course I will. Nicolas seems to be a fine young man."

Yubah shrugged. "He all right." But her eyes, gleaming with excitement, gave her away.

For all Yubah's worry about some mysterious voodoo queen arriving to harm Silas, nothing of the sort happened. Tiana slowly began to improve, but it was apparent she wouldn't be strong enough to manage the bakery for some time. She gave Jurissa her recipes, and it took three days of practice for Jurissa to be sure she'd mastered them.

Instead of repeating the same recipes over and over, she decided to gradually add ones she'd learned from Arabel for more elaborate French pastries.

"These were Tanguay's favorites," Arabel had told her, "so I learned to make them all, no matter how difficult. His pleasure was worth any amount of trouble."

As Jurissa stood in Tiana's tiny kitchen kneading dough for one of these pastries, she wondered, for the first time, the amount of time Arabel and her count had actually spent together. He must have had other obligations; an ill wife and an afflicted son; and there were the family vineyards to oversee, plus his chateau with its many servants.

Perhaps Arabel didn't see him any more often than

Jurissa saw Leon.

Arabel had lived under those conditions for seven years, the happiest of her life, she always insisted. Shaping the pastry shells, Jurissa tried not to think that she might be repeating Arabel's experience. Seven years of being with Leon only when he could get away from Dindon?

She shook her head. Leon wasn't married; the circumstances were entirely different. She must have patience. Leon's difficulties, as well as hers, were only temporary.

Bells tinkled as the bakery door opened. Jurissa wiped her floury hands on the bib apron Tiana had provided and passed through the curtained opening into the shop. A well-dressed man of about thirty stood on the other side of the counter, a Creole by the look of him.

"*Bon jour*," she said.

He inclined his head. "I seek a Madame Winterton," he said in French.

"You have found her," she replied.

He seemed taken aback but quickly recovered himself. "You are Madame Winterton?"

She nodded.

"My name is Anton DuBois. I am an attorney and—"

"Oh, yes, Leon—Monsieur du Motier—mentioned you'd be calling on me. You are *cousines*, I believe."

He didn't smile as he admitted this was true, and Jurissa remembered Leon describing him as being sober. He didn't look much like Leon except, perhaps, the eyes but he had a pleasant enough appearance and was dressed faultlessly.

"Leon didn't tell me you were working in the bakery," he said.

"He doesn't know. My landlady is ill and I'm taking her place until she improves."

Anton cleared his throat. "One Tiana LeMoine, free woman of color, I believe." His expression was as solemn as a preacher's.

"Yes. She—" Jurissa paused, sniffing the air. "Excuse me, please. My petite almond croissants are ready to come out." She hurried through the curtain and removed the pan from the brick oven. Struck by a sudden, mischievous notion, she eased one of the crescents onto a small blue plate and carried it back to the shop with her.

"Would you be so kind as to do me a favor?" she asked Anton DuBois.

"But of course."

"I've been experimenting with some Parisian recipes and I need your opinion." She proffered the plate. "Should I add these to Miss Tiana's offerings or not?"

Anton had no choice but to accept the plate from her. He stood staring down at the petite croissant.

"You have to taste it," she informed him. "Otherwise, how will you know?"

Looking extremely uncomfortable, Anton broke off a tiny piece and brought it to his mouth.

"More," she urged, suppressing a smile. "That's too small a bite."

He glanced at her, then lifted what remained of the crescent and bit into it, chewing thoughtfully. He finished the entire croissant, handed her back the plate and wiped his hands and mouth on his handkerchief.

Giving him the croissant had been originally aimed

at breaking through his stuffiness, but now Jurissa found herself waiting impatiently for his opinion.

"I haven't been to Paris, you understand," he said, as she hung on his every word, "so it's impossible for me to judge as a Parisian."

Would he never get to the point?

"I believe you said this was a petite almond croissant?"

"Yes. What do you—"

His upheld hand stopped her. "I've never before eaten a petite almond croissant. Therefore, I cannot compare yours to any others."

Jurissa, ready to burst with impatience, detected a suspicious gleam in his brown eyes. Stuffy or not, Anton *was* Leon's *cousine* and Leon was certainly a tease. Perhaps it ran in the family.

She lowered her eyes and did her best to appear downcast. "Alas," she murmured, "have my efforts been in vain?"

His laughter made her look up hastily. "Ah, madame, I concede."

Her lips curved into a smile. He *had* been teasing her. Leon was right. She quite liked *Cousine* Anton. "I really would appreciate your opinion," she confessed.

He brought his fingers to his lips, kissed them and, waving the fingers her way, bowed. "Perfection. I'll buy all you've made."

His appreciation warmed her. "I'd make you a gift of them but Miss Tiana needs the money."

Ducking back into the kitchen, she wrapped the still warm croissants, brought them to him, and accepted his coins.

"I came here to talk to you," he said.

"Unless a customer enters we are as private here as anywhere," she told him.

His eyebrows shot up but he nodded reluctantly. "It would be of help if you'd answer a few questions about your late husband. That is, if you don't mind."

Anton certainly slipped back into stuffiness easily, she decided. "My husband's name was Philip Winterton; he was thirty-five years old and formerly lived in Newtown, Virginia. I'm afraid I know little else about him."

"He never spoke of his relatives?"

"No. Yubah — she's one of the two slaves he owned — said Mr. Winterton was a cousin of her old master. His widow gave Yubah and Silas to Philip after her husband died. Their papers are among his belongings."

"Are you aware of any assets he might have had besides the slaves?"

"As far as I know he had none. And whatever money he left — it wasn't much — I've been forced to spend to support myself and the slaves."

Anton's brown eyes met hers, and for a fraction of a second she had the illusion that Leon was looking at her. Never, though, had Leon's eyes been so solemn.

"I'm afraid it will take me some time to discover if there are any other claimants to his estate beside yourself," he said. "In the meantime you may, of course, treat the slaves as though you owned them — although you cannot sell them."

"I understand that. But you haven't explained about me. Am I legally a widow?"

"Establishing your status will also take time."

Jurissa was tired of his legal pussyfooting. "If you mean no, say no."

His lips twitched but he didn't quite smile. "No."

"That's better."

His eyes gleamed again and this time she knew what it was. Anton DuBois found her interesting.

"I'll report to you when I have news," he said. "If you can bear it, I have one more question."

"I've told you everything I know."

"Not quite. Must you bake every day?"

Her eyes widened. "Every morning except Sunday."

"Is your female slave—Yubah, I believe you told me her name was—capable of taking care of bakery customers in the afternoons?"

"That's two questions," she said, smiling. "But I'll answer anyway. Yubah often waits on the customers."

"Good. Excellent."

She waited, but he didn't explain. "Monsieur DuBois, you do try my patience."

"I don't mean to. You must excuse my roundabout manner. It stems, no doubt, from the lack of a wife to mend my ways. I wanted to suggest that, perhaps, you need some time away from working. I'd be pleased to escort you about the city and show you our beautiful New Orleans."

Jurissa was taken completely by surprise. "Why I— it's kind of you to offer."

"You set the day, madame, and I'll have my carriage at your door."

She hadn't told him she'd go. Yet, why not? Since Anton was Leon's *cousine*, there'd be no misunderstanding on Leon's part. She'd love to see New Orleans with an escort who knew the city. Besides, though she enjoyed the baking, Anton was right; she'd appreciate time away from the bakery.

"Perhaps Thursday afternoon," she said.

"You make me a happy man, madame."

Watching Anton DuBois leave the shop with his croissants, Jurissa smiled. Solemn he might be, but he had the Creole touch for the right phrase to please a woman.

Not until she returned to her baking did it occur to Jurissa that she might miss a visit from Leon if she drove around the city with Anton on Thursday. She couldn't take the chance. Being with Leon was more important than anything else.

It was too late to tell Anton she couldn't go. She'd have to wait until he came by on Thursday. Leon, she was sure, hadn't confided in his cousin what was between himself and Jurissa, and she certainly wouldn't tell Anton the truth. Never mind, she'd find a plausible excuse.

The rest of Tuesday passed uneventfully. Tired from her day in the bakery, but feeling pleased that Miss Tiana's customers liked her baking, Jurissa fell asleep as soon as she stretched out on her bed.

She dreamed she was alone in darkness, the only light the red embers of a dying fire. Shadows danced above the embers, writhing and twisting in sinister patterns she didn't comprehend. She wanted to run, to flee from the peril she sensed lurking among the shadows, but she was afraid of the blackness surrounding the dying fire. Suddenly one of the shadows flung out a dark tendril and grasped her arm. She opened her mouth to scream—

Jurissa woke abruptly, gasping in fear, feeling a hand on her arm.

"Miss Jurissa!" The words were a strangled whisper

but, with relief, she recognized Yubah's voice. She'd been sleeping at Tiana's place in case the sick woman needed help during the night.

"You frightened me half to death," she scolded, sitting up. "I didn't hear you come in."

Moonlight slanting through the white curtains of the window gleamed in Yubah's eyes as she tightened her grip on Jurissa's arm. "Silas be gone, Miss Jurissa. I be feared."

"You're hurting my arm." Jurissa eased Yubah's fingers free. "That's better. Are you quite certain Silas isn't somewhere around?"

"I done looked everywhere. Called to him. He don't answer. He be gone."

Jurissa knew by now it was a serious matter for a slave to go anywhere off the property of his master without being ordered or granted permission to do so. "Where would Silas go?" she asked herself as much as Yubah.

"*Voodooienne* call him, he go, he can't help hisself."

Voodoo again. Jurissa didn't believe that for a minute. Thinking it over, she wondered how Yubah had discovered Silas's absence in the first place.

As though reading her mind, Yubah said, "I be dreaming bad. Seem like darkness gonna get me and I wakes up scared. Miss Tiana, she call to me, say something in the night come looking. We both be shivering. Pretty soon she say it go away and she tell me go fetch Silas.

"Don't want to go outside but she say I got to. He ain't sleeping in his bitty house. He ain't anywhere. I go back, tell Miss Tiana. She say *voodooienne* got Silas. She gonna make him dance. I got to come fetch you."

This was likely naught but nonsense. Still, a frisson of unease made Jurissa fold her arms across her breast. "I don't understand what Miss Tiana expects me to do," she said.

"Miss Tiana, she say you get dressed and come down to her."

She supposed she had to go to Tiana. She couldn't accept these voodoo tales but she had to find out what happened to Silas.

The April night was warm, and she hardly needed the Chinese shawl she'd settled over her shoulders. As she and Yubah descended the stairs into the courtyard, a full moon lit the night into a silvery semblance of day but failed to dispel the shadows lurking in the corners. Jurissa recalled her own unpleasant dream and involuntarily shuddered.

Stop that! she admonished herself. Shadows are only shadows; there's no harm in them. The next you know you'll be as fanciful as Yubah.

After verifying that Silas was not to be found anywhere, Jurissa followed Yubah into Tiana's quarters. Tiana sat propped up on pillows, her gaunt face skeletal in the lamplight.

"I'm too weak to go with you but I'll tell you where Silas is," she whispered, her words rasping in the night quiet.

"Did you know he meant to go?" Jurissa demanded.

Tiana nodded. "He had to go to that *voodooienne* from the time he coaxed her snake spell out of my stomach and flung it back at her. She hates me because I interfered between her and Nicolas. My brother grew up in France. He didn't remember voodoo. I had to show him how evil she was before he'd believe me. Then he didn't want her any more and she knew I was the reason why."

Besides Jurissa, Yubah caught her breath and Tiana gave her a half-smile. "Don't worry, girl, if Nicolas decides he wants you I'll keep out of the way."

"Tiana, I don't believe in voodoo," Jurissa said.

"What you believe doesn't matter. Better you don't. But you have to be the one to go. She's drawn Silas to her and he belongs to you so only you can help to save him."

"I don't understand any of this. I do know Silas is gone without my permission and that's a serious matter."

"He didn't want to go; don't you think he did," Tiana said. "He couldn't help himself when she called him. I felt her in the night but I don't have power enough to stand against her."

"Silas has power!" Yubah cried.

Tiana bowed her head. "We'll pray he has enough power to save himself once the one he belongs to finds him."

"Are you saying I should go and look for Silas tonight, alone?" Jurissa demanded.

"Yubah must go with you because she's bound to him by blood, but Yubah's not strong enough to save him. You are."

Jurissa glanced at Yubah and, seeing her pallor, knew how frightened she was, but Yubah met her eyes. "I be going with you," Miss Jurissa. We got to go. Silas gonna die if we don't."

"In the morning—" Jurissa began.

"You can't wait until morning." Tiana's voice was grim. "The snake dances under the full moon. Don't you hear the drums?"

Jurissa realized that for some time she'd been dimly aware of a deep, faint throbbing like the far-off beating of a giant heart.

"Voodoo drums," Yubah whispered.

"You go now or it's too late," Tiana said, her sunken eyes glittering shadows in the dim light. "In the morning the snake will sleep, fat from Silas's death. The drums beat in the swamp near Dindon. I will tell you how to go to them."

Dindon. The du Motier plantation. Jurissa didn't even know where it was. Tiana watched her with narrowed eyes. The woman must know Leon's a du Motier, Jurissa told herself, and she certainly knows Leon had visited her.

"Please, Miss Jurissa," Yubah begged. "I don't want Silas to die."

Whether she believed in voodoo or not it seemed she had little choice, Jurissa decided. If she refused and something happened to Silas, Yubah would never forgive her. She'd never forgive herself, for that matter. But, oh, how she longed to have Leon at her side. Venturing into the night alone—into the swamp, Tiana had said—was frightening enough. To make it worse, she had no notion of what awaited her when she did find Silas—if she did.

"So. You will go," Tiana said. "Lono waits to show you the way. Listen, now, while I tell you what you must know."


Awaiting Yubah and Jurissa when they eased through the gate leading to the street was a hunched-over aged black man. Where he'd come from or how Tiana had summoned him, Jurissa didn't know. Without speaking, Lono started off, limping on his right leg but setting a fast pace. Jurissa followed, Yubah trailing behind her.

I'm still dreaming, Jurissa told herself. I can't really be hurrying along the night streets of New Orleans, heading for the sound of drums and trusting that a hunchback Negro I've never seen before will bring me there and back safely.

What was in the swamp? Cypress trees, Leon had told her, with long Spanish moss hanging from them like beards. Alligators. Bobcats. Snakes.

The snake dances under the full moon, Tiana had said. But she'd meant the voodoo queen, hadn't she? Whatever else she might pretend to be, the *voodooienne* was a woman. A Negro woman who tried to harm others by making them believe she could kill them by evil spells.

The drums were real enough; the woman probably was, too. Jurissa refused, though, to believe in voodoo power or evil spells. If she found Silas, she meant to bring him home and insist he abstain from any more such foolishness.

Because of the late hour travelers were few, and whenever a carriage or horseman did pass Lono ducked into niches with Jurissa and Yubah crowded in beside him. On and on they traveled until Jurissa, tiring, felt she couldn't go on. A few minutes later, confronted by the gleam of moonlight on water, they halted. The throb of the drums was louder now, the beat invading her head, her body. Leon pointed to a dark shape on the water.

"Pirogue," he said in a low tone and motioned them to get in.

He poled the boat rapidly along the dark water and soon vegetation closed in around them. The moon shone through only intermittently, turning the journey into a dappled nightmare. Yubah said nothing but her hand reached for Jurissa's and clutched it in a death grip. Jurissa told herself firmly she'd trusted Lono this far; she wouldn't give way to panic now.

When Lono finally pulled the boat to a bank, Jurissa found her legs so stiff she could hardly climb out. It was as though the drum beat had settled into her bones. He secured the pirogue and started off along the trail running through heavy undergrowth.

A thought struck Jurissa and she caught his arm, slowing him. "Lono, where is Dindon?" she whispered. "Which way?"

He jerked a thumb over his shoulder, indicating it was in the opposite direction, and speeded up again. She hurried after him with Yubah, behind her, now clutching the belt of her gown instead of her hand. The heavy damp smell of greenery tinged with the scent of smoke surrounded her, and she saw a red glow up ahead.

Lono turned off the trail and eased through tangled growth, finally stopping. He motioned for them to come up beside him. Carefully he parted the vines in front of him and looked through. After a moment, Jurissa did the same. She caught her breath.

In a clearing, squatting dark bodies formed a semicircle about a fire. Within the half-circle, a brown-skinned woman, standing erect, weaved to the rhythm of the drums. Her long black hair flowed down past her waist and the brief red garment she wore reached scarcely to her thighs. Around her neck and over her bared breasts coiled a thick rope that shifted with her dancing.

"Snake!" The word hissed from Yubah who pressed against Jurissa, shivering.

Startled, Jurissa realized Yubah was right. The woman wore not a rope necklace but a huge, live snake! To her left a man sat astride a big drum lying lengthwise on the ground, slapping the skin head. Another Negro pounded a smaller drum as the dancer began a chant, calling out over and over: *"L'Appe vini, Le Grand Zombi. L'Appe vini pou fe gris-gris."*

The rhythm quickened with the chant and the crowd shouted, *"Aie, aie! Voodoo Magnan!"*

Jurissa, her attention focused on the dark dancer, felt a flicker of recognition. She'd seen the woman somewhere before; her features were familiar. But where? And when? Before she could try to remember, a gigantic, nearly nude black man jumped into the semicircle to face the snake-dancer. Silas!

## Chapter Nine

Concealed by a tangle of swamp vines, Jurissa, with Lono on one side of her and Yubah clinging to her on the other, stared at the brown-skinned woman and the black man swaying by the fire in the clearing. The throbbing of the drums grew louder, fiercer as Silas, wearing only a white loincloth, faced the *voodooienne*.

"*Aie, aie, voodoo Magnan,*" the semicircle of black watchers chanted. "*Aie, aie!*"

With an undulating thrust of her hips, the woman challenged Silas, her hands weaving patterns in and out of the coils of the live snake hanging around her neck.

Silas countered by leaping high in the air and coming down in a crouch. Slowly, keeping in rhythm to the drums, he began to dance around the *voodooienne*, his face always toward her. His skin glistened like black onyx in the firelight.

"She gonna bad-spell him," Yubah moaned, her fingers digging into Jurissa's arm.

Was this what Tiana expected her to stop? Jurissa asked herself, fighting to keep from being caught up in the seductive rhythm of the drums. How? Watching the giant black man gyrating around the brown-skinned woman, Jurissa couldn't imagine herself striding up to the fire and demanding that Silas come home with her.

At the moment Silas bore no relation to the obedient Negro slave left to her by Philip's death. His defiant dance denied that slavery existed, and she'd never felt less like his owner.

The feral intensity of both Silas and the woman convinced Jurissa that regardless of what she might think of voodoo, the two dancers believed in it heart and soul, as did the avid spectators. She felt she was in a strange country, alone amidst its alien and possibly dangerous inhabitants.

The *voodooienne's* gestures became an open invitation to Silas. He reached invoking arms toward the sky, fingers clutching as though trying to pull down the moon. Beside Jurissa, Yubah's trembling increased until Jurissa put a supporting arm around her.

*"Bomba, bomba, bomba,"* the crowd chanted.

Against her will, Jurissa was trapped by the struggle being enacted between the dancers. Her breath caught, and the blood ran faster in her veins as the woman offered herself to Silas again and again. But he kept refusing her. What would happen if he stopped resisting?

"He gonna die." Yubah's quivering lips could barely push the words out.

"Stop thinking that way!" Jurissa spoke low but vehemently, her eyes on the dancers. "Do you want to harm your brother? Silas is defying her but he needs your help. He might fail if you don't help him. You must tell yourself over and over how strong he is. You must say to yourself that his power is stronger than the *voodooienne's* and she can't force him to go to her, ever." She gave Yubah a shake. "Do you hear? Do what I say if you love your brother. Stand up straight and have faith in him."

Yubah gulped and pushed away from Jurissa.

Jurissa didn't know when or how she'd realized their purpose here; the reason Tiana had insisted they come; she only knew she was right. She might not believe in voodoo but she and Yubah had to believe in Silas's strength or he was lost.

Staring at the gigantic black man's struggle, she set her mind to belief in his triumph over the woman. And, as she did so, she remembered where she'd seen the *voodooienne* before. She was the woman who'd scowled at Jurissa from the cottage on the rue des Ramparts.

The drums beat on. The fire sent spirals of smoke and occasional bursts of sparks skyward, and still the dancers dueled. It seemed to Jurissa hours passed before Silas, his hands spread in front of him, began to challenge the *voodooienne* instead of merely resisting her. The first hint that he'd succeeded was the drums slowing their rhythm. Twisting, fighting her surrender, the woman sank to the ground where she writhed on her belly before Silas's feet. Plucking the snake from her neck, she offered it to him. After his abrupt gesture of refusal, a man sprang from the spectators and, grasping the snake, placed it in a slatted box Jurissa hadn't before noticed.

The drums ceased but their throbbing beat continued to echo in Jurissa's ears. Silas turned his back on the woman abasing herself before him, walked away and disappeared in the darkness.

"We go," Lono whispered and began to retrace his steps. Jurissa and Yubah followed him to the path in silence.

Before they reached the pirogue, Lono held up a

hand, saying, "Horse come." He ducked into the thick growth at the side of the trail as they joined him.

Concealed behind the greenery, Jurissa parted the branches to look out. Only now that the horse was almost upon them could she hear its hoofbeats thudding along the dank earth of the path, and she marveled at Lono's perception. Moments later the horse appeared, black as the night, coming from the direction of Dindon.

"Tigre!" Jurissa gasped.

The rider reined in the stallion and the animal reared, whinnying. Once the horse was under control, its rider brought Tigre's head around to face the undergrowth where Jurissa and the others were concealed.

"Come out!" Leon's voice demanded harshly. "I know you're hiding there. Come out, I say."

"Stay hidden," Jurissa whispered into Yubah's ear. "Go home with Lono." She stepped into the path. The horse whuffled and stepped back.

*"Mon Dieu!"* Leon exclaimed when she looked up at him and moonlight illuminated her face. "Jurissa! I thought you were one of the servants hiding from me. I can't believe my eyes." He slid off the stallion and grasped her hand, drawing her to him. "It's after midnight. What are you doing in this swamp?"

"Why are you riding Tigre so late at night?" she countered.

"It is, after all, du Motier land, whatever the hour. But you have no excuse for straying so far from home. And at night." He peered along the trail. "The drums have stopped."

How would she possibly explain what had happened? She'd tell him part of the truth but she hoped she'd never have to reveal all of it to anyone. Who, besides the Negroes she knew, would believe her? "I came to see the voodoo dance but it's over."

"You came here alone? You don't expect me to believe that!" He pulled her closer and frowned down at her.

"Of course not alone. How would I find my way? Silas and Yubah were with me. My landlady told us where to come."

"I see no sign of them."

"When I recognized Tigre I told them to go along without me."

His scowl didn't lessen.

She tugged at her hand, still fast in his. "If you free my hand I can overtake them."

He yanked her against him. "You know very well I'd never let you go home alone. As you should have known it was the height of foolishness to come here to begin with. Voodoo's for the people of color, not for us. And the hours of darkness are always dangerous in New Orleans, especially for a woman alone."

"Silas and Yubah—"

He covered her mouth with his own, effectively silencing her. His kiss was hard and angry. She met it with her own defiance, and when he released her they both breathed raggedly.

He sighed. "Your curious nature will be your downfall, *cherie*. I never dreamed you'd find your way to a voodoo ceremony. What am I going to do to keep you safe?"

Keep me with you and I'll be safe forever, was what she yearned to say. If only he could.

"This is no place for either of us," he muttered.

Scooping her into his arms, he lifted her onto Tigre's back, where she adjusted her skirts as best she could. It was impossible to be modest astride a horse. He eased up in front of her. "Put your arms around me," he ordered her as he urged the stallion back the way he'd come.

She clung to him, her cheek pressed to his back, her eyes closed. She refused to think ahead, relishing the feel of him. Leon, she was with Leon. Lulled by his warmth and the even gait of the horse, she eventually slipped into a reverie where she pictured herself and Leon riding Tigre home from a ball at a neighboring plantation.

Soon they'd reach their house at Dindon and he'd lift her down, holding her against him for a moment while his smile hinted of what awaited them upstairs in the privacy of their bed. She'd wake early after their night of love and, by the glimmering dawn light, watch Leon sleeping next to her, knowing that every morning would bring her the same pleasure. He would never leave her. They'd always be together.

"We're here," he told her and, still half dreaming, she smiled as he lifted her from the horse and held her briefly against him.

Securing Tigre, he pushed open the gate in the wall beside the bakery, ushered her into the courtyard and saw her up the stairs. At her door, he drew her into his arms. "More than anything in the world, I want to stay with you," he murmured, "but once I go inside that door I won't leave for far too long. I must get back."

She clung to him, her throat tightening with disappointment she tried not to show. "You haven't told me what brought you out so late at night."

"The same thing that forces me back so soon. *Maman* woke in the night, called for her maid, discovered she was gone, and became upset. I heard the drums and realized where Lilette was. I also knew she'd be back when the voodoo dance ended. But *Maman* wouldn't listen to reason—she's been distraught lately about Papa's condition—and she insisted I find Lilette and bring her home immediately. As it has turned out, Lilette will undoubtedly return sooner than I do and *Maman* will be beside herself with worry, certain something dreadful has befallen me. You understand why I must hurry home."

"I understand." Jurissa repressed her sigh. It wasn't Leon's fault he couldn't stay. She should be content with their unexpected meeting, but she could hardly bear to have him go so quickly.

He kissed her gently, the kiss warming and deepening as he held her to him. Her body flamed with need. "Leon," she breathed as he released her. "Oh, Leon."

"If I touch you again I won't be able to leave," he told her, "and I must."

"When will you be back?"

"Perhaps on Sunday, if Papa holds his own."

"No earlier?"

*"Cherie,* if *le bon Dieu* made it possible, I'd never leave you. As it stands—Sunday, at the earliest." He gave her one final, quick kiss, raced down the stairs and was gone.

Jurissa was positive she would never be able to sleep until Yubah and Silas were home so, as soon as she heard Tigre's hoofbeats fading, she slipped back down to Tiana's quarters to relive her all-too-brief moments with Leon in her mind as she waited for their return.

Leon urged the horse into a trot. What a night! First *Maman* in a tizzy about that wretched Lilette, then the shock of finding Jurissa in the swamp. Anything might have happened to her out at night without a man's escort. Silas might be strong but he was only a slave; didn't she realize that? Didn't she know how important she was to him? He couldn't bear to have harm befall her.

He couldn't stay angry at her, though, when he knew he should be the one to protect her and he could not. His longing for her grew with every hour they were apart; he'd had the devil's own time tearing himself from her side at her apartment. Sunday seemed a year away. He desperately needed to be with her, but when Sunday came, he was going to have to tell her. It couldn't wait any longer. He'd waited far too long.

If only he could find another way to raise money and keep Papa happy at the same time. Unfortunately, because of what had happened in the past and now with Papa hovering on the edge of death, there was no other way.

Jurissa was always so understanding; he counted on that. It wasn't as if he could have married her anyway, trapped as she was in the legal morass that kept her from being either wife or widow. Anton struggled to free her but he'd warned it would take time, perhaps a year or more. They could still be together often; he'd promise her they would be. He couldn't go on otherwise.

He'd wait for her forever if only Papa was well enough to listen, to understand about Jurissa. But

Papa was not well, and Leon was the only remaining son. How could he fail to honor his father's dying wish?

Whatever imp of perversity had persuaded Jurissa that she must view a voodoo ceremony? A dangerous proceeding for any not of colored blood. It was fortunate the dance had finished before she arrived; voodoo rites were not a sight for a gently reared young lady. Fortunate, too, he'd come along looking for Lilette so he was able to see Jurissa safely home.

What would she take into her head to do next? He worried about her being so curious and headstrong.

Leon smiled. Ah, but that was part of her charm. If she were as predictable as, say, Louise-Marie, she never would have fascinated him in the first place.

On Thursday, when Anton DuBois's carriage pulled up in front of the bakery, Jurissa saw no reason not to accept his gracious offer to escort her about the city. Hadn't Leon said that Sunday was the earliest he could come to see her?

After Anton had settled beside her in the carriage and given orders to his driver, he confessed, "I feared you might change your mind at the last moment. I'm delighted you did not."

"Ever since I first saw New Orleans from the ship I arrived on, I've longed to be shown the city," she told him. "It's most kind of you."

"If you had a look at New Orleans from your ship, you must have noticed the city is laid out as a rectangle along the riverbank."

"Something of the sort occurred to me, yes."

"Originally we were surrounded by a rampart with

forts at the corners for protection. Now that Louisiana is on the verge of becoming the eighteenth of the United States—perhaps this very month—New Orleans has grown beyond the ramparts with all the *Americains* pouring into the city. It's true we no longer need the wall or the forts—many years have passed since protection against the Indians was necessary." He frowned. "True, we have the English to worry us now, but they're more to be feared on the water than on land."

"The *Yarmouth* kept a sharp lookout for British men-of-war while we sailed down the East Coast," she said, "but we sighted none. We *did* see one of Lafitte's pirate ships in the Gulf."

He shrugged. "All too common a sight. We tell ourselves that at least Lafitte will be there to warn us when the English do sail against New Orleans."

"Do you really think New Orleans will be at risk?"

He nodded. "I am no military man, madame, but it's clear New Orleans is a strategic port. Already our goods languish in the eastern seaports because of the English blockade of the Atlantic, but at least we're still able to ship them east. What we fear is a blockade at the mouth of the Mississippi River by their warships. And it will come, I greatly fear. But enough. I am sure such gloomy talk bores you."

"No," she assured him, "I'm very interested. Coming from Boston, I'm quite aware of the havoc the British are causing with our shipping. From what you say, you expect it to become worse."

"I'm only surprised President Madison hasn't yet declared a state of war against England. I'm taking you first to the Place d'Armes, our parade grounds. Sooner than we think we may be seeing troops reviewed there in earnest."

The Place d'Armes was along the waterfront, a large grassy square with trees to either side. Three buildings overlooked the parade grounds: the Cabildo, the government building, and the matching *presbytere*, the church house, to either side of St. Louis Cathedral with its two domed towers.

Anton helped her from the carriage and they strolled around the square. Jurissa bit her lip as she gazed at the cathedral. "I'm afraid I've been remiss about attending Mass since I arrived in New Orleans," she admitted.

"You'd make me a happy man, indeed, if you'd permit me to accompany you on Sunday."

Jurissa found herself blushing as she remembered how she hoped to spend her Sunday. "Perhaps the following week," she said after a pause.

"Ah, of course, you still tend your ill landlady. You think of everyone except yourself."

Embarrassed by his assumption and wishing to change the subject, Jurissa said, "You know my landlady is a free woman of color. Do you have many other free people of color in the city?"

"There are several thousands in New Orleans. Most support themselves in trade."

"When you give me word I'm the legal owner of Yubah and Silas, I'd like to free them. I hope you'll help me with the necessary papers."

"It is, of course, your decision. But do you think it wise? Freeing a slave is giving away valuable property."

"I've been told that before. But I intend to free the two Negroes who've been left in my care as soon as I can."

He inclined his head. "Then, of course, it will be my pleasure to assist you. I hope you will call on me whenever you need help, in any way whatsoever."

His brown eyes, so reminiscent of Leon's, clearly told her how they admired her carriage dress of blue silk with its satin trim and the bonnet to match and hinted he'd like to know her better. She couldn't help but feel pleased, but at the same time she didn't want to encourage him.

Turning away, she remarked, "I do believe that's a steamboat on the river. I didn't think to see one here. They're very new in the East."

"She's the first we've had. They call her the *New Orleans* and she belongs to the *Americains*."

Jurissa shook her head. "You Creoles say that word as though Americans are your enemies. Haven't you considered when Louisiana becomes a state all the Creoles will be Americans?"

"But still Creoles."

"You sound like Leon — Monsieur du Motier."

"Like all Creoles, my *cousine* and I know what comes first."

It gave her such pleasure to hear anything about Leon that she searched for a way to keep the conversation focused on him. "Have you heard how the elder Monsieur du Motier fares?" she asked.

"He's gravely ill, I'm informed. *Docteur* Marchand holds out little hope for recovery. The family hopes, of course, he'll be with them at least until after the wedding."

The wedding? Surely she hadn't heard Anton right. Leon had no sisters or brothers. As far as she knew, there was no one of marriageable age in the du Motier family except Leon.

"Did you say wedding?" she inquired, marveling at how calm her voice sounded when her insides churned with dreadful speculation.

"*Cousine* Leon has been betrothed to Louise-Marie Rondelet for two years. It's his father's greatest wish to see them wed before he dies."

Jurissa swallowed. "A long betrothal," she managed to say past the lump in her throat. "When is the marriage to take place?"

"On the first Saturday in May."

She stumbled and he caught her, holding her upright.

"Madame Winterton, are you ill?"

"A touch of dizziness. If you don't mind I'd like to return home."

Her eyes were open but she was aware of nothing as he led her back to his carriage and helped her inside.

"You're face is as pale as skimmed milk," he told her when he was seated beside her. "You've been working too hard in that bakery. You must consider your health as well as that of your landlady."

"Yes, of course." She agreed to his words without really understanding what he'd said, intent only on her inner misery.

Please don't let me be sick before I get home, she prayed, her eyes closed, as she swayed with the motion of the carriage. She scarcely realized when Anton put a tentative arm about her shoulders to steady her.

"If there's anything I can do—" he began.

"No, please, don't bother. Yubah will take care of me."

She leaned heavily on Anton as she descended from the carriage and entered the bakery. Yubah rushed to Jurissa's side and put her arms around her mistress.

Mustering what strength she could, Jurissa turned to Anton. "Thank you for helping me. I'm sorry to have spoiled the outing."

"All that interests me is your rapid recovery," he said. "I'll be back to inquire about you, if you permit. Au revoir."

She nodded, incapable of uttering another word. He bowed and left.

"I must lie down," she whispered to Yubah. Then the darkness that had been dancing at the edges of her vision coalesced and she knew nothing more.

When Jurissa came to, she lay in her bed, a cool, damp cloth on her forehead with Yubah hovering over her.

"Miss Jurissa, how you be?" she whispered.

Tears welled into Jurissa's eyes. "Oh, Yubah," she wailed, "he's marrying someone else."

Yubah sat on the bed next to her and grasped her hand. "I sure do be sorry. Seem all along like you be the one he wants."

"He didn't tell me he was marrying her," Jurissa sobbed. "Why didn't he tell me?"

"He know you gonna be mad is why."

Yubah was right, Jurissa thought. Leon had been afraid to tell her. But why, oh why was he marrying another woman? Did he love this Creole woman he'd been betrothed to for two years? The bitter realization that he'd never once told *her* he loved her, not in so many words, dried Jurissa's tears. She sat up and mopped at her wet face.

"He's not worth wasting tears on!" she announced.

"Mama, she say no man be worth crying over but she say women, they does anyway."

"Well I'm not going to shed another tear." Jurissa swung her legs over the ledge of the bed and started to stand. A wave of dizziness made her grab at Yubah's shoulder and she hastily sat back down.

"Best you do rest," Yubah told her.

"I'm not sick, I'm only a bit light-headed."

After propping pillows behind her head, Yubah said, "Gonna fix you some of that hot tea you likes." She started to leave the bedroom but stopped when someone rapped on the outer door. She raised inquiring eyebrows at Jurissa.

"If it's Monsieur DuBois, back to find out how I am, I don't want to see him. Tell him I'm much improved."

Yubah nodded and Jurissa heard her open the door. She was startled when Tiana walked slowly into the bedroom.

"You shouldn't have climbed all those steps," Jurissa scolded. "You need to be in bed worse than I do."

"I wanted to see how you're feeling." Tiana advanced to the bed and settled into the chair beside it. "Is it you've been working too hard in the bakery?"

"No! I—I've had upsetting news, that's all."

"She finally be hearing what you told me," Yubah said to Tiana. " 'Bout Massa Leon."

Jurissa stared from Yubah to Tiana. "You mean you knew he was getting married? How?"

"They called the names in church like they do. I've been too sick to go to Mass but Nicolas told me."

Jurissa blinked tears back, determined not to cry. "You told Yubah but not me. Everyone knew but me!"

148

Tiana sighed. "You saved my life, you keep my bakery going—how could I bear to hurt you when it might all be a mistake, calling the names."

"I do anything for you, Miss Jurissa," Yubah put in, "but I don't be telling you what might not be gonna happen."

"It's no mistake." Jurissa's voice was bitter. "He's going to marry her the first Saturday in May. Louise-Marie Rondelet, that's her name."

"The Rondelets have one of the finest plantations on the river," Tiana said. "The girl brings a good dowry with her." Her deeply set eyes met Jurissa's. "Everyone knows the du Motiers are in debt."

The bitterness rose in Jurissa, scalding her throat. "You're saying he's marrying her for her dowry."

Tiana shrugged. "It's possible. Men do these things all the time. Creoles prefer marriages arranged by the families."

"And that accounts for the *placees*, I suppose."

"It's not for me but it can be a good life for a free woman of color who wants to keep house and raise children," Tiana pointed out. "She's protected and her children take their father's Creole name. My mother was quite satisfied to be a *placee*."

Jurissa stretched out a hand toward Tiana. "I didn't mean to insult your mother or you. Please forgive me. The custom is new to me. We don't have it in Boston and I'm not used to such arrangements."

Tiana pressed her hand briefly. "I'm not upset. Why should I be? What you really meant to tell me is that you'd never be a *placee*. And why should you? You're a lady. You're pretty and you've already attracted another man."

And, of course, though Tiana had tactfully not mentioned it, Jurissa wasn't colored. Everything she'd said had been meant to comfort, but Jurissa wasn't eased. What Leon had done to her was making her more ill by the minute.

"Bring me a pan, quick," she ordered Yubah. She covered her mouth with her hand and fought to hold back the retching.

After the vomiting was over and she lay back among the pillows, Jurissa smiled weakly at the two women who stared at her with concern. "I feel better. I'll be all right now."

Tiana glanced at Yubah questioningly and, after a moment, Yubah seemed to understand her wordless question for she frowned and shook her head. Both of them turned as one to gaze unhappily at Jurissa.

"What's the matter?" she asked, alarmed. "Are you keeping something else from me?"

"This isn't anything you don't already know." Tiana's voice was sad. "Although, perhaps, you haven't yet realized what it is."

## Chapter Ten

Jurissa sat on the upper gallery in the shadows of early evening, the scent of jasmine from a neighbor's courtyard sweet on the river breeze. The sleepy squawks of birds settling to roost in a nearby magnolia mingled with voices drifting up from the street. A quiet time of day, a time for relaxing.

As if she could!

Yubah and Tiana must think her an ignorant goose, but it had never once occurred to her she might be with child. Not until they spelled out all the symptoms to her: missed monthly courses, nausea, dizziness, fainting.

Leon's baby. She was going to have Leon's baby. And Leon was marrying Louise-Marie Rondelet on the first Saturday in May.

"You must tell him," Tiana had urged. "If he's any kind of a man he'll marry you instead."

Force Leon to marry her when he didn't want to? Never!

Tiana's next proposal was that Jurissa allow everyone to assume the child was her dead husband's, since who was to know it wasn't? Her reputation would be saved since no one could prove the child wasn't Philip Winterton's.

No one except the dead man. And Leon. Leon knew Philip had never truly been her husband. Still, Leon might be relieved if she named Philip as the father. But she feared he might not. What if he, married to another woman, insisted on claiming the child as his and raising it as a du Motier at Dindon?

Jurissa put her hands to her stomach. No! If the baby was hers to have, it was hers to keep. Leon didn't want her at Dindon and she'd see to it he wouldn't raise her baby there.

"You still be feeling poorly?" Yubah asked, coming out onto the gallery.

"I'm fine."

"Look like you be studying 'bout something," Yubah said after a moment.

"I wish I could disappear until the baby is born so that Monsieur du Motier would never find out about it. Because once he discovers I'm going to have a baby, he'll know it's his."

Yubah nodded. "I be thinking Massa Philip never touch you."

"You thought right. Oh, he tried to but he'd been drinking and he scared me so I ran off. That was the night he fell overboard."

"I told Silas that be what happen."

The two of them know as much about me as I do, Jurissa told herself resignedly. Maybe more.

"So Massa Leon, he know the baby be his soon's you start to show," Yubah went on. "Gonna be a problem."

"I can refuse to see him if he comes to call, but after the baby's born I'm afraid he'll find out and suspect that's why I hid from him. Besides, others will know I'm in a family way and he's certain to hear about it."

"He be married to that Creole lady by then."

"Yes, but what if he claims my child as his and takes

it away from me? If it's a boy, he's sure to. He told me once the first-born son of a Creole always becomes the chatelaine of the plantation when his father dies. It wouldn't matter if I was a *placee;* their children never inherit. But, as Miss Tiana pointed out, I'm not colored so I can never be a *placee*. My son *could* inherit if Monsieur du Motier decides he wants him to."

"You think Massa Leon be so cruel?"

Jurissa tightened her lips. "He's marrying another woman and he didn't have the courtesy to tell me. Is that kind? Worse, he knew all along he was going to marry her and yet he allowed me to hope—" She broke off, biting her lip.

"Me and Silas, we gonna think of something. Silas, he say he die for you if you be asking him."

Jurissa reached to squeeze Yubah's hand. "I prefer Silas alive. And you, too."

"Could be you have a baby girl," Yubah consoled.

"He'd still know she was his and might decide to take her from me to raise."

"Don't you be fretting. Gonna be all right."

I wish I could believe that, Jurissa thought, but things will never be all right for me, not ever again. How could Leon, knowing he was betrothed to another, make love to me the way he did? All his sweet words were lies, every caress a betrayal.

Below, a man's voice called a greeting and she stiffened. A moment later, realizing it was Nicolas LeMoine, she eased her breath out.

"I hear Nicolas downstairs," she said to Yubah. "I don't need you now if you'd like to go down."

Yubah sniffed. "Maybe I don't."

"Why? I thought you liked him and I know he likes you."

"Miss Tiana, she say her brother be like an artichoke. Got a leaf for every girl but keep his heart for hisself."

Jurissa, who'd thought nothing would ever amuse her again, smiled. "She's warning you not to trust him and that's good advice about any man. It doesn't mean you can't flirt a little with him."

After a while Yubah eased from the balustrade. "Maybe I mosey on by and just say hello."

Once Yubah left her, Jurissa was plunged into melancholy. She'd been far too trusting. No one had warned her not to be, but she wouldn't have listened anyway. Beguiled by his charm, his touch, she'd given her heart and soul to Leon.

The result was that he'd be acquiring a bride while she'd be having a baby. Certainly not what she'd expected. Betrayal by Leon had never entered her mind. Nor had the thought of a baby.

"Babies don't have to be thought of to be born," Tiana had advised her too late.

But she wouldn't have taken advice anyway. Not as long as she believed in Leon. What a fool she'd been!

He'd be here Sunday. Did he mean to tell her about the coming wedding or did he plan to keep his silence so she'd fall into his arms as usual?

I'll wait and find out just how traitorous he can be, she decided, before I let him know I never want to see him again. I certainly won't fall into his arms!

If only she had somewhere else to go. Even with enough funds to go back to Boston, though, her responsibility would remain for Silas and Yubah. Besides, she had no friends in Boston. Arabel had always wanted Jurissa's time for herself. The only friends she had in the world were here in New Orleans. Yubah. Silas. Tiana. And, possibly, if he never discovered the truth, Anton DuBois.

She had to remain in New Orleans, here, on the rue des Normandie. There was no place to hide.

By Sunday, Jurissa felt more like herself. She'd busied herself during the intervening days by baking in the mornings and napping a bit in the afternoons. At night, with memories of Leon haunting her, she had trouble sleeping.

She took special pains to choose a gown, deciding on a rose batiste with lace trim. The color, she felt, made her appear less pale. Yubah had dressed her hair in a new fashion, fastening it atop her head with rose ribbons and arranging strands to curl down artfully at the sides.

She'd expected Leon to ride Tigre and hitch the horse outside the bakery as he'd done before. Instead, he surprised her by walking up to the gate in the wall. Instantly she ducked into the apartment, not wanting to be caught watching for him on the gallery. Why hadn't he ridden in? Because people would recognize Tigre?

How thoughtful of him to consider his bride-to-be's feelings. Certainly he hadn't bothered to consider hers.

She heard him bounding up the stairs and, despite everything, her heart began to pound in anticipation as she opened the door to his knock.

*"Cherie!"* He strode to her, brown eyes alight and eager.

Before he could clasp her in his arms, she held up her hands, palms out. He took them in his, pressing the palms to his lips. The familiar tickle of his mustache almost did in all her good intentions but she managed to pull back.

"I've prepared Creole coffee," she informed him. "Just as you like it — what is the saying?" Black as the devil, treacherous as love—"

155

"No, no, you have it wrong," he insisted.

"Do I?" She shrugged. "I believe the coffee is right, though. Strong enough to stain the cup. And there are petite almond croissants for you to try."

"At the moment coffee and croissants are not what I'm hungry for." He tried to pull her into his arms but she resisted.

"I'll be upset if you don't at least taste what I've prepared."

"You know what I'd rather taste, *cherie*."

She gestured toward the table, a smile fixed firmly in place, her eyes not quite meeting his. "I'd prefer the coffee," she said.

"What's wrong?" he demanded, tipping up her chin with his fingers until she had to look at him.

"Why should anything be wrong?"

Her green eyes were cloudy, shutting him away from their depths. Leon leaned to kiss her but she jerked away.

"Is it that you believe I can't cook?" she demanded.

"I'm sure you're a wonderful cook but—"

"Then why won't you try what I've made for you?"

She was in a mood, certainly. He'd never seen her like this. She'd never been distant with him.

"*Cousine* Anton praises my croissants," she informed him. "When I went riding with him on Thursday he told me my baking showed a master's touch."

She'd been riding with Anton? Jealousy skewered him. He should have known better than to let his *cousine* get anywhere near her. It was true Anton didn't understand what was between him and Jurissa—that had to be kept secret—but who'd have expected old sobersides Anton to move so fast.

"He showed me the city," she went on. "I found your *cousine tres* amusing."

Anton had never amused anyone in his life. At least as far as Leon was aware.

"And so knowledgeable!" she continued. "Do you realize we should expect a declaration of war against England within days? Perhaps even before Louisiana becomes the eighteenth state."

Somehow she'd manuevered him to the table while she was talking. He had little choice except to sit down and accept the cup of coffee she proffered.

"What do you think about the chances for war?" she asked as she set out a plate of dainty crescents.

He had an almost irrepressible urge to sweep everything from the table and overturn it. To throw her over his shoulder and bear her off to some secret hideaway where no other man could ever come near her and to stay there with her forever.

Like everything else he wanted to do lately, it was impossible. Leon pulled himself together. So Anton was knowledgeable? If knowledge was what she prized, knowledge she'd get.

"It is true Louisiana will soon become a state," he said. "We Creoles insisted on the name, you know. The *Americains* wished to call our new state Jefferson, after the man who was president of the United States when this territory was purchased from Napoleon. Imagine having to call a pretty Creole girl a beautiful Jeffersonian!"

"I agree the name is not felicitous." Her voice was cool.

Perhaps he should praise her cooking. Leon picked up his cup and sipped the coffee. "Delicious. A true Creole brew."

"Although you claim I got the saying wrong."

"But you did. *Doux comme l'amour.* Sweet as love.'"

She shook her head. "I prefer *'traite comme l'amour.'*"

"*Cherie*, love isn't treacherous—" He stopped abruptly. *Bigre!* Why hadn't he understood when she said the words the first time? It explained her coolness, her refusal to let him hold her.

"You know," he said.

She stared at him in silence, her green eyes dark with accusation.

He spread his hands. "How could I tell you? *Le bon Dieu* knows I wish it didn't have to be but it doesn't matter what I want."

"Obviously I don't matter, either."

He reached for her hand and she drew back in her chair. "Don't you touch me!"

"You do matter," he insisted, still leaning toward her. "We matter. But I can't turn my back on Papa. On Dindon. I honor his dying request."

"You've been betrothed to her for two years. Why did you never think to mention that to me?"

"Because it had nothing to do with how I feel about you. I don't love Louise-Marie. It was an arranged marriage that I kept putting off for one reason or another."

"Until now."

He shoved his chair back, rose, grasped her hand and yanked her to her feet. He put his hands on her shoulders and gazed into her eyes. "I don't feel for Louise-Marie what I feel for you, *cherie*. It's you I want."

She was stiff and resistant under his hands. "Marrying another woman is a strange way to show your affection for me."

"Damn it, I thought you'd understand."

"But I do."

He sighed in relief. "Ah, *cherie*, I knew I could count on you. The marriage will make no difference between us, you wait and see. I'll be with you often and—"

"No!" She jerked free. Standing back from him, she folded her arms under her breasts and glared at him. "What I understand is you don't love me, you never have and you never will. I believe you're incapable of love — except, possibly, for Dindon. Like your father. Things mean more to you than people."

"*Cherie,* that's not —"

"Don't call me *cherie!* I'm not your darling, I won't be, ever again. Save your love words for your bride. Or, if not her, then the *placee* I'm sure you'll soon be acquiring."

Anger cast its dark net around him. Damn the woman. He took a step toward her. Quickly, she darted behind a chair, placing it between them.

"Don't come near me," she warned. "There's no longer anything between us. I don't want to see you again. I suggest you leave. Now."

"You're afraid to let me touch you," he growled. "You know as well as I do what's between us is too strong to die, no matter how upset you may be at the moment."

"I don't want you!" Her voice rose. "Get out!"

He half smiled. "You do want me. You fear if I don't leave, if I stay, you'll be forced to admit the truth." The truth for him was that he was fighting to keep his hands off her. Her breasts, rising and falling rapidly, her lips quivering with the intensity of her emotion — his urge to possess them, to possess her totally was overwhelming.

"The truth is you made your choice," she cried, "and it wasn't me. You chose her, now be satisfied with her."

*Dieu,* she was magnificent. Glorious. So beautiful in her righteous fury he was tempted to throw over everything he believed in for her.

Don't let him touch me, Jurissa prayed. Please don't let him touch me. I'll fall apart if he does and that must not happen.

She knew that somehow she had to find a way to make him want to leave her and anger wasn't the way. If he grew furious enough, he'd toss the chair aside and she'd be in his arms, where, God forgive her, she longed to be. Leon hadn't liked her speaking of Anton. Perhaps that was the best approach.

Taking a deep breath, she did her best to calm herself. "Leon," she said, keeping her voice firmly under control, keeping it even and reasonable, "I deserve to have a husband as much as you deserve to have a wife. Is that not fair?" Not waiting for an answer, she plunged on. "Why should I put my chance for marriage in jeopardy by allowing you to visit me after you're married?"

She could see she'd taken him aback. Good.

"Anton DuBois is attracted to me," she went on. "I like him. If all goes well, I believe he might eventually ask me to marry him once he's able to clear up the legal tangle surrounding me. Would you have me give up my chance for happiness to cater to your selfishness?"

Leon swallowed, staring at her. "Happiness? You'd be happy with *him*?"

She made herself look directly into his eyes. "As happy as you will be, anyway. And if I should marry him, I'd be a loyal wife, you can count on that."

"I can't believe you're saying this! I can't believe you mean it."

"I had the same trouble when I first heard about your coming marriage, but I've come to believe it. So will you, once you give yourself a little time. Don't you see, Leon, it's best for both of us this way."

"No," he muttered. "No, I don't see how it's best for us."

"If you think, you'll understand why it's best for me,

at least. Once a woman's reputation is ruined, she has nothing left. If I permit you to visit after you're married, soon everyone will know, Anton included. Do you wish to take every chance from me?"

"*Mon Dieu, mon Dieu,*" he muttered. "How will I go on?"

"One step at a time, just as I will."

His brown eyes held such a hurt, bewildered look it was all she could do not to reach out to comfort him. But why should he need comfort? Wasn't she more hurt than he? Didn't she still have her own ordeal to go through—alone?

"Adieu, Leon," she said, needing it to be over once and for all, needing him out of her life for good. When he was near her she wanted him, exactly as he'd suspected. It took all her will not to fling herself into his arms. "I'm sure you understand why it can't be au revoir."

"I'd have to be a selfish brute to force myself on you after what you've said." His voice was sad. He reached a hand to her but she shook her head.

He smiled wryly, a smile that didn't reach his eyes. "Can't trust yourself, can you? Ah, well, *cherie,* I do understand. I shan't trouble you again. Adieu, and may *le bon Dieu* truly be with you."

And with you, my traitorous love. The words remained unspoken. She had no more to say to him.

As he strode toward the door, she slowly followed him, knowing she'd be watching from the gallery until he was out of sight.

Without breaking stride, he reversed his steps and, before she could escape, she was in his arms. "One final kiss," he murmured against her lips. "Is that too much to ask?"

She had no chance to answer. His mouth covered

hers, warm and seductive, enticing her to retract everything she'd said. Her response was instinctive, out of her control. She pressed herself to him, her lips opening under his. Her blood raced with her need for him until she felt she would die with longing. What would it matter if she made love with him one last time?

"You belong in my arms," he whispered into her ear.

He was right; this was where she belonged. She, Jurissa, not the Creole woman he meant to marry. If she told him about their baby he'd surely change his mind. They'd be together, they'd be happy. She didn't need Dindon; she only needed Leon.

But what about Leon? Would he ever be truly happy without Dindon? If he lost it because she forced him to marry her, wouldn't he come to hate her?

As she'd hate herself if she used the child as a threat to make him marry her. No, she mustn't tell him. The baby must be her secret for as long as it was possible to keep her condition a secret. Leon had rejected her as his wife. So be it.

But pushing herself away from him was the most difficult thing she'd ever done in her life. "Go," she begged him, tears threatening. "If you have any feeling for me, please go."

Looking into his eyes, afire with passion, she thought for a moment that he meant to deny her plea, to sweep her into his arms again, and she was both exultant and afraid. Then without a word he turned on his heel, yanked the door open and strode through, kicking it shut behind him. Jurissa, her hands clenched together, didn't move. He was gone. She'd never see him again.

The first Saturday in May came and, as she sat on the upper gallery with Jurissa that evening, Tiana reported, from a friend's account, that Leon's marriage to Louise-Marie Rondelet had been celebrated in St. Thomas Cathedral.

"My friend says since the woman's not pretty, she must have an attractive dowry," Tiana added. "Didn't I tell you? Creoles are, above all, practical in money matters."

"So I'm learning." Jurissa had to force the reply. She hoped now that the marriage was a fact and she wouldn't miss Leon so much. Her longing for him was a constant ache.

In the courtyard below, Yubah's laughter punctuated Nicolas's sallies. Jurissa knew Silas was with them but he rarely spoke.

"My brother's quite taken with Yubah," Tiana said. "He might even be serious — if she were a free woman of color."

"I've told you I mean to free both Yubah and Silas when I can."

Tiana nodded. "I believe you, but life has taught me not to count any money I don't hold in my hand. Who knows what may happen to prevent you? Still, it won't harm Nicolas to wait and to learn patience. Silas approves of Nicolas but he watches over Yubah like an eagle with a single chick." She chuckled. "My brother's not used to such a formidable chaperon."

Jurissa couldn't bring herself to take an interest in the developing romance between Nicolas and Yubah. Nothing interested her. To keep herself busy, and because Tiana was still weak, she continued to help with the baking, an increased task since her Paris pastries had attracted new customers.

She wished Yubah well but she just couldn't care what happened. Anton DuBois had twice come to the bakery, hoping to persuade her to go for a drive with him. She'd politely refused. Though she'd had no compunction about misrepresenting her acquaintance with Anton in order to convince Leon he must stay away from her, she really had no feeling for *Cousine* Anton. None at all. She had no feeling for anything or anyone. Except Leon.

"I've been thinking," Tiana said. "It isn't fair for you to do most of the work and receive none of the profit from the bakery. Don't bother to argue, I won't listen. I've never taken in so much money and it's because of your fancy pastries. I plan to make you a partner."

Jurissa was jerked out of her lethargy. "A partner? Whatever are you talking about?"

"You have no money to invest, I know, but you please the customers with your baking and bring us new business, so why shouldn't you become my partner? I know you well enough by now to realize you don't mind working with a colored woman, and what other reason would you have to refuse?"

"But I—it's your bakery, not mine. I'm only helping out."

"At the moment you're carrying the business on your shoulders. Stop and think about what you're going to use for money after the baby comes. You'll need extra for him. Babies always cost more than anyone plans for. I'm offering you a chance to earn money for your child's future."

Jurissa was silent. She hadn't looked ahead; she couldn't summon the energy. Since Leon had left her, it was all she could do to get through each day, hour by hour. But Tiana was right; the baby would bring new responsibility.

"You're very kind," she told Tiana. "I promise I'll consider your proposal very carefully."

"You do that. After you agree, we'll get Monsieur

DuBois to make everything legal. As to the kindness, call it what you want but remember what I told you. Creoles are practical when it comes to business and money and I'm a Creole. Those born white don't like to hear us say so, but we free people of color are as much Creoles as any of them."

As if summoned by Tiana's mention of his name the night before, Anton DuBois climbed the steps to Jurissa's apartment early Sunday afternoon. Since Jurissa was sitting in plain sight on the gallery, she could hardly refuse to see him.

"I'm delighted to find you at home," he said.

It wouldn't do to say she was rarely anywhere else. "How kind of you to call," she murmured and motioned to a chair on the other side of a small iron table Silas had made for her. "Won't you be seated?"

"Thank you." He placed his hat and gloves carefully on the table. It was difficult for her to imagine Anton being anything but careful.

"Perhaps you'd enjoy some lemonade," she said. "My maid will soon be back from an errand, and I'll have her bring us some."

"It's not necessary. I've come because I wanted to see you before I traveled to Washington."

Jurissa sat straighter, interested despite herself. "Washington?"

"I don't believe I mentioned that I was one of those elected to the Constitutional Convention. Now that Louisiana has become a state, I'll be meeting with President Madison in Washington."

She stared at him, impressed. "I had no idea you were involved in the state-making procedure, although I did hear we were a new state."

"Louisiana joined the Union, just in time to be included in Madison's declaration of war against

England. No doubt he planned it that way. The president is a shrewd politician."

"I'm beginning to think you might be one, too."

Anton smiled. "I'm only a Creole who intends to see his people aren't overrun by *Americains*. I look forward to meeting the president. My one regret is I won't see you for months. Though our acquaintance has been of short duration, I shall miss you."

She couldn't honestly claim she'd miss him, too, but obviously something had to be said.

"I hope your trip is safe and you come nowhere near a British man-of-war," she told him, evading the issue.

"I was hoping you'd say that you looked forward to my return."

"I do. Of course I do."

His eyes, when they met hers, held a gleam of humor. "I'll have to console myself with your polite answer and be thankful you didn't say as far as you were concerned I might remain in Washington forever."

Jurissa smiled. She'd forgotten that she enjoyed Anton's company. "From what I've heard of the place, I'd wish that fate on no one."

"I admire your honesty, madame, more than you can know. I deal poorly with coquettes, perhaps because, though I know their behavior is mere affectation, I can't help noting the lies in their every word and pose. You are refreshingly direct. I can talk to you and trust what you tell me, a rarity in a woman."

Completely taken aback, she could find nothing to say.

"I must admit that's not all I admire about you, but others must have told you how very beautiful you are. My clerk will be doing his best to clear your legal status while I'm away, and I hope to find he has your affairs in order by the time I return. Not merely for your sake but for mine."

Good heavens, she thought in alarm, where is this leading? How can I stop him?

"I know this is premature," he said solemnly, "but, despite the way you've teased me about my circumlocution, I can be direct when I choose. I hope, once it's legally possible, you'll do me the honor of becoming my wife."

## Chapter Eleven

Tiana, seating herself in the chair vacated no more than an hour ago by Anton DuBois, stared across the iron table at Jurissa. "I can't believe you didn't agree to marry that fine man."

Jurissa shrugged. "How good a marriage could we have if it rested on lies? I'd not only have to pretend the baby was Philip Winterton's, I'd have to pretend I really cared for Monsieur DuBois."

"You said you liked him."

"Liking a man isn't enough for marriage."

Tiana shook her head. "I forget how young you are, hardly older than Yubah. You'll have to live a few more years before you realize a marriage is whatever a woman cares to make it." She waved a silk fan before her face, languidly stirring the warm afternoon air. "Monsieur DuBois is a rich man. You'd never have to worry about money. He'd make you a good husband yet you tell him no."

"I didn't refuse him outright. I hated to hurt his feelings so I simply said I wasn't ready to marry again."

Tiana fanned herself harder. "So you did show a little

sense. He'll try again, no doubt, and you'd best think carefully before you refuse the second time."

"I don't love him."

Tiana raised her eyebrows. "Do you intend to waste your life pining over a man who threw away his chance to marry you? Who chose another?"

"No!" Jurissa made a dismissing gesture. "He doesn't matter to me anymore. That's over and done with. But you know Monsieur DuBois is his *cousine*."

"If you married the *cousine* at least the child would have a blood relative as a father instead of no father at all."

"I can't do it." Jurissa shook her head. "I just can't."

Tiana sighed. "A mule has nothing on you for stubbornness."

Leon had called her stubborn, Jurissa remembered. Certainly her memories of him stubbornly refused to be put out of her mind. Her hand dropped to her lower abdomen where her body carried a more tangible reminder of him. She didn't show yet, but she fancied she felt a roundness there.

"I promised Yubah I'd talk to you," Tiana said, laying the fan aside. "She told me you wouldn't marry Monsieur DuBois, but I hoped she was wrong. She also said she didn't believe you could bring yourself to let the child be known as your dead husband's." Tiana glanced shrewdly at Jurissa. "Yubah says the man was evil."

"It's true he could be cruel especially to her."

"Is she right otherwise?"

Jurissa sat in silence for a while before answering. "Philip and I should never have married. It distresses me to think of pretending the child is his. I don't know if I can."

"Ah, well, in that case we must give consideration to Yubah's plan. What she proposes to do is have the baby instead of you."

Jurissa stared at Tiana. "That's clearly impossible."

"Be patient and listen. You may not have heard I was trained as a seamstress when I was young. I became an expert. Many of my clients begged me not to give it up when I bought the bakery but I prefer baking to sewing. I intend to design and sew gowns for you to hide your condition until close to the end. But *le bon Dieu* himself cannot hide the sudden appearance of a baby.

"Yubah's plan is simple but practical. She suggests she pad herself month by month so that when the child is born, everyone will assume it's hers by a Creole father. No one makes a fuss when a slave births a bastard; no one cares. You'll be able to keep the child as Yubah's and your reputation won't suffer. You could, if you can bring yourself to accept him, even marry Monsieur DuBois. Since you say you plan to free Yubah, the child could be freed at the same time."

Jurissa could only stare at her, aghast.

"I know the baby would be labeled as colored," Tiana went on, "but Nicolas, who lived in Paris, told me that coloreds are well accepted in France. The child could be educated there."

"I—I don't know what to say." Jurissa spoke from a choked throat. Yubah was willing to go through such a distressing charade for her? She couldn't consider letting Yubah do it, not for a moment, but she was overwhelmed by the offer.

Tiana held up a hand. "Don't make up your mind to say no. This isn't something you can decide quickly. I insist you promise me you'll at least think about it."

"Promises are cheap," Jurissa said. "I'll give you the promise but don't imagine I'll agree to this plan."

May eased into June. Anton DuBois was in Washington and Leon had been married for over a month when Jurissa heard that his father had died. By July, though her fashionable high-waisted gowns still concealed any betraying roundness, Jurissa knew she'd soon have to accept Tiana's offer to make her more concealing costumes.

No Boston July had prepared Jurissa for the damp heat that lay over New Orleans like a heavy hand. Baking in the tiny kitchen became a chore and, to free herself from the hot oven now and then, she painstakingly taught Yubah how to concoct the fancy pastries that were in so much demand. Tiana, her strength returning, also learned.

In mid-July Jurissa, encouraged by Tiana, purchased a horse and a small cabriolet so she might have the pleasure, badly needed, of taking the evening air. She drove herself with Yubah, who enjoyed the outings as much as she did, standing behind. Driving oneself unaccompanied by a gentleman was perfectly proper, it seemed, even though walking on the banquettes alone was not.

It was on one of these evening drives, after she'd passed St. Louis Cemetery, when she encountered Leon on Tigre. He raised his hat and she nodded, looking immediately away but feeling his eyes on her. Fear made her fingers tighten on the reins. The rounding of her abdomen suddenly seemed all too obvious, visible to him beneath her gown.

"You're looking well." His voice came from her left. She started, not realizing he'd turned to ride beside the cabriolet. Glancing at him, she saw his gaze intent on her.

"I was sorry to hear of your father's death," she managed to say while she wondered nervously if he'd notice the change in her figure.

"Papa's time had come."

Anger threaded into her upset. How dare he stare at her? "At least you can be sure he died happy." Her tone was tart.

He urged Tigre closer to the cabriolet and leaned from the saddle toward her. "I miss you, *cherie*," he said in a voice so low it barely carried above the rattle of the carriage and the hoofbeats of the horses.

Before she could decide whether to respond or not, he wheeled his mount and trotted away.

Back at home, Jurissa hastened to her mirror and stared into it, trying to decide if her condition was obvious to anyone but herself.

Yubah, watching her, shook her head. "You think he catch you out? He don't. But pretty soon everybody be knowing. Least you let me help like I say."

Jurissa turned to her. "Oh, Yubah, I don't know what to do. I'm so afraid he'll find out and yet I'll go mad if I have to shut myself up here from now on and hide so no one knows about me."

"Folk think I be having a baby. They don't pay heed to you the way Miss Tiana gonna make your gowns. Even Massa Leon ain't gonna know do he see you. Silas, he say I got to study on a way to make you let me do it. Only way I knows to help."

Jurissa shook her head. But, after three restless

nights where she kept rousing panic-stricken from dreams where she'd had the baby but couldn't find it anywhere, she told Yubah she'd changed her mind.

"I don't know whether this is the right thing to do or not," she said, "but I can't think of any other way." She flung her arms around Yubah. "You're a true friend."

Later, as she watched Tiana fashioning an undergarment to hold padding in place on Yubah, she had second thoughts. "What will Nicolas think?" she asked them. "Will he approve?"

"You don't think we're letting *him* into the secret?" Tiana demanded. "Never! Nicolas is a good boy but we can't trust him at a time like this. He doesn't know your condition. Why should he? It's none of his business."

"But he's fond of Yubah. If you don't explain, surely he'll be upset to find she's in the family way."

Yubah looked at Jurissa, her amber eyes unreadable. "He gonna have to understand. If he don't—" She shrugged. "Mean he don't be caring so much as he say."

"You're asking a great deal of Nicolas," Jurissa said. "Don't you agree, Tiana?"

"A boy's got to grow up and be a man," Tiana said. "Nicolas is coming along but he's not there yet. Maybe this will finish it, maybe not. He's no use to Yubah till he's a man, one way or the other."

"Maybe that's Monsieur du Motier's problem," Jurissa said bitterly.

Tiana shook her head. "He had a hard choice to make, a man's decision. You should have told him about the child so he could change his mind. You wouldn't."

Jurissa, stung by Tiana's criticism, cried, "I *couldn't* tell him!"

"You made your choice," Tiana said. "So now we do what we can to make it work."

In August the British stunned New Orleans by blockading the mouth of the Mississippi with two warships, cutting off the flow of goods by ship in and out of the city; just as Anton feared they would, Jurissa told herself, wondering how he'd be able to return from Washington. Overland could be a tedious and dangerous journey.

Life went on despite the blockade and, with Lafitte's brigs and barks slipping past the British to bring contraband goods to the merchants, New Orleans didn't suffer deprivation although cotton, sugar, and tobacco began to pile up on the docks.

Tiana's bakery continued to bring in money, so much so that, after consulting with Jurissa, she bought the building next door and moved the business into larger quarters with an expanded kitchen.

In September Nicolas noticed Yubah's changing figure, courtesy of Tiana's clever padding, and confronted her. Jurissa didn't know anything about it until she found Yubah weeping.

"What's the matter?" she asked in concern. "Are you ill?"

Yubah wiped her face. "Be nothing."

Jurissa put an arm around her. "Don't tell me that. Tell me what's wrong."

Yubah shook her head. "I don't be sick, I be fine."

Examining Yubah's woebegone expression, it dawned on Jurissa what was bothering her. "It's Nicolas, isn't it?"

Reluctantly, Yubah nodded.

"This isn't fair to you," Jurissa said. "I'm going to tell him the truth."

"No!" Yubah pulled away from her. "Me, I don't be wanting a man who don't listen. Was gonna say Massa Philip force me—ain't a lie, 'cause he sure try—gonna say that be where the baby come from. If I be forced, don't be my fault, do it? Nicolas, he just turn up his nose. Don't want no more to do with me. Don't want to hear nothing once he see this." She patted her padded stomach. "He don't give me a chance. He ain't gonna get one from me. Don't want you to be telling him nothing. Nicolas, he ain't worth it."

Jurissa, who'd suspected Philip had tried to rape Yubah, now had it confirmed. The poor girl—first a cruel master, then a mistress who caused her to lose the man she loved.

"I'm sorry," she said. "I'd try to change his mind, but if you don't want me to say anything to Nicolas, I won't."

Yubah shook her head fiercely.

It was a month before Jurissa saw her smile again, occasioned when Silas came home with the news that his employer at the forge, afraid he was going to lose the best helper he'd ever had to a rival blacksmith, had doubled Silas's wages. It was money Jurissa didn't need and she insisted on buying new clothes for Silas from the extra.

"Don't he look fancy," Yubah said proudly. "He gonna be swatting away women like flies."

Jurissa, who'd never forgotten seeing the nearly nude Silas dancing at the voodoo fire, had no difficulty understanding how women might be drawn to him, and she nodded in agreement. "Once this is over—" She touched her protruding abdomen and gestured at Yubah's padded one. "I'm going to buy you the finest clothes in New Orleans. It's little enough. You deserve more than I can ever give you."

As the year wound down toward December, Jurissa stopped appearing in public altogether, leaving even the baking to Tiana and Yubah. Her rapidly increasing girth made her grateful for the cooler weather.

In the middle of December Jurissa received a letter from Anton telling her that President Madison had been reelected on December 2 and had asked Anton to remain in Washington as one of his advisors.

"Congress hasn't been convinced we should have declared war," he wrote, "but now that the people show their approval by reelecting the president, I have confidence the tide will turn. We've lost battles but we'll win the war. As for New Orleans, every last Creole would die fighting before we'd submit to the English.

"I regret being parted from you for such an extended period. My only consolation is that, as time passes, you may be more willing to favor my suit when I do return."

It warmed her that Anton should think of her enough to write and that he still wanted to marry her. Luckily he couldn't see how she looked at the moment. She half believed she'd never have a normal figure again. Leon, if he saw her, would be cured of ever wanting her again—if he wasn't already.

It hurt to think of him in bed with his wife, touching her as he'd once touched Jurissa, perhaps calling her *"cherie."* How could he do it? She didn't think she could ever allow any man besides Leon to make love to her.

On Christmas Eve Jurissa felt her first pang. When the pains grew worse, around midnight, Yubah hurried down to fetch Tiana.

"I can't. It hurts too much," Jurissa moaned as Tiana insisted she get off the bed and walk back and forth.

"How many babies have *you* helped birth?" Tiana asked Jurissa. "Do as I say and it'll be over all the sooner."

Groaning, a hand to her swollen abdomen, Jurissa forced herself to her feet. She took two steps before another pain fixed her in place.

"Never mind how you feel, keep moving," Tiana urged. "Yubah, you take her arm and walk with her."

Leaning on Yubah, Jurissa began to pace slowly back and forth, moaning when each new pain lanced through her.

"Men." Tiana's voice was scathing. "If they had to go through this you can be sure there'd be fewer babies born. Men get all the pleasure and none of the pain."

In the midst of her travail, it struck Jurissa that she didn't know if Tiana had ever had a man of her own, but she was too miserable to pursue the thought. Back and forth she walked, forcing her attention on taking the next step to avoid screaming aloud with the pain.

Just when she thought she couldn't stand it any longer, Tiana stretched a white sheet on the floor, set the birthing stool, which she'd kept stored under Jurissa's bed, on top of it and draped a clean white cloth onto the stool. "Sit," she ordered.

"Can't I please lie down?" Jurissa begged.

"Babies come quicker and easier this way," Tiana insisted. "You can get into bed once the baby comes.

It's then you'll need to rest. Now, you have work to do."

Jurissa squatted awkwardly on the stool. The next pain was so strong that all she could do was grunt as it gripped her.

"Push," Tiana urged. "Take hold of the arms on the stool and push down hard."

Jurissa obeyed as best she could, gasping for breath in between pushing. The pain didn't ease but continued on and on. Sweat dripped from Jurissa's forehead as she bore down harder and harder.

"Good girl." Tiana's voice seemed to come from far away. Nothing existed for Jurissa but the pain and the need to push it out of her body.

"Be coming." Was that Yubah's voice?

All Jurissa knew for sure was that, after a long moment of such intense pain she thought she would die, she felt something slide from inside her, and the pain subsided.

"A boy!" Yubah cried at the same moment the baby began to squall.

Jurissa's lips curved into a smile. A son. She'd borne Leon's son. No, *her* son.

"The afterbirth's got to come out," Tiana announced, standing over Jurissa with a feather in her hand. "Open your mouth wide."

When Jurissa did, Tiana reached in with the feather and tickled the back of her throat. Surprised, Jurissa gagged, retching, feeling something else slide from her.

"You're finished with your work," Tiana told her. She lifted the screaming baby, afterbirth and all, from the sheet on the floor and held him for Jurissa to touch.

Reaching a tentative hand, Jurissa ran her forefinger over his cheek. He stopped crying and turned his face toward her hand.

"Already looking for something to eat, this one," Tiana commented. "Yubah will clean you up while I tie off the cord and wash him. Then you can nurse him in bed."

How well he fit into the curve of her arm, Jurissa marveled later as she cuddled her baby to her. Fingering the softness of his hair, she whispered to him, "As black and curly as your father's."

"He be born on Christmas, just like Jesus," Yubah pointed out. She knelt beside the bed to peer closely at the baby. "Never see such a fine-looking boy."

Jurissa smiled sleepily at her. "He's as much yours as mine, isn't he?"

"Nothing bad ever gonna happen to this boy!" Yubah momentarily startled Jurissa with her fierceness. "We all gonna watch over him, Silas and me and Miss Tiana. Be watching over you, too, Miss Jurissa."

"Thank you," Jurissa whispered. "Thank you for everything." Unable to keep her eyes open any longer, she drifted into sleep, her son held close against her.

She roused once when the baby began to cry and shifted him to her other breast. Tiana had told her the milk might not come in for a while but he seemed satisfied to suck. Jurissa crooned to him as he nuzzled against her and soon they both slept again.

She roused abruptly to find Yubah shaking her shoulder and crying, "Wake up, Miss Jurissa!" Men's voices, raised in anger, filtered through the closed door.

"Bad trouble. Massa Leon—" Yubah broke off as a man shouted.

"I *will* see her and no Negro's going to stop me. Let me by, damn you!"

Leon!

"Silas try to keep him out," Yubah said, "but Massa Leon, he done drink some and he be acting crazy."

Her worst nightmare! Jurissa thought, panic-stricken. Leon here and herself helpless. What was she to do? If she didn't think of something quickly Silas could be in serious trouble. No slave laid a hand on a white man without punishment. Pushing away her terror, she made a quick decision. After wrapping the baby's blanket so closely about him that even his face wasn't visible, she offered him to Yubah.

"Take him and try to keep him quiet. Remember, he's yours." Propping herself on pillows, Jurissa called to Silas, raising her voice to be heard through the door. "Silas, let Monsieur du Motier in."

"Get the baby down to Tiana as soon he comes in," she instructed Yubah in a half-whisper. "Stay with Miss Tiana until he leaves."

Yubah, the baby clutched to her chest, hesitated. "You gonna be all right?"

"Don't worry, he won't hurt me. Go!"

As Yubah slipped from the bedroom, the outer door opened and boots stomped across the wide planks of the floor. Leon, hatless, his hair in disarray, stood in the doorway to the bedroom. Silas loomed behind him.

"Please go out with Yubah, Silas," Jurissa ordered. "I'll be all right."

Silas, as Yubah had done, hesitated, but then turned away. When the outer door shut behind them, Jurissa let out her pent-up breath. She didn't know what would happen next but at least they were out of harm's way. Now that the baby was safe from Leon she wasn't afraid, even if he had been drinking.

180

He walked slowly to her bedside and stood looking down at her. Her heart contracted at the beseeching look in his brown eyes.

"I had to see you." He dropped to his knees by the side of the bed. "I couldn't stand being away from you any longer." He touched the back of her hand where it rested atop the covers. "I didn't mean to cause trouble but I went out of my head when Silas said you were sick and told me I couldn't come in."

"I—I'm better," she stammered.

His fingers trembled as he eased them along her cheek. "You're pale. You look tired." Tears glimmered in his eyes. "If anything happened to you my life would be over." He dropped his head onto the bed, his arms on both sides of her, and began to sob.

Easing herself up, she tangled her fingers in his soft dark curls. Like his son's hair. Tears filled her eyes and ran down her cheeks at the waste of it all. She loved him, she always would. Together they'd made a beautiful boy she could never show to him, never tell him about. Leon had done what he thought he had to do and so had she. And yet it seemed so wrong.

"I love you," he said, raising a tear-stained face. "I never knew it was possible to love anyone so much."

Once she'd thought she'd never hear those words from him. Even though he'd said them too late, her heart leaped with joy.

"I shouldn't have come to you but I couldn't help myself," he said. "It's Christmas, a time of celebration, of happiness. At the ball everyone laughed and danced and all I could think of was you. There's nothing in the world I want except you. How can I celebrate the season without you?"

"I think you celebrated it with wine," she told him, reaching for her handkerchief to wipe her tears, then his, away.

"Lafitte's smuggled champagne," he admitted, a rueful smile tugging at his lips. "Too much, I fear."

"What was it you once told me about Creoles? Their dignity prevents them from ever drinking too much in public, wasn't that it?"

"It sounds like the kind of pompous remark I've been known to utter." He sighed. "Ah, *cherie*, you're the only one who puts me in my proper place. How I miss it." He rose from his knees. "May I sit on the edge of your bed? Nothing more, I promise. I know you've been ill."

She nodded and he sat down on the bed, took her hand in his and pressed it to his cheek.

"To look into those sea eyes of yours, to breathe in your scent, to touch your hand—once it would only have tantalized me; now it's a pleasure beyond price. Tell me the truth. Do you miss me at all?"

"I don't think we should dwell on what can't be," she said. "I'd be lying if I said I wasn't happy to see you but we both know you must go soon and that you can't return."

"I hoped against hope you'd relent."

Slowly she shook her head.

"You always were stubborn." He moved her hand to his lips and kissed each finger, his eyes fixed on hers. "Remember?"

She ached with memories, with wanting. "You're not a man who's easy to forget."

"Promise me you won't try too hard."

If she ever could forget him, there'd be his son to remind her. Hardening her heart against the lure of what smoldered between them, she said, "The time is past for me to make promises to you, Leon."

The sadness in his gaze all but undid her. She wanted to cradle his head to her breasts, to stroke his head and croon to him as she had their son.

"You must go," she said firmly.

He leaned closer. "May I give you a Christmas kiss before I leave?"

It was unwise to say yes, but Jurissa desperately needed to feel his lips on hers. She raised her face to him in reply.

Gently, softly, his mouth covered hers in a yearning, bittersweet kiss that lingered on her lips long after the door closed behind him.

## Chapter Twelve

The new year of 1813 blew in on a chill wind. Nothing, though, could cool Jurissa's delight in her newborn son. Tanguay, she called him, after Arabel's count, but everyone shortened the name to Guy and vied to hold him. When she helped out with the baking, Guy came, too, sleeping in a basket tucked into a sheltered corner.

In February Jurissa was bringing newly baked rolls to the counter in the front of the bakery when a handsome Creole gentleman entered. Sweeping off his hat and bowing, he smiled appreciatively at her and asked to speak to Miss Tiana. Once she was summoned, he and Tiana spoke for some moments, their heads close together, their voices low.

Jurissa was returning to the kitchen when the man raised his voice and said loudly, "The English pigs be damned! Neither they nor anyone else has ever stopped Jean Lafitte. Rest assured the goods will be delivered to you as promised." With a bow that included both women, he strode from the store.

Jurissa, shocked, stared at Tiana. "Lafitte! Don't tell me we've taken to dealing with pirates?"

"Does he look like one?"

"Not as I imagined a pirate would look, certainly."

"I've heard Lafitte has a French letter of marque as a privateer," Tiana commented, "so perhaps he's not truly a pirate. Whatever he is, he's more of a gentleman than many who claim to be. Besides, with those ships bottling up the river, where else are we to buy the supplies we need?"

"I wish it didn't have to be from pirates."

"I keep trying to turn you into a practical Creole but you resist. Incidentally, *Capitaine* Lafitte asked me who the beautiful redhead was. I told him you were my partner and not available."

"To a pirate? I should think not!"


The following month, when the sacks of flour and other supplies were being unloaded and carried into the storeroom, Jurissa's curiosity about the pirates of Barataria led her to watch. Lafitte wasn't present. A stocky, swarthy man—Dominique You, Tiana said— shouted orders to two Negroes. When they finished, all three climbed back into the drover's cart. As it drove off, a blond man rushed from a coffee shop down the street and leaped onto the cart. She saw him only from the rear.

Jurissa caught her breath, staring after the cart before finally shaking her head and turning away. For a moment she'd imagined the man from the cafe was Philip Winterton. He was dead; it was impossible.

From the back, no doubt many blond men resembled him.

In August she received another letter from Anton. "The war," he wrote, "goes well despite the blockade. President Madison stands firm against surrender, though he's willing to negotiate with the British for a peaceful settlement. He's promised me a leave after October, so I hope to be home no later than December. If all goes well, we shall celebrate Christmas together."

Except for his eyes, Jurissa could hardly recall what Anton looked like, but his letter was welcome. Perhaps she might consider celebrating Christmas with him when he returned.

Guy grew as fast as sugarcane. By October he was walking with an unsteady gait, resulting in many spills, but he rarely cried as he climbed to his feet again. It had been apparent for months that, except for his mother, Silas was his favorite. Once he learned to walk, he toddled to Silas the moment he saw him and if Silas wasn't in evidence, Guy would go looking for him.

Silas always welcomed him, always treated Guy with kindness and with far more patience that Jurissa could manage. She often smiled, watching the huge black man with the tiny boy clinging to his forefinger as they took a stroll around the courtyard together.

"Gonna grow up to be a mighty fine gentleman, this boy," Silas would say. "We all gonna be proud."

Jurissa had kept her promise about buying new clothes for Yubah, and she was astonished to see how attractive Yubah was when dressed up. The pretty girl had matured into a beautiful woman. Men stared at Yubah when she walked on the banquettes; and when she waited on male bakery customers, they all tried to flirt with her.

Yubah had no objection to flirting but she'd have nothing to do with any man, colored or white, who ventured further. Nicolas's rejection of her had soured her on all men, it seemed. As for Nicolas; when he came to visit his sister, and Yubah was present, she ignored him. If Guy was around during Nicolas's visit, she made a great fuss over the boy.

"Nicolas watches you when he thinks you're not looking," Jurissa told her. "He can hardly take his eyes off you."

Yubah shrugged. "Let him look. He ain't gonna get any closer. Never. Where was he when I be needing him? Nowhere. Don't be wanting that kind of man."

Jurissa smiled sadly at Yubah, aware of what lay underneath her maid's apparent indifference. Yubah had no more forgotten her feelings for Nicolas than Jurissa had rid herself of her love for Leon. Each remained bound to one man, to the exclusion of any other.

December brought increased business to the bakery as customers planned parties and balls. Everyone worked to the point of exhaustion. Two days before Christmas, Jurissa, locking the bakery door late in the afternoon after a busy day, sighed when someone knocked. Another customer wishing holiday baked goods; a customer who'd be angry because she had nothing left to sell until tomorrow's baking.

She unlocked the door and opened it. A man stood framed in the doorway. He smiled and held out a hand to her before she realized who he was.

"Anton!" she cried, giving him her hand. "What a pleasant surprise."

Holding her hand tightly, he said, "I promised you we'd celebrate Christmas together. You didn't reply to my letter but I decided to take no answer as an acceptance."

She stepped aside, allowing him to enter and, at the same time, tugged her hand from his. Though surprised by how happy she was to see Anton, she didn't mean to encourage him unduly.

"The Lavalles, friends of mine, have invited me to a ball on Christmas night," he said, "and you are included." His brown eyes, Leon's eyes, were bright with hope. "Please don't tell me you have another engagement."

Should she accept? She'd never been to any kind of a ball and part of her longed for the brightness and gaiety she knew would be part of a Creole *balle*. Hadn't Leon described them to her? Arabel had carefully taught her the intricacies of quadrilles, though she'd never actually danced one. What harm could there be in accepting Anton's invitation?

She smiled up at him. "How can I say no to a presidential advisor?"

For a moment she thought he meant to sweep her into his arms but he checked the impulse, if such it was, and contented himself with grinning at her.

"You've made me the happiest man in the city. In the new state of Louisiana. No, in the entire United States and its territories."

Creole men had a way with flattery and she couldn't help enjoying it, as well as being excited about the ball. After Anton left, she hurried to tell Tiana.

"Monsieur DuBois has invited me to a Christmas ball!"

"That gives me but two days to work on your gown," Tiana said. "It will have to be enough."

Jurissa, who hadn't gotten as far as wondering what she'd wear, stared at her. "As busy as the bakery is, you plan to make me a gown?"

"I have a picture of a Paris ball gown I've always wanted to copy," Tiana went on, ignoring her. "I believe I'll make it in satin—green, to match your eyes. Ah, how the floating panels will whirl when you dance. You'll be the talk of New Orleans. All the women will be jealous, and all the men will fall in love with you."

The gown fit to perfection. On Christmas night Jurissa gazed at the elegant stranger in the mirror, unable to believe it was she. "Tiana, you've worked a miracle."

"It's true I design and sew well," Tiana replied, "but when I have a figure like yours to work with, I surprise even myself."

Jurissa gazed at the cot where Guy, tired by the day's festivities, lay sleeping, oblivious to the talking.

"Last December I couldn't believe I ever would have a figure again."

"It is, perhaps, a bit fuller, but that's to the good." Tiana tipped her head, critically examining the gold embroidery that looped around the bottom of the skirt. She bent and snipped off a thread.

The green satin of the gown reflected in Jurissa's eyes, deepening their color; the decolletage showed the upper curves of her breasts, her skin white as a pigeon's wing against spring grass. Gold embroidery also edged the bodice. Otherwise the gown was plain. The shimmering sweep of the satin hinted at the curves underneath. Gold cord outlined the high waist and two transparent silk panels of the same green as the gown fell from the shoulders to float behind her when she moved. Her kid slippers with the Grecian lacing were gold.

Yubah circled her, pulling at a curl here, tucking in a stray wisp of hair there. She'd arranged Jurissa's hair from a picture Tiana showed her. Apparently artless curls framed the face with the back hair twisted into an elegant chignon, held in place by a gold comb, one of the few belongings of Arabel's that Jurissa had been permitted to take with her. She wore no jewelry for the simple reason she owned none. Arabel's nephew and his wife had confiscated all the jewelry, even those pieces Arabel had given to Jurissa when she was alive.

"I hear the carriage in front." Tiana lifted a black velvet cape from the bed and draped it over Jurissa's shoulders.

"The cape is lovely," Jurissa said as she pulled on

long black gloves. "It's kind of you to let me wear it."

"I wore it one time only." Tiana's voice was tinged with wistfulness. "It was a happy time. I hope tonight will be as happy for you."

Someday I'll ask her about the cape and the man she must have worn it for, Jurissa told herself, listening to boots climb the stairs. Suddenly she was assailed by doubts. Would the Creoles Anton knew accept her? Would she, an outsider, be able to hold her own in their midst?

"I'm so nervous," she said to the two women. "What if—"

"No what-ifs." Tiana's voice was firm. "You'll have a wonderful evening. You'll enjoy every moment."

"Nobody gonna be as pretty as you, for sure," Yubah put in.

Anton knocked at the door and Yubah hurried to open it. He bowed to Jurissa. "As prompt as you are enchanting," he said. "A rare quality in a woman."

"If I'd known you expected to be kept waiting I could easily have arranged it," Jurissa replied.

"Ah, how you tease me." He smiled at her. "I look forward to introducing you to my friends. Shall we go?"

Jurissa said good night to Yubah and Tiana and went out with Anton. In the courtyard Silas stood waiting by the open door to the street, and she bade him good night, too. He grinned at her as she went past him.

All her friends were happy for her. As for herself, she was too excited about attending her first ball to know what else she was feeling.

"I've never been to a ball," she confessed to Anton when they were seated inside the carriage.

"A woman as beautiful as you?" He sounded amazed.

"My guardian was something of a recluse and wanted me by her side. When I married—" She broke off, not wishing to think of Philip. "The marriage was very short," she finished finally. "And since I've been in New Orleans I've been too busy." She smiled up at him. "Besides, no one has invited me until now."

"If I'd realized you might accept, I'd have overwhelmed you with invitations to every sort of gala. We Creoles enjoy parties. My friends dub me sober but compared to some *Americains* I've met I'm a veritable *bon vivant*. Why do Easterners eschew conviviality?"

"We know life is a serious matter, monsieur."

He glanced at her. "Of course. Which is why one goes to parties at every opportunity. To forget the seriousness for a few hours."

Anton continually surprised her. She liked him more every time they were together. If she could forget Leon, was it possible the liking might become something more?

Jurissa's excitement grew as their carriage joined the line of others waiting to drop guests at the porte cochere of the townhouse where Anton's friends were holding the ball. Lanterns atop the courtyard wall gleamed in the darkness, promising warmth and hospitality to come. Inside, chandeliers blazed with hundreds of candles, and bouquets of bright flowers enhanced the beauty of the foyer's rosewood paneling. A maid collected Jurissa's cape and Anton's hat and gloves.

"Madam Winterton and Monsieur DuBois," the Negro butler announced as they left the foyer to enter the already crowded ballroom.

Jewels winked from the breasts and ears of dark-haired women, and from their hair and wrists as well. Diamonds. Emeralds. Rubies. The soft glow of pearls. Jurissa felt positively naked without a single strand of anything around her neck, and she turned to Anton for reassurance. He was staring at her as though he'd never seen her before. Her eyes widened in apprehension. What was wrong? Was it the lack of jewels? Her gown?

*"Mon Dieu."* He spoke quietly, almost reverently.

She swallowed, watching his face for a clue.

"I knew you were beautiful," he said, "but tonight—" Words seemed to fail him. "As vibrant as a flame," he managed to add and she finally understood he was stunned with admiration for her.

Her confidence returned. If Anton approved of her appearance, she wouldn't worry about her lack of jewels, or her gown.

He introduced her to the Lavalles. Jurissa had no trouble interpreting the avid gleam in Monsieur Lavalle's eyes. His wife's gaze was considerably cooler.

"I can't think why we've never before met you," Madame Lavalle said to her.

Before Jurissa formed a reply, Anton answered for her. "As you know, Madame Winterton is a widow.

193

Only recently has she come out of mourning."

Jurissa's impulse was to be ashamed that she hadn't mourned for Philip, not at all, but reason took over. As Leon had once pointed out, it would be hypocrisy to pretend to mourn a man she scarcely knew, a man she'd been tricked into marrying; one who'd frightened and hurt her.

She waited a moment before saying, "Your home is beautiful. I especially admire the crystal chandeliers."

Madame Lavalle waved a deprecating hand. "The ones we have at Maroquin—our plantation, you know—put these to shame. Monsieur Lavalle's grandfather brought them over from the Lavalle chateau in France. I wished to have the ball at Maroquin but, with the English downstream, who knows what might happen? It's safer in town."

"This is not the time to speak of those pigs of Englishmen," her husband admonished. "With any luck a hurricane will sweep the river mouth free of them. In the meantime we will simply ignore their presence."

Anton excused them and took Jurissa on a tour of the room, introducing her to other friends. Most asked a variation of the hostess's question—about why they hadn't met her before—and she was grateful that Anton had provided her with a convenient answer.

"Here is an old acquaintance of yours," Anton commented as they came to yet another couple.

Jurissa felt her smile congeal in place as she looked up and met Leon's burning gaze.

"I don't believe you've met Leon's wife, the charming Louise-Marie," Anton continued.

Jurissa tore her gaze from Leon's face. Was she imagining it or did he look gaunt, as though he'd been ill? She desperately tried to fix her attention on the pleasant-looking brunette in blue standing next to Leon. Sapphires glittered from Louise-Marie's ears and surrounded the diamond pendant at her cleavage.

Somehow Jurissa managed the amenities of polite acknowledgement, unaware of exactly what she was saying.

"How lovely your gown is," Louise-Marie commented. "Is it from Paris?"

"A copy of a Parisian fashion," Jurissa admitted. She knew Leon was watching her. His eyes burned through to her heart. She didn't dare look at him again.

"You must employ a clever dressmaker. Mine would never be able to work such magic."

"She no longer sews but she made the gown as a favor to me."

Louise-Marie's light brown eyes narrowed in thought. "Tiana LeMoine," she crowed after a moment. "She was the best dressmaker in town until that man ran off with all her money. She refused to make another gown for anyone afterward. How clever of you to persuade her."

Louise-Marie turned to Leon and Anton. "You remember what a scandal it was when Pierre Lafreniere stole her money and decamped. To think a Creole would stoop so low as to take money from a free woman of color! Old Ignace LeMoine never spoke to the Lafrenieres from that day on."

So there *had* been a man in Tiana's past, Jurissa told herself. A Creole. One who'd betrayed her.

"Mademoiselle LeMoine made my gown because she is my friend," Jurissa said, determined to stand by Tiana.

Louise-Marie shrugged, evidently bored with any more discussion of the subject.

"I trust you've been well since last we met, Madame Winterton?" Leon asked.

Why did he have to say anything to her? Now she'd have to look at him, speak to him.

She focused her eyes to the left of his face. "I have. And you?" With great effort she kept her tone polite and nothing more.

"Only fair. That's how it is when you live each day one step at a time."

Her heart began to thud in alarm. Why was he reminding her of what she'd said to him in the past and of their times together? He must know it was all she could do to be in the same room with him and not give herself away. Was he deliberately trying to torture her?

"I didn't realize you'd met Madame Winterton before," Louise-Marie said.

"My husband and I were aboard the same ship as Monsieur du Motier a year or more ago," Jurissa put in before Leon could speak. God only knew what he might say or do. She made herself smile at Louise-Marie. "I've enjoyed talking to you." After nodding, but not looking at Leon, she turned expectantly to Anton, hoping he'd understand she wished to move on.

"If you'll excuse us," Anton said and she breathed a sigh of relief.

"Are you all right?" he asked as he led her away. "You seem somewhat distraught. Is it because of what was said about Tiana LeMoine?"

Jurissa seized on that explanation gratefully. "She's my best friend but I've never pried into her life. It upset me to hear about the Creole who stole her money."

"You have remarkable loyalty. And Tiana's a good woman. It's time, though, you began to meet people of your own kind—" He gestured about the room. "So you can find other, more suitable, friends."

She opened her mouth to protest—that friendship rested on more than suitability—but the orchestra, having tuned up, launched into *La Marseille* and everyone in the room began to sing: *"Allons, enfants de la patrie . . ."*

Stirred by the enthusiasm of the Creoles, Jurissa searched her memory for the words, taught to her long ago by Arabel.

*"Le jour de gloire est arrive,"* she sang, joining in.

*"Vive la France!"* a man cried as the French anthem finished. Approving cheers rose from countless throats.

After the guests quieted, they began to form up for a quadrille, Jurissa and Anton included. Her excitement about the ball had been shattered by the meeting with Leon, and she worried about what might happen if she came face to face with him once again in the intricacies of the dance.

Soon she was separated from Anton by the changing of partners, twirled this way and that by various men until, eventually, what she dreaded came to pass, and Leon stood in front of her. He grasped her waist and, before she could protest, whirled her not only free of the pattern but entirely out of the ballroom.

Leon knew he was being reckless beyond all sense. It had been building in him ever since he'd seen Jurissa enter the room, her glorious hair flaming above the very gown in which he'd once dreamed of seeing her descend the staircase at Dindon; even to the panels floating behind her. She wore not a jewel, and the splendor of her unadorned white skin outshone every precious stone in the room.

By the time *Cousine* Anton brought her to him, Leon was almost past control. Every man in the room stared at her, wondering who the beautiful woman was, wanting her, when, damn it, she was his! He burned to challenge every one of them, Anton included. How dare they lust after her?

A soupcon of sanity remained and somehow he managed to get through the introduction and the babble of inanities, even though she refused to look at him. But when the quadrille began and one man after another put his hands on her, he lost all restraint, barely able to wait until he came to her in the course of the dance. When he touched her he was lost.

Clasping her hand tightly in his, he pulled her from the ballroom and along a corridor toward the back regions of the house, past startled black faces to a storeroom he once recalled Lavalle having shown him. He opened the door and pushed Jurissa inside. Lifting a lamp from a work table, he followed her in and shut the door behind him.

They stood in a long, narrow room lined with shelves stacked with various household necessities. He set the lamp on an empty shelf and yanked her into his arms. She stiffened and her lips refused his at first, but soon she began responding to his urgency, opening to him so he could taste the sweetness of her mouth. Her body softened against his until he trembled with need.

So long. A year. He had thought in that time a man could wipe any woman from his mind and his heart. But he hadn't even begun to forget her. Everything about her excited him, from the topmost curl of her red hair to the smallest toes of her feet. His body exalted in the familiar feel of hers, demanding further remembered pleasures. Now. Here.

She wrenched her lips from his. "You're mad!" she whispered.

He nuzzled her ear, not bothering to answer. *Dieu,* how he'd missed her special fragrance, the honeyed taste of her. His fingers caressed the side of her breasts, the smooth satin of her gown, no substitute for the softness of her skin. How he longed to strip her clothes away and feel her naked beneath him.

She moaned and pressed closer.

"*Cherie,*" he groaned, his hand seeking the fastening of her gown.

Suddenly she began to struggle. "No!" she cried. "We must go back to the ballroom, Leon. Think of your wife. And Anton."

"Damn Anton!"

"This is wrong."

"Tell me you don't want me, then."

"You know I can't. But we mustn't remain here. You must let me go."

"How can I when we belong together?"

"I won't let you hurt either of them. It's not fair." Thrusting her hand hard against his chest she broke free and, opening the door, fled from him.

Against his will, he let her escape. She was right and he knew it. Anton could go to hell for all he cared but he owed something to Louise-Marie, who didn't deserve to be hurt, especially after what she'd told him last week. He leaned his forehead against a shelf and tried to bring himself back to the reality of Dindon and the heritage he must one day pass along.

Would he never stop wanting that witch-woman? Beside her, everything else faded to nothing. It was plain his *cousine* desired her and would ask her to marry him, if he hadn't already. She must never marry Anton. He couldn't bear it. But how could he stop them? What a tangled mess he'd made of his life.

Jurissa fled upstairs, searching for a room with a mirror so she could smooth her hair and have a few moments to compose herself before she returned to Anton. She didn't blame Leon. How could she? Once she'd seen him the same terrible need had pulsed through her until she'd felt she'd die if she couldn't be in his arms and have his lips against hers. Where she'd gotten the strength to stop before it was too late, she had no idea. Even now she regretted leaving him.

Through an open door she saw a mirror and entered the upstairs room. Intent on fixing her hair, Jurissa didn't notice the woman stretched out on the chaise longue in the corner until she spoke.

"Your hair is such an unusual color," Louise-Marie said. "And that style is most attractive."

Jurissa turned to face Leon's wife.

Louise-Marie swung her feet over the side of the chaise longue and sat erect. "I'm quite recovered. Perhaps we can go down together when you're ready. I've been feeling a bit light-headed and I feared the press of people in the ballroom might make me faint."

Jurissa's heart seemed to stop. Light-headed? About to faint? Those words had only one meaning for her after her own experience. Without thinking, she blurted out, "When do you expect the child?"

Louise-Marie blushed. "Oh, you guessed. I didn't mean to mention it to anyone except the family this early but I don't mind you knowing. In July."

Jurissa managed to smile and nod though anger at Leon thundered in her head. He knew! He'd whirled her off into that dreadful little room to make love to her and all the time he knew his wife was going to have a baby. The du Motier heir. How could he do such a thing to her? To Louise-Marie?

There'd be no more kisses between them, not ever again. She'd forget Leon and go on with her life.

## Chapter Thirteen

Jurissa wasn't sure how she managed to get through the rest of the evening at the Lavalles nor how she'd responded to Anton's conversation on the drive home. To make him leave without argument, after he saw her to her door, she agreed to go for a drive with him the following Thursday if the weather permitted.

Inside the apartment, Yubah rose from her cot, yawning, ready to help Jurissa take off her gown.

"Go back to sleep," Jurissa told her. "I'll manage."

Yubah paid no heed and Jurissa submitted to her ministrations in silence.

"Where you be putting that fancy comb?" Yubah remarked as she began to undo Jurissa's hair. "Lucky I fix that chignon tight so it don't come loose anyway."

Jurissa raised a hand to the back of her head. Arabel's comb wasn't there. She hadn't missed it until now. Where had she lost the comb? When? She was afraid she knew the answer. In the Lavalle's storeroom, in Leon's arms.

The tears she'd held back for hours welled into her

eyes. "The comb was all I had of Arabel's," she wailed, crying for more than the loss of a keepsake.

Yubah put her arms around Jurissa, murmuring wordless sounds of comfort until the tears stopped and Jurissa pulled away, reaching for a handkerchief.

"What happen at that ball make you so sad?" Yubah asked gently.

Jurissa hadn't meant to tell anyone but in her misery the words slipped out. "I met his wife. She's going to have a baby. The du Motier heir."

Both women glanced toward the sleeping Guy, then at each other. Yubah's yellow eyes gleamed tiger fierce. "Gonna take his place, that baby. Ain't right."

"There's nothing to be done," Jurissa said, "except to forget about it."

"Like Miss Tiana say, men be bringing bad trouble to women. She right."

Jurissa sighed, thinking of all the trouble men had brought to Tiana, to Yubah, and to herself. She hated Leon for what he'd done to her tonight.

"If Massa Leon don't be married, seem like you and Guy might could be living at Dindon," Yubah said.

Jurissa shook her head. "No, it's far too late for anything like that."

"Mama used to say never be too late do you study 'bout it a while."

"All the studying in the world can't change this, Yubah. Set your mind to something else; don't waste time fussing over the impossible."

Yubah's expression said she was unconvinced but Jurissa was too tired and upset to go on.

Thursday dawned fair and sunny. Jurissa had little enthusiasm for a ride with Anton but it was easier to go than to find a reasonable excuse not to.

"I've made every man in New Orleans envious of me," he told her when they were seated in the carriage. "Since the ball at Lavalle's my friends can talk of nothing but how attractive you are. They've even accused me of deliberately keeping you hidden."

She smiled, pleased despite herself.

"You were the undeniable belle that night," he went on. "Even Madame Lavalle admits it. 'What can we poor Creoles do up against that glorious hair?' is how she put it." His gloved hand touched a curl by her ear. "She's right."

"I can take no credit for what I was born with, though I imagine madame might have hinted the color didn't come from nature."

He laughed. "How did you know?"

"The way she looked at me conveyed a good deal. I do not think she'll be one of the new friends you've told me I should make."

"The way you say that conveys to me that you don't approve of my suggestion."

"Suggestion? Why, sir, I thought it was an order."

He turned toward her, all trace of humor gone from his face. "I hadn't realized you took my remark so seriously. One makes friends by choice, of course. I merely felt you haven't had the opportunity to meet women of your class. Whether you find friends among them when you do meet them is not up to me to say."

"It seems I misunderstood."

"The tone of your voice suggests that, in actuality, you don't believe you misunderstood me. Regardless of what you think, I did not intend to imply Tiana LeMoine wasn't a proper person to have for a friend. She is, as I said, a good woman, but she is colored."

"Her father was a Creole, her mother a *placee*."

Anton looked sharply at her. "Creole women don't speak of such things. I admit, though, that our customs can seem strange to one from the East." He reached for her hand and captured it before she could think to draw it away. "Please forgive me if I've offended you. The last thing I wish is to quarrel with you."

Anton was so reasonable, she thought, unable to understand why this would annoy her. Perhaps because she was being unreasonable? Jurissa took a deep breath.

"Tell me how you found Washington," she said, taking back her hand, "and what you think of President Madison."

He gazed at her for a long moment before settling back in the seat. "I am pleasantly surprised at the thought the *Americains* have given to laying out the capital of the United States and to the architecture of the president's home and the offices of Congress. Washington is at present little better than a morass of mud, but one can see what it might become someday. President Madison is in height a small man but a giant in vision. He, more than anyone else, brought about the union of the states. I admire his tenacity of purpose and am honored he asks me for advice concerning the Missouri Territory, Louisiana, and Spanish Florida. Florida may prove to be our Achilles heel."

"I know little of Florida. Why do you say it's a vulnerable spot?"

"If the British assume control there, and I fear they will, it gives them a base all too near New Orleans. I've urged President Madison to take action but he can't march troops in to take over the Spanish garrison without the danger of incurring Spain's wrath. Having the British warring with us is more than enough."

"I can't help but notice how often you say 'us' referring to the United States. When I first met you it was otherwise. As a Creole, you held yourself aloof from 'the *Americains*.'"

"Ah, well, there are Creoles and there are *Americains* and we will never look at things with quite the same eyes, but since I've been with President Madison in Washington, I accept the fact Louisiana is a part of a union of states that, only together, are strong enough to be a country. And that is enough, I believe, from me. I'd much rather listen to you speak."

"You haven't yet pointed out the Theatre St. Phillipe to me. Do you know I have never been to a theater?"

Anton called to the driver, who changed direction. "If you will go with me, I'd be delighted to take you, perhaps to a French opera. Someone is sure to have a theater party before the performance and someone else afterward, so be prepared for a very long evening."

"You are kind," she said, without committing herself.

"Kindness has nothing to do with my desire to be

"The tone of your voice suggests that, in actuality, you don't believe you misunderstood me. Regardless of what you think, I did not intend to imply Tiana LeMoine wasn't a proper person to have for a friend. She is, as I said, a good woman, but she is colored."

"Her father was a Creole, her mother a *placee*."

Anton looked sharply at her. "Creole women don't speak of such things. I admit, though, that our customs can seem strange to one from the East." He reached for her hand and captured it before she could think to draw it away. "Please forgive me if I've offended you. The last thing I wish is to quarrel with you."

Anton was so reasonable, she thought, unable to understand why this would annoy her. Perhaps because she was being unreasonable? Jurissa took a deep breath.

"Tell me how you found Washington," she said, taking back her hand, "and what you think of President Madison."

He gazed at her for a long moment before settling back in the seat. "I am pleasantly surprised at the thought the *Americains* have given to laying out the capital of the United States and to the architecture of the president's home and the offices of Congress. Washington is at present little better than a morass of mud, but one can see what it might become someday. President Madison is in height a small man but a giant in vision. He, more than anyone else, brought about the union of the states. I admire his tenacity of purpose and am honored he asks me for advice concerning the Missouri Territory, Louisiana, and Spanish Florida. Florida may prove to be our Achilles heel."

"I know little of Florida. Why do you say it's a vulnerable spot?"

"If the British assume control there, and I fear they will, it gives them a base all too near New Orleans. I've urged President Madison to take action but he can't march troops in to take over the Spanish garrison without the danger of incurring Spain's wrath. Having the British warring with us is more than enough."

"I can't help but notice how often you say 'us' referring to the United States. When I first met you it was otherwise. As a Creole, you held yourself aloof from 'the *Americains.*' "

"Ah, well, there are Creoles and there are *Americains* and we will never look at things with quite the same eyes, but since I've been with President Madison in Washington, I accept the fact Louisiana is a part of a union of states that, only together, are strong enough to be a country. And that is enough, I believe, from me. I'd much rather listen to you speak."

"You haven't yet pointed out the Theatre St. Phillipe to me. Do you know I have never been to a theater?"

Anton called to the driver, who changed direction. "If you will go with me, I'd be delighted to take you, perhaps to a French opera. Someone is sure to have a theater party before the performance and someone else afterward, so be prepared for a very long evening."

"You are kind," she said, without committing herself.

"Kindness has nothing to do with my desire to be

with you. Surely you're aware of that, since you know I wish to marry you."

She was fond of Anton but now that she knew what marriage involved she couldn't imagine herself in his arms, or allowing him the intimacies that were a husband's right. Hate Leon she might, but her heart belonged to him.

Jurissa shook her head. "I can't think of marriage. Please don't press me."

He was silent a few moments. "Well, if you won't be convinced to share my home, I'd like to show you a house I know of that might suit you." He lifted a hand. "No protests. I've discussed the matter with Tiana LeMoine and she informs me you're doing well enough financially to afford to buy a larger place in a more fashionable location."

Jurissa stared at him. How dare he!

"In fact," he went on, "she told me the house would be a good investment for you. Property, unlike money, she says, cannot be easily stolen."

Jurissa was astounded. He and Tiana talking behind her back, discussing her future — she never would have thought it of either of them.

"I can see I've upset you," Anton said. "I hope you'll consider the matter carefully before you decide. You ought to look at the house, too. How can you make an informed decision without all the facts at your fingertips?"

Her protests died on her lips. She didn't want to leave the familiar apartment on the rue des Normandie, but she'd noticed it did seem smaller now that Guy was growing. She wouldn't go so far as to think about moving but perhaps she could satisfy Anton and Tiana by at least viewing this house they were so eager for her to have.

By March Jurissa had furnished her new house in the Faubourg Ste. Marie, above Canal Street, and moved into it with Yubah, Silas, and Guy. It was what she'd come to think of as a New Orleans house: two-story with galleries, on the street with a walled courtyard. There was a small room off her bedroom for a nursery and a room above the stables for Silas's use. The courtyard was unusually large, a fine place for Guy to run and play.

Though she wasn't terribly far from the bakery and, though the women of color Tiana had hired were working out well, Jurissa still went in to help out. She felt she'd left part of herself in the old apartment, and she did miss having Tiana living close by.

Later she wondered that if she'd stayed on the rue des Normandie, the tragedy might have been avoided. Surely the shrewd Tiana would have suspected what Yubah was up to if she'd been only a courtyard away, suspected and stopped Yubah's rash impulse. Jurissa, herself, busy with fixing up the new house, had no notion that anything unusual was going on until it was too late, and Silas, if he knew, remained silent.

How sadly ironic that it was Guy who gave Jurissa the first clue. Since the curious little boy now got into everything, he was a nuisance around the bakery. It became common practice that, if Yubah was to help with the baking, Guy stayed home with Jurissa and if it was Jurissa's turn, Guy was left with Yubah.

The last Wednesday in March, Jurissa came home early to find Yubah and Guy gone. She wasn't alarmed; her son adored going for walks around the neighborhood. When they did come home, Guy, as usual, was full of chatter about everything he'd seen, speaking in a mixture of French and English. (Jurissa always promised herself she'd have to do something about that but never got around to doing it.)

"Me ride *cheval*, Mama," he said. "Black, black, black. Me like."

"I'm glad you liked the black horse," she told him. Turning to Yubah she asked, "Was he really on horseback?"

"*Chevalier* lift me way up," Guy went on before Yubah could say anything. "Way, way up."

"Did you thank the man?" Jurissa asked her son.

He shook his head, intent on climbing into a chair to see if there was anything interesting on the table.

Jurissa thought no more of it until, after the evening meal, when she was getting Guy ready for bed, he suddenly said, "Dindon." She froze.

"Dindon," he chanted, obviously enchanted with the sound. "Dindon, Dindon."

She gripped his shoulders. "Where did you hear that?"

He stared up at her, frightened, his face wrinkling to cry, and she eased her grip and tried to smile. "Dindon is a funny word," she said as calmly as she could. "Tell Mama where you learned it."

He pushed a thumb into his mouth and wouldn't answer, no matter how she coaxed him. When he was in bed, Jurissa went to find Yubah, who hadn't come in to say good night to Guy as she usually did.

Yubah, down on her hands and knees scrubbing an already spotless kitchen floor, didn't look up when Jurissa came into the room, and Jurissa knew something was very wrong.

She crouched beside her and put her hand over Yubah's, holding the brush until Yubah was forced to stop. "Why does Guy say 'Dindon'?" she asked.

Yubah sat back on her heels, pulling her hand from Jurissa's and leaving the brush on the floor. " 'Cause he go there." Her voice was sullen. "I got to take him with me. Never think Massa Leon see me and go to picking up Guy like that and setting him on that old black horse and be talking to him 'bout Dindon."

A chill crawled along Jurissa's spine. "You took Guy to Dindon? Good God, why?"

"Massa Leon think Guy be mine, that what I say. He don't know, Miss Jurissa. I never be telling him the truth."

Jurissa, her terror somewhat eased, got up from the floor and sat in a chair. She motioned to Yubah to do the same but Yubah stayed on her knees.

"I can't think of any reason for you to take Guy there," Jurissa said. "What if Leon had noticed that Guy resembled him?"

"He think Guy be mine," Yubah repeated. "He don't notice nothing. I go there 'cause you say yourself she be having a baby."

It took Jurissa a moment to work this out. "Louise-Marie? Are you talking about Monsieur du Motier's wife?"

210

"You say that, you be crying 'bout it, so I knows I got to be stopping her. Long time ago I hears you tell Miss Tiana where the *voodooienne* be living. Scare me to go to her but I be doing it for you. She laugh, say she got no love for du Motiers, give me the potion."

"Oh my God! What potion?"

Yubah rose to her feet and crossed her arms over her breasts. "To make her lose that baby. *Voodooienne* say it be strong, maybe she get sick, too. If that happen she got to swallow another potion or maybe she die." She stared at Jurissa defiantly. "Better she die."

"Tell me you didn't give Louise-Marie any voodoo concoction," Jurissa begged.

"I did and she swallow it 'cause I be telling her Massa Leon send me with it and he say she got to take if for the baby."

Jurissa sat unmoving, speechless, one thought spinning frantically around and around in her head. What am I going to do? What am I going to do?

Finally she pushed herself to her feet. "The voodoo queen told you there's an antidote, am I right?" The words came out in a hoarse whisper.

"You be meaning a potion to keep her from dying? She told me that, yes."

Could the *voodooienne* be believed? Was it possible she'd sold Yubah some harmless concoction instead of what she claimed it was? Jurissa couldn't take the chance. She'd have to go herself to the rue des Ramparts and find out. And from there? It didn't bear thinking about.

"You stay with Guy," she ordered Yubah.

Wrapping herself in a dark shawl, Jurissa went into the courtyard to where Silas was chopping wood. When he understood where she was going his brow creased.

"She bad. Can't trust that woman."

"Unfortunately, Yubah bought a potion from her. I have to try to find out exactly what might happen to Madame du Motier."

"I don't let you be going to no voodoo woman by your ownsome."

Jurissa hadn't argued. She was glad of Silas's company as she drove the cabriolet through the darkening streets toward the rue des Ramparts.

Because she ordered him to, Silas waited by the horse while Jurissa knocked at the cottage where she'd once seen the *voodooienne*. No one answered but there was a lamp lit inside so Jurissa knocked again, harder.

Finally the door opened a crack and Jurissa looked into the face she'd last seen at the voodoo fire. Not waiting for permission to enter, she pushed the door far enough open to go inside.

"I'm Madame Winterton," she said, "and I expect you to help me."

The woman stared at her. "I know you. What do you want that you burst into my house?"

"You sold my maid a potion to rid a woman of the child she carries."

"Maybe I did, maybe I didn't."

Jurissa eyes narrowed. If this woman wouldn't deal with her openly, then she had to take the consequences. "I brought Silas," she said. "He's out there. Should I invite him in?"

The brown eyes widened until white showed all around the irises.

"Tell me your name," Jurissa demanded.

"Don't have to."

"You want him to ask you?"

"Vivian Pinot."

Jurissa couldn't shake off a strange feeling she knew Vivian Pinot from somewhere else besides the voodoo fire. Something about her face was inexplicably familiar.

"I sold your maid a potion, like you said." Vivian's tone was sulky.

"Will it do what it's supposed to?"

Vivian smiled thinly. "You think I don't know anything? What I put together works."

Could she be believed? Jurissa wondered, then decided quickly that she had to believe the woman. It was too much of a risk not to. "Will the woman who drinks the potion get sick?"

Vivian shrugged. "Some do. I give them another potion to make them better."

"Sick enough to die?"

"It happens."

"Sell me the antidote. The potion to prevent death."

Vivian was silent, her eyes on the door. Jurissa didn't know what Vivian saw or felt but she suddenly knew Silas stood outside that door.

"Anything you want." Vivian almost ran from the room in her haste to fetch what had been asked for. She came back quickly and thrust a twisted paper at

Jurissa. "Don't offer money. I refuse your money."

"What must I do with this?"

"Mix it in brandy and convince Madame du Motier to swallow the brandy." Vivian glanced at the door again. "If he wasn't with you I swear I'd let her die like my brother died. I wish they were all dead."

It was then Jurissa realized just who the *voodooienne* resembled. The woman looked like Leon!

She had no time to pursue it. Opening the door, she was surprised not to find Silas in front of her. Instead, he stood by the horse where she'd left him. Had he ever moved? Pushing away her confusion, Jurissa hurried to the cabriolet.

"We're going to Dindon," she said.

As the small carriage rolled along the dirt road leading from the outskirts of the city to the du Motier plantation, Jurissa felt her resolve oozing away with every turn of the wheels. How was she to accomplish her mission? What excuse could she possibly offer to Leon's wife that would convince the woman to drink what Jurissa offered? God forbid she wasn't too late to offer Louise-Marie anything.

By the time they arrived in front of the plantation house, night had settled over the countryside. Lights blazed from inside, both up and downstairs. She alit from the cabriolet and lifted her chin determinedly. She'd find a way to do what had to be done.

"I don't know how long I'll be," she said to Silas. "You'd best take the horse around to the stables."

"Yes'm."

"And, Silas, thank you for what you did at the rue des Ramparts."

He nodded without replying.

She marched up the steps to the wide front door. She'd never dreamed she'd come to Dindon for such a terrible purpose, and she prayed she wouldn't encounter Leon.

The old Negro who'd met Leon at the dock opened the door to her knock. "Francois," she said, recalling his name, "I must see Madame du Motier." He started to shake his head and she quickly added, "I know she's ill. That's why I'm here. I've brought something to help her."

Francois hesitated, at last motioning her inside.

Jurissa handed him her shawl. "I'll need brandy," she said, feeling small and lost in the vast gloom of the paneled foyer that had not a candle lit in its massive chandelier.

Francois watched her, obviously puzzled.

She straightened her back and stared directly into his eyes. "I must take the brandy and a small glass—not a snifter—to the madame's room. Be quick, do you hear? There's no time to lose. Bring me what I've asked for and direct me to her."

He bowed slightly and hurried away. Not, she hoped, to fetch the master. She eased her breath out when he returned with the brandy and a stemmed glass on a silver tray. She followed him up a magnificent curving staircase with carved mahogany banisters. At the top he turned to the right along a lamplit corridor and stopped at the fourth door. He knocked.

Jurissa lifted the tray from his hands. "Thank you, Francois. I won't need you any longer." Without waiting for an answer to his knock, she pushed open the door and walked into the room, making sure to close the door behind her.

A Negro maid, halfway to the door, stopped and stared at her. Louise-Marie lay propped on pillows in a large four-poster, canopied bed. Jurissa hurried to the bedside and set the tray on a table. She stared down at the sick woman's pale face. Turning to the maid, she said crisply. "What's your name?"

"Tutie, ma'am."

"You must help me, Tutie. You must do exactly as I say if you want your mistress to get well. Do you understand?"

"Yes'm." Tutie looked frightened but resolute.

"Pour a bit of brandy into the glass. Not more than a swallow or two." When she saw Tutie intended to obey, Jurissa sat on the edge of the bed and put her hand to Louise-Marie's forehead.

Cold, almost a death chill. Was she too late? Leaning close to Louise-Marie's ear she called her name. The blue-veined eyelids flickered. She called louder. Slowly the lids parted.

"I'm here to help you," Jurissa said. "You'll have to take me on faith but I'm your only hope. Do you hear me?"

"Yes." The word was a breath of sound.

"Tutie, hold the glass in front of me," Jurissa said to the maid. When Tutie did so, Jurissa pulled the twisted paper from where she'd tucked it under her waistband. Opening the paper, she poured the contents into the brandy and took the glass from the maid.

Why hadn't she thought to ask for something to stir

with? Glancing at the table, she saw a fluted medicine spoon and asked Tutie to fetch it.

"I'm going to dribble some brandy into your mouth," she told Louise-Marie. Swallow every drop." Belatedly she wondered if the potion might have a bitter flavor. "Never mind the taste," she added, "you must swallow."

Very carefully she poured some of the brandy mixture into the medicine spoon and put the spoon to Louise-Marie's lips. "Open," she ordered. The lips parted slightly and Jurissa tipped the concoction very slowly into Louise-Marie's mouth. "Swallow," she coaxed. "Be a good girl and swallow."

At last the sick woman's throat moved and Jurissa sighed in relief. She refilled the spoon and repeated the dosing. As she dribbled the last few drops into Louise-Marie's mouth, the bedroom door crashed open. Jurissa steadied her hand and continued without turning around. Only one person would burst into the room like that: the last person in the world she wanted to face at the moment.

"What in hell are you doing here?" Leon demanded.

"Keep quiet and don't interfere if you want you wife to live," Jurissa said sharply. She made certain the last drop was swallowed before she removed the spoon. Setting it aside, she rose from the bed and faced Leon.

"As best I could, I've undone what was done to her by no wish of mine," he told him.

"You expect me to believe that?"

"I don't care what you believe." She stepped to one side to head for the open door and he gripped her arm, stopping her.

"You're going nowhere." His voice was ragged with anger.

Jurissa glanced toward the bed. Louise-Marie's eyes were closed but Tutie stared at them, her mouth wide open.

Leon, who'd followed her gaze, gave a curt nod and strode through the door, towing Jurissa willy-nilly after him. He dragged her to a room two doors down and across the hall, jerking a lamp from the corridor wall on the way. He opened the door, thrust her inside and slammed the door behind them.

Jurissa made a quick survey of the room. Though clean, it appeared not to be in use because the bureau and tabletops were clear of toilet articles. "You might release my arm," she said coolly. "Unless you think I intend to run off."

"I don't put anything past you," he said with anger. But he let her go. They stared at one another, Leon scowling, Jurissa with her head held high.

"What have you done to her?" he demanded.

"I gave your wife the antidote. I'm told she'll now recover." She took a deep breath and let it out slowly. "If I'd know what Yubah intended to do, I certainly would have put a stop to it. Unfortunately I learned what she'd done after the fact."

"I don't believe you. Yubah's been a slave all her days. She wouldn't dare act on her own." He took a step toward her. "This is *your* doing. You're the one who planned it. Yubah only carried out your wishes."

"I'd never poison anyone," she cried.

His next step brought him so close she edged back.

He grasped her shoulders before she moved out of his reach. "Louise-Marie told me you'd guessed she was carrying a child. How could she know you might be jealous? Everyone in New Orleans knows there are voodoo potions for getting rid of unwanted babies — with your curiosity you'd soon learn this. You sent Yubah here with such a potion, and when you found out I'd seen her at Dindon, only then did you try to rectify what you'd done."

"No!"

He shook her. "Don't lie to me."

"I'm not lying. I've never wished your wife ill or tried to harm her. When Yubah confessed what she'd given your wife and I learned Louise-Marie might die as a result, I went immediately to Vivian Pinot to buy an antidote."

His hands fell away from her shoulders. "Vivian Pinot! *Mon Dieu!*" His gaze swept the room as though searching for something or someone.

Jurissa, remembering the *voodooienne's* hatred of his family and her strange resemblance to Leon, said, "She's one of you, isn't she? She's a du Motier."

## Chapter Fourteen

Leon stood in the middle of the room, his eyes fixed on Jurissa but not, she felt, seeing her.

"Denis," he muttered. *"Dieu,* with all of Dindon's rooms, why should I have chosen Denis's old bedroom."

Jurissa looked around the room once again. Who was Denis? And what did he have to do with Vivian Pinot? The walls, covered in green-flocked paper, and the fine mahogany furniture, bare of all personal belongings, gave her no clues.

"To think, after all this time, Vivian found a chance to revenge herself." Leon shook his head. He blinked and seemed to come to himself. "You have no idea what old hatreds you stirred with your meddling," he said to Jurissa.

"Your family's past has nothing to do with me," she snapped. "I came to try to save your wife once I learned Yubah had put her life in danger. I hope what I gave her helped remedy the damage."

"You were too late—the child was lost."

Jurissa, knowing the joy of bearing a son, felt a pang

of grief for Louise-Marie. "I'm sorry."

"Louise-Marie herself lies at the door of death. Vivian's poisons are potent, it seems."

Jurissa clasped her hands together between her breasts. "I pray I came in time to save her, if not the child."

Leon snorted in disbelief. "You can't be serious. Vivian Pinot would prepare only death potions for any du Motier."

"I threatened Vivian. I'm sure she was too frightened to deceive me." Uncertainty rose in Jurissa even as she said the words, adding to her guilt over what Yubah had done.

"I must look in on Louise-Marie," she said, wanting reassurance Leon's wife was still alive. She started for the door.

Leon stepped in front of her. "You're going nowhere."

Her temper flared out of control. "If you're so worried about your wife you ought to be at her bedside, not in Denis's room—whoever he was—arguing with me."

"He was my brother!" Leon shouted.

She stared at him, aghast. "Long ago you told me you were an only child."

"Papa expunged Denis from the family records. He insisted I'd never had a brother and forced everyone to his point of view. My mother never got over it."

"But why?"

Leon leaned an elbow against the closed door and rested his head in his hand. The familiar urge to comfort him rose in Jurissa. Firmly, she squelched it.

"Denis was seven years older than I, and Papa's favorite. Why not? He was the heir. From an early age

Denis took an active hand in running the plantation. As for me, I was the idler. I thought of nothing but having a good time. Denis was more like—well, perhaps *Cousine* Anton. Sober. Responsible. That's why what happened was so unbelievable. Papa could have understood if I'd transgressed; I was always in trouble. Denis, never."

Leon raised his head and looked at her, his brown eyes filled with pain. "Denis taught me to fence, to ride, to hunt. I admired him. I wanted to be like him but knew I'd never be."

"You are yourself," she said quietly.

He shrugged. "After it happened I was all Papa had left, whatever I was like."

"What did happen?"

Despite his obvious distress, a half-smile quirked Leon's upper lip. "Always the curious one."

"You don't have to tell me," she said hastily. "I don't mean to pry."

"I find I want to tell you. It's one of your charms that a man can talk to you. It began, though he would never admit any of it could be his fault, when Papa took a *placee*, a beautiful colored woman who looked as white as any Creole. She bore him two children, twins, shortly after my mother had Denis. One was Vivian, the other a boy named Jean. She died of yellow fever not long after the twins were born. Papa never took another *placee*."

"I don't approve of the custom."

"As you've told me more than once." He took her hand and led her to a straight-backed chair near the bed. She saw no alternative but to sit, so she did. Leon sat on the side of the bed, facing her in silence.

"Is it so difficult to speak of?" she asked.

He sighed. "The twins were raised by an aunt, a free woman of color, and took her name. She moved to Santo Domingo when they were very young. When she died there, they returned to New Orleans. You must understand neither Denis nor I knew anything of Papa having had a *placee,* much less of her children. Even Papa wasn't aware when the twins came back to live in the city.

"Perhaps you see what's coming. Denis met Vivian at a quadroon ball and fell in love with her. She lived with her twin, Jean, found life *tres agreable* as a coquette and refused to be Denis's *placee.* My brother became absolutely besotted with her; he had to possess her. And so he did, finally, although she wouldn't move into a cottage but continued to live with Jean."

"And none of the three knew they were half-brothers and sister?"

"Denis hadn't the slightest notion. Jean must have known from the start and I've always thought Vivian did, too. Denis had a terrible awakening. He told me himself how it came to pass. He called on Vivian and found her making love with her twin, Jean. Shocked and disgusted, Denis shouted that they were worse than animals. Jean laughed and told him, in that case Denis, himself, was no better since all three had the same father. Denis went berserk. The two men fought and Denis broke Jean's neck. Killed him."

"How terrible!"

"Once Papa heard the story, he turned Denis out of the house, even though by that time my brother had a festering wound from the knife Jean had used on him." Leon drew a shuddering breath. "I was sixteen. I defied Papa's edict and searched for Denis to try and help him. I found him in the swamp. He died in my arms and I had to bury him there because even then Papa would not relent."

Jurissa could find nothing to say. What good were words to heal the pain Leon must have carried since that day? Unable to stop herself, she stood and reached for Leon, cradling his head against her breasts. His arms went around her.

His shoulders heaved. "I loved my brother," he said brokenly. "Why couldn't I save him?"

She crooned to him in soothing sounds, holding him.

After a time he eased away and rose to his feet. Before she could retreat, he took her face in his hands, his eyes bright with tears.

"I was all Papa had left," he repeated. "I thought I had to save Dindon, and so I betrayed you." His thumbs caressed her cheeks. "And again tonight, I did the same. In my heart, where I know you best, I realized you couldn't, wouldn't hurt anyone and certainly not poor Louise-Marie, but I counted on the child and lost my judgement when I found there was to be none."

You have a son, she longed to say. I've given you an heir for Dindon, but she was silent. Louise-Marie was Leon's wife.

"She will soon be well," Jurissa said. "May I see her before I leave?"

His hands dropped. "Yes, of course. We'll go to her now."

Get a **Free** Zebra Historical Romance

*a $3.95 value*

Affix stamp here

**ZEBRA HOME SUBSCRIPTION SERVICES, INC.**
**P.O. BOX 5214**
**120 BRIGHTON ROAD**
**CLIFTON, NEW JERSEY 07015-5214**

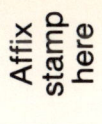

# ———— FREE ————

## BOOK CERTIFICATE

## ZEBRA HOME SUBSCRIPTION SERVICE, INC.

**YES!** Please start my subscription to Zebra Historical Romances and send me my free Zebra Novel along with my first month's Romances. I understand that I may preview these four new Zebra Historical Romances Free for 10 days. If I'm not satisfied with them I may return the four books within 10 days and owe nothing. Otherwise I will pay just $3.50 each; a total of $14.00 (a $15.80 value—I save $1.80). Then each month I will receive the 4 newest titles as soon as they come off the press for the same 10 day Free preview and low price. I may return any shipment and I may cancel this arrangement at any time. There is no minimum number of books to buy and there are no shipping, handling or postage charges. Regardless of what I do, the **FREE** book is mine to keep.

Name _____
(Please Print)

Address _____ Apt. # _____

City _____ State _____ Zip _____

Telephone ( ) _____

Signature _____
(if under 18, parent or guardian must sign)

Terms and offer subject to change without notice.

9-88

---

## *MAIL IN THE COUPON BELOW TODAY*

**GET FREE GIFT**

To get your Free **ZEBRA HISTORICAL ROMANCE** fill out the coupon below and send it in today. As soon as we receive the coupon, we'll send your first month's books to preview Free for 10 days along with your **FREE NOVEL**.

# *ACCEPT YOUR* **FREE GIFT** *AND EXPERIENCE MORE OF THE PASSION AND ADVENTURE YOU LIKE IN A HISTORICAL ROMANCE*

Zebra Romances are the finest novels of their kind and are written with the adult woman in mind. All of our books are written by authors who really know how to weave tales of romantic adventure in the historical settings you love.

Because our readers tell us these books sell out very fast in the stores, Zebra has made arrangements for you to receive at home the four newest titles published each month. You'll never miss a title and home delivery is so convenient. With your first shipment we'll even send you a FREE Zebra Historical Romance as our gift just for trying our home subscription service. No obligation.

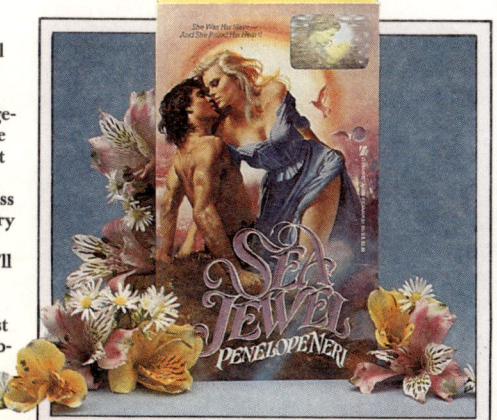

## *BIG SAVINGS AND* **FREE** *HOME DELIVERY*

Each month, the Zebra Home Subscription Service will send you the four newest titles as soon as they are published. (We ship these books to our subscribers even before we send them to the stores.) You may preview them *Free* for 10 days. If you like them as much as we think you will, you'll pay just $3.50 each and *save $1.80 each month* off the cover price. *AND you'll also get FREE HOME DELIVERY.* There is never a charge for shipping, handling or postage and there is no minimum you must buy. If you decide not to keep any shipment, simply return it within 10 days, no questions asked, and owe nothing.

# Zebra Historical Romances Make This Special Offer...

## IF YOU ENJOYED READING THIS BOOK, WE'LL SEND YOU ANOTHER ONE
## FREE

*a $3.95 value*

### No Obligation!

—Zebra Historical Romances Burn With The Fire Of History—

When some days later, Leon send a brief note to Jurissa saying Louise-Marie was recovering, she thought that would be the end of it. She was surprised, the third Sunday in April, to find Louise-Marie calling on her. Though pale, Leon's wife looked quite fit in her blue pelisse trimmed in ermine.

"My husband tells me you saved my life," Louise-Marie said, once they were comfortable in the sitting room. "I've come to thank you in person."

Jurissa, certain Leon would never have told her the truth of what happened, made up a story on the spot. "Oh, no, I can't claim that. I just happened to recall a cure my guardian swore by and felt you might profit from it. I can't tell you how pleased I am that you're well again."

Louise-Marie looked long at her. "Yes, I really believe you mean that. I'm so glad. It means my anxieties have been foolish. I don't quite know what I thought might have happened, but you're so very beautiful while I've always been plain. I wouldn't have blamed him, really I wouldn't."

With great effort Jurissa managed to keep her gaze merely politely inquiring.

"You see, I found this." Rummaging in her reticule, Louise-Marie brought out a gold comb. Arabel's gold comb. "Leon's man found this in a pocket when he hung up his master's clothes and handed it to my maid, Tutie, to give to me because he thought it was mine. I'd noticed you wearing it at the ball so I knew who the comb belonged to and I couldn't help but wonder how

Leon came to have it."

Jurissa rose to take the comb from Louise-Marie, hoping she appeared more tranquil than she felt. "I'm so grateful to have this back. It's a keepsake from my guardian and I treasure it. I was heartbroken when I lost the comb at the ball. Your husband must have picked it up from the floor. Please thank him for me."

Louise-Marie smiled at her, apparently willing to accept the explanation—true, after all, as far as it went.

*"Maman!"* Guy's voice rang out clear and sweet and Jurissa froze. He'd be in here in a moment looking for her. Guy did call both her and Yubah *Maman* indiscriminately and perhaps Louise-Marie would believe that. But what if she noticed that Guy resembled Leon, as, increasingly, he did. Jurissa didn't dare take the chance.

"Please excuse me," she said to Louise-Marie. "My maid's little boy must have gotten out of his room. He's not allowed in here. I won't have it!" She hurried out just in time to sweep Guy into her arms and bear him off before Louise-Marie caught a glimpse of him. Depositing him with Silas, she asked him to take Guy for a walk.

After Louise-Marie's departure, Jurissa made up her mind that she'd never give Leon's wife any cause to be jealous or suspicious of her. She couldn't bear to think of hurting Louise-Marie any more than she had already. It was best for all three of them if Jurissa and Leon never again met.

The tragic story of Denis haunted her. No wonder Leon had behaved as he did when his father insisted he marry Louise-Marie. She still wished with all her heart

Leon had made a different choice but now, at least, she understood why he'd decided as he had.

Anton hadn't yet been able to clarify her legal status and sometimes she despaired of it ever happening. He persisted in his courting, and Jurissa agreed to go out with him now and again. Somehow, and she wondered if it could be the coincidence it seemed to be, Leon and his wife were never present at the parties she and Anton attended. The last Saturday in August, Anton took her to a dinner at a plantation upriver and it was there the news from the East reached them.

"Washington taken over by the British?" their host exclaimed. "What next?"

"What *will* happen?" Jurissa asked Anton privately. Of all the men present, she believed him to be the most knowledgeable.

"It's true the Capitol and the White House were burned," he said, "but buildings can rise again. The president escaped safely; that's more important. What worries me the most has nothing to do with Washington."

"Spanish Florida?" she asked, remembering what he'd told her about the Achilles heel.

"I heard a rumor today that British warships are anchored offshore at the Spanish garrison in Florida. After all, Spain and England are allies. It was bound to happen."

Would New Orleans be the next target for the British, as Anton feared? Jurissa shivered, though the evening was very warm.

After dinner the guests were invited to dance, but Anton led Jurissa into the gardens at the side of the mansion where lanterns strung between magnolia trees cast a soft glow. Finding a bench between two giant camellia bushes, he asked her to sit with him. The night air was heavy with perfume, and orchestra music drifted from the open windows. It seemed impossible war could disrupt this peacefulness.

"I've made up my mind," Anton told her, his voice grim with purpose. "I must go east, find President Madison and convince him to send troops to take over the Spanish garrison in Florida. I only hope I'm not too late."

"Will the president listen to you?"

"After what happened in Washington he can't afford not to. Naturally, I'll try to return as quickly as possible. In these perilous times my place is in New Orleans." He clasped her hand in his. "No doubt you're bored with the repetition, Jurissa, but if you'd promise to marry me before I leave, the journey would go that much faster."

Sometimes she was tempted to agree to marry him, but when she considered it, she knew she couldn't. Perhaps someday, when Guy grew old enough to be taken to France for his education and she'd come to terms with her love for Leon, perhaps then. It wasn't fair to Anton, though, to make him wait years for her.

"You'd do better to find a more willing woman," she told him. "I can't promise you anything, not even that someday I will."

"My problem with your solution is that I don't want any other woman, be she ever so willing." He leaned closer. "At least allow me to kiss you in farewell."

She could find no reason to refuse and he stood, drawing her to her feet. He took her in his arms and held her carefully, his lips warm and gentle on hers. If nothing about Anton's kiss thrilled her, she was pleased to find she wasn't repelled. Perhaps someday.

Anton left the following Tuesday. September and October passed and still he hadn't returned. Nor did a letter come. Although Jurissa didn't mean to marry him, she missed his company.

When he did come home, it was in mid-November, on the heels of the news that Gen. Andrew Jackson had defeated the British in Mobile Bay and had taken over Pensacola, ousting the British who were "guests" of the governor of Spanish Florida. Jackson was rumored to be marching toward New Orleans to command its defense.

"I suspect it's your doing," Jurissa told Anton as they sat sipping coffee at one of the cafes on Canal Street.

"I can't claim credit. President Madison had made up his mind before I spoke to him." He leaned closer and lowered his voice. "Peace commissioners from England and the United States are meeting in Ghent, trying to find a way to end this war but they won't be in time to save our city. There'll be fighting here and soon. I only hope General Jackson arrives in time. He may not be the type of man you'd wish to invite to your home but, as a general, he can't be faulted."

On the first day of December, Jurissa stood in a cold drizzle among other spectators, the cannon of Fort St. Charles thundering in her ears, in greeting to General Jackson as he rode into New Orleans. Along with everyone else, she stared up at the tall thin man, erect on his horse, his blue gaze raking the crowd. Would this gaunt-faced general, with his iron-gray hair sticking up from his head like porcupine quills, save New Orleans from the British? She prayed Anton was right about him.

An air of excitement blew through the city as Creoles, *Americains,* and free men of color alike, sought to enlist in the force gathering to stand off the British. Tiana told Jurissa that even Jean Lafitte and his pirates had offered their help.

Guy was thrilled by the sight of marching men and so, for a treat, Jurissa, with Yubah and Silas, took him to the Place d'Armes to watch the militia groups drilling. Seated atop Silas's shoulders, Guy surveyed a group of mounted men in blue hunting shirts and wide-brimmed black hats. Suddenly he pointed.

*"Cheval!"* he cried bouncing up and down so that Silas had to grip his legs tightly to prevent a fall. "Black *cheval!"* His piercing child's voice carried over the other sounds as he waved at the soldiers. *"Chevalier! Chevalier!"*

Leon heard a child calling and turned to look. He smiled as he recognized the boy he'd taken onto Tigre that day at Dindon. He found it difficult to forgive Yubah for what she'd done, but her son was not a part of it. He was a handsome lad and brave. He hadn't been a bit afraid to be lifted onto a horse. No doubt the father was a Creole.

He raised a hand and saluted the child, realizing it was upon Silas's shoulders the boy sat. Leon glanced quickly at the faces near the giant Negro, hoping. It had been so long since he'd seen her.

There she was! Her small-brimmed jade-green bonnet showed off the fire of her hair and, he knew, would deepen the green of her eyes if he were close enough to look into them. His gaze lingered on the curves of her breasts, her hips under the close-fitting jade pelisse. How could he ever lose his need for her when the mere sight of her triggered potent desire?

His heart quickened as her hand went up in a quick wave. She still acknowledged him, despite everything. Why didn't his *cousine* marry her? Surely Anton had hurdled the legal obstacles by now; she must be officially a widow. He could hardly bear to speak to Anton these days, knowing his *cousine* was escorting Jurissa to parties, to the theater. Did he kiss her as well? Hold her? Leon gritted his teeth. He'd given up his own right to her, but couldn't control his jealousy when he thought of her with any other man.

John Beale, their *capitaine*, called for attention and Leon brought himself back to order. He was a Volunteer Rifle under Beale, along with thirty other Creoles, and they were learning formations. All were excellent marksmen, else they wouldn't have been chosen, but not a one knew anything about military drill either on or off horseback.

They were part of General Jackson's army, along with other local militia volunteers; plus General Coffee's twelve hundred Tennessee troops, eight hundred of them mounted; Major General Carroll's three thousand Tennessee militiamen; Major Hind's Mississippi dragoons, and Major General Thomas's Kentucky militia. New Orleans would not stand alone. There was much to be said for becoming a state in a federated union.

With such an army on land and Lafitte's men guarding the bayous and coulees below the city, let the British come! They'd soon be sent howling off like the dogs they were.

After the close of the day's drilling, Leon looked for Jurissa but, of course, she was gone. He'd remounted Tigre to head back to Dindon, when Beale stopped him.

"General Jackson has asked me to recommend one of my men as his aide," Beale said, "to be a liaison between the Creoles and his staff. With your excellent command of English, you're the obvious choice."

"An honor," Leon told his *capitaine*, saluting.

Beale gestured toward the Cabilde. "The general wants to see you immediately."

Jackson was pacing when Leon arrived at the room the general was using. He introduced himself, speaking in English, and Jackson nodded.

"Good to have you on my staff," he said. "I need your help." He swept his hand in a broad gesture toward the window. "Those plantations downriver. You know who owns them?"

"Yes, sir. I own one myself."

Jackson stared at him a moment. "Then you'll appreciate the problem. With British warships anchored in the Gulf, their attack must come by water. I've planned how to stop the ships coming upriver; that's not my immediate concern. The British troops aboard those ships are another matter. If I were the British general, Packenham, intent on deploying my foot soldiers to best advantage, I'd move the men in small boats, at night, up several of the bayous—there must be hundreds of small waterways in those swamps—and mount a surprise attack.

"To be successful, the British soldiers will first take over those plantation houses nearest the bayous Packenham chooses for his invasion. I want every owner alerted to the danger and instructed he must send immediate word to me if and when this occurs."

"Yes, sir, I understand and will carry out your order." Leon spoke crisply despite his heavy heart. Had he gone through his own hell to save Dinson, only to have the British swarm over his land and burn his house?

It hadn't occurred to him that they could be successful against the British, win the war, and yet he could lose Dindon all the same.


Jurissa accepted an invitation to an afternoon soiree at Madame Lavalle's townhouse because the card carried a handwritten message at the bottom: "We will be discussing what the women of New Orleans can do for our brave volunteers."

Both Leon and Anton had joined up. Nicolas Le-Moine had too, Yubah had told her.

"He come struttin' in the bakery," Yubah had said. "He be knowing Miss Tiana not there, be knowing who is. Me. He act all surprised, say he mean to tell her he joined up. He gonna be a sharpshooter, like that. Maybe I tell her for him, he say."

"What did you do?" Jurissa asked.

Yubah tossed her head, and Jurissa could all but see her doing the same thing to Nicolas. "I say I be telling her. Then I starts to turn away and he say, 'Wait.' "

" 'Don't you care I might get shot?' he say."

" 'Don't reckon sharpshooters get shot,' I tells him. 'Supposing they be good at it.' "

"I imagine he wasn't happy about that."

Yubah had affected indifference. "He get mad but I don't care. What he think, I be forgetting what he do to me just 'cause he gonna be a soldier?"

Jurissa wondered, as she dressed for the soiree, if in her heart Yubah wasn't as worried about what might happen to Nicolas if the British did attack as Jurissa was about Leon. And Anton, too, for that matter.

Fifteen women came to Madame Lavalle's, including Louise-Marie du Motier, who seated herself next to Jurissa. Jurissa was pleased to see the color had returned to Louise-Marie's face. In fact she looked quite plump.

"We must face the unpleasant fact of war," Madame Lavalle announced to her guests after they'd been served an afternoon meal of crayfish bisque, baked squabs, assorted vegetable and rice dishes, and *batons amondes* for dessert. The plates had been cleared away and they were sipping coffee.

"We must not be faint of heart," the hostess continued, "for we have to prepare ourselves to tend wounded men if the British attack."

"I, for one, don't wish to dwell on such unpleasantness," a sharp-chinned woman announced.

"How can you avoid it with the streets full of *Americain* soldiers and our own husbands drilling in the Place d'Armes?" Madame Lavalle challenged.

"Our plantation is upriver. I daresay the British will

never come near us," the woman persisted.

"So you will allow those of us downriver to bear the brunt of any attack and not lift a finger to help, is that what you say?" Madame looked at the others. "Do we have any other cowards among us?"

A squabble broke out between the sharp-chinned woman and the one sitting next to her. In the midst of it, Louise-Marie leaned toward Jurissa and whispered, "I feel ill. I must get home. Could you help me from the room?"

In the foyer, a Lavalle maid rushed to assist Louise-Marie but she clung to Jurissa's arm. "Have Madame du Motier's carriage brought around," Jurissa told the maid.

Even when the carriage came, Louise-Marie refused to let Jurissa go. "Please come with me," she begged. "I'm frightened to be alone."

Jurissa felt she had little choice but to agree, though the last place in the world she wished go to to was Dindon. Inside the du Motier carriage, Louise-Marie leaned back and sighed, not relinquishing her hold on Jurissa's hand. "If anything happens to this one, Leon will never forgive me."

A spasm of pain gripped Jurissa's heart. Leon's wife carried another child. Yet, at the same time, she was happy for Louise-Marie, so unfairly deprived of the first baby.

"This time everything will be well," Jurissa said. "You must try not to worry."

"I know worry isn't good for the baby but I can't help it. These pains come and go and I fear what may happen." With her free hand she touched her abdomen.

"My mother-in-law says all women experience such things." She glanced at Jurissa for reassurance.

"I'm sure Madame du Motier knows what she's talking about," Jurissa said. She, herself, hadn't had any pains until Guy was ready to be born, but she certainly couldn't tell Louise-Marie that.

Louise-Marie sighed again and closed her eyes. They rode in silence until, as the carriage neared the outskirts, Louise-Marie moaned and her fingers tightened on Jurissa's hand.

"I have a terrible pain," she whispered. "I can't stand it."

To Jurissa's horror, she saw blood staining Louise-Marie's gray gown. "Stop!" she called to the driver, remembering the jolting ride to Dindon. Wouldn't such jolting be the worst thing for Louise-Marie? Yet what was she do to now?

"Where are we?" she asked the driver.

"Be right by Joyau," he answered.

*"Docteur* Marchand," Louise-Marie gasped. "He lives at Joyau; he'll help me. Take me there."

The driver, hearing her, turned in at the gates. When they reached the house, Jurissa sent the driver to the door. Moments later, a portly white-haired man, followed by a very black woman in a yellow tignon, descended the steps toward the carriage.

Jurissa leaned out. *"Docteur* Marchand?" When he nodded she explained what had happened.

"We'll get her inside," the doctor said. "She needs to be put to bed immediately."

He supervised two hastily summoned servants as they carried Louise-Marie up the steps and into the house.

"I'll go on to Dindon and tell them where she is," Jurissa told the doctor.

"She must remain here until the bleeding has stopped," he warned. "Any motion might be fatal."

"I'll explain everything," Jurissa promised.

Back in the carriage, riding down the dirt road toward Dindon, she faced the dreadful irony that she must be the one to bring the news to Leon that his wife was about to lose another baby.

She didn't know how she could bear to tell him.

## Chapter Fifteen

Neither the driver nor Jurissa suspected anything amiss as they drove through the lengthening shadows toward Dindon and finally turned into the road that circled to the front of the plantation house. As Jurissa allowed the driver to help her from the carriage, she glanced around at the semicircle of oaks that truly did seem to hold the house in a protective embrace, just as Leon had once told her. She climbed the steps and, for the second time in her life, knocked on the door of Dindon.

Francois opened it and agitatedly gestured to her to enter. Wondering what was wrong with him, she stepped into the foyer and stopped dead. Facing her, in full uniform, was what she knew had to be a British officer.

"You are my prisoner," he said in halting and very poor French.

About to protest in English, Jurissa paused to think. Maybe it was better to let him believe she knew no English. *"Allez-vous en!"* she said sharply.

*"Laissez-moi tranquille."*

He frowned, either not liking to be told to go away or not understanding her rapid speech. Turning her back on him she faced Francois.

"How long have the English pigs been here?" she asked the old servant, still speaking French.

From the corner of her eye, she watched the officer's face. He didn't seem terribly upset to be called a pig so she assumed he hadn't understood. Evidently his French was limited.

"Several hours," Francois muttered, also in French. "Both master and young mistress are not in the house," he added.

"That'll be quite enough!" the officer ordered in English. "You—" He pointed at Francois and gestured. "Go."

Jurissa did her best to look confused while Francois, correctly interpreting the gesture, retreated toward the back reaches of the house.

"Major Smith," the officer said, and waited for her name, obviously.

Winterton didn't sound Creole and she dared take no chances. Translating it into French she announced haughtily, "Madam d'Hiver."

"Come with me." He gestured her ahead of him. Had he given up his meager French entirely? Perhaps he'd learned only the one phrase he'd spoken originally.

Shrugging her shoulders, she obeyed and he led her into a sitting room where an older woman, dressed in black faille, was propped on a sofa, her head on pillows, her eyes closed. Leon's mother,

Jurissa decided. Two maids hovered over her, casting frightened glances at the major. Another British soldier stood by the door.

Recognizing one of the maids, Jurissa said to her, "Tutie, what's the matter with Madame du Motier?"

Leon's mother opened her eyes and stared up at Jurissa. "You ask such a question," she demanded, "when you can plainly see I am menaced by these unspeakably rude British soldiers?"

Jurissa was relieved by the tart reply. Apparently nothing was wrong with the older woman, who now sat up and fixed bright brown eyes on her.

"I don't believe I know you," Madame du Motier said. "I trust you are not in league with these English pigs."

"No, certainly not! I am a friend of Louise-Marie's."

Major Smith's eyes flicked to one, then the other of them during their conversation in French as though he suspected they were sharing secrets dangerous to his and his men's welfare. The soldier by the door, from what Jurissa could make out by surreptitious glances, didn't understand French, either.

"And where is she, my daughter-in-law? They haven't dared harm her, have they?"

"She's ill and in pain. I came here to tell you I left her at *Docteur* Marchand's."

"I suspected all was not well this time." *Madame* sighed and shook her head. "At least she's been spared this indignity." She stared up at Major Smith. "Is this how you English wage war—against helpless women and servants?"

The major might not have understood her words but he didn't miss the sense of them. Shifting his shoulders, he looked away. For some reason, perhaps only because he was blond, he reminded Jurissa of her dead husband.

"How many soldiers are at Dindon?" Jurissa asked Leon's mother.

"Who knows? Scores, certainly. Hiding, skulking like dogs outside. Ten or more inside. And this one here, stalking about the house as though he owns it. I thought to send a servant to warn my son what had happened but I was too late; the soldiers had rounded up even the field servants. Now we are all under guard. Prisoners!" She spat the last word at the major.

Sketching a bow to her, he stalked from the room, stopping to give orders to the soldier at the door. "None of them are to leave this room unless I say so."

"What a barbaric tongue," Madame commented. "I could never understand why my son insisted on learning it."

"I understand English," Jurissa admitted. "I thought it best not to tell them."

Madame du Motier's eyes again assessed Jurissa. At last she gave a little nod and patted the seat of the sofa. "Come sit next to me."

Jurissa obeyed. Leon's mother leaned close to her and spoke in a low tone. "How brave are you, child?"

Jurissa had to think about it. "I don't believe I can answer sensibly since I've never had to test myself. I do hope I'm not a coward."

"Keep your voice down," Madame advised. "They pretend not to understand our language but who knows what tricks they may have. I have a plan but there was no one I could trust to carry it out. Your arrival was an answer to my prayer. My son, as you may know, is General Jackson's aide. Leon must be warned of the calamity that has overtaken Dindon. The British must not capture him!"

Jurissa nodded in agreement. She shuddered to think of Leon subjected to God knew what cruelties by Major Smith to make him divulge General Jackson's plans.

"It's up to you to warn him," Madame went on.

"How? Even if I could leave the house unobserved, you say British soldiers guard the entire plantation."

"Ah, my dear, we shall outsmart them. Mine is a woman's plan and therefore devious." Leaning closer, she whispered into Jurissa's ear.

A few minutes later, Jurissa rose and made for the closed door of the sitting room, her gait unsteady. Just before she reached the soldier standing as sentry at the door, she moaned, swayed, and crumpled gracefully to the floor, where she lay motionless. Tutie gasped and ran over to her while Madame du Motier rose to her feet and called imperiously, *"Majeur! Majeur!"*

Major Smith burst into the room. With a torrent of French, accompanied, Jurissa had no doubt, by furious gesturing, Madame conveyed that Jurissa must be taken upstairs and put to bed immediately, that she was with child and in danger of losing the baby. How much of this Major Smith grasped, Jurissa had no idea.

When Jurissa felt herself being lifted by the major, she made her body as limp as possible, keeping her eyes closed. She didn't open them even when she was eased onto a bed. Madame, who'd followed them up the stairs, proceeded to send both maids off on errands—to heat bricks to be placed at the invalid's feet, to fetch brandy spiced with cloves—and shooed the major from the room.

"We're alone." Responding to the older woman's whisper, Jurissa opened her eyes.

"I can't trust either of those girls, not in a perilous affair like this. Lilette is a fool and Tutie's afraid of her shadow. It's best they know nothing so they can tell nothing if asked."

"I know nothing, either," Jurissa reminded her.

Madame sat on the edge of the bed. "Leon was a rowdy young boy, even wild, at times. He was the despair of his father. Many times when my husband had confined Leon to his room for some transgression, I knew perfectly well Leon didn't remain there. A locked door didn't stop the boy, no. He used the oaks. You've seen how they hug the house and loop away to the swamp? Noticed how the limbs of one intertwine with each neighboring tree? Leon would climb out his window into the trees and travel through them like a monkey to the swamp. He was as familiar with the swamp trails as any wild creature. No one ever knew except me and I never told. My husband always feared I'd spoil the boy but *le bon Dieu* knows he gave me little enough chance to spoil either of—that is, Leon."

Jurissa's heart went out to her. I know about Denis, she wanted to say, and how you must have suffered over his loss. The impulse died as she realized what Madame must be leading up to.

"You want *me* to climb through the trees?" she asked, aghast.

"The limbs are broad; you will manage." Madame rose and crossed to a chest against the far wall. Opening it, she rummaged through the clothes inside. "Ah, here they are. I knew I'd saved them."

Jurissa stared in astonishment at the pair of brown breeches and a boy's heavy shirt that Leon's mother dropped on the bed.

"These were mine. Before I was married, of course. Oh, what a scandal it caused! Someday, when we have less to accomplish, I'll tell you the story. I feel you would be amused. Anyway, they should fit reasonably well. I once was as slim as you." She gestured impatiently. "Don't just lie there; put them on."

Jurissa did as she was told, finding the fit near perfect. How strange it felt to wear men's clothes. Madame tied a black scarf over Jurissa's hair so the color was hidden and stood back to admire the result.

"You should fare well in the trees," she said. "When you reach the swamp, be careful. Go into it far enough to be hidden and then use this." Reaching into a small drawer in the highboy next to the bed, she pulled out a bone whistle on a leather thong.

"Use it?" Jurissa was confused.

"Blow into it. Wait. Someone will come; an old black man named Lono. He'll—"

"Lono?" Jurissa was wide-eyed with amazement. "I've met Lono."

"Good, then his appearance won't frighten you."

"But what is he doing in the swamp?"

"He lives there. He was a du Motier slave—it's said he was once an African chief—and Leon's grandfather freed him after Lono saved his life. This bone whistle came from Africa, and Leon's grandfather used it to signal to Lono. It was passed on to Leon's father, who gave the whistle to me when he became ill. Lono will come when you blow the whistle, and he'll lead you through the swamp safely. Without him, you'd lose you way and, perhaps, your life."

The trees were bad enough. If she managed not to fall out of one or another of them and reached the swamp, she had worse perils to face. Quicksand. Snakes. Alligators. In darkness. What would she do in the swamp if Lono didn't appear? Jurissa repressed a shiver of dread.

"You're frightened, I know," Madame said, "but Leon must be saved from the British and you are the one to save him."

Looking into the older woman's wise brown eyes, Jurissa thought she read an understanding of what was in her heart. But how could that be?

"My son told me once about a beautiful red-haired widow he'd met on the ship from Boston."

Madame's voice was barely audible. "He said no more but he is my son and he did not need to. You will do this for him. You would go through any danger for his sake. I see it in your eyes."

Jurissa didn't trust herself to speak. Madame pressed her hand. "We must hurry before the maids return. I have yet to fashion a convincing body from pillows so it will seem you are still in the bed." Without bringing a lamp to light their way, she led Jurissa through a connecting door into another bedroom. "You see how the branches grow up against the house here. No one below can possibly see you in the darkness." Carefully and quietly, she opened the window.

Taking a deep breath and easing it out, Jurissa straddled the sill, groping for a foothold as she clutched a branch with her hand. A moment later she was outside, in the tree.

"Good luck," Madame du Motier whispered. She closed the window.

Jurissa forced herself to loosen her grip on the branch she held and to search for another hold. She'd never climbed a tree in her life, yet here she was high up in an oak, expected to travel monkey-wise from one tree to another until she reached the swamp. The only thing to be thankful for was that, in the dark, she couldn't see how far down it was.

A vision crossed her mind of Leon, still a boy, perched, as she was, in a tree, outwitting his father. If as a boy he had been able to do it, why couldn't she? Certainly the breeches gave her an amazing freedom of movement. She wondered why Madame du Motier had worn them. It was hard to picture the matronly, graying woman creating a scandal when she was young.

Night frosts had stilled the peeping of frogs and the strident chorus of insects. As Jurissa transferred herself from oak limb to oak limb with increasing confidence, the only sound she heard was the occasional far-off barking of a dog. When there was the clink of metal on metal below her, she froze in panic. British soldiers!

"You hear something?" a man's voice asked. "Sort of a rustling-like?"

They'd heard her! She held her breath.

"I been hearing worse ever since it got dark," another voice answered. "Bloody country. Nothing but swamps."

"Ain't seen naught but a bunch of Frenchy frogs so far. Frogs like swamps, so I always heard."

Both men laughed.

She was too relieved to be annoyed over their derogatory remarks. Move on, she urged them silently. It seemed hours before they did. Jurissa crept into the next tree, doing her best to be as quiet as possible. When she reached the last oak of the loop to the swamp, she could hardly believe she'd made it all the way.

A new apprehension seized her when she saw by the feeble light of a quarter moon that there was a gap between the tree she was in and the tangle of swamp vegetation that would hide her. When she dropped out of the tree she'd be plainly visible for some seconds as she crossed the cane field stubble.

She listened, her eyes searching the darkness for the slightest glimpse of a flame. Apparently the soldiers had been instructed not to show a light for she saw none. An animal screamed from the depths of the swamp, and she tensed in fright but she heard no man-made sounds.

Holding her breath, she hung from the lowest branch of the oak and let go. The ground was far enough beneath her so the landing shook her. She staggered and regained her balance, glancing around apprehensively. Nothing moved.

Now or never, she told herself and, crouching, dashed toward the swamp, expecting to hear shouts, the sound of pursuit.

Jurissa plunged into a tangle of vines and tripped, falling heavily. Hastily, she climbed to her feet and forced her way into the cover of the swamp. Damp soaked through her slippers and oozed over her feet. Quicksand? Foliage closed her in; she could see nothing. Terrified, she halted and fumbled for the leather thong around her neck. She raised the whistle to her lips, blew, and its shrill sound pierced the night's quiet.

Please, Lono, she prayed under her breath.

"What the hell was that?" The man's voice was close. Jurissa shrank in on herself, expecting to see a British soldier materialize in front of her any second.

"Some bloody bird." The second voice didn't sound any too certain.

"Ain't like any bird I ever heard."

"This ain't like any country you ever been in,

either."

Their voices sounded different from the first two soldiers she'd heard. How many men did Major Smith have on patrol?

She didn't dare move, though ooze covered her slippers now and edged up her ankles. The soldiers didn't speak again, and she had no idea whether they were still close or had moved away. The damp chill of December struck through the shirt she wore and she shivered, frightened and miserable, certain she'd either be discovered or be sucked down forever into the dismal depths of the swamp.

When a hand closed over her arm, she screamed but the sound only squeaked out.

"Lono," came the whisper.

She clung to his hand. "Q-quicksand," she stammered.

"Mud." He tugged her loose and she was grateful she'd worn slippers that tied or they'd have been left behind in the mire.

Quickly, she whispered what she wanted from him.

The trip through the blackness of the swamp, following Lono's steps by holding onto the rope he wore tied around his waist, was worse than the most horrible nightmare she'd ever had. Once something large slithered off into invisible water, and she was afraid to ask what it was. Unseen things brushed her face and she couldn't tell what they were. With every step she took the ground squished ominously underfoot. How could Lono possibly tell where they were going? He must be lost and wouldn't admit it.

They were doomed.

When he finally stopped, she saw the glint of the moon on water. Could they actually be out of the swamp?

"Pirogue." He pointed.

Jurissa clambered into the boat and Lono poled along a bayou that snaked in and out of the swamp until at last he pulled in to the bank. She scrambled out, blessing the breeches she wore for their convenience. To her surprised relief, the two domes of St. Louis Cathedral thrust into the night sky almost straight ahead.

"Lono, I know where we are," she said. "I can find my way now if you want to go back."

He said nothing but when she started off, he walked behind her and she was grateful for the company of this strange hunchbacked old man who lived in the swamp and had once been the chief of his tribe in far-off Africa.

Jurissa hugged herself against the chill, damp breeze off the river as she hurried toward the Calbido. At least the cold weather kept most people off the streets so her bizarre costume didn't attract attention beyond a few stares. Lights glimmered from the windows of General Jackson's headquarters, and she prayed Leon was still there and not on his way back to Dindon.

Lono left her outside the door and she called her thanks after him. A uniformed soldier opened the door to her knock, and she cringed back before she realized he was American, not English. What was the matter with her? Her brain must be addled from that hurried trip through the swamp.

"I must see *Capitaine* du Motier immediately," she said.

The soldier didn't move, staring at her incredulously, and she suddenly realized how very peculiar she must look to him. Whipping off the black scarf, she said crisply. "Madame Winterton is here to see the *capitaine* and she's in a hurry."

He blinked at her red hair, nodded and muttered a "yes, ma'am." Turning, he called Leon's name and her message.

Leon appeared from an inner room and stopped in his tracks when he caught sight of her. Moments later, he had her inside, seated, with a cup of hot coffee at her lips.

She cradled the cup to warm her cold hands, suddenly so tired she could hardly get the words out. "Your mother sent me. British soldiers at Dindon. Don't go home."

Leon seized her by the shoulders. "What do you say?"

"British. At Dindon."

*"Mon Dieu!"* Leon shouted for General Jackson.

After the general had gotten all she knew about the invading force from her, Jurissa was ignored as the general and his staff poured over a table cluttered with maps. She sipped the coffee, watching, and must have slipped into a doze because the next she knew, Leon was lifting her onto Tigre.

"It would take too long to locate a carriage," he told her, "and I need to get you home as quickly as possible."

The breeches proved themselves astride the horse, too. As she held to Leon, her face pressed against his back, she thought sleepily that men's clothing did have some excellent qualities. It felt so good to be close to Leon again, so right.

He carried her toward the house despite her protests that she could walk. Silas loomed up before them as Leon entered the courtyard.

"Thank the Lord you be home safe, Miss Jurissa," Silas said. "We don't be knowing what to think."

Yubah threw open the door and rushed toward them. "Oh, Miss Jurissa!" she cried.

"Heat some water," Leon ordered. "She'll need a bath. And warm some bricks for her bed. She's chilled to the bone."

But she wasn't, not anymore, not now that Leon held her in his arms.

"I can't stay," he murmured to her. "I'll be back to hear the full story when I can." He bent his head and kissed her gently. "There's your decoration for bravery."

He set her on her feet just inside the door and was gone.

When Leon returned it was barely light. Jurissa woke to find him sitting beside her bed. "I didn't want to wake you," he said, "but I don't know when I'll be free again."

She propped another pillow under her head and gazed into his weary, stubbled face. "You haven't slept at all, have you?"

"It doesn't matter. Tell me what happened. Every detail."

She began the story at Madame Levalle's and ended it with Lono in the priogue. "I'm sorry I can't tell you more about Louise-Marie's condition but at least she's getting expert care," she added.

He nodded. "From what you say *Maman* is in fine fettle. I can't get over the breeches. Are you certain she said they were hers?"

"Not only that but she seemed quite proud of having worn them on whatever occasion it was. I admire your mother greatly. She was so convinced I could make the journey through those trees that I didn't dare fail her." She smiled at Leon, and suddenly he was on the bed and she was in his arms.

"Don't tell me it's wrong," he murmured as his lips hovered over hers. "I'll only take a little of your sweetness; you must grant me that much."

The taste of him went to her head like wine, and for a few blissful minutes she didn't think at all, much less worry about what was right and what was wrong. She only knew Leon was holding her and she loved him.

*"Chevalier!"*

Guy's piping voice startled them apart. The boy ran toward the bed, then stopped short, staring in awe at Leon. *"Cheval?"* he asked finally. "Black *cheval?"*

"I left Tigre outside," Leon told him, easing away from Jurissa until his feet were on the floor.

"I'm afraid Guy has the run of the house," Jurissa said hastily, her pulses jumping in alarm. "I spoil him more than Yubah does." Would her words fool Leon? Surely he couldn't fail to see himself in Guy.

And what would she do then?

"He's a Creole, by his looks," Leon said to her. "I could wish for a son as sturdy and handsome." Bending down, he looked Guy in the eye. "Would you like to come outside and sit on Tigre again before I go?"

Guy was so excited he could only nod vigorously.

Jurissa released her pent-up breath. Leon didn't see the resemblance. "Find Yubah and tell her to put some shoes on you first," she ordered Guy.

When he ran out of the room, Leon turned to her. "It's as well he interrupted because I couldn't have stopped myself." He traced her lips with his forefinger. "Au revoir, *cherie*. Never again will I say a final adieu to you."


Just before two o'clock in the afternoon, the signal gun at Fort Charles roared three times and the bells of St. Louis began to toll. All over the city soldiers sprang to arms but there was no fighting until dusk. The battle began when General Jackson sent the navy schooner *Carolina* downstream to bombard the entrenched British from the water while his troops struck from land.

Leon, listening to the thunderous roars of the *Carolina's* cannon, cursed under his breath. It was an honor, yes, to serve General Jackson, but *Cousine* Anton had taken his place in Beale's Volunteers and was now in the thick of the fighting. Leon longed to be beside him. Or in place of him. Diplomatic Anton, who'd never been the world's best shot, should be on the general's staff and Leon with Beale.

Thinking about his mother, still at Dindon, with shells crashing about her ears, drove him frantic with worry. He had to put her and Dindon out of his mind or go mad. Louise-Marie was safe enough at Marchand's and Jurissa, thank *le bon Dieu*, was safe, too.

How brave she'd been struggling through the night and the swamp to reach him. True, she'd also warned Jackson that the British had landed troops and pinpointed where they were, but Leon knew she'd done it for him. She loved him; he'd seen the love in her eyes and, tired as he was, it invigorated him. He would always love her even though they could never be together.


Christmas Eve dawned with a mist chilling the city. By afternoon the mist had turned to rain. Jurissa, Madame Lavalle, and the other Creole women who volunteered to help, waited for the call to take care of the wounded. After the initial skirmish the night before there'd been no fighting, and everyone was tense with waiting for the real battle to begin.

The British troops still held Dindon as well as a neighboring plantation, but they'd made no move to advance toward the city. Jackson's troops, she knew, were dug in near the edge of the city by the Rodriquez Canal, an old, abandoned mill run. The general himself was in command, so Leon was sure to be with him. Anton and Nicolas LeMoine, too, for all the American forces were deployed there.

In her mind she knew men fought, men died, but in her heart she couldn't believe that could possibly happen to any of the men she knew. Especially not Leon. Oh, never Leon!

Tomorrow, Guy would be two years old. She'd been tempted for a moment, when Leon praised the child, to tell him Guy *was* the son he wished for. But she couldn't be cruel to poor Louise-Marie, ill at Marchand's, perhaps losing her own child once again. Nor did she dare risk losing Guy.

Tonight, at Mass, she would pray for them all.

## Chapter Sixteen

By New Year's Day American and British troops had skirmished a few more times, but no major battle had yet occurred. In the relative calm, General Jackson invited the people of New Orleans to attend his review of the troops at the army encampment near the outskirts of the city. Since the rain had ceased and the day was fine, though chilly, Jurissa decided to go. She left Yubah at home with Guy and, driving her cabriolet, she picked up Tiana, then stopped at *Docteur* Marchand's on the way to inquire about Louise-Marie.

Louise-Marie, lying on a chaise longue in an upstairs bedroom, greeted Jurissa with tears in her eyes. "Have they told you I lost the baby?" she asked.

Jurissa took her hand and pressed it. "I'm sorry about the child but happy you are recovering."

"Again I have you to thank for insisting on bringing me here. I might very well be dead if I'd gone on to Dindon that day as you did. I swear I'd have been frightened beyond recall if the British had captured me. Your escape from Dindon seems quite extraordinary. I can't think how you managed."

"Without the help and encouragement of your remarkable mother-in-law, I wouldn't have had the courage. Have you heard how she fares?"

"When he visited two days ago, Leon told me he could find out nothing about his mother. I pray she hasn't been killed. And that he hasn't. My brother is fighting, too, and I worry about him. Oh, this horrid war! When will it end?"

Jurissa murmured a few more words of what comfort she could and said good-bye. Leon, then, knew his wife had lost another child, she mused as she left the house. Poor Louise-Marie.

"Maybe Madame du Motier will never carry a child long enough for it to be born," Tiana said after Jurissa rejoined her in the cabriolet with the sad news. "Sometimes it happens that way."

"I feel sorry for her," Jurissa said as she took up the reins. "Deprived of the child and of being able to go home to Dindon at the same time."

At the encampment planks had been laid over the mud for the assemblage. Jurissa scanned the troops who waited to march as soon as the general appeared at the crude stand constructed for the review, but her search for either Leon or Anton was unsuccessful. The bands tuned up in not unpleasant discord as the Creoles chatted and laughed with one another, treating the occasion in a seemingly frivolous fashion. Jurissa knew by now that Creoles were anything but frivolous; they simply enjoyed gathering together and showed it.

"There's Nicolas," Tiana said, gesturing toward one of the volunteer groups of free men of color. "I hope they've taught him how to shoot a musket properly. If soldiers fought with rapiers he'd be the equal of any and the master of most, but what good is skill with a rapier when you face another's man's bullet?"

Cheers went up, signaling General Jackson's appearance, and the American band burst into "Hail Columbia." The soldiers stood at attention, ready to march as soon as he reached the stand. As the notes died away, a Creole band began *Le Chant Du Depart.* Suddenly a fearsome hiss sliced through the music.

"British rocket!" a man's voice cried.

Jurissa and Tiana clutched each other as the rocket exploded in a crashing burst overhead. Confusion reigned as women screamed, men shouted, horses panicked, and soldiers broke ranks. The musicians frantically packed up their instruments. British cannon roared by the time Jurissa and Tiana reached the cabriolet and Jurissa, struggling with the terrified horse, wondered if they'd ever get back to town.

"So the big attack finally comes," Tiana said, tears in her eyes. "What chance do men have against cannon? Ah, Nicolas, may *le bon Dieu* watch over you."

Tiana was wrong about a big attack, as they both discovered later in the day. After an hour's cannonade, the British guns ceased and none of their troops advanced on the American embankment. There were casualties from the shelling. Some of the wounded Creole soldiers were moved from the field hospital to the house on the edge of town, set up as a hospital where Creole doctors volunteered their services to the wounded and New Orleans women, including Jurissa, served as nurses.

In the late afternoon Jurissa helped Dr. Marchand treat a stocky soldier with an injured arm. The man looked familiar and she soon realized where she'd seen him before. He had been the one giving orders to unload the pirate cart at the bakery.

"*Miserables*," he muttered as the doctor fitted his arm into a sling. "They will pay for shooting at Dominque You, those English. *Nom de Dieu*, how I will make them pay!"

Like most of the less seriously wounded, he was intent on returning to the battle line. The doctor shrugged and didn't argue. A half hour later, Jurissa, taking a moment's respite by a window, noticed Dominque You, his arm in a sling, being helped onto a horse by a blond man with a bandage around his head. She stared in consternation before assuring herself it couldn't possibly be Philip Winterton. He was dead. Drowned. Nevertheless, she hurried to the door, determined to get a closer look at Dominque You's companion.

Jurissa almost collided with two men who came in bearing a wounded man on a litter. One glance at the bloodstained face of the soldier they carried and she forgot everything else. Leon!

When they deposited him in a vacant spot on the floor, she knelt beside him and laid her hand on his chest. Was he breathing? She was too upset to tell. Fumbling for his neck pulse, Jurissa prayed desperately. Leon couldn't be dead; he mustn't die. If he did, how could she go on? A world without Leon was unthinkable.

Relief spread through her when she felt a throbbing under her fingers. She called his name; he didn't respond. He gave no sign he lived except the rapid beat of his pulse. Was he dying? Frantically she looked around for the doctor and saw him bending over another wounded soldier.

"*Docteur* Marchand, please!" she begged. "This man needs you."

He turned toward her, nodded, and returned his attention to the patient in front of him. Jurissa bit her lip to keep from screaming at him to hurry. It seemed hours before he finished and moved to Leon's side.

"I'll need some water to wash away the blood," he told her, and she hurried off to fill a basin and find a clean sponge.

By the time she returned, the doctor was leaving Leon to head for the next casualty. As far as she could see, he hadn't done anything for him. She tensed in renewed dread. Was the doctor abandoning Leon because there *was* nothing he could do for a dying man? In desperation, she clutched the doctor's arm.

"Be calm, my dear," he instructed. "You are becoming far too agitated. I sent you for the water to give you a chance to recover yourself."

"Leon," she managed to gasp. "Is he—"

"A bullet or a shell fragment creased his skull. He's suffered a concussion but should recover rapidly with nothing more than a bad headache. Remember, you can't provide efficient help if you go to pieces over every wounded soldier you happen to recognize. Wash the blood away, bandage his head and let him rest. Then go home yourself. You've done more than enough for today."

Gently, Jurissa sponged the blood from Leon's face and more gingerly from the caked mass on the left side of his head. She wound a bandage around the injury as she'd been taught, then knelt beside Leon, waiting. No matter what Dr. Marchand advised, she had no intention of leaving before Leon roused.

She had no idea how long it was before he moaned and raised his arm as though reaching for his head. Grasping his hand so that he couldn't reach the bandage, she murmured, "Leon."

His head turned toward her, his eyes opening. He looked at her in confusion.

"You're in the temporary hospital," she told him. "*Docteur* Marchand says you have a concussion from a bullet that creased your skull. There's a bandage around your head—don't touch it."

"Jurissa." She leaned closer to hear him. "Stay with me. Don't go away. Please don't go away." He closed his eyes again.

"I won't," she whispered, uncertain whether or not he heard her. "I won't leave you."

When he roused the second time, Leon refused to stay still and made Jurissa help him to his feet. "I can't lie here while the others fight," he muttered. When he grimaced, clenching his teeth, she knew he had the headache the doctor had predicted.

"Do you hear any gunfire?" she demanded. "Any cannon? The fighting's over for the moment and you can't go back to the encampment until you give yourself the chance to recover."

"I'm not staying here." He tried to walk, swayed against her, and finally accepted her support.

As much as she longed to, she couldn't bring him home with her. War or no war, everyone would know, including Louise-Marie.

"I'll take you to Tiana's," Jurissa told him. "You can sleep there overnight. And don't you dare protest! Your comrades have enough to do without having to take care of you."

Leon meant to argue but it took all his strength just to put one foot ahead of the other as she led him out of the building. He couldn't remember being hit; he only knew his head hurt like the devil himself was piercing his skull with a red-hot rapier. With Jurissa's help he managed to climb into the cabriolet. As she urged the horse on, each turn of the wheels brought another thrust of the devil's cursed *epee*.

It took both Tiana and Jurissa to support him as he staggered into Tiana's quarters. He all but fell onto the bed they brought him to. Throughout the next few hours he slipped in and out of a half-sleep, dimly aware that someone had put a damp, cooling compress to his wound and that Jurissa's soothing voice coaxed him to swallow the most foul-tasting potion he'd ever encountered.

He woke fully to an unfamiliar room where a single aromatic-scented candle burned. By its flickering light, he saw Jurissa sitting in a chair drawn up to the bed. She leaned to him.

"You're at Tiana's, Leon. How do you feel?"

"Why is it you never call me *cher* as you once did on the ship?" he asked.

A smile brightened her tired face. "I thought you'd taken possession of that word for your exclusive use."

He reached for her hand and pressed it to his lips before releasing it. Her skin was rougher than he remembered, no doubt from her nursing duties. What a woman she was! Slowly he eased to a sitting position, bracing himself for the searing pain he was sure would strike. When all he felt was a dull throbbing ache, he smiled in relief.

"If you can smile Tiana's concoction must be working," Jurissa said.

He grimaced. "Why is it cures never taste good?" Testing his recovery, he swung his legs over the edge of the bed and rested his feet on the floor.

She stood up. "You're not going anywhere. There's been no more fighting. They don't need you. Even if they did, you deserve a good night's sleep first."

He grinned at her. "If they left wars up to women there'd never be any soldiers at the front lines."

"In other words, no wars. Would that be so bad?"

He reached out for her, pulling her close to him, resting his head against her breasts. "Back there in the hospital, when I opened my eyes and saw you, I knew I'd be all right if only you'd stay with me."

"I wanted to take you home with me," she said, her hands gently caressing his shoulders. She didn't explain why she hadn't; she didn't have to.

She felt so warm, so soft. He longed for the exquisite joy she alone could bring him, the suspension of all worry and pain. Why must he deprive himself and her, too, of what they both desired?

"You might have died today," she murmured. "For a few terrible moments I thought you had." Her fingers dug into his shoulders while, in his ear, her heart beat wildly. "I couldn't bear it if anything happened to you."

Didn't she know he felt the same? All the joy would leave his life if she was gone. He rose to his feet, his arms still holding her, and gazed into her face, shadowed by the flickering candle. *Dieu*, he was starved for the look of her, the feel of her, the smell and taste of her.

Before he could kiss her, she raised her fingers to touch his lips. "We can't." Her voice was heavy with regret, with longing, with determination.

For an instant his arms tightened around her, then, reluctantly, he released her.

"Now that you're on the road to recovery, I must go home," she said. "Yubah and Silas will be worried."

He sighed. "Even Yubah's little boy—what's his name, Guy?—must miss you when you're away. It was plain to me how fond you are of him. I'm sure he adores you."

She gave him a long look. "Guy—" she began and paused. "Guy is—" She stopped again. "I do love Guy," she finished finally, but he had the impression that wasn't what she'd meant to say at first. Had she been going to tell him who the father was and decided it wasn't wise? Ah, well, he wouldn't push her. What did it matter?

"Guy's a charming child. Yubah can be proud of him." Leon tipped her chin with a forefinger. "I'm certain you wouldn't refuse *him* a good night kiss."

"You're not a little boy."

"Ah, but that means I need the kiss all the more." He bent and brushed her mouth with his, fighting to keep himself from crushing her to him. The tip of his tongue met hers in a brief caress, and he lifted his head before temptation overcame him. "I'll see you safely home before I return to the encampment. Perhaps the British will be kind enough to allow me the good night's sleep you insist I deserve."

Outside of sporadic gunfire, no more skirmishes occurred until bursting rockets roused New Orleans before dawn on the eighth of January. Jurissa dressed in the gown Madame Lavalle had devised for the volunteer nurses—black, with a white apron—and hurried to the makeshift hospital. By the time she arrived, the roar of cannon, interlarded with the popping of gunfire, was continuous, and casualties were already being treated. She discovered they were no longer receiving only the less seriously wounded Creoles.

Doctors and nurses alike were soon busy. The nurses, rushing from one wounded man to another, had no time to be upset by shattered limbs or eviscerated organs as they did their best to assist the doctors and care for the patients. Death hovered on every side.

As the mists of late afternoon began to creep in from the river, Jurissa became aware that the cannonade had ceased and she was hearing only sporadic gunfire. Which way had the battle gone? she wondered, as she coaxed a dose of laudanum down the throat of a wounded Creole youth who looked no older than sixteen.

Tiana came up to her. "I'm here with my crew." Glancing from Jurissa's bloodstained apron to the crowded room they stood in, she said, "It's bad this time, isn't it? Did you see him?"

Knowing she meant Nicholas, Jurissa shook her head. "No one I recognized, thank God. And I thank God, too, that you recruited your friends among the free women of color to help out here. I'm ready to drop."

"I just told them if those pampered Creole ladies can nurse the wounded, it must be easy." Tiana grinned at Jurissa who shook her head.

Outside, the winter mist had begun to shroud the city with its winding sheet of damp chill. Men and horses appeared and disappeared as it thickened and thinned. A wagon of wounded was pulling up in front as Jurissa headed for the shed that sheltered her horse. The Negro hostler hurried to hitch him to the cabriolet and assisted Jurissa in. As she directed the horse onto the road, two men suddenly appeared out of the mist, the light-haired one half carrying, half dragging his dark-haired companion. Another casualty.

The blond one, who wore the grimy bandage on his head, tilted at a rakish angle, looked up at her when she passed them and her heart stood still. This time there was no mistake. She stared into Philip Winterton's blue eyes. Eyes that widened in recognition.

Jurissa flicked her horse with the reins, urging the animal into a trot while the cabriolet swayed perilously on the rough road. All she could think of was that she must get away from him; she must escape.

Silas met her at the courtyard gate and looked at her, to the lathered horse, and back again. Without waiting for his help, she scrambled down from the cabriolet and stared back through the open gate.

"Close it!" she cried, hugging herself. "Bolt the gate!"

"Yes'm." He looked into the misty darkness as she had, the huge muscles in his arms flexing. "Something be wrong?"

Silas was strong but all his strength was of no use against what she'd encountered. Her impulse was to hide but what use was that when he'd recognized her? With the British blocking escape there was no way to flee. Nothing was any use.

Jurissa swallowed the bitter bile that rose in her throat. When she spoke her voice trembled. "Silas, I bring terrible news. He's not dead. I saw him."

Silas's eyes widened until white showed around the deep brown. "Can't be him lest he be a devil-man."

He hadn't asked her who it was she meant. He hadn't needed to. Philip Winterton was the one person they all feared. She shook her head. "I thought I saw him before, with the pirates. This time I'm sure. He's alive."

"Should be knowing a devil ain't that easy to kill," Silas muttered.

Jurissa moved toward the house on leaden feet.

How long would they be safe here? Perhaps until the war was decided one way or the other. Perhaps not that long. It wouldn't be difficult for Philip to trace a redheaded woman in this city of dark hair. There was no use in trying to run. Where could she and the others go?

Yubah took one look at her face and led Jurissa to a chair. "Look like you done see a ghost," she said.

Jurissa gazed sadly at Yubah. "You speak more truly than you know. The dead have come back to haunt us. Philip Winterton is alive."

Yubah stared at her as though she'd lost her mind.

"I saw him. He recognized me." Jurissa's tone was flat, hopeless.

"What gonna happen?" The apprehension in Yubah's voice showed her fear.

"Monsieur DuBois was still working on my legal status," Jurissa said. "The court hadn't yet declared Philip Winterton dead but even if it had, I wouldn't necessarily have gotten clear title to the estate. Monsieur DuBois told me that apparently there's a distant cousin in Virginia who may have had a claim. I wanted to free you both but the law said I couldn't. Because Mr. Winterton isn't dead, he still owns you. And Silas. And I'm not a widow either legally or in fact. I'm still his wife."

"*Maman?*" Guy's sleepy voice called from the bedroom.

The two women glanced at each other in terrified speculation. Jurissa had been so devastated by seeing Philip that not until this moment had she thought of what might happen to Guy. Philip would think he was Yubah's. But that made Guy a slave, as Yubah was. Philip's slave. So Philip could do as wished with Guy—even sell him. What could she do? Jurissa closed her eyes in pain for an instant before hurrying in to Guy's room.

After she'd settled her son into sleep again, she returned to the kitchen where Yubah and Silas shared a silent communication.

"Been thinking you got to take the boy to Massa Leon," Yubah said.

Jurissa spread her hands. "How can I? He's a soldier. I don't even know where he is. And the British hold Dindon—if it still stands."

"You know where Massa Leon's wife be," Yubah said.

"How can I do such a thing to her?" Jurissa demanded. "And even if I could, she might refuse to accept Guy. After losing two babies of her own, she won't want another woman's."

"You got to try."

After a long silence, Jurissa nodded. She couldn't allow Philip to get his hands on Guy. She had no choice but to try.

At first light bells woke Jurissa from a fitful sleep. She recognized the deep tones of the St. Louis Cathedral bells, joined by what must be every other church bell in the city. The agreed-on signal for an American victory. The British were defeated!

Jurissa's momentary elation faded as she recalled her own dilemma. She rose and dressed, with Yubah hovering over her and Guy at her skirts. "I'll go to her now," she told Yubah.

But when she arrived at Dr. Marchand's, Jurissa was told Louise-Marie's father had come for her as soon as he heard the victory bells. He'd taken her to her childhood home on the Rondelet plantation up and across the river, to wait there until Leon could discover what had happened to Dindon.

The difficulty of crossing the river and finding the Rondelet plantation was a problem in itself. Once she managed to solve that, she'd have to face trying to explain the situation to Louise-Marie in her parent's home. From her short acquaintance with Leon's wife, Jurissa knew Louise-Marie was a woman who leaned on others. Whatever Louise-Marie might have decided on her own, Jurissa felt certain her parents would convince their daughter to have nothing to do with any such scandalous claim. Also, by Creole custom, the matter must be handled by the husband, not the wife.

Tiana! Surely her friend would help. Jurissa hurried to the rue des Normandie and woke Tiana to explain the problem.

"Bring Guy here immediately," Tiana said. "He can stay as long as necessary—forever, if it comes to that. I love the child as my own."

Jurissa hugged her. "What would I do without you?"

"You forget I live because of you. Perhaps you mean what would we do without each other?" She eyed Jurissa, frowning. "If the man is as evil as Yubah has told me, I hope for the boy's sake this husband of yours never discovers there had been a child at all."

"Who would tell?"

"No one who loves you. But many people know of the child, believing him to be Yubah's. We'll do our best, but it is very difficult to keep a secret."

After she left Tiana, Jurissa was tempted to search for Leon and tell him everything. He'd take Guy, she knew, and keep him from harm. But where would she find Leon? And might she not put herself in Philip's path by venturing near the encampment? Before she made such a dangerous move, she must spirit Guy away to Tiana's, where he'd be safe even if Philip found her.

As she rushed back home, Jurissa tried to come up with another plan if she couldn't find Leon. Could Anton help her? He'd know if there was any legal way out. Why, oh, why hadn't she married him when he'd asked her? Upon Philip's return, the marriage might not have been legal but Anton would surely have found some means to keep Philip away from her. And, if she'd had the courage to confess the truth to Anton, he'd have been able to keep Guy safe, too.

Perhaps, though, if Anton had known the truth, he wouldn't have wanted to marry her. Would he agree to help her now if she told him the truth?

If I have to ask him, I will, she vowed.

Guy, who was fond of "*Tante* Tiana," accepted going to stay with her—if he could bring his *cheval*, the ebony rocking horse that Silas had fashioned for him, and also the African horn whistle he'd found among Jurissa's belongings and wouldn't part with.

Hoping he'd lose interest if it wouldn't make any

noise, Jurissa had asked Silas to make a stopper so the whistle wouldn't blow, but Guy refused to give it up, even sleeping with the whistle clutched in one hand.

Whistle around his neck on a shortened thong, the horse and his clothes in the cabriolet behind him, Guy chattered to Jurissa all the way to Tiana's about how he was going to help in the bakery. When she parted from Guy she held him so tightly he yelped in protest, wriggling free and giving her a quick wave before he ran across the courtyard to see if the frog he remembered still dwelt in the tiny pool by the banana tree.

She watched him with tears in her eyes, wondering when she'd next see him.

The city swarmed with people, everyone celebrating the victory over the British and making plans to honor the *Americain* general who'd saved New Orleans. Though she was glad the war was over, Jurissa's mood was uncertain and fearful. How could she bear to accept Philip Winterton as a husband?

Something that hadn't before occurred to her popped into her mind. Perhaps he wouldn't want her as his wife. He hadn't married her for love; hadn't even wanted to marry her. He'd been with the pirates. Maybe he meant to remain with them. Perhaps the situation wouldn't be as bad as she feared. Except for Yubah and Silas. They belonged to him, and Jurissa didn't think Philip would easily give up his possessions. She did have money put away, though. Was it possible he'd sell them to her?

She might not have liked him but he was simply a

man, after all, not the devil Silas called him. He hadn't returned from the dead. There was a reasonable explanation for what had happened to him and where he'd been since the night she last saw him on the ship.

Even putting the best of interpretations on his reappearance, though, Philip must never learn of Guy's existence.

## Chapter Seventeen

Anton DuBois, in the blue hunting shirt and ebony hat of Beale's Volunteers, was waiting in the courtyard for Jurissa when she returned from Tiana's.

"I heard you'd been nursing the Creole wounded," he said, helping her from the cabriolet and taking hold of her hands. "I tried to find you at the temporary hospital but you weren't there so I came to the house. I had to make certain you were all right."

"Thank God you were spared injury, Anton. As for me, I should have gone in to work at the hospital today but I couldn't bring myself to. Something happened as I was leaving there yesterday—" She paused and, easing her hands from his, laid one on his arm. "I—I saw my husband, Philip Winterton, bringing in a wounded man."

Anton stared at her. "Surely you must be mistaken."

"I thought I'd seen him before with Lafitte's men but I convinced myself it wasn't possible. This time there was no mistake. Philip Winterton is alive."

"*Cousine* Leon, as well as yourself have told me how the *capitaine* of the *Yarmouth* entered Philip Winterton's disappearance in his log as a fall overboard."

"I know who I saw. And though it's true my husband wasn't to be found aboard the ship, no one saw him go over; no one saw him drown. I tell you he's in New Orleans. He recognized me." Jurissa shivered.

"Did you confront him?"

"Good God, no!"

"And he said nothing to you?" When she shook her head, Anton raised his eyebrows. "Don't you feel it was strange he didn't speak? Why hasn't he come forth in all this time? Do you realize it's but two months short of three years? I don't understand how any man could leave you alone and in distress." He covered her hand with his own. "How upset you must be."

She took a deep breath. "I'm more than upset, I'm terrified. When I told you I couldn't marry you, Anton, you made the assumption it was because I held Philip's memory dear. I didn't disillusion you but now I'm forced to tell you it was the exact opposite. I feared him. Marriage to him was a nightmare. He tried—" She bit her lip, uncertain how to explain.

Anton frowned. "I don't know quite what to say. You've taken me by surprise."

"Even if the court had made me a widow by law, it would make no difference now. I can't be a widow if my husband lives, is that correct?"

He nodded.

"Philip can walk into my house and claim me as

276

his wife as though no time had passed?"

His eloquent brown eyes were sympathetic. "He can. Furthermore, anything you've acquired in the meantime will become his."

She stared at him in horror. "My house? The money I've saved? My partnership in Tiana's bakery?"

"Everything. I'm sorry, Jurissa, but it's the law. Women aren't considered capable of managing property or money. Quite correct in most cases. The law is designed to protect women from themselves."

Jurissa, bridling at Anton's defense of such a law, took her hand from his arm. "Are you saying you don't think I'm capable of handling my own financial affairs? Or that Tiana LeMoine is not?"

"Free women of color, by necessity, frequently learn to become businesswomen. It's extremely unusual for a women of your social status to involve herself in business and actually handle money."

"You make it sound demeaning. Why should conducting a business be demeaning for women if it isn't for men?"

Anton's expression suggested he'd just swallowed a noxious potion. "Creole gentlemen do not involve themselves in business; they own plantations. Occasionally one, like myself, will enter the profession of law. Or medicine."

"But running a plantation *is* a business," she protested.

"We Creoles don't consider it so. You're from Boston, where the customs are different. Even our law differs. Here in New Orleans we base our legal system on the French civil code."

She clenched her fists. "So, because I'm a woman, I'm expected to sit back and do nothing when my husband walks in after a three-year absence and takes over everything I've earned. Is there no way to prevent this? I want Tiana protected, if nothing else. Because she's a woman of color Philip will regard her the same as he does his slaves. That is to say—like an animal."

Anton looked uncomfortable. "You can assign your half of the bakery interests to her, but is that wise? You'd best wait and see how this develops. Perhaps he won't appear."

"No! I want the papers drawn up immediately. Is someone in your office available today?"

He shook his head. "Everyone is celebrating the victory and so—"

"Anton!" Her fingers dug into his arm. "Please take me to your office now and draw up the papers. Please!"

He spread his hands. "Be reasonable. I stole a few minutes to come here but—"

"Then you can steal a few more to help me. The war is over, after all."

Impatiently, she watched as he pondered. She could almost see his mind weighing one possibility against the next. Fond as she was of Anton, this particular trait annoyed her. Would he do the same if she asked him to help with Guy? She feared he would. The fact that Guy was a helpless child might even weigh less with him than other considerations.

"I can't refuse you," he said at last. "Though, mind you, I advise waiting."

"I can't wait. You don't know what Philip is capable of."

"My reasoning is that the man has stayed away for three years. Why? You have no way of knowing whether he means to go back into hiding instead of reclaiming you as his wife. Jurissa, you know how I feel about you. Believe me, I hope Philip Winterton never approaches you. If he doesn't, in four more years the law will agree he's deserted you and you'll be free. I hesitate, first because I know you are Catholic, and secondly, because under Louisiana law it would be difficult to mention divorce."

"Divorce?" Jurissa stared at him. "I truly believe that if Philip means to claim me as his wife, he'd kill me before he allowed me to divorce him. I dare not take the chance he'll stay away, either. If I can't protect myself or Yubah and Silas from him, I can at least arrange to protect Tiana's business."

He inclined his head in surrender. "If you insist, I'll fill out the papers."

"One moment before we go." Jurissa left Anton and crossed the yard to where Silas worked on a chest he was making to hold Guy's toys. "Silas, after I leave with Monsieur DuBois, I want you to dig up the money we buried and take it to Miss Tiana. All of it. Tell her she must say the money's hers, otherwise it will belong to my husband. And tell her I'm signing a paper to return my part of the bakery to her for the same reason. She's not to tell anyone I was ever her partner. Do you understand."

"Yes'm. I fears I do."

She put her hand on his. "Silas, if I could have freed you and Yubah, I would have. I'd hoped one day the legal tangle would be settled. I never expected him to return from the dead."

He shook his head. "Gonna be bad times."

"Monsieur DuBois seems to think Mr. Winterton might want to remain in hiding but I can't believe it. We must prepare ourselves for his return as best we can."

"I do what you say. Only thing be—ain't no way to get ready for the devil."

Anton had ridden his horse to her house, so Jurissa drove herself in the cabriolet to his office. After the necessary papers had been signed and they were ready to part, he grasped her hands in his.

"I'll help you all I can," he said earnestly.

Jurissa summoned a smile. "I know you will, Anton. You've helped me already."

On the way home alone—Anton insisted he must return to his unit—she wondered if he could possibly be right. Maybe Philip was no more eager to see her than she was to see him. But even if this were true, now that she knew Philip was alive, she'd be living with a sword over her head—the threat of his return to her.

She couldn't be sure that Guy was more than temporarily safe at Tiana's. Even if she confessed to Anton that she, and not Yubah, was Guy's mother, she feared he was too slow-moving, too concerned over legalities to find a solution in time. At the worst, he might decide he wanted nothing more to do with a woman of her social status, as he called it, who bore a child not her husband's.

Leon was her only hope. If she sent Silas to find

Leon and bring him to her, she wouldn't be risking another encounter with Philip. Once Leon knew the boy was his son she could be sure he would never allow Philip to get near the boy, must less lay claim to him.

The courtyard gate was closed when she drove up in the cabriolet. Silas always had it open for her but perhaps he hadn't returned yet. As Jurissa prepared to dismount and open the gate herself, she heard the catch rattle. The gate swung open. Her heart sank.

Philip Winterton stood there in black trousers and a white shirt with a red neckerchief knotted at the throat. He looked lean and fit. There was no sign of the paunch he'd had when she married him. The bandage around his head was fresh, and she noticed an old puckered scar along his right temple.

He smiled and sketched a bow. "Won't you come in, my dear?" he asked, his blue eyes watchful.

For a moment she couldn't move. She'd been telling herself to expect this but nothing she'd said or done had prepared her for facing Philip. Pulling herself together, she drove the cabriolet through the gate and heard it clang behind her, shutting her in with her husband.

She halted the horse and, head held high, accepted his help to descend from the cabriolet. Apprehension clogged her mind; no plan for dealing with him occurred to her.

"What, no loving greeting for a long-lost husband?" He said as she stepped back from him.

"I thought you were dead," she countered. "What else was I to think when I was told you fell overboard? There was little affection between us at that time, as seems obvious since you've waited three years to let me know you were alive."

"The three years has sharpened your tongue, at any rate." He looked her up and down.

This morning, without thinking, she'd pulled on another of the black gowns designed for nursing, a dowdy affair with no claim to style. Her bonnet, brown with black ribbons, was far from her newest. She was obscurely grateful not to be looking her best.

His eyes left her and he glanced around the courtyard. "You've done well for yourself. Who is he?"

She blinked. "I don't understand."

"I know the house is in your name; a friend of mine found that out for me. You didn't have any money when you arrived in New Orleans so you certainly didn't buy the house on your own. What other way does a woman acquire a house? In New Orleans, I believe the term is *placee*."

"I am no man's *placee!*"

His eyes narrowed. She'd forgotten how chilly a blue they were, the color of icicles seen in the dusk of a Boston winter. "I'll have to teach you not to lie to me. In any case, I know who he must be. That Creole bastard who threw me over the rail into the sea to drown."

Jurissa was shocked into silence. It couldn't be true; Leon wouldn't do such a thing! But if he hadn't, why would Philip say so?

"You seem surprised," he said. "Either you didn't know, in which case you can't trust him, or the two of you planned it but you didn't realize I knew he was responsible." His hand snaked out and grabbed her wrist, twisting.

Jurissa cried out.

"So. Tell me the truth this time."

"He wouldn't do such a cowardly thing." She spoke between her teeth. "You fell, more likely."

"The hell I did. He lifted me over the rail."

"It was dark. How could you tell who it was?"

"He'd already pushed me down on the deck—as you'll remember. I know very well who it was. And why he did it. The bastard wanted his chance at you. Which he got, by all appearances. Where is he? I've got a score to settle with Monsieur Leon du Motier."

Jurissa jerked her arm free and cradled her bruised wrist in her other hand. "If you plan to wait here for him you'll have a long wait. There's nothing between Monsieur du Motier and me. He doesn't come here."

The iron knocker on the gate banged. "Silas!" A man's voice called.

Oh, God, it must be Leon, she thought in horror.

Silas emerged from the horse shed and Philip waved him back. "My pleasure," he said to Jurissa, smiling in triumph. He strode to the gate and flung it wide.

Jurissa caught her breath as the horseman rode into the courtyard. "Wait!" she cried to Philip. "You're making a mistake."

She was too late.

"Monsieur du Motier, I believe." Philip's voice was silky with menace.

"You have the wrong man, sir," the horseman announced, dismounting. "My name is Anton DuBois."

Taken aback, Philip stared at Anton who gazed coldly at him. "You look just like the bastard," Philip muttered.

How could he think that? Jurissa wondered. Except for their eyes, there was little resemblance between the cousins. Philip must not remember Leon very well. And why, she wondered, had Anton returned to her house?

"I beg your pardon?" Anton's tone was stiff with outrage.

"Monsieur DuBois, this is my husband, Mr. Winterton," Jurissa put in, since it was evident Philip had no intention of being polite enough to give his name. "Monsieur DuBois is my attorney," she said to Philip. "I retained him when I believed you to be drowned."

"You're to be congratulated on your remarkable resurrection, Mr. Winterton," Anton said. "I'll admit to some curiosity about why it took you three years to surface. Your wife has had a most difficult time of it."

"She seems comfortable enough to me." Philip's tone was just short of insolent.

"I hope you've communicated with your second cousin, once removed, in Virginia," Anton went on. "A Mr. Tompkins. He's filed a claim to your estate."

Philip snorted. "Bill always was a greedy pup. I'll let you send him the bad news of my survival, since you're the lawyer." His gaze slid speculatively between Anton and Jurissa.

"I'd appreciate an explanation," Anton persisted, "of your extraordinary reluctance to inform your wife you were alive."

"I wasn't aware it was illegal."

"Common courtesy—" Anton began.

"Let's say I had that knocked out of me with the rest of my senses when I was thrown overboard."

Philip crossed to Jurissa and wound his arm around her waist. She forced herself not to shrink away from him.

"As I was about to inform my dear wife," Philip continued, "I injured my head in the fall." He touched the scar on his temple. "The first I knew, I was sprawled on my belly on the deck of one of Lafitte's ships with a crewman pumping water out of me. As far as memories were concerned, I had none. No name, no past, and no knowledge of how I came to be where I was."

Jurissa remembered the pirate ship that had trailed the *Yarmouth*—and, apparently, plucked Philip from the sea.

"Jean Lafitte is quick to accept a willing recruit, so I became a pirate." Philip grinned at the two of them. "They called me *Poisson* because I was pulled from the water like a fish. That's been my name from then until the first of this year when a British shell fragment knocked me cold and all but took my scalp off. After I came to, the old memories gradually filtered back. A miracle, wouldn't you say?"

Jurissa was stunned. Philip living the life of a pirate? It was difficult to believe.

All expression had left Anton's face. It was impossible to tell how he felt or what he was thinking. "A remarkable tale, indeed, Monsieur Winterton."

"Naturally I immediately set off in search of my dear wife and was delighted to find her living comfortably." Philip gestured. "Such pleasant surroundings to come home to. *Our* home, from now on. She will, of course, have no need of your—services in the future, as I'm sure you understand."

Anton's gaze gave away nothing. He nodded curtly to Philip. "Madame," he said to Jurissa, "it is possible I will need your signature on papers terminating the probate procedure since I obviously will not be continuing it. With that in mind, au revoir."

The way he'd worded his farewell, she knew Anton was saying he wouldn't desert her if she needed him. He'd come back to see her for some reason—she wished he'd been able to tell her what it was. Not that he could help her. How could anyone? "Au revoir, monsieur," she said.

Philip shut the gate behind Anton and barred it before returning to her side. "I've had to learn a bit of French to get by. Adieu, not au revoir is the proper word. You won't be seeing your attorney friend again; he's been warned off. As your husband, I'll make certain you don't regret losing his—services."

Again he emphasized the word and this time Jurissa realized he used the word in the sense of a stallion servicing a mare. Indignation roiled inside her. She and Anton had never been lovers but even if they were, how dare Philip compare her to an animal? Then the full meaning of what he'd said penetrated, and dread overcame her anger.

She'd never forgotten the cruel way Philip had tried to bed her aboard the ship. How could she bear it if he claimed his rights as a husband?

"You haven't yet said you're pleased I'm alive, after all," Philip said.

She determined to be as truthful as possible and chose her words carefully. "Like everyone else aboard the *Yarmouth*, I believed you'd drowned. Your sudden reappearance is unsettling but I have never wished anyone dead."

"Hardly a wife's warm welcome."

"I don't believe you expected warmth from me. We scarcely know one another."

He eyed her consideringly. "We'll soon remedy that." He bowed. "I told Yubah to prepare a meal. May I have the honor of escorting you to the table, madame?" In a parody of courtesy, he offered Jurissa his arm. Not knowing what else to do, she took it and they walked to the house.

The rich aroma of chicken gumbo filled her nostrils as Philip opened the door. Yubah had taken to Creole cooking as though born to it, and even Tiana declared her gumbos couldn't be surpassed. I'll concentrate on getting through the meal, Jurissa told herself; only that; not what might come next. If I think ahead I'll fall apart. I must take it one step at a time.

Jurissa had no idea if Yubah's gumbo was as rich and good as usual since she found it impossible to force anything down her throat. She did her best to conceal this by pretending to eat. Philip's appetite was excellent. He enjoyed several large servings of gumbo plus a half dozen of the freshly baked *petit pains* that Silas must have brought back from the bakery.

Not once did Jurissa look directly at Yubah as she served the meal. It was as well not to see her own fears mirrored in Yubah's eyes, Jurissa thought, bitterly aware she could no more protect Yubah from Philip than she could herself.

"Excellent," Philip pronounced, pushing back his

chair but not rising from the table. "You've trained her to cook a tasty meal, my dear wife."

"You be wanting coffee, Massa Philip?" Yubah's voice quivered as she asked the question.

"I've gotten used to that devil's brew of the Creoles."

"Yes sir. Be the kind I makes."

"Pour me a cup, then. And one for your mistress."

Yubah seemed steady enough as she poured for Philip, but her hand shook so that much of the coffee intended for Jurissa's cup splattered onto the table.

"You clumsy bitch!" Philip angrily waved Yubah away.

Jurissa opened her mouth and shut it again without a word, fearing anything she might say would only make it worse for Yubah. Philip might have improved his outward appearance but inside he hadn't changed. He was still impatient and short-tempered, and she feared, every bit as cruel as she remembered.

Lifting the cup to her lips she pretended to drink but she could no more swallow coffee than she could the gumbo. At last Philip finished his and rose to his feet.

"Any rum in the house?" he asked.

"No, only brandy," Jurissa told him.

"I'll remedy that tomorrow. Brandy will do well enough for a nightcap. Get it for me, Yubah. Jurissa, you may lead me to the master's bedroom. Or, to be correct, the master and mistress's bedroom. I find myself quite fatigued. And you look a bit tired, too, dear wife." He held out his hand to her.

Jurissa hung back. "I am not accustomed to retiring as early as five in the afternoon, sir."

He caught her hand, squeezing her fingers together until she winced. "I'll set the customs here from now on and I don't tolerate objections. Is that clear?" Without waiting for an answer, he pulled her with him toward the stairs.

When he unerringly chose the right bedroom, Jurissa realized he'd made a tour of the house before she came home.

"Did your paramour choose this fine wide bed or did you?" he asked, running his fingers over the graceful curves of the rosewood footboard. "Delicate, yet strong. Like you, Jurissa?"

"I ordered the bed myself," she said, keeping any emotion from her voice. "I have no paramour."

"That's correct. Not anymore. You have a husband instead. You'll find me an improvement over that foppish Creole lawyer." His suggestive smile sickened her.

She could insist he was wrong about Anton but why bother? He'd believe what he chose no matter what she said. Besides, if he focused on Anton, perhaps he'd forget his animosity toward Leon.

Philip sat on the bed, eased back and, propping his head on the pillows, looked up at her. "Get into your nightgown."

Jurissa's eyes widened. She didn't move.

"I'm forgetting," he said. "The pirate life has its compensations but one does tend to forget how civilized people live. A lady doesn't dress or undress herself, as I recall. Her maid does it for her." He raised his voice. "Yubah!"

Yubah entered the bedroom carrying the brandy

bottle and one snifter on a silver tray. She set the tray on the top of the rosewood writing desk and faced Philip.

"I'll have the brandy while I wait," he told her. "Don't be stingy when you pour."

Yubah filled the snifter without spilling a drop and handed it to him. "Go to your mistress," he ordered, putting the glass to his mouth and swallowing rapidly. "No way to treat fine French brandy; that's what you're thinking," he said to Jurissa. "As I've mentioned, it takes time to get over playing the buccaneer."

Yubah stood beside Jurissa, her eyes downcast, but Jurissa stared at her husband defiantly. Philip's gaze examined them as though they were horses he contemplated purchasing. Jurissa's blood ran cold when she heard his gloating laugh. "As pretty a pair as I've ever seen."

He lolled back against the pillows. "Yubah, your mistress requires your assistance in preparing for bed."

Yubah rolled her eyes at Jurissa and looked quickly away. Neither woman moved.

"Didn't you hear me?" Philip demanded.

"Yes sir," Yubah whispered.

"Then do as you're ordered."

Yubah hurried to the dresser and removed a white batiste nightgown embroidered in blue along the neckline and laid it across the back of a chair. She edged behind Jurissa, swallowing audibly as her hand reached to the fastening of the black gown Jurissa wore. Slowly she undid the first button, then the next and the next. Jurissa clenched her teeth and fixed her eyes above Philip's head. She would not plead with him, she would not cry, she would not shake in fear. Neither would she look at him.

With the release of the waist belt, the gown slid to the floor. Jurissa, clad only in her cambric chemise, her stockings, and her slippers, didn't step out of the gown. Yubah didn't try to pick it up. Instead, she lifted her arms and detached the comb holding Jurissa's chignon in place. Jurissa heard Philip catch his breath as the masses of red curls tumbled over her shoulders. Yubah's fingers tried without success to coax order into the tangled strands. She reached for the brush atop the dressing table and began to smooth Jurissa's hair but after a minute Philip ordered her to stop and get on with the undressing.

Jurissa knew he was deliberately keeping Yubah in the room to witness her humiliation, and that he knew Yubah was as upset as she was. She knew he wanted to hurt them both. It pleased him to show them he was the master and that they must obey his every whim.

Rage, mixed with fear, simmered inside her, resulting in a smoldering but impotent brew. She could do nothing. He'd enjoy having her scream and fight or crawl on her knees, begging. He'd relish her telling Yubah not to obey him because he could use it as an excuse to beat Yubah. Silence was the weapon she must use — ineffective, perhaps, but the only weapon she had.

Yubah plucked the nightgown from the chair and approached Jurissa with it, bunching the garment to draw over Jurissa's head.

"What do you think you're doing?" Philip demanded. "Your mistress isn't fully undressed."

"Miss Jurissa, she be keeping on her shift when she sleep," Yubah said.

Jurissa blessed her for the outright lie. She cringed at the idea of standing naked in front of Philip while he stared at her with gloating, lustful eyes. Yubah's lie might help her avoid such a horror.

"I don't care how she sleeps," Philip roared. "Take the damn thing off!"

## Chapter Eighteen

Clad in a thin cambric chemise, Jurissa stood in her bedroom doing her best to ignore Philip Winterton, sprawled on her bed, watching Yubah undress her. Gooseflesh studded her exposed skin. His lustful gaze crawled along her body, leaving, she felt, slime trails like the slugs in the courtyard garden.

If only she could walk out and never return. But she couldn't leave. Where would she go? If she fled to Tiana he'd find her there and Tiana might well be punished for sheltering her. Besides, Guy was at Tiana's. She couldn't jeopardize Guy.

She'd already refused to undress in front of Philip. What good had it done? Philip had simply ordered Yubah to do it. If she balked now, he'd blame Yubah and punish her. Jurissa couldn't allow that to happen.

She knew Yubah didn't want to undress her with Philip watching but what choice did she have?

Yubah knelt in front of Jurissa. She lifted Jurissa's foot and slid off one kid slipper, then the other. Reaching under the chemise, she slowly and carefully rolled down Jurissa's stockings, one at a time, before removing them. She stood up and hesitated.

Only the chemise was left. Yubah shot Jurissa an unhappy glance before bending to take the hem of the garment in both hands. I won't flinch, Jurissa resolved. I won't give him the satisfaction of showing any emotion.

Inexorably, the white chemise rose past her knees, her thighs. She heard Philip draw in his breath as the chemise crept higher, but kept her gaze fixed over his head. The garment rose over her head and off. She was naked, her body exposed to a man she feared and distrusted. Yubah reached for the nightgown.

"We can do without that." Philip spoke lazily. "Get out, Yubah."

Jurissa stood without moving until she heard the door close behind Yubah, then she grabbed the nightgown and yanked it over her head. He protested but she paid no attention now that Yubah was out of the room and couldn't be blamed. As far as she was concerned the rights of a husband didn't include standing naked in front of him.

"Come here," he ordered before she could tie the ribbons at the front of the gown. She ignored the command.

He rose from the bed, took a wobbling step toward her, grasped her arm and fell back onto the bed with her sprawled across him. He reeked of brandy. She'd been careful not to look at him so she didn't know if he'd poured himself more than the one glass, but he'd certainly been unsteady on his feet.

Remembering how he'd hurt her when he was drunk aboard the *Yarmouth*, she repressed a shudder. This time there'd be no escape from Philip's cruel caresses, no Leon waiting outside to rescue her.

Could she do anything to save herself? Before she

could try to roll free, Philip twisted her beneath him, pinning her there with the weight of his body. One hand yanked down the open front of her nightgown, exposing her breast. His hand closed over the tender flesh, squeezing. She swallowed her gasp of pain.

I can't stand this, she thought, revolting against the abuse of her body. Husband or not, I can't stand him.

Philip mumbled something, his words so slurred she couldn't understand what he'd said. He laid his head on her breasts and bile rose in her throat. If he put his mouth to her nipple she'd vomit.

No matter what the law said and despite her vows before the priest, she couldn't convince herself that Philip had the right to do what he wished with her when she loathed his touch. And no man had the right to hurt her.

"No!" she cried. "Let me go!"

He said nothing, lying with his body heavy and unwelcome on hers.

"Did you hear me?" she asked after long moments passed and he didn't move.

Silence.

"Philip?" She pushed at his head, moving it sideways until she could see his face. His eyes were closed. Asleep? She couldn't believe it.

Jurissa writhed, trying to twist her body from under his, shoving at him as she fought to free herself, expecting him to rouse and capture her again. But he didn't move, remaining a dead weight as she struggled from beneath him. At last she wriggled free, slid to the floor and turned to look at his limp form sprawled over her bed. He must be drunk. Nothing else would explain such a sound sleep. Lifting the brandy bottle, she checked what was left and frowned. Almost full.

Tiptoeing to the door, she eased it open and peered out. Yubah's yellow eyes gleamed at her from the open door across the narrow hall. Jurissa slipped from her bedroom, shut the door and ducked into the room where Yubah waited, the room that had been Guy's.

"He fell asleep," Jurissa whispered. "I don't know why but I thank God."

"Best to thanking Miss Tiana," Yubah whispered back. "She give Silas two potions for me, say one go in what Massa Philip eat; it be taking away his manhood. The other go in his coffee; he sleep, no matter what. I didn't get no chance to be telling you and I sure be scared when he say to give you coffee."

"So that's why you spilled most of mine." Jurissa smiled reassuringly. "I didn't drink what was left."

"Miss Tiana tell Silas she be studying what to do. She say if you be giving her Guy and all that money to keep, Massa Philip got to be evil. She be knowing you gonna need her help so she say she gonna fix Massa Philip so he don't make no trouble for you."

"She certainly did." Jurissa's eyes widened as a thought struck her. "I don't mean him to die!"

"Miss Tiana say he just sleep a long time. I undress you slow's he let me 'cause I be thinking he close his eyes if we takes long enough. Only he don't. I be waiting here, scared lest he hurt you."

"Tiana's potion worked. He didn't get the chance."

"What we do now?"

"Try to get some sleep ourselves. While he's asleep."

Uneasy about remaining in her nightgown, Jurissa gathered her courage and returned to the bedroom to retrieve her clothes. She spent the night fully dressed, huddled on the bed in Guy's room with Yubah on Guy's trundle bed, listening tensely for any sound that might mean Philip was awakening.

He hadn't roused yet when Dominique You knocked at the gate at mid-morning and Silas came to get Jurissa.

"Ah, madame." The stocky pirate, his arm still in a sling, swept Jurissa a bow. "I seek your husband. Is he here?"

"If you mean Philip Winterton, he's still sleeping," she said.

"Such a name. I can't help thinking of him as Poisson, you know. I never dreamed, when you helped *Docteur* Marchand with my arm, that Poisson would regain his wits and find you were his wife. A miracle."

Jurissa refrained from comment. "Will you wait?" she asked.

Dominique pursed his lips before shaking his head. "I fear I must wake your husband. It is imperative he come with me immediately."

"Of course." She directed Dominique to the bedroom and left him there.

A scowling and sleepy Philip grumbled down the stairs a short while later, Dominique in his wake. "Yubah," Philip called. "I need food."

"When the *capitaine* orders, 'come!' there is no time to eat," Dominique put in. "I tell you as a friend he was not pleased to find you missing last night."

The *capitaine* must be Jean Lafitte, Jurissa decided. Evidently the pirate captain kept his men under his thumb. She still had difficulty picturing Philip as a pirate. Would he continue as one now that his memory had come back? At the moment he didn't seem to have much choice. Perhaps Captain Lafitte wouldn't allow him to leave the ranks of the pirates even if Philip wished to.

Philip plucked a *petit pain* from the covered basket and turned to Jurissa. "I trust you won't forget me, dear wife. Never fear—I'll be back."

"Not before those British pigs sail away, you won't," Dominique added, earning himself a black look from Philip.

When the two of them rattled off in the cart Dominique drove, Jurissa sighed in relief. A half hour later she was eating rice and peas as though she were starved. When Yubah poured coffee for her, Jurissa glanced from the cup to Yubah.

"Nothing of Miss Tiana's in this, I trust?"

Yubah grinned and shook her head.

Tiana, with Yubah's assistance, had saved her from Philip for one night and she was grateful. But what about the nights to come? Jurissa wondered. Yubah couldn't go on feeding Philip sleeping potions without him suspecting something was wrong. At present, though, she was too tired to worry about the future.

To make up for her sleepless night, Jurissa napped in Guy's room until early afternoon, when a man's voice from downstairs woke her. She leaped up in alarm. Had Philip returned so soon? Easing the door open, she listened.

"You must hear me out." Jurissa recognized Nicolas LeMoine's voice and relaxed.

"Don't have to do nothing you say." Yubah's tone was cool.

"Aren't you even glad to see me?" Nicolas demanded.

"Well, I guess I be glad you ain't dead from fighting in the war."

"Waiting in that *fosse*, that ditch, for the redcoats to charge us, that's when I understood I'd made a terrible mistake." Nicolas paused but Yubah didn't comment. "I knew that the next minute I might die. And what did I regret? You. I regretted turning away from you. I've come to understand you're the only woman for me. You're the woman I want."

"I don't hear you saying I be your woman back when I be needing *you*."

"Ah, Yubah, I was wrong, I admit it. Can you ever forgive me? I know none of it was your fault. I knew it wasn't then. A man who owns you can do what he likes; it's not right but it's so and I know it is, but it hurt me there'd been another man for you, even though you didn't choose him. I turned against you, I admit it, and I'm sorry."

"Seem like it be a waste of time for a free man like you to come around here 'cause I still belongs to Massa Philip."

"I'll challenge him if he forces you again," Nicolas declared angrily.

"No, don't you be talking like that." Yubah's voice rose. "Don't mess with him; he be the devil."

"I'd face him for you. *Mon Dieu*, girl, what must I do to convince you I love you?"

There was a silence. Jurissa, ashamed of eavesdropping, told herself she ought to shut the door. Now that Nicolas had declared himself, though, she had to know what Yubah would say in return. The silence lasted so long Jurissa finally realized that Nicolas must be trying to convince Yubah with his kisses, and Yubah must be letting herself be convinced. As she'd suspected all along, Yubah really did love Nicolas.

Jurissa smiled. Nothing was sweeter than being in the arms of a man you loved. Her smile faded as she remembered her own circumstances. What was worse than being forced to accept the caresses of a man you could never love?

When Nicolas left, Jurissa came downstairs. Yubah was dreamily dribbling rice into a simmering soup pot.

"Did I hear Nicolas just now?" Jurissa asked.

Yubah swung around. "Oh, Miss Jurissa, he say he be wanting to marry me; don't matter 'bout Guy." Shadows darkened her amber eyes. "Trouble is, Massa Philip ain't gonna let me. He ain't never gonna let me."

Jurissa couldn't deny it. Philip would never permit a slave of his to marry a free man of color. "I wish I could help," she said. "As it stands, I'm afraid I can't even help myself."

"Ain't your fault he come back from the dead like some bad-spell voodoo. I tell Nicolas to stay away from Massa Philip and I pray he do. Only he stubborn, Nicolas; I be feared he don't listen."

Philip didn't come back that night. The next morning, Jurissa decided she wasn't going to huddle in the house waiting; she was going about her business as though the threat of his return didn't hang over her. Dressing in the black nursing gown, she drove to the Creole hospital.

Many of the wounded had been discharged to the care of their families. There were few patients left to watch over.

"You must go home," Madame Lavalle insisted. "You're very pale. I do believe you're sickening for something."

Jurissa couldn't bring herself to tell Madame Lavalle about Philip's miraculous return. Sooner or later all New Orleans would know, she supposed, but not through her telling.

"I'll stay on for a bit," she said. "I really feel quite well. I haven't heard any gunfire today. Is the war truly over?"

"Those British haven't left. I heard our troops killed thousands of them in the big battle but still they don't sail for home. General Jackson, it's said, claims the battle won and the war over, but he maintains his troops and stays vigilant and insists he'll do so until the enemy packs up and vanishes from our shores."

As long as the British ships remained at anchor, Philip would be forced to stay with Captain Lafitte — or so Dominique You had said. Could she believe him? Jurissa hoped so.

After an hour she realized there wasn't enough to keep her busy, and she was preparing to go home when Anton walked into the hospital.

"I hoped you might be here today," he said. "I wanted to see you alone." He glanced around.

"I'm just leaving."

"Is there a place inside here where we might speak privately? I hesitate to compromise you in your husband's eyes by being seen in public with you."

Jurissa smiled without humor. "Especially since he believes I'm your *placee*."

"*Nom de Dieu!*"

"He doesn't believe I could have acquired the house any other way. I dare not tell him I made enough money to buy it myself." As she spoke she led Anton into what had once been the pantry but now was storage for medical supplies. The small room reminded her of being in Lavalle's storeroom with Leon the night of the ball. She sighed. When would she see Leon again? Never?

"Jurissa, I apologize for not taking your antipathy to Monsieur Winterton seriously enough. Since I have met him, it is now clear to me he's no gentleman."

"I believe he came from a good family in Virginia."

"His family is not in question. If ever you need protection from him, you must notify me immediately."

What could Anton do? Challenge Philip to a duel? What a scandal that would be. And how terrible if Anton was killed. No, she couldn't run to Anton for help.

"Thank you," she said. "I don't believe that will be necessary."

"Jurissa—" He paused and took her hands in his. "It pains me to see you with him when I know you're afraid."

"There's nothing you can do." She drew away her hands. "I did wonder why you returned to my house yesterday after we said good-bye at your office."

"I came back partly because I'd forgotten to give you the news about Dindon. As you know, the British quartered troops there. Our cannon shelled their position from both land and water, and the house itself is ruined, the outbuildings burned, the fields trampled."

"Madame du Motier?" Jurissa whispered fearfully.

"It seems the British had the decency to move the women out before the shelling began. She and most of the house servants are aboard the British flagship."

Shocked at first, Jurissa pictured Leon's mother, undismayed by her forced visit to the ship, berating her reluctant hosts for their barbaric treatment of her, and she smiled a little. Madame, she had no doubt, had made herself mistress of the situation.

"I've worried about her," she said. "I'm glad she's safe. And, of course, Louise-Marie is safe with her parents. But what about your *cousine*? Where is he? Dindon was his life."

"Leon's living in an old cottage of his father's. Temporarily, of course."

Memories flooded over Jurissa. The terrible quarrel she'd had with Leon over that cottage where he'd expected her to move. Their lovemaking later. Those wonderful, passionate caresses she'd never experience with any other man. It had been so long ago.

"Don't look so sad," Anton said. "Houses can be rebuilt."

"Yes, of course. I'm happy all the du Motiers survived Dindon's destruction. But your *cousine* loved Dindon beyond reason. Something rebuilt is never the same as the original."

Anton shrugged. "War is destructive. *Cousine* Leon should have anticipated such a blow. He'll do what he has to, like the rest of us."

It wouldn't be easy for Leon, Jurissa told herself. Dindon was gone, destroyed. What happened to a man when he lost everything that was important to him?

"I had another reason for returning yesterday," Anton said. "I'd thought of a way to transfer ownership of your house so it would seem you didn't own it. Unfortunately, I arrived too late. I'm sorry I didn't realize the urgency." He shook his head. "To think any man could boast of being a pirate."

How like Anton to be too late. Was it because he was an attorney or was it just his nature to be methodical and uninclined to act swiftly? In any case she couldn't berate him; he was who he was.

"I wish there was more I could do for you." Anton leaned toward her.

Did he mean to kiss her? That would never do. She stepped back and said firmly, "We really must leave this room. Though I've told no one but you, everyone will soon know my husband has come back from the dead. Neither of us can afford scandal."

Slowly he nodded, his gaze fixed on her face. When he stepped aside she thought it was to allow her to precede him, but as she eased past, he caught her arm. "How can I give you up?" he muttered.

"Anton—"

He pulled her closer. "That animal doesn't deserve you. I can't stand the thought of you living with such a man." Before she could protest, he kissed her.

As before, the pressure of his lips against hers wasn't unpleasant. She didn't want Anton to kiss her but she didn't struggle, knowing he'd soon release her. Nor did she respond.

The sound of the door opening startled them into jerking apart.

"Oh!" Madame Lavalle's eyes were round with astonishment. "I beg your pardon. I didn't mean to interrupt—"

"You haven't," Jurissa said when it became clear

that Anton, the eloquent attorney, had nothing to say. "We were just leaving." She knew the words were idiotic but they were as good as any others since there was no reasonable excuse for her being in the supply closet with Anton.

She walked past Madame Lavalle, who now wore a knowing smirk, hearing Anton's boots behind her. Her reputation wasn't ruined, not yet. An engagement announcement between Anton and herself would save it. But, of course, that was impossible. After viewing the scene in the closet, and after hearing about Philip's return, she'd label Jurissa a scarlet woman.

Anton, on the other hand, wouldn't be an outcast. Men never seemed to be at fault in such cases. She'd been a fool to take him into the closet.

But what did it matter? Once Philip's connection with the pirates was known, the Creoles would have nothing to do with him socially so what difference did it make what they thought of her?

"I'm sorry," Anton said, catching up to her by the door. "I wouldn't for the world have anyone think you—"

"It's all right, Anton. Don't be upset."

He followed her to her cabriolet, apologizing all the way, and she knew he stood staring after her when she drove off. Even if she wanted Anton, there was no way for them to be together.

She hoped he'd have the sense to stay away from her and from Philip. Nothing good would come of any further meetings, and she dreaded to think of the terrible consequences that might result from a quarrel between Anton and Philip.

When she arrived home, Philip hadn't come back,

nor did he return the next day or the next week. As January neared the end, Jurissa grew brave enough to visit her son, carefully making the occasion seem no more than a trip to the bakery in case somebody Philip knew might notice.

Guy was in the kitchen kneading dough.

"Since we can't keep him out," we decided to teach him to bake," Tiana said.

The two free women of color, whom Tiana had hired to help, laughed. "He does fine," one said, "when he remembers to wash his hands first."

Guy took his mother into the courtyard to show her his new kitten, all black with bright green eyes. La Belle, he called her because, he said, she was pretty. While Jurissa sat on the white-painted iron bench, Guy dangled the whistle on the thong for Belle to play with and, when the kitten tired and curled up to sleep in Jurissa's lap, he fingered the whistle himself, picking at the plug.

"Won't make noise," he said, speaking entirely in French. "Silas broke it."

"I asked Silas to fix the whistle so you couldn't blow it," she said. "There's a very important reason. Shall I tell you?"

He nodded and climbed up to sit beside her. She put her arm around his shoulders and he leaned against her, petting the kitten.

"The whistle is very old. It comes from a country far, far away. A black man brought it here when he came to New Orleans. Now he's old, too. An old black man named Lono who lives in the swamp."

"With alligators?"

She nodded. "The whistle belonged to Lono but a long time ago he gave it to a man who was his friend. He told the man to blow the whistle if he ever needed help and Lono would come."

Guy looked down at the whistle, then up at her. "My whistle."

"Yes. You have the whistle now. But Lono doesn't know you do. And if he hears it blow, he'll think someone's in trouble and he'll come. Now the swamp is a long way off and Lono is a very old man. He's all hunched over he's so old. Do you think you should bring him out of his swamp just because you want to blow the whistle?"

Guy thought this over. "Can I see Lono?"

"Maybe sometime. But not by blowing the whistle. It's wrong to make Lono come if you don't need help." She hugged Guy to her. "You're my good boy."

"Belle come home with me?" he asked. "Want to show her to *Maman* Yubah."

"You have to stay here a while longer. You and La Belle. Stay with Tiana."

His lip quivered. "Want to go home with you. Want to see *Maman* Yubah."

Jurissa fought her own tears. Lifting the sleeping kitten carefully, she laid it on the bench and slid Guy onto her lap, her arms around him. "Listen," she said. "When I come back to see you the next time, we'll have a party, just you and me and maybe Belle. We'll serve hot chocolate and the rolls you've baked that day. So you have to work hard and learn to be a good baker. With clean hands, because Mama doesn't want to eat dirty rolls."

He pulled away from her to show her his hands.

"Cleaner than that," she said. "You have to wash them."

"Belle washes like this." He licked his grubby palm

with his tongue.

"But you're not a kitten. People wash with water."

"Meow," he said, grinning at her. "Meow, meow." He climbed off her lap, got down on all fours and crawled over the bricks. "Meow!"

Jurissa raised her eyebrows, wanting to laugh but knowing better than to encourage him. Inspiration struck her. "Kittens grow up to be cats, they don't grow up to be *chevaliers*. Only little boys grow up to be *chevaliers*."

Guy stood up. *"Moi chevalier,"* he announced, prancing around on an imaginary horse. "Me. Me!"

He looked so much like Leon that her heart twisted. Nothing must ever hurt Guy. He must have the chance to grow up and ride as straight and proud as his father.


On the twenty-third of January the citizens of New Orleans celebrated General Jackson's victory with Creole enthusiasm. In the Place d'Armes an arch of triumph curved imposingly atop Corinthian columns. Jurissa, with Yubah and Silas—she hadn't dared bring Guy although she longed to—watched and cheered with the rest of the crowd as the general marched down the carpeted path.

Two pretty girls, representing Justice and Liberty, one Creole, one *Americain,* stood on pedestals on either side of the arch. Other beauties graced pedestals between the arch and St. Louis Cathedral, each holding the name of a state or a territory. Jackson marched between them to the arch, where he stopped. Cannon salvos and cheers rang out as Justice and Liberty crowned him with the laurel wreaths of a victorious hero.

Abbe Dubourg, standing at the entrance to the cathedral, welcomed the general, and they entered the church to celebrate a High Mass. Because of the crowd, Jurissa couldn't even get near the church, much less inside, but she stood outside and made her own prayers. Thank God the war was over and those she loved were still alive.

She expected Philip that evening or the next day but he didn't come. On the twenty-sixth, she decided she must take steps to assure Guy an untroubled future and the only way to do that was to talk to Leon.

While she didn't know exactly where his father's cottage was, she remembered him saying it was near the rue des Ramparts. She ought to be able to find the cottage, and Leon, without much trouble.

What would he say when she told him they had a son?

## Chapter Nineteen

Jurissa set out alone in the rain for the rue des Ramparts, telling Yubah she meant to visit a friend. Surely it was better to leave Yubah and Silas at the house in case Philip returned and better to keep the truth from Yubah so she wouldn't be forced to lie to Philip.

It isn't because I want to be alone with Leon, Jurissa assured herself. Or was it? She shook her head. No, she and Leon must not indulge themselves in any passionate interludes. Would not. She was going to him only because of Guy.

Leon had to be heartsick over losing Dindon. She found no satisfaction in the fact retribution had overtaken him. He'd done what he felt he had to, not what he'd wanted to. Though she'd suffered because of his decision, so had he.

The rue des Ramparts was a mass of mud, and when she turned into the narrow unnamed dirt lane leading off it, the wheels sank so deeply into the mire her horse had to struggle to pull the cabriolet at even a slow walk. The chill and gloomy day with its incessant drizzle depressed her spirits. The thought of seeing Leon was the only brightness to focus on.

Noticing a peaked-roof cottage to the right, she tried to decide if it was Leon's. No smoke came from the single chimney—surely he would have a fire on this cold day. He must have a servant with him—or did he? The du Motier slaves had been taken captive by the British. What had happened to them when Madame was whisked off to the British flagship? Anton had said some of the house servants went with her. What of the others and of the field slaves?

Perhaps Leon wasn't at home. Or maybe this wasn't the right cottage. There was no way to find out except to drive in and ask. Her gray gelding picked up his ears as she directed him into the cottage yard. As she halted him, he whickered, and a horse answered from the shed behind the cottage.

Jurissa waited a moment but no one came to the door. Pulling her blue wool shawl over her head and shoulders, she climbed to the muddy ground and made her way toward the shed. One glance at the horse and she'd know whether or not she was at the right place.

When she looked in, the black stallion inside snorted and shifted, restless, watching her. Tigre, beyond doubt. Moments later, Jurissa, her slippers wet and heavy with mud, knocked on the cottage door. Her heart quickened as she waited, picturing Leon's delighted surprise when he saw her. "*Cherie*," he'd say, "it's been so long." He'd hold out his hands and take hers, he'd draw her inside. And then—

Then she'd tell him about Guy. She must remember that that was her purpose in coming here. Her only purpose.

He didn't respond to her knock. She knocked

louder. No one came to the door. He must be here—Tigre was in the shed. Was he sleeping? Jurissa hesitated. She *must* see him; she'd have to wake him. Making a fist, she thumped on the door, creating enough noise, she felt, to rouse the soundest sleeper.

Nothing happened.

Hesitantly, she tried the door. It opened under her hand. Pushing it ajar, she poked her head inside.

"Leon?" she called tentatively.

There was no answer.

Jurissa eased all the way in. "Are you here, Leon?"

A glance around the sparsely furnished main room showed it was uninhabited. Ashes on the hearth smelled damp. The room had a musty, unused odor. The wide-brimmed black hat of Beale's Volunteers lay on a table. Unpolished black boots stood beside the cold hearth. Apprehension gripped her.

"Leon!" she cried. "Leon!"

Was that a groan? Jurissa hurried across to a curtained door leading off the main room, pushed the curtain aside, and walked into a small bedroom.

"Oh my God," she whispered.

Leon was sprawled naked across the bed, one arm hanging off the side, his fingers trailing on the floor beside a crumpled blanket. Several days' growth of beard darkened his face. His eyes were closed. The fetid odor of illness permeated the room.

She flew to the bed and put a hand to his forehead. Burning hot. The injury to his head seemed healed but a suppurating wound on his right thigh drained green pus. He desperately needed help. What should she do first?

Warmth. She straightened him on the bed as best she could. Searching the room, she found another blanket on a shelf and covered him with it, tucking it around him. She added the blanket from the floor, dirty as it was. He groaned and opened his eyes momentarily but didn't seem to see her. She bent and brushed her lips against his before rushing into the main room to lay a fire on the hearth with sticks and small logs, which she found in a cubicle.

Once she was certain the fire had taken, she dashed out to her cabriolet. Much as she hated to leave Leon, he needed more than she could give him. She urged the gray on but the mire hampered the horse, and she thought they'd never get through to the main streets, to Tiana's.

Nicolas was with his sister and listened as Jurissa breathlessly explained what had happened.

"I can't stay with him. What if Philip found me there? Oh, Tiana, will you help him? He mustn't die!"

"I cured him once, I guess I can again." Tiana's calm voice eased Jurissa's anxiety.

Tiana turned to Nicolas. "Here's what you'll have to do," she said.

"Me?" He looked astonished. "I'm no doctor."

"Time you learned something beside sticking other men with *epees*," Tiana said tartly. "He needs someone to stay there and take care of him. I'm busy, you're not. You told me yourself your unit has disbanded and it will be a month before you begin teaching again. Any man who can thrust a sword into another man certainly isn't one to flinch from a wound. You'll do fine."

Jurissa had her doubts but felt it best not to let Nicolas know she feared he wasn't the right person to care for Leon. Nicolas was someone and right now

Leon had no one. Nicolas would report to Tiana if anything went wrong, and Jurissa trusted Tiana above anyone she knew.

"I'll give you what you need," Tiana told Nicolas, "and instruct you in the proper use of each potion. You'll have to make certain he eats—soup at first. And keep the bed clean—I'll send blankets along. Don't forget to feed the horse. When Monsieur de Motier improves, make him use that leg—maybe a bit of fencing practice. And—"

"Enough!" Nicolas spread his hands. "I'll do it. I'll never hear the last of it if I don't. But, please, not all the details at once."

"I can't tell you how grateful I am, Nicolas," Jurissa said.

He smiled at her. "What are friends for?"

"I'll send food to the cottage." she told him. "And firewood. There wasn't much."

"Maybe Yubah could bring it," he suggested.

She smiled in return. "If I can, I'll make certain to send her."

It went against every instinct Jurissa possessed to return home instead of hurrying back to Leon. But she didn't dare risk Philip coming in search of her. She shuddered to think of what might happen if he found her with Leon while Leon lay helpless, unable to defend himself.

To her relief, Philip hadn't yet come back to the house. She set Silas to loading their supply cart with firewood while she and Yubah piled on sheets, blankets, and food.

"You both go," she said after giving Silas directions. "Be sure and stop at the bakery on the way back to bring fresh bread for dinner and buy fish if you can find any for sale because that's what I'll say I sent you after if it comes to that."

No excuse was necessary. Philip didn't come. The next day went by without him. The following day, Silas brought news that the British ships had weighed anchor and sailed away after sending a small boat ashore with a Creole woman and her servants. Several of Captain Lafitte's barques, he'd been told, were escorting the ships from the Gulf to make certain they left.

Jurissa hoped the woman was Leon's mother. She prayed Philip was aboard one of the pirate ships and, apparently he was, because February arrived without him appearing. In the second week, Yubah came back from a visit to the cottage and gave Jurissa the most encouraging report yet on Leon's condition.

"Massa Leon, he be fencing with Nicolas. Nicolas, he say Massa Leon be good even with his sore leg. Massa Leon, he stop me when I be leaving. He say to tell you he owe you his life twice over and he wish he be saying so in person."

"You mean he wants me to come and see him? You told him about my husband's return, didn't you?"

"I tell him last week, just like you say. So he ask me today 'bout Massa Philip and I say he ain't come back. You don't be knowing when he do."

Jurissa felt her pulses race. Dare she visit Leon? She longed so to see him again, to see with her own eyes he was recovering.

"Massa Leon, he know 'bout Nicolas and me," Yubah went on. "He tell us to take what happiness we can." Tears filled her eyes. "I be remembering what happen to you, 'bout Guy, and I knows if Guy truly was my baby, Massa Philip would own him just like he does me. Ain't gonna have that happen, so Nicolas and me, we can't never be happy."

Jurissa put her arm around Yubah.

"Nicolas, he say he coming to ask Massa Philip 'bout marrying me. Nothing I be saying make him change his mind. I just knows Massa Philip gonna kill him." She buried her face in Jurissa's shoulder and sobbed.

Yubah's unhappiness made up Jurissa's mind. Leon wanted to see her. Being with him would be wonderful beyond anything she could imagine. Once Philip returned she'd never dare visit Leon, under any circumstances. Why shouldn't *she* take what happiness she could, while she could?

The sun was out, birds sang, the breeze spoke of spring. It was a beautiful day, made even more marvelous by her destination, Jurissa thought, as she drove the cabriolet over to Tiana's. She wore a riding gown of blue percale with a darker blue spencer and matching jockey cap because she meant to borrow the elderly chestnut mare Tiana rarely rode.

Guy didn't ask about Yubah this time. Had he come to accept Jurissa as his real *maman*? She feared so. He knew she was the one who made the rules, the one he looked to for answers. If only this didn't place him in jeopardy. She'd have to make certain it didn't.

Guy was delighted to help Tiana and Jurissa put the side saddle on Yvette, thrilled to think his *maman* would be on horseback just like his *chevalier*. He was ecstatic when she led him around the courtyard on Yvette's back before she mounted.

The chestnut stepped out briskly, enjoying the fine

weather as much as Jurissa. The roads were dry, and they were soon at the cottage. Tigre, cropping new grass in the back yard, greeted the mare with enthusiasm, and the chestnut behaved as if she were a colt again. Jurissa tethered her and went to the door, which stood open. There was no sign of either Nicolas or Leon inside.

Recalling what Yubah had said about the fencing, Jurissa came back outside and circled the house. In a small grove of oaks to the far side of the house, she saw them. Walking quickly, she made her way toward the trees.

Neither man saw her, so involved were they with the rapiers. She caught her breath as she saw the *epees* were without protective shields over the points. If she didn't know better, she could imagine Nicolas and Leon were fighting a duel in earnest.

Advance, thrust, retreat. Thrust, parry, feint, thrust, circle. She stood entranced, caught up in the graceful rhythm of their fencing. Leon, she thought, was well nigh the equal of Nicolas in spite of his slight limp.

Leon, circling, caught a glimpse of her and broke stride. "Enough," he called to Nicolas, "we have company." He tossed Nicolas the rapier, hilt first, and hurried toward Jurissa.

She longed to hold out her arms to him, to feel the strength of his body pressed against hers. Instead, she didn't move. He reached for her hands but she shook her head slightly and his arms dropped.

"I can't tell you how glad I am to see you," he said, his gaze warming her more than the sun. "How lovely you look. I don't believe I've ever before seen you in a riding costume."

"I'm exercising Tiana's mare. It's good to see how you've improved, Leon."

"I'm quite well. Nicolas is needed now only to teach me the finer points of fencing. He's a true master."

Glancing toward where she'd last seen Nicolas, Jurissa noticed he'd disappeared. Turning her head, she saw he was walking away.

Following her gaze, Leon smiled. "He's also a gentleman." He captured her hands, ignoring her attempt to stop him, and gazed into her eyes. "Ah, *cherie*, you saved me in spite of myself. When I heard Dindon was gone—" He didn't continue. "Yubah told me about Winterton's return. It seems unbelieveable. The man leads a charmed life. I suppose it's asking too much to hope his brush with death changed him for the better."

Had Leon tossed Philip over the rail of the *Yarmouth?* No, she wouldn't entertain such a thought. "So far I haven't seen much of him," she admitted. "He's been gone for almost a month."

Leon's eyes darkened. "If he hurts you I'll kill him."

"You mustn't say such a thing. He's my husband just as Louise-Marie is your wife."

Leon's scowl told her she hadn't convinced him. The last thing she wanted was for Leon to approach Philip. She sought a change of subject. "I heard a Creole woman was set ashore before the British sailed and I hoped it was your mother."

"I believe the British were glad to be rid of *Maman*. She does speak her mind no matter what the circumstances. She's well and staying with Dr. Marchand, an old friend and admirer of hers. Marchand and his sister have taken in our field hands and house servants, too. I'm welcome there but I wanted to be alone for the time being, here at the cottage."

"And Louise-Marie, is she well?"

"She prefers to remain with her parents at present. I received an invitation from them to stay there until—" He paused and shook his head.

He avoided speaking of Dindon. Jurissa took a deep breath and asked bluntly. "Will you rebuild Dindon?"

Leon smiled wryly. "How do I manage to live without you? I've been wallowing in self-pity, haven't I? And you won't let me go on doing it." He squeezed her hands. "Since I know you won't desist until I tell you, I suppose I must. I've had time to think while I was laid up here and I've decided to— no, on second thought I won't tell you, I'll show you. What luck you didn't bring the cabriolet today. I'll saddle Tigre and we'll ride there."

"Ride where?"

"I want it to be a surprise. Tell me you'll come with me."

She'd promised herself this day. Her day with Leon. Quite probably the last time they'd ever be together. A bright memory to carry into the darkness that would be her life with Philip.

Throwing caution to the winds, she said, "Why not?"

He saddled Tigre and, after assisting her onto the chestnut, mounted and led the way, heading north, up the Bayou Road toward Lake Pontchartrain. His face was thinner. He'd lost weight during his illness, but he was still the most handsome man she'd ever seen, and she couldn't get enough of looking at him.

She hadn't yet told him about Guy and she decided to let him show her his surprise before she sprang her own. In the meantime, what harm could there be in pretending she and Leon were the only two people in existence and that neither of them had a care in the world?

"If the weather continues this warm, we'll have mosquito bites by March," Leon said, dropping back to ride with her.

"I never dreamed a true Creole would be bothered by mosquito bites!"

He grinned at her. "You haven't learned everything about us."

She slanted a gaze at him. "I know *one* of you quite well."

"You refer, of course, to me."

She raised an eyebrow. "I believe one trait I've noticed is arrogance."

"You wound me. I'm the most humble of men."

Jurissa laughed. "I've yet to meet a humble Creole and certainly you're not!"

"I insist on being humble!"

"You'll have to find someone to give you lessons because it will never come naturally to you."

"You mean I can learn it, like fencing?"

"I doubt that. As far as fencing goes, you didn't look to me as though you needed any lessons. You were Nicolas's equal."

"Not quite. My timing's off. I need practice. He's good, very good. He tells me he wants to marry Yubah. They're obviously in love."

So much for pretending, Jurissa thought sadly. The real world always intruded. "Yubah knows Philip will never permit her to marry a free man of color.

She and Nicolas have no chance for happiness together."

His gaze sought hers. Like us, his brown eyes told her. No chance.

The road narrowed to follow the Bayou St. John, becoming a trail they rode along single file, Leon in the lead, the bayou to their left, the swamp to the right. A damp odor of decay tinged the breeze that whispered through the gray moss on the cypress trees.

At last they came to Fort St. John at the mouth of and across the bayou. Beyond, the sun glittered on the blue water of Lake Pontchartrain. Leon swept his arm to the right. "Here," he said.

"I see the lake," she told him. "I see the fort, I see the swamps."

"The swamps hide the higher ground." He turned Tigre and walked the horse east along the lake shore.

She trailed him along the shore but hesitated when he finally plunged into the swamp. After a moment, she shrugged and followed. Wherever he was taking her, she'd be safe with Leon. She breathed easier when she saw they were on a rough path until the thought came to her that it might well have been made by animals. Branches caught at her clothes, and she had to duck to avoid low-lying limbs. Just when she thought she couldn't take another moment of the swamp, her horse, on Tigre's heels, broke into the open. She pulled up beside Leon.

Dry land stretched out in front of her. Wild, uncultivated land. Far beyond she could see the deep green of the swamps.

"I'll have the field servants build quarters for themselves first," Leon said. "They'll have a place to live, then, while they ready the ground for planting."

She had the feeling she'd missed the beginning. Was Leon saying he meant to start another plantation here?

"This is du Motier land," Leon said, "won by my grandfather years ago in a wager. It's never been cultivated. Until now."

She gazed at the wild growth, at the surrounding swamps, at the lack of houses, of any sign of civilization. "I imagine this is what Louisiana must have looked like when the French first landed here," she said.

He smiled at her. "I knew you'd understand." Dismounting, he held up his arms to her. She fell into them, and he slid her down his body until her feet touched the ground, then let her go.

Jurissa tried to ignore the desire he'd ignited inside her as she listened to him explain his plans.

"I'll situate the house there—" He pointed to the highest ground. "To face the lake. We'll cut through the swamp and drain the wet land. I intend to name the plantation Frere."

Brother. For his dead brother, who'd been expunged from the family records. For Denis.

"Well, what do you think?" he asked.

"It's a wonderful plan. To be the first to cultivate this land, to make the plantation a permanent reminder of your brother—Leon, how marvelous. But what of Dindon?"

"Dindon is finished. I can't go back, only forward. The soil here is good for both cane and cotton. Of course it takes time for money to start coming in with new plantings. With luck those hogsheads of cured sugar and the cotton bales stored in that Boston warehouse will be shipped across the Atlantic soon. Even then, I won't have enough to build the main house for a while."

"Where will you live?"

"In the cottage for the time being. *Maman* and Louise-Marie are happy enough where they are. Eventually I'll have to find a house in town, I suppose, though I hate to spend money on that when I'll need it here."

"Surely your wife will want to be with you."

His smiled was one-sided. "In the cottage? Can you see Louise-Marie there?"

"I don't know her well enough."

"She can't even understand how *I* can bear to live in such 'meager circumstances' as she calls them. That I might expect her to is beyond consideration entirely." He caught Jurissa's hand and drew her to him. Looking into her eyes, he said, "You'd live there with me, if things were different, if there were no Louise-Marie, no Winterton. Yes, you'd live there with me, I know you would."

"If it were possible, I'd live anywhere with you," she told him.

The warmth in his eyes fired her. She had to touch him, she couldn't help herself. Reaching her hand to his face, she trailed her fingers along his cheek. He turned his face so his lips brushed her palm.

"Your mustache tickles," she whispered, so breathless she could hardly speak.

"You've told me before. I thought I'd never hear you tell me again." His voice was hoarse with repressed desire as he leaned closer and closer.

"Leon—"

He swept her into his arms, his kiss cutting off her

words and the moment his mouth was on hers, she lost all sense of what she'd meant to say. His lips, warm and vital, carried a more important message. An urgent message of love and passion, of long-denied need. A message she answered by parting her own lips in welcome.

How wonderfully familiar to feel the strength of his body pressed against hers. How beautiful and right. She would never leave his arms. She would stay within them forever while he held her and loved her.

Jurissa was his woman; she had been from the beginning. Leon lifted his lips from hers long enough to jerk the jockey hat from her head and bury his fingers in her glorious hair. His, all of her, from head to foot. He kissed her closed eyes, her nose, trailed kisses along her cheek to the waiting eagerness of her lips.

She told him with her kisses, with her sighs that she wanted him as much as he wanted her. Countless nights he'd dreamed of caressing her beautiful body only to come achingly awake knowing he'd lost her. Now she was here; she was in his arms. No other woman would ever satisfy him.

"*Cherie*," he murmured. "Only you."

She trembled as his fingers unbuttoned the short jacket she wore and found their way to her breast. He had a desperate need to touch every inch of her, to cover her with kisses. He could never have enough of her. There'd never be enough time in all eternity to tire of making love to her.

Nothing else mattered when he was with her. She loved him, she understood him. With her he reached heights he'd never imagined existed until they'd met. He loved her as he'd never loved another. He'd love her until the day he died.

A memory surfaced and he drew away from her to cradle her in one arm while he removed her left glove. He brought her bared fingers, one at a time to his mouth, tasting them, her gasping breaths fueling his passion. Mastering his urgency, he removed the other glove, deliberately tickling her palm with his mustache as he kissed her fingers.

"Leon," she breathed. "Oh, Leon." She stroked his hair, his nape, molding herself to him until he thought he'd lose all control.

He took off her jacket and pulled her gown, then her chemise, down over her shoulders until her breasts were free. Such lovely white breasts, with pink tips like flowers. Ah, the taste of her was like nothing else in the world. More heady than the finest brandy, sweeter than honey. She moaned, arching against him.

He had to have her, he would have her, nothing could stop him, not the devil himself.

Cupping the enticing rounds of her derriere, he lifted and pressed her against his aching need. She wriggled her hips, showing him she felt the same desperate urgency. Now! It had to be now!

"Monsieur du Motier!" The cry was faint, filtered through the swamp from the lake. "Halloo!"

With a long, shuddering sigh, Leon let her go. He recognized Nicolas's voice. Why would Nicolas be calling him?

Jurissa stepped back, pulling up her chemise and gown and smoothing her hair. "Who is it?" she whispered.

"Nicolas. I don't know what he wants."

"He must know where to find you if he's come this far."

"I showed him this place, yes. But why he's come after me—"

Fear darkened Jurissa's green eyes. She hastily donned her spencer and hat and smoothed on her gloves. "Leon, I'm afraid."

He put an arm around her but she edged away.

"I shouldn't have come here with you," she said. "It's wrong."

"*Mon Dieu*, how can you say that when it's the first right thing I've done in years? I don't live without you, *cherie*, I merely exist."

She bit her lip. "I understand. But we both know we can't be together."

"Monsieur du Motier!" Nicolas was closer.

"I'm here!" Leon called to him.

"Help me onto my horse," Jurissa said.

He did, then mounted Tigre and headed for the swamp path to the lake shore.

They met Nicolas halfway.

"I went to my sister's," he said without preamble. "Silas came to her with a warning. He has friends who work at the docks and one of them sent word that Monsieur Winterton was on his way home."

## Chapter Twenty

Tiana had loaded the cabriolet with bakery goods, fresh fish, and two live, trussed-up chickens by the time Jurissa arrived there, flushed and overheated from her frantic rush to get back. She slid off the lathered mare and, after hurried thanks to Tiana, climbed into the cabriolet and set off for home. It wasn't until she reached her gate when she realized that, in her desperation to reach home before Philip, she'd forgotten all about revealing her own secret to Leon. She hadn't told him Guy was his son. Dear God, when would she get another chance now that Philip had returned?

Jurissa hurried to change from her riding dress, lest Philip think it odd she wore riding clothes to drive a cabriolet. Putting on a long-sleeved, high-necked gown of tobacco brown she'd never cared for, she asked Yubah to do up her hair. At her bidding, Yubah twisted it into a severe chignon, leaving no curls to fall over the forehead, as was the style.

The gown was not becoming but Jurissa couldn't contain her worry. "Do you think I look plain enough?" she asked Yubah.

"Miss Jurissa, truth be you never be looking plain. You too pretty."

"Right now I wish I were the ugliest woman in New Orleans. If I were, he wouldn't—" She bit her lip and stopped.

Yubah nodded, understanding what wasn't said. "I got some of Miss Tiana's potion left. Gonna put it in Massa Philip's food again. Might be it do help."

When Philip finally did arrive, it was dark and he wasn't hungry. He didn't need to bang on the gate for admission. His farewells to the friends who'd driven him home were loud enough to be heard not only by Silas, but inside the house and, Jurissa thought, all along the block as well. Philip entered with an uneven stride, the fumes of rum preceding him. Her heart sank. She feared him more when he was drunk than she did sober.

He shouted for coffee but by the time Yubah brought a cup to him, he was snoring in Jurissa's favorite cane-seated rocking chair. He slept on into the night until Jurissa finally sent the drowsy Yubah to bed. She didn't dare go to bed herself; neither did she care to stay in the sitting room watching Philip sleep. While he'd been away, she'd considered getting a lock for her bedroom door but, in the end, had not. A lock wouldn't deter Philip, who'd more than likely kick down the door or order Silas to.

After turning the lamp low in the sitting room, Jurissa settled into a chair in the dining room and, laying her arms on the table, put her head down and drowsed, starting awake at the slightest sound. It was well after midnight when she roused to hear the creaking of the rocker. She raised her head and listened. Philip was muttering. She couldn't make out his words.

She rose and, hugging herself, waited.

"Yubah!" he shouted.

Jurissa walked into the sitting room. "I sent her to bed."

Philip stood staring at her for a long moment. "Well, get her up. I want a drink."

"I'll get it for you."

"Rum, that's what I want." He held up a hand. "No, don't tell me, I know, you only have brandy. I brought some bottles of rum, where are they?" He glanced around. "Where did you put my rum?"

"I've seen no rum," Jurissa said. "When you came in you weren't carrying anything."

He shrugged. "Must have drunk them all, my friends and I. Wouldn't the folks back home be surprised at my drinking companions? And afraid of them. Afraid of me." He grinned at Jurissa. "You're afraid of me, too, admit it."

"I never expected to have a pirate for a husband," she said as calmly as she could. "Do you intend to remain one now that you've regained your memory?"

His eyes narrowed. "What I decide to do is my own business. You ask too many questions. When I marry a little rabbit, I expect her to stay a rabbit."

A rabbit? Is that how he saw her? She was certainly no rabbit, frightened of her shadow and with no voice of her own, though to tell the truth his presence did make her feel hunted.

"I'll have a swallow or two of the brandy," he said. "Then we'll go up to bed. I notice you were properly reluctant to retire without me." His bloodshot blue eyes examined her.

Jurissa did her best to keep her face expressionless. She said nothing as she got out a snifter and the brandy bottle.

"Pour it, dear wife," he said. "A full glass, if you please."

She had no idea what Yubah had done with Tiana's sleeping potion. Even if she knew where it was, Jurissa thought, his watchfulness would prevent her from using it. She poured the brandy and handed the nearly full glass to him.

"He didn't come here while I was gone," Philip said, "your lawyer lover. I put the fear of the devil into him, all right."

Jurissa tensed. Did Philip have someone watching the house?

He downed the brandy as though it were water. "You went out quite often, though," he said, setting the glass down. I wonder where? Perhaps, with a little persuasion, you'll tell me later." He smiled thinly and offered her his arm.

Having no choice, she laid her hand on his sleeve and went with him up the stairs. I won't let him frighten me, she told herself firmly. No matter what happens, no matter what he does. But apprehension quivered along her spine.

Yubah had folded down the coverlet as she always did but she hadn't laid Jurissa's nightgown on the pillow. The lamp was turned low. Philip sat on the bed and removed his boots, then his shirt. He glanced up at her. "No need for the bedtime ceremony we had on my homecoming. Get into your nightwear however you please."

Jurissa lifted her nightgown from the drawer. Her back to Philip, she took off her dress and slid the nightgown over her chemise before slipping off her shoes and stockings. Unable to avoid it any longer, she turned to face him. He sprawled on the bed naked, and the sight of him turned her stomach. Quickly, she averted her eyes.

"You've forgotten to take down your hair," he said. "I don't go to bed with a woman unless her hair is loose. A man never knows what may be hidden in those coils."

She had no idea what he was talking about. Slowly, trying to postpone the inevitable as long as she could, Jurissa undid the chignon and began brushing her hair.

"Come here," he ordered, his voice thick.

She set down the brush and walked to the bed, careful not to look directly at him.

"On the bed, little rabbit," he said. "Beside me."

Jurissa obeyed, lying next to, but not touching him, every muscle in her body tense.

"Turn toward me," he ordered. When she did, he said, "Now put your arms around me."

I can't, she thought. I can't stand to touch him.

"Maybe you didn't hear me." As he spoke he reached over and grasped a handful of her hair, pulling her head back until her neck arched painfully. He let go and repeated, "Put your arms around me."

He meant to hurt her each time she didn't do as he asked. Jurissa put out her arms until her hands touched his naked flesh. Her stomach lurched uneasily.

"Kiss me, dear wife."

How could she? It just wasn't possible! It would be awful enough if he forced himself on her, but she'd done her best to convince herself she had no choice, as his wife, except to submit. She didn't look forward to it but she was resigned. Never in a thousand years had she expected him to insist on her touching him, kissing him.

"I can't," she whispered.

"I think you'll find you can." Grasping her hair again, he twisted his fingers in it, pulling until the pain filled her eyes with tears. "This is only the beginning, little rabbit," he told her. "Now kiss me."

Bile rose in her throat as she brought her lips to his, barely brushing them. His hand on the back of her head pushed her lips hard against his. He tasted sour — an unpleasant mixture of rum, brandy, and something worse. When he thrust his tongue into her mouth she gagged.

"The rest of the lesson can wait until the next time," he said hoarsely, reaching down to pull up her nightgown, her chemise. "It's my turn now."

He crouched over her, one knee thrust between her bared thighs. She had no way to stop him, no way to avoid what was to come because it was his right as her husband. She knew he'd hurt her but it wasn't the pain she minded as much as the humiliation and indignity of having to submit to a man she didn't want, a man she didn't love.

As he shoved her legs apart and fumbled between them, she closed her eyes so she wouldn't have to look at him and clenched her teeth against the nausea threatening to overwhelm her. She braced herself against what she knew would be a painful thrusting and the heavy weight of his unwelcome body.

It didn't come.

"What the hell are you doing here?" Philip demanded in French as he shifted from her.

Jurissa's eyes flew open. Freed of Philip, she quickly pulled down her clothes and slid to the far edge of the bed, her startled gaze on the strange woman standing in the bedroom doorway. Who was she? How had she gotten in? Jurissa hadn't heard a sound.

"And where should I be but with you?" the woman countered, also speaking French. "You thought to leave me in Barataria, did you? No one promises Merlette one thing and does another. Why are you with her?"

She was as tall as Philip, her skin bronze, her dark hair an elaborate mass of coils and braids. She was strikingly beautiful. Her gleaming black eyes shifted from Philip to Jurissa and back as her long fingers smoothed her hair.

To Jurissa's surprise, Philip put up his arms as though to shield himself. "Merlette, I told you I was married. She's my wife." His tone was placating.

"You belong to me," Merlette said, flicking something shiny from a coil of her hair. Sharp and shiny.

Jurissa bit back a gasp. The woman had a dagger in her hand!

"Dammit, woman, I told you no more knives!" Philip grabbed for his trousers and slid into them but took care not to move toward Merlette.

"You told me many things, many lies." She smiled, a feral baring of teeth. "I told you one thing, no lie. Betray Merlette and I use the knife, you know where."

Philip reached for his boots.

"Stop!" Merlette warned him. "You think I've forgotten you carry knives in your boot sheaths?"

333

"Will you listen?" Philip sounded desperate. "How can you call yourself betrayed when I married this woman before I ever set foot on Barataria? You knew I'd lost my memory when we met. Now it's come back, you knew that, too. Is it so wrong for a man to bed his wife?"

"I'm the only wife you need." Merlette glared at Jurissa.

Merlette looked as dangerous and as unpredictable as a wild animal. She only faintly resembled the black women Jurissa knew. Even her color was different. Could she be an Indian?

Jurissa moistened her lips, wondering if she should speak. What could she say that might calm this menacing woman?

Philip spread his hands. "Of course you're the only wife I need, the only one I really want. But she—" he nodded toward Jurissa without glancing her way, "has this fine house for us to stay in. Here we have two servants to do the work."

"If she was gone, you would still have the house and the servants, is it not true?"

Philip shook his head. "Do you want to see me hanged? Use your head. Jurissa's lived here three years and has many powerful Creole friends. Do you think they wouldn't notice if she died suddenly or disappeared? I value my life. Be reasonable, Merlette."

"How can I be reasonable when I can't trust you out of my sight?"

"Put the knife away," he said.

"I'm not convinced I shouldn't use it on you."

He grimaced. "I wouldn't be much good to you then."

She tossed her head toward Jurissa. "Or her, either."

She'd never believe me if I told her I don't want Philip, Jurissa thought. It's the truth but she wouldn't accept it.

The woman frightened her. Philip, too, from all indications. She had no doubt Merlette would use the knife if she decided to. It was plain that he felt the same.

A flicker of movement behind Merlette widened Jurissa's eyes. Apparently Merlette sensed something because she started to turn. She was too late. Silas's huge arms wrapped around her, trapping her arms at her sides, rendering the knife useless.

"Drop the knife," Philip ordered. "If you don't, I'll tell Silas to squeeze. He's strong enough to crack your bones like twigs."

Merlette twisted her head for a quick glance at her captor and then, glaring at Philip, let the knife fall from her hand. Yubah's frightened face peered around Silas.

"Come here, Yubah," Philip said. "I want you to search Merlette's hair for more knives before Silas lets her go."

Obviously fearing to touch Merlette, Yubah timidly did as she was ordered. "Ain't no knife, Massa Philip," she reported.

"Bring me the dagger she dropped." After Yubah obeyed, Philip said, "Let her go, Silas, but stay here." The command had returned to his voice.

As soon as Silas's grip relaxed, Merlette, ignoring the rest of them, whirled and stared at the giant black man for long, silent seconds before she turned back to face Philip.

"He's yours?" she asked.

Philip nodded.

Merlette smiled. "I will agree not to use any knives while I stay in this house with you," she said to Philip. "Not on you or on her." She gestured toward Jurissa. "Unlike you, I do not break my word."

Philip glared at her. "You can stay if you behave yourself. But I tell you now, keep away from Silas."

"Whatever would I want with a servant?" Merlette asked, crossing the room to wrap herself around Philip in a manner that reminded Jurissa of the voodoo snake.

"You may help your mistress remove her belongings," Philip told Yubah and Silas. "From now on she'll be using another bedroom. Miss Merlette will be in here with me. And Yubah, you are to obey any orders Miss Merlette chooses to give you. That goes for you too, Silas. Do you understand?"

"Yes sir," they replied in unison.

Silas left after he and Yubah had brought everything of Jurissa's into the bedroom across the hall. Yubah set about putting garments in drawers and in the wardrobe with Jurissa aiding her.

"Where she come from?" Yubah whispered, jerking her head toward the closed door.

"The pirate stronghold in Barataria." Jurissa kept her voice low. "I don't know how she got in the house unless Silas—"

Yubah shook her head. "Her carry-on done woke me up. I creeps down and fetches Silas. He don't know she here till then. He say must be she somehow climb over the wall."

Jurissa wouldn't put anything past Merlette. She wondered if Philip had actually gone through a marriage ceremony with the woman or was she merely his *amoureuse*. Not that it made any difference. Since he was already married to Jurissa, any subsequent marriage would be invalid. Whatever the circumstances, though, Merlette meant to fight for her place in Philip's bed.

"She's welcome to him." Jurissa didn't realize she'd spoken aloud until Yubah nodded in fervent agreement.

"Only thing be," Yubah said, "she gonna make trouble."

"Silas can manage her." Jurissa spoke more confidently than she felt.

Yubah shook her head. "That be where the trouble gonna come from. She look at him like ole snake look at bitty bird it gonna swallow up."

Recalling Philip's warning to Merlette to leave Silas alone, Jurissa sighed. Merlette was likely to do exactly as she wanted, warning or not. She certainly wasn't going to be a comfortable companion to share the house with, even if she did keep Philip to herself. Jurissa didn't want Merlette in her house at all—but then she didn't want Philip here, either. Not that she had a choice about the matter. Thank God Guy was safe, for the moment, at Tiana's.

After Yubah returned to her own back bedroom, Jurissa stretched out on the bed and wondered how her life had come to this terrible state of affairs. She was separated, perhaps forever, from the child she loved, from the man she loved. Instead, she must live with a man she hated, a man who openly installed another woman in his bed. The house she'd bought with the money she'd earned was no longer her house; it was his to command. As Silas and Yubah were. She'd come to love them and she lived in dread that Philip would decide to whip one or both, with her helpless to prevent him. How could she bear it?

In her mind she could hear herself answering Leon long ago when he'd asked the same question. One step at a time. Tears squeezed from under her closed eyelids and trickled down her cheeks. So much mire bogged her down that even one step seemed impossible.

The days passed somehow, February easing into March. Philip all but ignored Jurissa and she avoided Merlette as much as possible. Merlette gloated over her possession of Philip but, since Jurissa didn't begrudge her that, she could remain, if not calm, at least outwardly impassive.

The second Saturday in March, Philip went off with Dominique You. As soon as he disappeared, Merlette sauntered into the courtyard where Silas was putting new rushes on a chair seat. He no longer worked at the forge. Philip had put a stop to outside work for either of the servants.

Yubah stomped in from the courtyard where she'd been laying Silas's shirts, newly washed, on a wooden rack to dry. Her amber eyes sparked angrily.

"She tell me to go in the house and don't be bothering her," Yubah fumed. "Wasn't doing nothing to bother her."

Jurissa absorbed in baking *petit pains*, looked up. "I saw her go out."

" 'Cause Silas is there and Massa Philip be gone. She sliding round Silas to make him be wanting her, that be what she doing."

"Silas knows better."

"He only be a man, Miss Jurissa, and she got sneaky ways."

Jurissa searched her mind for a way to intercede without seeming to, unwilling to break the unspoken truce between herself and Merlette. As she covered the dough to let it rise, she thought of something.

"I've been wanting Silas to whitewash the outside of the wall before it gets too hot," she said, heading for the door.

Yubah's word was apt, Jurissa thought, her gaze on Merlette and Silas. Merlette wore a low-necked yellow gown, her bronze skin gleaming in the sunlight. Her long arms twisted sinuously as she spoke, her hips swaying as she edged first to one side of him, then the other, pretending to check on his repair work. Sliding around him, yes.

Silas still spoke no French and Merlette didn't speak English. Jurissa couldn't imagine why she bothered to talk to him. Merlette didn't need words. She used her body in a language universally understood.

Before Jurissa reached them, the recently installed bell on the gate clanged. Silas rose to answer it while Jurissa held her breath. Who waited outside? She had no doubt Merlette would report on whoever the visitor was to Philip later.

When Nicolas came through the opened gate, she relaxed. That he'd come to call was unfortunate but, unlike Leon or Anton, at least he could pretend to be delivering a message for Tiana.

Nicolas saw Jurissa and smiled, striding toward her. He stopped abruptly when Merlette blocked his path, staring at her in surprise mixed with wary admiration.

"I'm Merlette St. Martin," she said, looking at him from under her eyelashes. "And who are you?"

Nicolas introduced himself. Jurissa, coming up to them, saw with dismay he was responding with enthusiasm to Merlette's seductive gaze.

"Mademoiselle St. Martin is a friend of my husband's," Jurissa said to Nicolas, emphasizing the "friend" ever so slightly. "Have you come with a message from your sister?"

Nicolas blinked, obviously at a loss as he transferred his attention to her. "From my sister?" he repeated.

She'd never considered Nicolas slow before. Did it take Merlette such a short time to bewitch a man? Jurissa resisted the impulse to grab his arms and shake him into sensibility.

"Won't you come inside?" she said. "I'll have Yubah make coffee."

Merlette slanted her a quick glance, then smiled up at Nicolas and laid her long, sharp-nailed fingers on his arm. "Please do have coffee with us. It's not every day such a handsome man comes to visit."

Inside, confronted with a scowling Yubah, Nicolas had the grace to look shamefaced and he refrained from gazing so avidly at Merlette.

Jurissa watched unhappily as Merlette's black eyes shifted from Nicolas to Yubah and back to Nicolas, obviously making connections, coming to conclusions. She also seemed taken aback when Jurissa sat down at the table with Nicolas, as no Creole woman would have with a man of color, free or not.

"How is Mademoiselle LeMoine?" Jurissa asked

when she, Nicolas, and Merlette were seated, with Yubah serving them. "I trust she's feeling better."

Nicolas's blank look was belatedly replaced with understanding. Unfortunately, Jurissa thought, not before Merlette had noticed his confusion.

"My sister is much better," he managed to say. "She thanks you for your interest in her condition."

Why was he here?" she wondered. Just to see Yubah? Guy couldn't be ill or Nicolas would be more nervous, eager to get away from Merlette so he could tell her something was wrong. Wouldn't he? Or had Merlette addled his wits completely?

"Nothing else is amiss, I hope," Jurissa said to him.

"What? Oh, no, nothing." He gave her a reassuring smile. "We're all fine."

Jurissa, relaxing a trifle at this news, noticed Yubah's increasing upset and tensed all over again. She had to do something before Yubah exploded and revealed more than Merlette might have guessed.

"Nicolas, would you mind taking a mug of coffee to Silas?" Jurissa said. "I think he could use your advice on repairing chair seats?"

He had himself under better control for he nodded and said, "I'll be happy to give what help I can."

Yubah, looking as though she'd prefer to pour the hot coffee in Nicolas's lap rather than into the mug, slapped the filled cup ungraciously on the table in front of him.

"Yubah!" Merlette's tone was sharp, her eyes watchful. "Is that any way to treat a guest?"

"Sorry, Miss Merlette," Yubah muttered.

Nicolas's eyes widened at the exchange. Apparently he hadn't before realized Merlette's favored status in the household. Jurissa hoped it was beginning to penetrate through his strangely thick head that he'd better walk very carefully where Merlette was concerned.

Merlette jumped up as Nicolas reached the door. "I'll go with you," she told him.

She was *not* going to give Merlette a chance to be alone with Nicolas. Getting to her feet, Jurissa followed them out. "I forgot to give your sister the bakery order for next week," she said to Nicolas. "Perhaps you'd tell her for me."

"Of course."

Jurissa took care to draw out the order while they crossed the courtyard to Silas. When Nicolas had handed him the mug, she said. "Enjoy the coffee, Silas. Never mind letting Nicolas out—I'll do it."

For a moment she thought Nicolas would hang back but, confronted by her determined gaze, he changed his mind. "A pleasure to meet you, Mademoiselle St. Martin," he told Merlette.

"Au revoir, Nicolas," she replied, her smile inviting him back as soon as possible.

Merlette showed every intention of trailing them to the gate until Silas looked up at her and made an intricate motion with his fingers in the air between them. Merlette's mouth dropped open as she stared at him.

Jurissa hurried to the gate and Nicolas had no choice but to keep up with her. She opened it and, as he started through, she hissed, "Stay away. From us. From her. She's trouble."

Banging the gate shut behind him, she looked over at Silas and Merlette, greatly fearing the sign he'd traced in the air was related to voodoo and Merlette had recognized it as such. The two of them hadn't moved, remaining in the same position as if in a trance.

She'd thought, after his terrible experience in the swamp, voodoo was the last thing in the world Silas wished to practice again. Apparently she'd been wrong. What was the matter with him? Didn't he realize the situation was perilous enough without adding the unpredictable dangers of voodoo?

Whatever he was up to, she'd certainly let him know she was violently opposed to any more encounters with voodoo.

## Chapter Twenty-one

To Jurissa's surprise, Philip made no mention of Nicolas's appearance at the house while he was away. She wasn't certain whether Merlette had failed to tell Philip or whether she'd told him, but he considered the information unimportant because Nicolas was merely a man of color.

What did make her uneasy was that, when Philip was at home, Merlette didn't go near Silas but the moment he went off with one of his pirate friends, Merlette sought Silas out, displaying herself to him as blatantly as she dared in public. She knew Yubah would never dare speak of it to her master and, apparently, she didn't worry that Jurissa would say anything to Philip either.

Did she think Jurissa was a timid rabbit, too? Or did she suspect Jurissa would keep her mouth shut for fear of getting Silas into trouble? Either way, her behavior showed her contempt for Jurissa and there was nothing she could do about it.

Philip went out often during the day but never at night. By evening, he always returned home if he'd gone out earlier. Then, on March 15, Dominique You appeared.

"The *capitaine* needs you on his new venture," Dominique told Philip. "Not many of us speak English well, not like a gentleman."

Philip scowled. "What about his promise I could stay ashore?"

Dominique shrugged. "I have no knowledge of such an agreement. He told me to bring you back with me; that's all I know."

Philip argued, but in the end, he agreed to go, confirming Jurissa's opinion that Captain Lafitte's hold on his men was a powerful one. Philip kissed Merlette good-bye, as usual. Jurissa expected nothing more than a nod of farewell to her, if that, but to her amazement he took her arm, forcing her to walk to the gate with him. Merlette stared speculatively after them.

"I don't want her going out at night," he muttered to Jurissa.

She gazed at him in surprise. "I'm not Merlette's keeper."

"I realize you can't stop her but I want you to tell me if she does go out at night."

Did he actually expect her to act as his spy? "I'm no informer, either," she said.

"You will tell me!" His fingers dug into her arm. "I've made things easy for you but that can change any time I feel the need to. And don't you forget it."

Easy for her? How? By bringing his fancy woman into her house and giving Merlette the right to command Yubah and Silas as though she were the mistress of the house instead of Jurissa? If, by easy, he meant he hadn't insisted on bedding her, Merlette wouldn't allow that and they both knew it. Or could he be referring to something more sinister? Jurissa hadn't forgotten how Merlette had suggested she be killed. It was Philip who'd dissuaded Merlette either because he didn't want to kill his wife or he truly believed he'd be in danger of being hanged if she disappeared.

Jurissa swallowed. She might be in more danger than she'd thought if she refused to oblige Philip in this matter. The trouble was she found spying distasteful.

"I'll do my best to see Merlette doesn't leave the house at night," she said finally, temporizing.

Later, Merlette confronted her in the kitchen. "He wants you to watch me." Her smile was scornful. "You'd rather not but you're afraid not to."

"Monsieur Winterton hopes you won't find it necessary to leave home at night," Jurissa retorted.

Merlette laughed. "Isn't it charming how he trusts me? He expects everyone to behave as he might. Madame Winterton, I give you my word I'll remain on the premises every night. I do not make promises lightly." Though she spoke mockingly, there was an underlying ring of sincerity to her final words. She turned away from Jurissa, only to look back over her shoulder and add, "Don't you wonder if the so-mistrustful *Monsieur* Winterton hasn't also asked me to watch you?"

Merlette didn't wait for an answer but stalked out the door into the courtyard.

You've found out precious little if you've been watching me, Jurissa thought.

Yubah, tossing shrimp into the gumbo pot, snorted. "Massa Philip ain't looking where the trouble be. That be right here. She be working on Silas. Silas, he know he can't be touching that woman but she gonna drive him crazy with wanting her."

Jurissa nodded. Silas had shown remarkable restraint but it couldn't last if Merlette kept after him. He was a man, after all, and Merlette was a beautiful woman who made it very clear she was his for the taking. Had the voodoo symbol been meant to warn her away? If so, it hadn't been effective.

"I hope he doesn't resort to voodoo," she said.

"No! Only bad-spell voodoo stop a woman like her. Silas, he never do that." Yubah sounded more hopeful than certain.

That night Jurissa woke from a terrible dream where Guy's black kitten, La Belle, transformed into a gigantic monster, pinned Guy in a corner of the courtyard where she threatened him with huge claws and fangs. No matter how hard Jurissa tried, she couldn't reach him, couldn't save him from the monster closing in for the kill.

She sat up in bed, her heart pounding. Even though she knew it was a dream, the vestiges of terror clogged her mind. When she heard the stairs creak she started in fright, choking off a gasp.

It's nothing dangerous, she told herself firmly. Even if what you heard is Philip coming home, he won't bother you. Not with Merlette waiting for him. But she couldn't relax. Finally she rose, crossed the room without lighting the lamp and eased her door open. All was in darkness. When her eyes adjusted, she saw Yubah's door was ajar, as always, in case someone called for her. Merlette's door was closed, as usual.

What was that noise from downstairs? It sounded as though someone had shut a door. She waited and heard nothing more. Had Yubah gotten up and gone downstairs? Merlette? She'd never to able to go back to sleep until she knew for certain everything was all right.

Taking a deep breath, Jurissa crept down the stairs one at a time, holding her breath lest a creak betray her. The night was warm, a spring night. If it lasted, they'd soon have to put up netting against the mosquitos. She recalled Leon speaking of mosquito bites in March and smiled. What a day that had been, a wonderful day. If only it had never come to an end. Her smile disappeared as she remembered regretting her lost chance to tell Leon about his son and assure Guy's safety.

Reaching the bottom of the stairs, she saw no lamps lit in the lower rooms and realized she hadn't really expected to. If someone had closed a door, it had to be the one to the courtyard. She opened it and stepped into a night that smelled of new growth and was lit by a quarter moon. The frog chorus stopped when she opened the door and resumed again when she didn't move. If the frogs sang there was no one in the courtyard.

Go back to bed, she told herself. You're upset over nothing, over a dream.

Jurissa turned to go inside but stopped abruptly when she heard a woman's laugh, low and intimate. She whirled. The sound had come from the far end of the yard, from Silas's quarters over the stables. After identifying the location, she stood irresolute. She was almost certain the woman was Merlette. What Silas did was his own business, as far as Jurissa was concerned, but she couldn't believe he'd invited Merlette there.

So what should be done about it? Jurissa shook her head, sorry she'd come downstairs. She wouldn't tell Philip. Not only was she reluctant to involve Silas but she had no reason to tattle on Merlette. Still, she wished she didn't know the two of them were together. Nothing good would come of—

"You black dog!" Merlette screeched. "You son of a pig!"

Someone stomped heavily down the stairs that led from Silas's room. Remembering Merlette's fondness for knives, Jurissa flinched. Was Silas all right?

"Gonna put you where you belongs and you gonna stay there." Silas's voice, thank God.

Jurissa ducked back inside, retreating to the kitchen where she waited in darkness. She'd forgotten to close the outside door, but it was too late to rectify her error.

Silas loomed in the doorway and, but his silhouette, Jurissa could tell he had Merlette draped over his shoulder.

"Told you I ain't for you," he muttered as he climbed the stairs. "You don't be a listening woman. Hear me now. You and me, we ain't gonna be together, no matter what. You ain't gonna fasten on me, woman, no, never."

Merlette was uncharacteristically silent. Silas must have shut her up somehow. Without hurting her, Jurissa hoped, for his sake.

She waited, hearing Silas climb the stairs, open Merlette's door and dump her on the bed. Then he closed the door and came back down.

"Silas," she whispered.

He stopped. "Miss Jurissa."

"What happened?"

"Don't mean to be waking you. Miss Merlette, she made a mistake 'bout me. I brings her back."

"I heard. I think you're wise."

He sighed. "Don't know. Ain't good, no matter what I does."

She whispered good night, let him go and tiptoed up the stairs. About to enter her room, she stopped, hearing a voice from Merlette's room.

"You'll be sorry, you black dog. Sorry. You'll beg for mercy. No mercy. Dogs grovel, you'll grovel. Crawl on your belly. No one turns Merlette away. Never. Black dog. Not good enough to lick my feet. Dog. Dog." On and on, like a chant, Merlette spoke of punishing Silas for his rejection of her.

Jurissa shuddered, went into her room and closed the door. Even then she could hear Merlette droning on, but at least the words weren't clear enough to understand. She spent the rest of the night in uneasy sleep, waking up time and again for no apparent reason.

Shortly after noon Merlette appeared downstairs in the dining room, wearing a gold silk gown and a gold bonnet to match. It was the first time Jurissa had seen her with anything covering her head. She looked flamboyant, stunning.

"I'll be taking the cabriolet," she announced, "to visit a friend. Naturally, I'll be home before dark." With a regal toss of her head, she sailed from the house.

From the way she acted, Jurissa thought, it was as though last night never occurred.

"What she up to now?" Yubah asked, coming in from the courtyard. "She tell Silas to harness your horse. She going out."

"Like everything else here, the cabriolet is hers to use if she wishes."

"Don't make it right."

"Nothing's right anyway."

Yubah's glance was sharp. "Something worse happen?"

Jurissa didn't intend to discuss last night with Yubah. "I worry about Guy," she said. "I miss him so but I don't dare go visit him."

"Might be you could send me to Miss Tiana's for rolls, bread, like that."

Jurissa hadn't risked asking either Silas or Yubah to visit Tiana's since Merlette had arrived but today Merlette was gone. And Philip wasn't home. It might not be safe for her to go to Tiana's but surely she could send Yubah without risk.

"That's a wonderful idea, Yubah. If you hurry you ought to get there and back before Miss Merlette returns. Tell Guy—" She paused. If she had to give him up permanently, it would be easier for him if he forgot her as soon as possible. She blinked back tears. Crying didn't change what had to be.

"What you want me to be saying to Guy?" Yubah asked.

"Just give him a kiss. And don't tell him it's from me."

"I do what you say." Yubah's sympathetic look nearly shattered Jurissa's control.

After Yubah was gone, Jurissa, afraid if she remained by herself she'd break down, wandered into the courtyard to seek Silas's company. He sat in the shade of a tall hibiscus bush, his back propped against the wall of the stable.

"Don't get up," she called to him when he started

to rise upon seeing her. He did anyway, bringing her a stool from the stable to sit on.

"It's hot for March," she said, breaking a long silence.

"Yes'm."

She didn't want to talk about last night; there was no point. They both knew what had happened and neither could foresee what the consequences might be, if any. Silas had to be aware that Merlette was furious with him. She wasn't about to mention Merlette's angry chanting.

"I done dreamed," he said after a time.

"That makes two of us. I had a bad dream last night."

"Ain't just a plain ole dream I be having. Be a seeing dream."

"I don't understand what you mean."

"Seeing dream gonna happen. Only thing, I can't be telling when."

"You mean you think your dream is going to come true?"

He shook his head. "Don't be thinking. I knows it. Ever since I be a bitty boy, I be having them. Ain't no way to stop them from happening once I dreams them."

After the night in the swamp by the voodoo fire, Jurissa couldn't easily dismiss as superstition what Silas told her. "What did you dream?" she asked, almost afraid to hear.

"Saw how I gonna die." His voice was calm, without emotion.

Jurissa's eyes widened as a chill ran along her spine.

"Bad times be coming down on us, Miss Jurissa.

You got to be lasting through them, 'cause if you goes under, we all does."

Bad times? They were already living in bad times. She hated to think something worse might be at hand.

"Did your dream tell you what the bad times would be?" she asked.

"Nothing be real clear; be dark and the devil be hanging round. He be waiting to pounce."

"I dreamed a terrible animal was after Guy," she said, struck by the similarity.

Silas nodded. "Bitty Guy, he be in the dark with us all. It gonna happen, Miss Jurissa. Nothing I can do, nothing you can do."

"Silas, I came outside because I felt so sad and alone. What you're telling me certainly doesn't make me feel any happier."

"Be telling you happy things if there be any, Miss Jurissa." His dark eyes held compassion.

"I know you would." She leaned over and touched his hand. "You're my friends, you and Yubah. Without you I couldn't survive. I hope that death you saw in your dreams is many, many years away because Yubah and I would be lost without you."

"Gonna watch out for you both and for the bitty boy till ole death come looking for me; no matter what I be having to do." His voice was grim. "No matter what."

Jurissa shook her head. "No voodoo, Silas."

He didn't reply.

"Silas?"

"When I be just a bitty boy, I knows I be different," he said, looking up at the blue of the sky. "Don't be knowing why. Ole woman, she from another place, come to me. She tell me I be born with the power; got to be careful. Use the power careful or it gonna kill me. The power be for good, not bad, she say, and I got to use it that way. Never hurt people, don't kill, or the power go bad inside you. Ain't easy, but I tries. All my life I be trying." He sighed.

"Something happen. Now it don't be working right, the power. I be studying on what to do. Wish I could be promising what you want, Miss Jurissa. Can't be." His voice was heavy with sadness.

What had happened? The confrontation with the *voodooienne* in the swamp? Silas never talked much, and Jurissa was touched he'd wanted to share his problem with her.

"I won't hold you to any promises," she told him. "I only hope whatever you do is for good."

He turned to face her. "I always be wanting good for you and Yubah and the bitty boy. Seem like wanting ain't enough; got to be doing. I sees bad all around. I be thinking only way to fight bad is using the power. Only it don't work right no more. There be bad in here—" He thumped his chest. "So looks like I only got bad-spell power now."

"Oh, no, Silas, you're not bad. I don't believe it."

He smiled. "You be a gracious lady, Miss Jurissa."

What good was graciousness in her present circumstances? Jurissa wondered. But its uselessness didn't prevent her from treasuring Silas's compliment.

Yubah returned before the shadows grew long, her basket full of baked goods. She said nothing when she came into the house, but Jurissa could tell from the way Yubah thumped the basket onto the table that she was thoroughly upset.

"Is Guy all right?" Jurissa asked.

"He be fine. Worrying 'bout that cat of his; is she gonna catch his frog."

Jurissa smiled, picturing Guy trying to chase La Belle away from the little pool where the frog lived.

"I hope Tiana's well," she said.

"Miss Tiana, she all right."

It it wasn't Guy or Tiana, what had upset Yubah? It had to be Nicolas.

"Did you happen to see Nicolas?" she asked.

"I don't be seeing him, no." Yubah's tone was bitter. "Not me. Somebody else see him, that be who."

Tiana often said Nicolas had too many women friends for his own good. Jurissa thought the women had been discarded once he had asked Yubah to marry him, but apparently she was wrong.

"Be *her*," Yubah muttered, tossing food from the basket.

Jurissa frowned, puzzled. Her? An uneasy suspicion wormed its way into her mind. "You can't mean Miss Merlette."

"Be who I said—her. Miss Tiana, she just come from visiting Nicolas and she see the cabriolet, think maybe it be you, so she stop to look. Miss Merlette, she sashay up to where Nicolas live. She go in and she don't come out."

Jurissa didn't know what to say. She was almost as shocked as Yubah, but apprehensive, too. What was Merlette up to? She might simply find Nicolas an attractive man, one unlikely to reject her, as Silas had done. That was bad enough, but what if Merlette had a more sinister motive? If she was cultivating Nicolas to learn all she could about this household, it could be a disaster. Though Nicolas didn't know the truth, he *did* know about Guy. He might not tell on purpose but if he let anything slip—

"Ain't enough she got Massa Philip and Silas—" Yubah began.

"She doesn't have Silas," Jurissa said without thinking, her mind still busy with the possible consequences of a liaison between Merlette and Nicolas. "That's why she went after Nicolas."

Yubah stared at her.

Jurissa realized she'd have to explain. "Silas turned her down last night."

The anger left Yubah's eyes and was replaced by fear. "Miss Merlette, she ain't gonna let that go by. Gonna make terrible trouble for Silas."

"What can she do? She promised not to use her knives while she lived here."

"I don't be knowing how she do it, but she gonna. And now she catch hold of Nicolas; gonna hurt him, too."

Jurissa put an arm around Yubah. "Just because she went there doesn't mean Nicolas welcomed her."

"I be seeing how he looked at her when he come here. Like she be sweet sugarcane, that be how. Silas, all his life he be different, but Nicolas, he just a man."

Jurissa, who'd also seen how attracted Nicolas was, greatly feared that Yubah was correct. Silas, with the power he believed he had, might be a match for Merlette but Nicolas wouldn't be. "If he betrays Guy to that woman—" she began.

"No! Nicolas, he never do that!"

"Not knowingly, maybe. But she's clever. If she finds out she'll tell my husband. Then what?"

Yubah hugged Jurissa. "Ain't gonna happen," she said fiercely.

Jurissa wished she could be sure as Yubah.

Merlette arrived in time for the evening meal, coming in with a smug, satisfied expression. She spoke little and retired early. The wakeful Jurissa heard no unusual sounds during the night.

Philip came home at noon the next day, surprising the three women when he appeared in the dining room.

"Captain Lafitte postponed the venture," he said as he pulled off his hat, looking from Merlette to Jurissa. "I trust all's gone well here."

Merlette pushed back her chair and flung herself into Philip's arms, sobbing. "Thank *le bon Dieu* you're home," she gasped. "The most frightful—oh, I can't go on."

He pushed her back a bit so he could look into her face. "What happened?"

"Silas!" she cried. "He tried to—no, I can't tell you, it was too awful."

Philip glared at Jurissa. "What's she talking about?"

Jurissa shook her head, her heart filled with dread. She should have known this was coming. Yubah had been right. Merlette meant to revenge herself on Silas, by using Philip. How could she possibly be stopped?

"He raped me!" Merlette sobbed. "Silas. He came to my room and he—" She covered her face with her hands.

"Philip," Jurissa began but he brushed past her, rushing upstairs.

She started after him but Merlette grabbed her arm, holding her back. "You don't interfere," Merlette warned. Jurissa struggled to break away but Merlette's grip was firm.

Philip stomped down the stairs without paying any attention to the women and, whip in hand, hurried to the door. As he opened it, he shouted for Silas.

Yubah ran after him, ignoring Merlette's order to stop. Abruptly releasing Jurissa, Merlette headed for the door. Rubbing her bruised arm, Jurissa followed. She had to do something.

By the time Jurissa reached the stables, Yubah was crouched on the ground weeping, blood on the hand she held to her face. Merlette stood over her while Philip lashed Silas to one of the posts that held up the extended roof at the stable front.

"Hurt him," Merlette cried as Philip stood back from Silas. "Beat him like the dog he is. Do it! Do it! Do it!"

Jurissa's protest was lost in Merlette's wild shrieking.

The whip snaked out and flicked back to lash across Silas's back. Yubah screamed and Merlette kicked her. Jurissa hurried to Yubah, lifted her off the ground and forced her away, hearing the whip crack sickeningly and flinching from the unforgettable sound of it striking flesh.

She all but dragged Yubah to the house and pushed her inside. "Stay here. You can't help Silas. She'll torment you out there—don't let her."

"She wants him dead," Yubah moaned.

"Stay here," Jurissa repeated, hurrying back to the door.

She ran across the yard, Merlette's screeches ringing in her ears. Jurissa saw, as she watched, horrified, that the woman was unrecognizable as the well-dressed lady who'd driven out in the cabriolet yesterday.

"Kill him! Kill him! Kill him!" Merlette, standing near the post, ran her fingers through her hair until it stood out wildly around her head in a dark mane. Her black eyes glittered with hate and the lust for blood. "Kill the black dog!"

Philip's lips were drawn back from his teeth, making him look evil and deadly. Between them they meant to kill Silas.

"No!" Jurissa's voice rose above the screaming, the crack of the whip, but neither Merlette nor Philip paid her the least attention.

Silas's back was a mass of red. His blood dripped onto the ground. So far he hadn't made a sound.

Dear God, help me, she prayed. Help me stop him.

Words were useless. She was smaller and weaker than Philip. But if she took him by surprise? Taking a quick look at Merlette, whose eyes were fixed avidly on Silas, Jurissa edged to one side of Philip and backed up, raising her skirts high. She'd have to judge carefully or get caught in the whip's backlash.

The whip uncoiled and she ran, swerving so she was directly in back of Philip. Before she reached him, she bent at the waist, keeping her head thrust out. Without breaking stride, she rammed him with her head as hard as she could in the middle of his back.

Philip thudded onto his face, grunting as his breath was knocked out of him. Jurissa landed on top of him. She sprang to her feet, fighting dizziness.

"She's lying," Jurissa cried to Philip. "I saw what happened and Merlette's lying. She wants you to kill

Silas because she offered herself to him and he turned her away." From the corner of her eye she saw Merlette start toward her.

"I've never lied to you, Philip, I don't now," Jurissa continued, shifting to face Merlette, who clutched a knife in her hand. Jurissa had gone too far to be stopped. "You told me to watch her at night and I did." she shouted at the still recumbent Philip. "I saw her. She went to Silas and he refused her. I heard her promise to kill him for rejecting her. She lied to you so you'd beat him to death. She wants him dead because he wouldn't have her."

Philip groaned and sat up, one hand going to his back. Merlette reached Jurissa, spat in her face and, ducking around her, ran toward Silas.

"She's got a knife," Jurissa warned. "She means to kill Silas."

## Chapter Twenty-two

Philip grasped his dropped whip and jumped to his feet. The whip snaked out and tangled around Merlette's legs as she raced toward Silas, knife in hand. She staggered and sprawled on her face. Philip ran toward her and, before she could rise, stomped on her knife hand. Merlette screamed in pain.

"Once a slut, always a slut," he snarled, reaching down to grasp her by the hair and drag her to her feet. The knife lay half buried in the ground.

She tried to claw him and he slapped her across the face with his palm, then with the back of his hand. Once, twice, three, four times. Her head twisted back and forth with the force of his blows.

"I warned you — no knives. You broke your promise." His words punctuated the slaps.

"No!" Merlette gasped. "I never promised not to use a knife on him."

Philip, still holding her by the hair, continued to slap her. "He's property. You don't kill property. The whip is one thing, a knife another. I've a good mind to drop you into the river for lying to me. I should have known he didn't rape you. He's got better sense."

Jurissa, appalled by Philip's violence, dared not intervene. For all she knew, she'd be next for interfering with Silas's whipping.

Yubah darted by her, leaned down and dug the knife free, then rushed to Silas and cut the rope binding him to the post. He slid down onto his knees. Without a glance at anyone else, Yubah helped him to his feet and led him toward the house.

Jurissa took one last, horrified look at Philip beating Merlette before following Yubah and Silas. In the kitchen Yubah washed her brother's back and applied a poultice made from dried leaves, which she said Miss Tiana had given her. While she tended Silas, Jurissa heard the gate clang shut. Moments later Merlette staggered into the house, her face swollen and bleeding, and pulled herself up the stairs by the banister rail. She closeted herself in her bedroom.

Jurissa looked into the courtyard to make certain the clang of the gate meant Philip had left. He was nowhere in sight. She helped Yubah steer Silas across the yard and up the stairs to his quarters above the stable where he sprawled facedown on his cot.

The only sounds he'd made were groans when Yubah washed his back; he hadn't said one word. Jurissa couldn't help but wonder if his dream had shown him he'd die from Philip's whip. If so, he'd cheated death. Though it sickened her to look at his battered back, thank God Silas was far from dying. Perhaps Philip, as he'd told Merlette, had never meant to kill Silas and lose a valuable property. Jurissa would never be sure. She did know Philip's cruelty had turned her stomach, and she hated and feared him more than ever before.

If only there was someone in authority she could appeal to. But a constabulary, as she'd known it in Boston, didn't exist in New Orleans. Anton had told her all too clearly that any civil authority would recognize the right of a husband to regulate his wife and control his slaves. Because she had no male relative to intercede with her husband, she had no one to protect her.

Somehow she had to save herself and her son. And Yubah and Silas, if she could. Now that the British were gone and ships sailed freely from the city once again, might not she try taking passage aboard one? It would all have to be done in the utmost secrecy and, at the moment, she didn't see how she could manage. Nevertheless, she had to try.

"What do you mean you don't know how she is?" Leon stared in disbelief at his *Cousine* Anton. "Has no one at all seen Madame Winterton for two months?"

"Tiana LeMoine reports Jurissa's well enough," Anton said. "She's heard from Yubah that—"

Leon brushed away his words. "I've heard all Tiana knows. She hasn't seen Jurissa since I last did. In case you aren't aware, April's upon us."

Anton, perched on the edge of his office desk, rose and confronted Leon. "You seem unduly perturbed, *cousine*."

"Unduly? Winterton was a full-fledged bastard when I first met him. *Le bon Dieu* knows three years among the pirates never improved any man. He's brought his Baratarian consort to live with him, as I suppose you're aware. Those pirate wenches are sav-

363

ages. When I think of what may be happening to Jurissa—" Leon broke off and took a deep breath.

Anton put a hand on his shoulder. "It worries me, too. I agree the man is impossible and her position untenable. But what I meant was, you are extremely concerned about a woman with whom you have only a limited acquaintance. Or so you've led me to believe."

Leon looked into Anton's eyes. "I love her. It's hopeless, I know that, but I love her. How can I stand by and allow that pig to mistreat her?"

Anton considered him a moment. "I should have guessed there was something between the two of you. It explains—" He broke off. "Well, it doesn't matter now, since neither of us can have her. From what Tiana LeMoine hears from Yubah, it's Winterton's woman who mistreats Jurissa—in his absence. If only she had relatives here, a father, a brother to stand up for her. I've tried in vain to discover any legal precedent I could use to intervene." He spread his hands. "What would you have me do?"

"Go there and see for yourself."

"He's told me I'm not welcome. Would you have me call him out? Challenge him to a duel?"

Leon shook his head. "He's no gentleman. From what I know of him, he'd probably shoot you with a hidden pistol while pretending to duel with a rapier. Surely, though, you, as her lawyer, can dream up some legal excuse to call on her whereas I have no reason at all."

"But he hasn't forbid you to call as he has me."

"He would if I tried to see her. He disliked me aboard the *Yarmouth*, and I'm certain nothing's changed his mind since."

"I hesitate to mention it but, perhaps your wife . . ."

Leon shook his head. "Louise-Marie is fond of Jurissa and has asked me about her but Louise-Marie hasn't been well. As you know, she's been staying with her parents in their townhouse since the first of the month. She hasn't felt able to accept any invitations. I don't know if I'd ask her to venture into that place even if she were in better health."

"I'm sorry to have suggested it. I didn't realize she'd been ill. No doubt things will improve once you're able to build your new home on the lake."

Leon swept that aside. "We will go together," he announced. "The two of us will beard Winterton in his den."

"I don't know if that's wise. As you say, I might be able to concoct a reason for the visit but not for bringing you along."

"Very well, I'll wait outside the gate, prepared to come in and rescue you if necessary." Leon grinned at Anton. "I haven't rescued you since that time in the swamp when we were boys."

"I think you've forgotten just who pulled whom out of the quagmire."

"If you insist, I'll admit old Lono rescued the two of us. But I think we can survive without him on this venture."

"He's still alive, old Lono?"

"Yes. Francois, who's staying with *Maman* at Marchands, brings him food. Lono claims the alligators don't touch him because they know he's gotten too tough for them to chew. He says the snakes don't bother him because he's a friend of their king, whatever that means. You remember, he was supposed to have been an African chief."

"He must be a hundred years old. Remarkable."

"So, shall we go?"

"Now?"

"Anton, I can't bear to wait any longer. I thought you were fond of Jurissa. I don't know how you can wait."

"Whatever my feelings, I've never been as impetuous as you, *cousine*. But, yes, we'll go."

Leon on Tigre and Anton on his strawberry roan, Rouge, set off together for the Winterton residence. Anton carried a portfolio of papers he meant to claim needed Jurissa's signature so he could close her file.

As they approached, the gate opened and Yubah came out carrying a basket. Leon spurred his black and pulled up before Silas could shut the gate. *"Bon jour* Silas," he said, noting with dismay the Negro's healing welts.

"Massa Leon!" Silas smiled. "You be coming in?"

"Better I wait out here," Leon told him, "while Monsieur DuBois calls on Miss Jurissa."

Yubah had stopped, listening to the exchange. "Massa Philip be home," she warned.

Anton halted Rouge and looked down at her. "I wouldn't call otherwise," he said.

Yubah nodded and began walking away, looking back apprehensively over her shoulder.

Anton dismounted and, handing Leon his reins, walked through the gate. Silas shut it behind him.

He'd give everything he owned to be Anton at this moment, Leon thought. He was so starved for the sight of Jurissa that he could hardly stand to wait outside, to be this close and yet not able to catch even a glimpse of her. Dismounting, he tethered both horses and began to pace and down along the outside of the wall.

Since Silas's whipping last month, and when her own bruises had faded, the vindictive Merlette had plagued Jurissa. She had used words, pinches, and punishing blows when Philip was gone or sleeping. Merlette well knew Jurissa was too proud to complain to Philip, but she was careful never to hit Jurissa where a bruise could be readily seen.

Provoked beyond endurance one day in the kitchen, Jurissa grabbed the knife Yubah had been using to bone fish. "I made no promises not to use knives," she cried to Merlette. "Touch me again and I swear I'll stop you with this."

Merlette tried to hide her involuntary withdrawal. For a moment Jurissa thought she meant to challenge her but Merlette sneered. "My time will come," she threatened. "Meanwhile, why should I bother with such as you?" Turning her back, Merlette stalked off.

After that the physical punishment stopped but Jurissa, wary of Merlette, tried to avoid her as much as possible. She was successful until the afternoon when, after Philip went upstairs to nap, Jurissa, not realizing he wasn't in the sitting room, reentered the house after seeing Yubah off to the bakery.

As soon as she noticed Philip wasn't around, Jurissa started back outside but Merlette slid out of the dining room and blocked the door.

"Someday I'll run off with you to Barataria," Merlette threatened. "Just you and me. They don't know you there, no one, so they don't care. Philip won't be with us. He can't save you. There, it won't matter what I promised him. With my knives I'll start on your hands. Finger by finger, little by little, I'll feed you to the alligators. What do you think of that, little rabbit?"

The vicious intensity of Merlette's tone chilled Jurissa, and she began edging slowly backward.

Merlette pushed herself away from the door and lunged at her, grabbing Jurissa's arm above the elbow, where the sleeve of her gown covered her skin. "You deserve to die very slowly," Merlette hissed. "Painfully. And soon you will. I promise. Very soon." Her fingernails dug through the cloth into Jurissa's skin.

"Maybe I'll scalp you first. My mother was an Indian, did you know that? I'll wear your red hair at my belt as a trophy."

Neither woman had noticed the door edging open. Now it was thrust wide. "Take your hands off Madame Winterton, woman!" Anton ordered.

Merlette released Jurissa's arm and whirled, her mouth agape. Jurissa stared at Anton, unable to speak.

"I heard you," Anton accused Merlette. "What gives you the right to speak to Madame Winterton in such a hideous fashion?" His eyes flared with fury as he grasped Merlette's forearm. "Have you forgotten who she is? Who you are? I suggest you get on your knees and beg her forgiveness."

"Who are you?" Merlette asked, her voice quivering slightly. Jurissa knew that she was remembering a woman of color had no right to lay her hands on any white person.

Anton glared at her, his expression plainly saying she had no right to ask him, much less to know.

"Down on your knees, I said!"

Jurissa, now aware that Philip was probably upstairs, shook her head. "Anton, that isn't necessary."

"I say it is. This woman is lucky I don't insist she be publicly whipped."

"No!" Merlette's voice rose. "You'll never have me whipped. He won't allow it!"

"What the hell is going on down there?" Philip demanded from upstairs.

"This man is threatening me!" Merlette cried before either Anton or Jurissa could speak. "Threatening me in your house."

Philip clattered down the stairs. "You!" he said when he saw Anton.

"I came to call on your wife and what did I find?" Anton said angrily. "I found this—this *sauvage* threatening to kill her by various hideous methods. Is this how you run your household?"

Philip shoved Merlette aside so roughly she almost fell. "Get upstairs where you belong," he ordered. He watched her, waiting until the bedroom door closed before he confronted Anton again.

"I'll run my house however I choose, Monsieur DuBois," he said, "and you have nothing to say about it. Absolutely nothing."

"Does that include having your wife threatened by a woman like that one?" Anton jerked his head toward the stairs. "We don't approve of such practices in New Orleans, sir."

"Get out," Philip ordered. "Out of my house, out of my sight. And don't come back."

Anton's fists clenched as he stared at Philip. "I warn you—"

Philip jerked the door open. "Out! I don't tolerate

interference. Especially from my wife's former lover."
He whirled and strode into the sitting room.

Jurissa seized her chance. "Go," she whispered. "Please. It'll only make it worse if you don't."

Anton walked toward the door. "I hate to leave you in this—"

"Go!" she begged.

Anton stepped through the door and started across the courtyard. He was almost to the gate, when Philip pushed past Jurissa and hurried after him. She drew in her breath. Philip had a dueling pistol in his hand!

Jurissa ran out the door after the two men.

"Dubois!" Philip called.

Anton stopped and turned. Philip level the gun. Silas, standing by the gate, swung it open. Jurissa gasped, stopping in her tracks.

Leon strode into the courtyard and paused beside Anton. "I expected better of you, Winterton," he drawled, "then to shoot an unarmed man."

Philip, taken aback, dropped the muzzle of the pistol. "I—the gun—" he began.

"I suppose I should be grateful you didn't shoot him in the back," Leon went on. "At least you had the courtesy to call his name so he'd turn around."

"The gun was a warning," Philip snarled. "I don't want him here. You, either, du Motier. I'll shoot you both on sight if you come here again. Do you understand?"

"Jurissa," Leon said. "You can't stay here." He held out his hand to her.

Her gaze fixed on Leon. She took a step toward him, another and another. He'd come for her; she'd be safe with Leon, and so would Guy. She should have known Leon would never desert her.

Philip reached out and grabbed her arm, pulling her to him. "In case you've forgotten, she's my wife, and she's going nowhere."

Leon started toward him and Philip jerked up the muzzle of the pistol until it nestled at Jurissa's breast. "I'll kill her rather than see her go with you. Get out, both of you. Now."

Her eyes burning with unshed tears, Jurissa watched Leon's agonized face as, along with Anton, he slowly backed toward the open gate.

"If anything happens to her, I'll kill you, Winterton. That's a promise." Leon's voice was as cold as a Boston midwinter night.

"Shut the gate and bolt it!" Philip ordered Silas as soon as the two men were through it. When the gate clanged closed and the bolt dropped in place, Philip dragged Jurissa into the house.

"So you'd go with that bastard du Motier, would you?" he accused her. "It's been him all the time, hasn't it?"

She jerked free of him, so angry she was beyond fear. "Why would I want to stay here? Your fancy woman does her best to make my life miserable. I don't know from one day to the next whether she's going to kill me or not."

"You knew I'd put a stop to her threats if you told me," he growled. "Why didn't you? You and your stinking pride—you're as bad as those damn Creoles. Let me tell you this. You belong to me the same as Silas and Yubah, and I have no intention of letting you go. Du Motier will never put a hand on you again as long as I live, and neither will that bitch in the bedroom." He turned to the staircase. "Merlette!"

he bellowed. "Get the hell down here and listen to me."


Jurissa's life improved after Anton and Leon's visit. Merlette no longer spoke to her or came near her at all. But Merlette made it plain by her scowls and angry glances that she hated Jurissa more than ever.

The day after Easter, Philip announced he'd be gone for a week. "A friend of mine, Henri the Hook, will stay here while I'm gone," he said. "I'm afraid his manners aren't too refined so he'll sleep in the stable. Henri's instructions are to admit no visitors and to shoot any if they try to enter by force. He's also been told no one leaves for any reason—except Yubah, when she needs to shop."

"I do some of the shopping," Merlette reminded him. "You know Yubah can't pick out fresh shrimp and fish like I can."

He shrugged. "Very well. I'll tell Henri you're to be allowed to shop in the mornings." He smiled thinly. "Remember, he'll let me know how long you're gone. And, while I'm at it, I might remind you there's nothing you can do to entice Henri. His tastes don't run to women."

Merlette grimaced. "I've heard of him. Pah!" She turned to Jurissa, forgetting her animosity for the moment. "You've no notion what kind of animal Philip leaves to guard us. The man has an iron hook for a left hand and a patch over a missing eye. He's ugly, mean, and he fancies boys instead of women."

Jurissa, who'd never heard of such a thing, stared from Merlette to Philip.

He shrugged. "I trust him; which is more than

I can say about anyone else in this household."

Merlette drove out in the cabriolet the morning after Philip left. Henri opened the gate and bolted it after her. Silas, following Philip's orders, had cut a spy hole in the wall so it was now possible to see who stood outside the gate. There was no chance Henri would open the gate to anyone but Merlette or Yubah, if she went shopping.

Philip had also, after discovering how easily Merlette had gotten over the wall on her first visit, made Silas install iron spikes along the wall's top. The place was rapidly becoming a prison, complete with Henri the Hook as jailer.

Jurissa had no idea if Henri's personality was as unappetizing as his looks, and she had no desire to try to find out. She didn't doubt he'd follow Philip's orders exactly.

"She ain't just going for shrimp," Yubah observed bitterly. "Not her. She be looking for a man. I knows what man."

Nicolas. Jurissa wished she could reassure Yubah but could not, since she believed that's exactly who Merlette had in mind. Jurissa was sure Merlette hoped Nicolas would reveal some secret, something Merlette could use as a weapon.

"You can't trust a man with a secret," Tiana had warned long ago, apropos of Nicolas.

In the week Philip was gone, Merlette went out three mornings in a row, coming home at noon. After that, she told Yubah it was her turn to do the shopping. Yubah brought back news that Bronze John, as the Creoles called yellow fever, had appeared early this year, not waiting for summer. Already two people had died of the disease.

"Miss Tiana, she say people who live in New Orleans since they be bitty, Bronze John pass them by. We be the ones she worry 'bout."

"We've lived here three summers without Bronze John coming for us," Jurissa reminded Yubah.

"Miss Tiana she be giving me some packets just in case. And she say don't you be fretting 'bout Guy, he be fine. She keep him safe."

Philip returned eight days after he'd left but he didn't immediately send Henri off. Merlette greeted him with enthusiasm, winding herself around him as she'd done when she first arrived. Philip needed little encouragement to go upstairs to the bedroom with her.

He came down forty-five minutes later and strode into the sitting room, where Jurissa sat sewing. "Yubah!" he shouted. "Get in here!"

Merlette sidled in ahead of Yubah, looking smug. Jurissa's heart sank.

"There's a boy at that bakery you patronize," Philip announced coldly, his eyes flicking from Yubah to Jurissa. "The LeMoine woman keeps him for someone. Who?"

Jurissa swallowed, fighting not to show her panic. "Why are you asking me?"

"Because I suspect you know." He turned to Yubah. "And you do, too."

Yubah couldn't conceal her fright and Philip pounced on her. "Whose child is he?"

Yubah shook her head. Philip grasped her arm. "You'll tell me!"

"I—don't be knowing." Her voice quavered with terror.

He hauled her from the room and out into the courtyard, Jurissa on his heels and Merlette sauntering behind. She told Philip, Jurissa thought. Merlette. Nicolas let something slip and Merlette went to Tiana's and saw Guy.

As Philip dragged Yubah across the yard, Henri came out of the stable. "Tie her to that post," Philip ordered him.

Without a word, Henri obeyed. Silas came around from the back and stared at what was going on.

"You can't whip Yubah!" Jurissa cried.

"Merlette, shut her up," Philip ordered.

Merlette, coming up behind her, twisted Jurissa's arm behind her back and clamped her hand over Jurissa's mouth, her long fingernails digging into Jurissa's cheek. Henri fetched the whip from where it was hanging in the stable and thrust it at Philip.

Tell him, Jurissa wanted to cry to Yubah. Don't let him whip you—tell him! But, when she tried to twist free, Merlette increased the pressure on her arm until she grew faint from the pain.

Philip's whip lashed out and Yubah screamed. Someone banged on the gate and Henri scurried away to look through the spy hole.

"Whose child?" Philip demanded, sending the whip snaking out for the second time.

Yubah screamed again. The banging on the gate redoubled. Silas started for the gate and Henri blocked his path. Philip readied the whip for another stroke.

Everything happened at once. Silas swept Henri from his path. Henri flew into the air, thudded to the ground and didn't move. The whip struck Yubah's back. Blood spattered her clothes.

"Mine!" she shrieked. "My child!"

Silas unbolted and flung open the gate. Nicolas LeMoine ran in, rapier in his hand, and rushed at Philip. Silas strode to his sister and, protecting her with his body, began to untie her. Philip turned the whip on Nicolas, who evaded the lash and continued to advance. Merlette's grasp loosened and Jurissa jerked free.

As she ran to Yubah, Jurissa noticed that Philip was unsuccessfully trying to fend off Nicolas's rapier with the butt of the whip. For an instant she felt the urge to stop and call to Nicolas, "Run him through!"

Jurissa reached Yubah just as Silas freed her. He caught his sister in his arms, but she fought to put her feet on the ground. "Be all right," she gasped, leaning against him.

Jurissa looked back at Nicolas and Philip. Nicolas's thrusts had jerked the whip from Philip, and Philip retreated as the point of the rapier threatened him.

"Kill him," Yubah muttered under her breath.

Merlette, in a sudden burst of speed, dashed toward the two men and flung herself on Nicolas's back. The surprise attack dropped him to his knees. The rapier slipped from his grasp and Philip kicked it away. On the ground, Henri the Hook stirred and sat up.

"Run!" Yubah shrieked. "Run, Nicolas, for your life."

Nicolas twisted away from Merlette, springing to his feet. He took in the situation with a glance and raced for the open gate. Henri was a moment too late to intercept him as Nicolas passed through the gate. The clatter of hooves revealed he was safely away. Henri banged the gate shut.

Yubah, clinging to Silas, began to sob.

Philip picked up the whip and walked to her. "Your child," he said. "By him?" He jerked his head toward the gate.

"No," Yubah sobbed. "A—a Creole. Don't be knowing his name, Massa Philip."

"It doesn't matter who he was," Philip said. "What matters is you hid the child from me." He turned to Jurissa. "You knew about this."

She nodded.

"It's your doing, hiding Yubah's bastard. She wouldn't have the nerve. Did you think I wouldn't find out?"

Desperately, she sought for a protective screen of words. "I—you know Arabel raised me to despise slavery," she said.

"So you sought to deprive me of what's legally mine. I own that child and you know it." His glare lashed her and passed on to Yubah and Silas. "All of you were in on it."

"I told you they were hiding something," Merlette said.

He whirled on her. "Yes, and you damn near got me killed. LeMoine came here because of you. Don't you deny it. Henri told me how long you were out every one of those three mornings. Four hours. To shop for a few shrimp?"

"But I only saw Nicolas LeMoine to find out what their secret was," Merlette protested.

He snorted in disbelief and turned his back on her. "Silas, you lay a finger on Henri again and I'll beat you within an inch of your life. Yubah, whipping you

377

isn't enough. I'm going to punish you in a way that will last for the rest of your life. And you can remember it was your dear mistress's advice that brought it on. D'you hear, Jurissa? You caused this." He smiled, his gaze flicking over the three of them.

"I'm going to send Henri to bring the boy here where he belongs. After that, I'll register him as Yubah's child, establishing my ownership, and then I intend to put the boy up for sale."

## Chapter Twenty-three

"Take Yubah with you," Philip ordered Henri the Hook. "It'll avoid trouble at LeMoine's when you pick up the child. Don't just stand there—go."

Jurissa, still in shock at Philip's announcement that he meant to sell Guy, rallied enough to find a lightweight shawl to throw over Yubah's shoulders to hide her torn dress and the slashes on her back. She knew better than to try to do anything else for Yubah now, but she managed to walk with her to the gate without Philip preventing her.

As the supply cart rattled off with Henri and Yubah, Jurissa found the chance for a word with Silas.

"Don't let Henri near Guy," she whispered. "Merlette says Henri has strange tastes and I'm afraid."

"Be knowing 'bout that man," he said. "He ain't gonna bother that bitty boy, no, never."

Jurissa walked slowly back to the house, trying desperately to think of a way to convince Philip not to sell Guy. Surely once he realized Guy was so young, hardly more than a baby, he'd change his mind. Before she said anything, though, she had to find a way to get rid of Merlette so she could talk to Philip alone.

As she entered the house, she heard loud voices from upstairs. Merlette and Philip were fighting again. If he got angry enough he'd slam out of the bedroom and stomp downstairs. Even if he stopped long enough to give her a chance, though, it would be folly to approach a raging-mad Philip. Usually he marched through the gate and disappeared for a few hours. Maybe when he came back.

Jurissa stood irresolute at the foot of the stairs while the sound of their voices grew louder. She shook her head. She'd have to wait. As she turned away, Merlette screamed. Seconds later, the bedroom door slammed and Philip ran down the stairs. He headed for the outside door without so much as glancing at her.

She hoped he left the house. Henri was gone and, if Philip left, she could send Silas with a message to Leon. Once Leon knew Guy was his son, she knew he'd find a way to rescue the boy.

Jurissa listened in vain for the clang of the gate. After a few minutes, she eased the door open and peered out. Her heart sank. Philip paced around the courtyard, banging a fist into the palm of his other hand, his face contorted in fury.

Merlette flew down the stairs and Jurissa stepped aside. Merlette yanked the door open, looked out, and slammed it shut.

"Bastard," she muttered, stalking into the kitchen.

Merlette should know Philip better by now, Jurissa

thought. Didn't she realize her only reward for bringing him the information about Guy would be angry words and a blow or two because she'd spent too many hours with Nicolas LeMoine? Philip was neither grateful nor kind.

He's angry, but this may be my only chance to talk to him alone, Jurissa told herself. Now, while Merlette is too annoyed to go near him.

Making up her mind, Jurissa hurried into the courtyard and crossed to where Philip was scowling up at a branch of the camphor tree that overhung the wall. He turned when she neared.

"Well?" he demanded.

"I don't think you realize Guy's only two years old," she said. "Surely that's too young to be sold."

"Guy?"

"That's his name. Tanguay."

"What do I care how old Yubah's bastard is? I said I intended to sell him and I will."

"You can't!"

He gave her a thin-lipped smile. "Are you going to stop me? I'd like to see how."

Jurissa crossed her arms over her breasts. "He—he isn't Yubah's," she said.

He laughed. "You can't convince me otherwise. Didn't I have to whip her to get the truth?"

"Yubah was covering up for me."

"You? I don't believe it."

"It's true! Yubah's idea was that she had no reputation to be ruined, whereas I did. She padded herself and pretended to be carrying a child. I hid from everyone. No one knew except the midwife." She dare not endanger Tiana by using her name. "Tanguay is my child, born on Christmas Day, 1812."

He stared at her. "You expect me to swallow that?"

"It's the truth. It's why his birth isn't registered. I named him after the man Arabel loved."

Philip said nothing for a long time. Finally he reached out to grasp her shoulders, looking intently into her face. "If the brat was born by Christmas and he was yours, you could have claimed he was posthumous. Though we both know he couldn't have been my child, no one else would. Your reputation wouldn't have suffered. Everyone would have pitied the poor widow, left with a fatherless baby."

Jurissa bit her lip. "I didn't want anyone to know I had a child."

He gave her a shake and released her. "If you're trying to save Yubah's son from being sold with your absurd confession, you're wasting your time."

"It's true! Guy's my son."

"Then who's the father?"

Jurissa tensed. How could she tell him? But she had to. Philip must be convinced Guy belonged to her, not Yubah, and therefore couldn't sell the boy as a slave.

She swallowed and, raising her chin, said, "Leon du Motier."

Philip's expression of supercilious amusement faded. His eyes narrowed. "If you're telling the truth the son of a bitch must have bedded you as soon as he was sure he'd drowned me . . ." He raised his hand menacingly and she flinched from a blow that never came.

His hand dropped. "I don't put it past du Motier. I also don't put it past you to have made up this tale to protect Yubah's child." He focused his eyes on the limb of the camphor tree, ignoring her.

"I assure you I'm telling the truth," she said after long moments had passed.

He turned his gaze on her again. "Truth or lie, it makes no difference. I've made up my mind. If the story is true, you're the one who needs punishing, not Yubah. You and that bastard du Motier. I've decided not to sell the boy but I *will* register him as Yubah's since I'm not convinced he isn't hers. Registered as her son, he's my property. If he isn't Yubah's, think of the pleasure I'll have ordering du Motier's son to do my bidding and whipping him when he displeases me." He smiled at Jurissa, the cruelest smile she'd ever seen.

A knock came and they both hurried toward the gate. Silas opened up. The gray pulled the cart inside and the gate closed behind it. Silas reached in and lifted Guy out. Philip put out a hand to stop Jurissa before they reached the cart.

"Set the boy down, Silas," Philip ordered. When Silas obeyed, Philip said, "Guy, come here. Come here to your mother."

Guy glanced at Yubah, still in the cart, then ran across the courtyard and hugged Jurissa's legs. She bent down and lifted him into her arms.

"Who is your mama?" Philip asked.

Guy stared at him and stuck his thumb in his mouth, not answering.

"He calls both Yubah and me *Maman*," Jurissa explained.

"You have an answer for everything." Philip took Guy from Jurissa's arms and held him at arm's length. "You are to call me Master Philip. Do you understand?"

Guy's brown eyes widened as he gazed into Philip's scowling face.

"You're frightening him," Jurissa said.

"He may as well get used to it. Master Philip," Philip repeated, giving the boy a shake. "Say it."

"*Maman*," Guy protested, wriggling to get loose, his eyes fixed on Jurissa.

"Please," she begged. "Don't hurt him. I'll teach him to say it."

"He'll learn from me and he'll learn it now!" Philip's angry voice was too much for Guy, who'd never been mistreated in his life. He burst into tears.

Philip opened his hands and deliberately dropped the boy onto the ground. Guy hit the ground, screaming. When Jurissa reached for him, Philip backhanded her across the face, sending her staggering.

"*Maman!*" Guy shrieked.

Philip crouched down and yanked him to his feet. "*Maman* won't help you. Not anymore. That was your first lesson. Do as you're told or you'll be punished. Stop that blubbering and say my name."

"Philip," Jurissa pleaded, "he doesn't understand English very well. He speaks mostly French." Before Philip could prevent her, Jurissa quickly told Guy, in French, to call the man Master Philip.

"Massa Phip," Guy sobbed.

"He'll have to learn English," Philip warned. "I don't speak French unless I have to." He picked up the whistle Guy wore around his neck and studied it. "What's this?"

"Be a slave whistle, Massa Philip," Yubah said before Jurissa could answer.

"Very appropriate." Dropping the whistle, Philip looked from Jurissa to Yubah and back, then shifted his gaze to Silas. "He's your charge, Silas. I don't want the women near him. Do you understand?"

"Yessir." Silas crossed the courtyard, picked up the sobbing child and carried him toward the stable.

"There's no doubt the boy favors du Motier," Philip remarked to Jurissa. "But for all I know the bastard bedded Yubah, too. I'll certainly not get the truth from either her or you."

That night Jurissa couldn't rest for worrying about Guy. He had to sleep in Silas's quarters above the stables without any netting to protect him against the mosquitoes, without any comfort from his mother. The poor baby must think she'd deserted him, that she didn't love him anymore. God only knew if he'd gotten anything to eat. She realized Silas would do his best, but Guy was so little and defenseless and Silas was Philip's slave, subject to his orders.

This couldn't go on. Somehow she had to get Guy away to Leon. It seemed an impossible task. She'd only made things worse for poor little Guy by trying to tell Philip the truth. What was she to do?

Near dawn she dozed off and woke with a start, a woman's scream ringing in her ears. Rising to her feet, Jurissa pulled on a dressing gown, slid her feet into slippers, and stood waiting. She hated this listening at doors, loathed having to sneak around to discover what was happening lest she be taken by surprise.

Her door eased open and Jurissa stepped back in

alarm. Yubah slipped into the room and she breathed easier again.

"He gonna kill her some time, the way he beat her," Yubah whispered.

"I don't know why Merlette stays with him. She doesn't have to. *She* isn't married to him."

"Some women, they likes a mean man."

Jurissa shuddered. Laying a hand on Yubah's shoulder, she asked, "Is your back hurting you?"

"The poultice you done fix be helping," Yubah said. "Miss Tiana, she sure be—" She broke off as they heard the door across the hall open.

"If you so much as stick your nose out the gate," Philip shouted at Merlette, "you'll be the next one tied to that post."

He slammed the door and Jurissa caught her breath. He was coming toward her bedroom! She motioned to Yubah to get behind the door.

Philip pushed the door partway open and stuck his head into the room. "What, not asleep?"

She said nothing, watching him warily.

He grinned. "D'you think I've come to bed you?"

She didn't answer.

"I trust you haven't forgotten it's my right, dear wife."

"How can I forget I'm your wife?"

"See you remember it while I'm gone. I'll be back in a week. Henri stays here. He'll see to it no one goes out, not you, Merlette, Yubah, or Silas. I've arranged for supplies to be sent in. When I return I've a little surprise for all of you. We'll be moving."

Jurissa bit back her exclamation of dismay. "But this house is mine—ours."

386

"Prices are up. I should do well on the sale. I've decided it's time to move."

Her clenched fists were hidden by the folds of her gown. "Where?" she asked as calmly as she could.

"I'm saving that as the surprise. In the meantime, you are not to go near the boy. Henri will tell me if you do, and I'll provide appropriate punishment. Directed toward the boy, not you. Do you understand what I'm saying?"

"You've made it unpleasantly clear."

"The little rabbit has a tart tongue." He stepped into the room and put a forefinger under her chin. "I think it's time you started sending your husband off with a good-bye kiss." Before she could move, his mouth covered hers.

Jurissa stood rigidly, every muscle tense, her lips stiff under his. He hadn't tried to caress her for so long she'd almost forgotten how she detested his touch, how his kisses sickened her.

After what seemed an eternity, he pulled away. "That's a sample of what's in store for you one of these days, little rabbit." He pinched her cheek and turned on his heel.

Jurissa listened to him descend the stairs. She'd gone from mere dislike of Philip to hating him as she'd never thought to hate another human being.

Yubah crept out from behind the door. "Where he gonna be taking us? To that pirate place *she* come from?"

Living among pirates could hardly be any worse than living in prison as she was now, Jurissa thought. Yet the idea of being taken to Barataria appalled her. If that happened she'd never have a chance to save

Guy from Philip.

"I don't know what he plans to do," she said.

"Miss Tiana, she tell me Nicolas, he safe. He be hiding someplace where Massa Philip ain't gonna find him."

With everything else that had happened, Jurissa had forgotten Nicolas's life was in danger for trying to kill Philip. "I'm glad Nicolas is safe," she said.

"I be wanting to tell Miss Tiana to let Massa Leon know 'bout Guy," Yubah went on, "but ole Hook, he don't be letting me say nothing."

Would Tiana send a message to Leon on her own? Jurissa shook her head. She had no way to be sure, but she doubted Tiana had.

"Poor bitty boy," Yubah mourned.

What was she going to do about Guy? Jurissa asked herself in desperation.

Later that morning, Merlette came down to breakfast wearing a bright red gown of lawn so sheer her chemise was clearly visible, its fine lace edging showing at the extremely low decolletage. Her defiant gaze dared Jurissa to comment.

Jurissa wondered for whom the display was intended. Silas had spurned Merlette once already. Henri wouldn't care, nor would he allow her out the gate to impress any other man. Merlette wasn't such a fool that she expected a fine dress to have any influence on Jurissa.

"That boy—he's yours," Merlette said.

Jurissa didn't reply.

"Philip isn't sure," Merlette continued. "I am. I watched yesterday and I know." Her eyes held Jurissa's. "I don't like you, I never will. I wouldn't lift a finger to save you under any circumstances but I can't stand to see a child tormented. If I had it to do it over I wouldn't have told Philip about the child."

Surprise kept Jurissa silent and, after a moment, Merlette shrugged and turned away.

In the late afternoon there came a single knock at the gate. Jurissa, who'd been sitting in the courtyard near the house, hoping to catch a glimpse of her son, watched Henri look through the spy hole, then open the gate and bring in a squirming bag tied at the neck. Live chickens, from the look of it — the promised supplies.

Silas plucked the bag from Henri and carried it up the stairs into his quarters. When he emerged he brought Guy with him, and at the sight of her son, Jurissa forgot all about the bag of chickens.


Anton glanced around Leon's cottage with ill-concealed distaste. "This is no way to live, *cousine*," he said.

"I need to be alone while I am here," Leon explained, as he had before. "*Maman* wanted to send Francois to look after me but I couldn't imagine old Francois adapting to this place at his age. To satisfy her I told her I'd take Guinon instead. He's young and can put up with a few hardships."

"I don't understand, but I bow to your right to live as you see fit. Still, you might keep in mind that tomorrow I'm off to Washington and you could be alone in much more comfort at my place."

"Your servants would be all too solicitous. Not to mention your dear sister-in-law, Eloise, who'd be calling every day to make certain I was being taken care of adequately. Plus all the other callers who'd never dream of stopping by here but would consider me fair game at your townhouse. Thank you, Anton, but no. Bon voyage and good luck in Washington."

"May *le bon Dieu* smile on your endeavor against Winterton. You know I'd be riding with you and the others if President Madison hadn't requested my presence so urgently."

Leon clapped Anton's shoulder. "I'm aware your heart is with us. With her. We'll succeed, never doubt it. Besides, you've contributed magnificently by making the arrangement with Lafitte. I've word that he's called Winterton to Barataria and will keep him there for at least a week."

Anton grinned. "As an attorney I've been compared to a pirate so many times I ought to know how to deal with Lafitte."

"You know the plan. Two days' hence three of my comrades from Beale's Volunteers will assemble here before dawn. By sunrise we'll be stationed near the Winterton house—fortress is more appropriate—waiting for the signal to storm the place. Tiana LeMoine, carrying a packet of bakery goods, will knock at the gate. When it swings open Jurissa will be mine." He sighed. "For the moment anyway."

"She'll be free of Winterton, at least."

Leon grimaced. "I'd prefer to run him through but I can't take the chance. He threatened to kill her first and I'd put nothing past him."

"Rescue her and keep her safe, *cousine*. I'll be waiting."

"Nothing, not death itself, will stop me."

After Anton rode away, Leon ran through the plan in his mind for the hundredth time. He and his friends, all former war comrades, would be dressed as pirates to confuse Henri the Hook even as they overwhelmed him. The masks they'd be wearing would prevent identification. Once Jurissa was safe, Leon had to keep her from discovery until her ship sailed. He decided she'd camp out at Dindon. No one would think of looking for her at a ruined plantation house. Or Yubah's little boy, either. Tiana had stressed that the boy must be rescued, must go with Jurissa without fail. The woman had been quite agitated about it.

But, of course, he'd save the child from Winterton. He was a fine boy and he knew how fond of the child Jurissa was.

She and the boy would remain at Dindon for a day or two at the most. Then he'd put them on the eastbound ship. Once the ship docked, she'd travel to Washington where Anton would see to her safety.

He, himself, would never set eyes on Jurissa again. Closing his eyes, he remembered when he first met her. She'd been standing at the rail of the *Yarmouth*, the sea breeze teasing tendrils of her glorious hair out from under her bonnet. He'd admired her trim figure as well as the color of her hair and was determined to meet her. When she turned at his greeting and fixed her green eyes on him, he was lost.

He was jolted from his reminiscing by Guinon's knock.

"A servant come from Monsieur Rondelet, sir," Guinon announced.

Leon sighed. Another message from Louise-Marie,

begging him to give up the cottage and come to live at her father's townhouse. She didn't seem to understand he could not accept her family's hospitality; he wanted to remain his own man.

"Send him in," he told Guinon.

A young Negro he didn't recognize stepped inside. His skin glistened with sweat and he breathed heavily as though he'd run all the way. He bowed his head and held out a folded paper to Leon.

"Louise-Marie is ill with the fever," her father wrote. "She calls for you."

Poor Louise-Marie. Intent on setting up the new plantation on the lake and distracted by Jurissa's impossible situation, he'd been neglecting his wife. He didn't blame her for using what was likely a minor illness as an excuse to send for him. He'd go to see her and if, as he suspected, she wasn't very sick, he'd continue as planned with Jurissa's rescue. Once Jurissa was safely on her way east, forever lost to him, he'd do all he could to be a better husband to Louise-Marie. It was never too late to make amends.

Jurissa didn't know whether she woke because she'd had a bad dream or whether something had roused her. She listened but heard no unusual sounds. Once her eyes were adjusted to the room's darkness, she glanced toward the trundle bed where, Yubah, saying she was scared, had insisted on sleeping that night. Yubah was gone.

Slipping down the stairs, Jurissa checked the downstairs rooms. Yubah wasn't in any of them. The outside door was ajar. As she eased it open, Jurissa became aware of a humming in the courtyard. The moon was full, its light silvering the trees and shrubbery. No frogs sang in the warm May night.

The night-blooming jasmine that scented the spring darkness didn't quite mask another, less pleasant, smell, familiar to Jurissa, yet one she couldn't quite place; a smell that sent a quiver of apprehension along her spine. She stepped into the moonlight. A dark figure rose in front of her and she gasped, holding out her arms to ward it off.

"Miss Jurissa!" Yubah whispered.

"You scared me," Jurissa told her. "What are you doing out here?"

Yubah found Jurissa's hand and clung to it. "Too late to be stopping him," she whispered. "Bad gonna happen, I smells it. I feels it all around."

"Stop who? What are you talking about?"

"Silas."

Jurissa opened her mouth to ask Yubah what Silas was doing when she finally recognized the unpleasant odor. The scent of blood. Of death.

"Silas, he need a black cat for bad-spell voodoo," Yubah whispered. "And Miss Tiana, she done send bitty Guy's cat in a bag."

Not chickens in the bag but La Belle, Guy's black kitten. Jurissa looked at Yubah in horror. Was she saying Silas had killed the cat?

Yubah nodded toward the camphor tree and Jurissa saw a huge dark figure tending a tiny fire blossoming near its trunk. Silas. The humming came from him.

"He say he got to save us," Yubah muttered. "Ain't no other way."

Jurissa gripped Yubah's arm. "Guy," she demanded. "Is Guy all right?"

"Silas bring him to my room. He be sleeping in there."

"But Henri—"

"Silas, he ask me for Miss Tiana's medicine. That ole Hook, he ain't gonna be awake for a long time."

If Henri had been given a sleeping potion, now was the time to bring Guy to Leon, Jurissa told herself. There was no one left to stop her except Merlette.

At that moment, as if conjured up by the thought, Merlette slipped out the door into the night. Jurissa held her breath but Merlette drifted past her and Yubah as though they didn't exist and trod a moonlit path toward the voodoo flames, toward Silas.

"Silas, he be binding her," Yubah half sobbed. "Be wrong. Bad."

With an effort, Jurissa broke the spell of fascination that kept her focused on the fire. "I'm going to get Guy and take him to his father where he'll be safe," she told Yubah.

"No!"

"Why not?"

"Silas say Massa Philip gonna claim the bitty boy be his. You be Massa Philip's wife. The law ain't gonna let Massa Leon keep Guy, and you got to stay with Massa Philip."

Jurissa was shocked. Silas said that? How could he possibly know?

"He say he dream," Yubah said as though answering. "He dream what he have to do so we all be safe."

Was it true Leon would have to give Guy up to

Philip? Jurissa asked herself. She could almost hear Anton's solemn voice citing chapter and verse of the law, telling her a wife's husband, if he claimed to be, was considered the father of any child she bore. The law aside, Philip would kill in order to keep Leon from having either her or Guy; she was sure of it.

Slipping through the gate tonight with Guy was no solution. It could lead to death for both Guy and Leon. Oh, dear God, was there no way out?

"She dancing," Yubah whispered.

Jurissa looked back at the fire. Merlette, clad in the red dress she'd worn earlier, swayed to Silas's low-voiced chanting. He faced her across the fire, wearing the white loincloth he'd had on at the other voodoo ceremony. He drank from a cup before extending it across the fire to her. Merlette took the cup from him and drank.

"Blood," Yubah whispered, clinging to Jurissa. "She bound to him, he bound to her. Forever."

Jurissa shivered. She didn't understand how Silas expected to save anyone by this monstrous voodoo ceremony—how could he kill La Belle? The sound of his chanting, the sight of them dancing caught her in a dark web. His movements urged Merlette to come to him, to give herself to him, and her tall willowy body, silvered by moonlight, writhed in invitation.

Silas flung out a hand and threw something on the fire. Sizzling flames flared for an instant, then a foul black smoke hid the dancers from view. Jurissa gagged from the odor. When the smoke cleared, the dancers had disappeared and the fire was guttering out.

"Bad all around us," Yubah moaned. "Coming for

me. Coming for you."

"I don't believe in voodoo, I won't believe in bad spells," Jurissa muttered under her breath. "Nothing's in this courtyard except Silas and Merlette and poor dead La Belle."

But she pulled Yubah inside the house, shut the door against the night and ran up the stairs to where Guy slept.

## Chapter Twenty-four

Leon stood in a bedroom of the Rondelet townhouse, looking down in distress at Louise-Marie's face, yellow against the white pillow. He glanced at her mother, who stood near the door. "You mentioned a fever, but I had no idea she—"

"It's merely a fever," Madame Rondelet interrupted. "Nothing else."

"But her skin has turned—"

"Louise-Marie has always been sallow. When she's ill, naturally her complexion becomes less attractive."

Leon stared at his mother-in-law. Bronze John had slipped into New Orleans early this year, and it was obvious he'd visited Louise-Marie. She lay gravely ill with yellow fever. How could her mother deny it?

"Leon," the sick woman murmured and he turned to her as her eyes fluttered open. He took her dry, hot hand and pressed her fingers gently.

"I'm here," he said.

Louise-Marie didn't seem to see or hear him but

397

her fingers clutched weakly at his. He eased into the chair beside her bed. "I'm here," he repeated, appalled by how ill she was. Why hadn't they let him know sooner? Because her mother refused to admit to herself or anyone else how sick Louise-Marie was?

He held her hand between his, gazing down at her. He'd seen enough deaths from yellow fever to know she was dying. Poor Louise-Marie. Even if he hadn't met Jurissa, he should never have married her. Without love and understanding, a marriage was empty. He'd tried to be kind to her but he feared he hadn't always been.

Although she didn't enjoy the marriage bed, she'd desperately wanted to bear him a son. He hadn't thought it a good idea to try for a child again, so soon after she miscarried the first time, but she'd wept and fretted for days, saying she couldn't bear to fail her wifely duty.

In trying to satisfy his father and keep Dindon intact, he'd married Louise-Marie and made the greatest mistake of his life. He'd lost Jurissa, the only woman he'd ever love; the war had taken Dindon from him; now Bronze John was about to claim Louise-Marie.

He'd wronged both women and there was no way to make amends. It was too late, after all. Jurissa was forever beyond his reach, and all he could do for Louise-Marie was to stay with her until the end.

In Yubah's bedroom, Jurissa hovered over her

son. Guy still slept though the sun was high. He didn't feel feverish to her touch but he should have been awake by now. Unless Silas had given him some of Tiana's potion to be certain the boy wouldn't rouse during the night.

Merlette was not in her room or anywhere else in the house. Was she with Silas in his quarters? There'd been no sign of Henri. Was he still asleep, too? Last night seemed a vague nightmare, one Jurissa would rather not recall.

Downstairs, Yubah simmered bouillabaisse, the rich smell of the fish chowder drifting up to Jurissa. Whatever happened, Yubah never forgot people had to eat. Stroking Guy's sweat-dampened curls, Jurissa realized on this hot day he'd be more comfortable downstairs, but she was afraid to bring him there in case Henri appeared. She hadn't forgotten how Philip had threatened to punish Guy instead of her if she dared approach the boy.

Reluctantly, she left him and descended the stairs, knowing that, for Guy's safety, she had to find out where Henri was.

She discovered Henri lying on a straw pallet in the stable, head back, mouth open, breathing harshly, a pool of dark vomitus on the ground beside his head. Staring down at his slack face, she recalled Tiana's words.

"If Bronze John's victim vomits black, nothing will save him from death."

Gingerly, she pressed the tips of her fingers to Henri's forehead. Fever-hot.

Hurrying outside, Jurissa shouted for Silas.

Some moments later he appeared on the stairs, naked to the waist.

"Henri's got yellow fever," she told him. "I think he's dying. Are you all right?"

"Bronze John, he ain't never gonna catch me." Silas turned back to his quarters.

"What shall we do about Henri?" she demanded.

"Nothing gonna help him. Or her."

"Her? Do you mean Merlette's sick, too?"

Silas looked down at Jurissa. "She gonna be. I talk to Bronze John last night, tell him what I be wanting. Henri, he gonna die. Her—" He paused, tilting his head as though listening. "Best I bring her to the house, Miss Jurissa."

Jurissa took a deep breath. Did Silas actually believe he had the power to choose who took the fever and who didn't?

Silas carried Merlette down the stairs from his quarters and across the courtyard, with Jurissa trailing behind. From the glimpse she'd had of Merlette's face, Merlette looked dazed rather than ill. After Silas had deposited Merlette in her bed, though, Jurissa discovered the woman was feverish. She stared down at Merlette, worried now about her son.

"Guy's still sleeping," she told Silas.

He nodded. "Bitty boy gonna wake up soon. Nothing be the matter."

With two of the household sick with fever, Jurissa wasn't reassured. She hurried into Guy's bedroom and sighed with relief when she found him sitting up in bed, the bone whistle clutched in one hand.

*"Maman!"* he cried, holding up his arms.

She hugged him to her. He felt warm but not hot. "Massa Phip?" he asked, his body tense as he wriggled in her arms in order to search the room.

"He's not here," she told Guy.

"Want down," he demanded. When she set his feet onto the floor he ran to where Silas stood in the hall, grasped one of the big man's fingers and tugged toward the stairs. "Eat!" he announced.

"Wait," Jurissa said. "Silas, I want you to go to Monsieur du Motier's cottage with a message." Whatever came of it, she was determined to reveal the truth about Guy to Leon. She'd been wrong to keep Guy her secret as disaster had been the only result.

Before Silas left, he returned to the house to report Henri was dead. "Don't you be worrying 'bout what to do," he added. "I be taking care of ole Hook when I gets back."

Jurissa felt no grief for the man who'd been her jailer. The sick woman upstairs was a different matter. Merlette needed nursing. Was she to stand back and do nothing?

"Miss Merlette, she don't be caring 'bout you if you be sick," Yubah pointed out when Jurissa mentioned her concern about Merlette. "That woman be no good; be better if she die."

Jurissa wasn't sure why she felt the need to try to help Merlette. She didn't like her and she knew Yubah was right. Merlette wouldn't nurse her if she were ill. All the same, she readied a tray with brandy, lemon water, and a packet of the yellow fever medicine Tiana had sent over the month before.

As she carried the tray upstairs, she asked herself if she was doing this because Merlette had shown sympathy for Guy and admitted she was wrong to tell Philip about him? Whatever the reason, Jurissa was driven to help the sick woman.

Merlette's condition worsened rapidly. By the time Silas returned, the sick woman was delirious, raving about being fed to the alligators.

"Massa Leon, he ain't at the cottage," Silas reported. "Nigra there, Guinon. He say Massa Leon go see his wife. She be sick."

Was it yellow fever? Jurissa wondered. Poor Louise-Marie. It would be cruel to send Silas to the Rondelets with a message at a time like this. But now that she couldn't get in touch with Leon, what was she going to do? She glanced from Silas to the muttering, tossing Merlette.

There was no place for her to go, no place to take Guy. Philip would only come looking for them. Besides, how could she leave Merlette alone to die?

"Forget the message, Silas," she said.

"I do what you say, Miss Jurissa. If you don't be needing me, best I get to burying ole Hook."

That night Jurissa had Silas bring the trundle bed across the hall so she could sleep in the sick room in case Merlette needed her. Merlette, in her delirium, kept trying to climb out of bed, even though she was too weak to walk. Jurissa's voice and touch seemed to calm her.

Merlette couldn't eat and had trouble swallowing liquids. Spoonful by patient spoonful, Jurissa fed the sick woman Tiana's potions, mixed with the brandy and lemon water. She napped when

Merlette did, ate when Yubah brought her food and stood over her until she finished it.

Assured by both Yubah and Silas that Guy was fine, Jurissa continued to nurse the gravely ill Merlette while one day merged into the next and the next. Sometime during the night of the third day, Merlette's fever broke and she came to herself.

"You," she whispered, looking up at Jurissa. "I dreamed you saved me from the alligators."

"I've been taking care of you. You've been sick with yellow fever."

"So Bronze John almost got me." Merlette managed a weak smile.

"Henri died."

"You wouldn't let me die. Why?"

"I couldn't. I don't know why."

"I wouldn't have nursed you," Merlette admitted.

Jurissa shrugged.

"What day is it?" Merlette asked. Jurissa told her. "Then Philip will be back soon." Merlette sighed and closed her eyes.

"Rest," Jurissa suggested.

Merlette's eyes flew open. "You and the boy get out of here. Then I'll rest."

Jurissa stared at her.

"Do what I say." Merlette waved a limp hand. "The boy's not safe with Philip. Take Guy away from here. Go."

"There's no place—" Jurissa began.

Merlette cut her off. "Any place is better for Guy than with Philip. Find a ship, leave New Orleans. Just you and the boy. Not Yubah. Not Silas. They stay, they belong to Philip."

She had planned to take a ship if only she could have found a way, Jurissa thought. Who'd have ever thought that Merlette, of all people, would have urged her to go. She could book passage for herself and Guy with the money Tiana had kept for her. What did it matter she had no place to go? She'd take Guy away from New Orleans, take him where Philip would never find them.

"Leave while you can," Merlette whispered and closed her eyes.

By dawn, Jurissa had packed a bag with clothes for her and for Guy. She yearned to bring Yubah and Silas with her. How she hated to think they would be left at the mercy of Philip.

But Merlette had warned her not to take them, Jurissa told herself, afraid Merlette would tell Philip where she'd gone if she risked it. And what would happen to Guy if they were caught? For his sake Yubah and Silas had to stay behind.

She decided not to drive the cabriolet or the cart, fearing her identity and destination could be easily discerned. She planned instead to take Tiana's chestnut mare, holding Guy in front of her.

"Don't know how we be getting on without you," Yubah said, tears running down her face. "But you got to go. You got to save the bitty boy."

Jurissa hugged her, tears in her own eyes. "I hate to leave you. If there was any way to take you with me, I would. You're more than a friend, Yubah. You're my dearly beloved sister."

Turning to Silas, who stood in the bedroom doorway, Jurissa said, "Silas, my dear friend, how I'll miss you." The words caught in her throat. "I'll miss you both for the rest of my life."

Silas said nothing, his dark eyes mournful.

Pink-tinged clouds in the eastern sky heralded the sunrise as Silas drove the cart toward Tiana's. Already the day was warm. It would be hot before noon. Guy, only half awake, nestled in Jurissa's lap.

"Go see Belle," he murmured.

Jurissa couldn't think of what to tell him so she said nothing. She stared reproachfully at Silas's back. Poor La Belle, sacrificed because Silas believed in some invisible power.

As they turned into the rue des Normandie, a black wagon passed them. "Death cart," Silas muttered. "He don't be knowing when to stop."

"What are you talking about?" Jurissa asked.

"Bronze John. I done turn him loose. It be on my head."

"Nonsense." Jurissa spoke tartly. "Yellow fever happens ever summer in New Orleans. How could you possibly have anything to do with it?"

"I done conjure up a bad-spell."

She hadn't been able to convince Silas his voodoo wasn't the cause of Henri's death and Merlette's illness. It was hopeless to try to make him understand he had nothing to do with it.

Tiana greeted Jurissa with an enthusiastic hug. "I thought I'd never see you again!"

Jurissa blinked back tears. How could she bear to leave her good friends? Tiana would be all right, but she couldn't bear to think of what might happen to Yubah and Silas. If only there was a way to bring them with her. But she couldn't; she'd be lucky to get herself and Guy away. Sighing, she told

Tiana why she'd come.

Tiana, in turn, told her about Leon's plan to storm the Winterton house and free her, postponed because his wife was dying of yellow fever. "He made all the arrangements for you to sail the day after tomorrow, under a false name. Madame D'Artagnon."

Jurissa smiled. How like Leon to choose the name of Arabel's lover, knowing it would amuse her. She should have realized he'd never rest until he found a way to release her from Philip's prison. Her smile faded. She wouldn't see Leon again. She'd never love anyone as she did Leon, and she couldn't even bid him a last farewell.

"I told him you wouldn't go without Guy," Tiana added. "I didn't tell him why because I wasn't sure you'd want me to. Monsieur DuBois will meet you in Washington," Tiana went on. "He'll see to your comfort there."

So I won't be alone in an unfamiliar place, Jurissa thought. *Cousine* Anton was a good friend. Leon had thought of everything.

"So we must find a place for you until the ship sails," Tiana said.

"Not here!" Jurissa exclaimed. "If Philip arrives home and finds me gone, he'll come to you first. I don't dare go to Leon's cottage, either. If Philip doesn't already know where it is, he'd soon find out."

"Monsieur du Motier thought if you didn't mind the inconvenience you could camp out in what's left of his old plantation house. He told me he'd stored blankets, mosquito netting, jugs of water, and other supplies there for you. Who'd ever think to look among the ruins?"

Dindon. Was she to spend her last few hours in New Orleans at Dindon? How ironic. "It's the perfect place," she agreed. "Guy will enjoy the novelty and I won't have to worry about keeping him quiet."

"I've saddlebags for Yvette to carry the food I've packed for you," Tiana said. "There's enough to last for the two days."

Silas had saddled the mare and left her tethered in the courtyard. Tiana helped Jurissa cover her auburn hair with a dark, opaque scarf, held on by the jockey cap of her riding costume. She also added a see-through black veil to the cap before Jurissa mounted the chestnut.

Looking around for Guy, Jurissa saw him sitting on Silas's lap on the rim of brick bordering the pool. Though she could hear the low rumble of Silas's voice, he spoke too quietly for her to make out the words.

As she approached them on Yvette, Guy nodded vigorously, his eyes fixed on Silas's face.

"You gonna grow up and be a fine *chevalier* just like your daddy," Silas told him. He gave the boy a hug and rose with him in his arms.

Guy was agog with excitement when Silas lifted him to the saddle in front of his mother. Though he managed a farewell wave to Tiana and Silas, his full attention was on the chestnut mare.

"*Maman*, me ride," he cried. "*Moi chevalier.*"

There was no way to reach Dindon without traveling through a part of the city. Though Jurissa preferred not to attract undue attention, she knew she'd be noticed. All she could hope was that no one would recognize her with her hair covered and her face veiled. But even if they did, how could they know where she was going? She and Guy would be safe at Dindon for the two days they had to wait for the ship to sail.

Hearing that the plantation house was in ruins and seeing what the war had done to Dindon was vastly different. Jurissa well remembered riding up to the mansion in the du Motier carriage after leaving Louise-Marie at Marchands—her first sight of Dindon. She recalled the elegant lines of the house, the well-tended shrubbery, the brilliant flowers, the carefully kept circular drive leading to the massive front door.

Now the mare picked her way along the overgrown drive where exploding shells had left huge holes. The shrubbery had either been blasted or burned away except for a few surviving plants that grew rankly, their bright flowers garish against the shell of what had once been a gracious home. Leon had been right. Dindon was dead. Looking at the ruins, she understood why he couldn't bring himself to rebuild.

Telling Guy to hold to the saddle, she slid to the ground, then lifted him off. Leading Yvette, she circled what remained of the house, finding, in the back, a place to tether the mare inside the walls where she wouldn't be seen. Rubble littered the ground floor but, to her surprise, the curving staircase remained intact.

Guy thought it great fun to explore the ruined house, and she had to hold his hand firmly to keep him from running off to investigate on his own. The downstairs rooms, with their gaping holes in walls and floors, were totally uninhabitable, even for camping. She found none of Leon's supplies there.

"We'll see how the stairs look," she told Guy.

She noticed how clean the staircase was. Obviously someone had cleared it. Leon? As a sign it was safe to climb to the second floor?

She found no holes in the steps and the staircase itself was as solid as when she'd first climbed it. She had no way of knowing where Leon might have stored the supplies, but her instinct led her to Denis's room. The room still had its door on the hinges, a closed door. She opened it, looked in and smiled. She was right. Leon had been here before her. She'd seen smashed and burned furniture littering the lower rooms and the other bedrooms she'd passed but there was no debris in Denis's room. By some miracle the bed remained intact. Sheets and covers were piled on it. While there was no sign of dressers or wardrobe, an octagon marble-topped table sat next to the bed. Atop the table was a candle in a holder. The table's drawer held more candles.

Against the far wall stood a long, high table that might once have graced the library. Water jugs and other supplies were placed on its scarred but still serviceable top.

"Nobody home, *Maman*," Guy said.

"That's because no one lives here now. We're guests ourselves."

No glass remained in the windows but Leon had tacked mosquito netting over them. The roof, open to the sky in many sections of the house, was intact here. Leon had seen to it his guests would be as comfortable as possible under the circumstances. Of course he hadn't known she'd have Guy with her. She hated to leave New Orleans without letting Leon know they'd had a child together, but perhaps it was for the best.

"Massa Phip not here?" Guy asked, apprehension in his voice.

"No." She would never allow Philip to get his hands on Guy again. Never.

Guy examined everything on the tables, in the drawer, climbed on and off the bed and finally peered under it.

"Look, *Maman!*"

Jurissa bent down to see what he'd found. A long slender case lay on the floor under the bed. She grasped its tarnished silver handle and pulled it out. A thick layer of dust grayed the black, hinged cover, making her wonder how long the case had been there. She'd never seen a case like this one, very long but not wide or high, and she couldn't imagine what was inside.

"Open up," Guy demanded.

Jurissa, as curious as he, unlatched the lid and raised it. They stared down at two rapiers, the steel blades as bright as if they'd been polished yesterday.

"Nicolas!" Guy exclaimed, reaching for the hilt of one.

Jurissa pushed his hand away and quickly shut the lid. "Swords are not for little boys to play with.

And these don't belong to Nicolas, though I know he has some like this. They don't belong to us, either, and so we must put the case back where you found it—under the bed."

"Who?" he asked.

Realizing he meant who owned the rapiers, she said, "I think they belong to your *chevalier* on the black horse."

Guy's eyes widened.

"This is his house though he can't live in it anymore. I think the swords were put under the bed a long time ago and he doesn't know about them. If he were here I'd tell him because I believe they belonged to his brother."

"*Chevalier* come here?" Guy asked hopefully.

She shook her head. Leon was where he belonged, beside Louise-Marie's bed. She hoped Louise-Marie would be as fortunate as Merlette in resisting the fatal embrace of Bronze John. She liked Leon's wife and wished her nothing but good.

Guy climbed onto the bed again. "Mine?" he asked.

"We're both going to sleep in it tonight. You and me, the two of us together."

He grinned, happy with the idea. Sliding to the floor, he walked to the window and looked out. She followed him. The bright green of the swamp seemed closer, encroaching on the no longer cultivated fields where weeds grew among the shell holes.

"That's the swamp out there beyond the fields," she told Guy.

"Where Lono live." Guy fingered the bone whistle

dangling from his neck.

She glanced at him, surprised he'd remembered the story she'd told him about Lono and the whistle. "Yes, Lono lives in that swamp."

How solemn her son looked, as though he pondered matters of great importance. Guy should be laughing and playing with other children, not shut away in hiding. I'll see he has friends and the chance to play, she vowed, as soon as I know we're beyond Philip's reach.

"Silas," he said.

"What about Silas?" she asked when he didn't go on.

Guy looked at her and she caught her breath. The expression on his face was exactly the same as one she'd often seen on his father's, a "should I tell her?" expression.

By the time it occurred to her to wonder what Guy was concealing from her, he'd run across the room to the high table and was demanding a drink. She shrugged and went to pour him some water.

By evening, Guy, thoroughly tired out from the day's excitement, fell asleep. Jurissa decided against lighting a candle. She didn't want anyone suspecting someone was in the house. Bolting the door, she got into bed beside her son, fearing she wouldn't be able to close her eyes. The next thing she knew, it was morning.

They breakfasted on Tiana's *petit pains* and orange marmalade. Knowing Guy needed to move around, she planned a game where they'd explore the entire house, hand in hand, and see how many interesting things they could find. They were in a bedroom facing the road and Jurissa, crouching down, was extracting an unbroken silver-backed hand mirror from the rubble on the floor when Guy, who'd been looking out the window, ran to her and buried his face in her shoulder.

"What's the matter?" she asked in alarm. "Did you hurt yourself?" She held him away to see if he was bleeding anywhere.

"Massa Phip," he whispered, his voice quivering with fright.

For a moment she couldn't move. Forcing herself to her feet, Guy's hand in hers, she dashed to the window. A man rode a bay horse with a white star on his nose toward Dindon. She'd never seen the horse before but the man was blond. Though she couldn't be positive at this distance, she feared Guy was right. Philip had found them.

Before she could decide what to do, Guy broke away from her and ran out of the doorless bedroom toward Denis's room. She hurried after him. They could bolt themselves inside but eventually Philip would find that door locked and would break it down. The other choice was to run and hide somewhere else. It was too late to saddle the mare. The only place to hide was the swamp, deadly as it was. But Philip would see them running. Could they reach the swamp on foot with Philip chasing them on a horse?

A shrill, high whistle pierced her ears. She raced through the doorway and into Denis's room. Guy leaned out the window, the netting billowing about him, the bone whistle in his mouth. Somehow, he'd removed the plug and he blew again and again, the piercing blast cutting through the humid air. If Philip hadn't known where they were, he certainly would now.

Jurissa pulled Guy back from the window and took the whistle away. "Why did you do that?" she asked.

"Silas tell me. He fix my whistle. Got to blow it when Massa Phip come. So Lono hear."

Jurissa shook her head. Had Silas actually told Guy that? He must have. Guy wasn't likely to have made it up. But what use would Lono, an old, crippled man be against the cruel and wily Philip?

## Chapter Twenty-five

In Louise-Marie's bedroom, *Docteur* Marchand straightened and turned away from her bed, shaking his head. "There's nothing more I can do," he said, glancing from her parents to Leon. "She's gone."

Louise-Marie's mother screamed and threw herself on the bed. Dr. Marchand restrained her from flinging herself across her daughter's body and beckoned to the maid. Monsieur Rondelet helped the maid bear his wife from the room, leaving Leon alone with the *docteur*.

"In all my years here I've never seen this sickness strike so early in the year," *Docteur* Marchand said, placing a comforting hand on Leon's arm. "Some say it's because of the war but of course it is not. The heat of summer brings bad air from the swamps, and this year summer has arrived in May."

Leon nodded, hardly aware of what was said. He couldn't pretend to inconsolable grief but he mourned the loss of Louise-Marie. She was so young to die, and he had never really tried to make her happy.

A servant appeared in the open door. "*Pardon,* Monsieur du Motier," he said. "Your servant Guinon comes with a man of color named Silas."

His words jerked Leon from his preoccupation and filled him with apprehension. "Take me to Silas," he ordered, excusing himself to the *docteur*.

Silas waited in the foyer as Leon strode to him. "Why are you here?" he demanded.

"Miss Jurissa, she say don't be bothering you, Massa Leon. I got to. She in bad trouble. She be needing you. Guinon, he don't want to be bringing me where you be. I makes him."

"Never mind all that. What's happened to Miss Jurissa?"

"She take Guy and go to Dindon. Massa Philip, he come home. He go looking for her. He gonna find her."

Winterton had come back early, Leon thought. Why? Did he suspect something? "When did Miss Jurissa leave home?" he asked Silas.

"Yesterday. Massa Philip, he bang on the gate afore the sun come up this morning. I be there by my ownsome. Ole Hook, he dead. Yubah, she tote Miss Merlette in the cart to Miss Tiana 'cause Miss Jurissa say to. Massa Philip, he mad, he ride off. Say he gonna whup Miss Jurissa and the bitty boy, too."

Leon stared at the giant Negro without focusing on him, his mind sorting through possibilities. Why had Jurissa taken Yubah's son with her? Winterton must have been abusing the boy. Would Winterton go to Dindon? The old plantation had seemed the perfect place when he'd tried to find a safe place for Jurissa to stay temporarily. He'd counted, though, on Winterton being away until her ship had sailed.

He couldn't take the chance that Winterton wouldn't head for Dindon. *Mon Dieu,* it was past noon and the man had been searching since early morning. Had he found Jurissa? Was it already too late?

He grasped Silas's arm. "Come, help me saddle Tigre."


Jurissa gave up any thought of locking herself and Guy into the bedroom. Even if Guy hadn't blown the whistle and given away their presence here, once Philip entered the house and found the mare, he'd know. A locked door wouldn't stop him, whereas it would trap Guy and herself. They'd be better off on the ground floor. It was a slight chance, but perhaps they could elude Philip by slipping from room to room.

She started for the door, then remembered the rapiers. If she was forced to, she'd kill to protect Guy. Hurriedly dragging the case from under the bed, she lifted Guy, carrying him and the case down the stairs.

There was no need to caution Guy to be quiet; he was terrified of Philip. The heavy case slowed Jurissa, so she hid it in a cubbyhole under the staircase, unlatching the lid. She might need to grab a rapier in a hurry. Still carrying Guy, she picked her way through the rubble until she reached the center of the house. Peering through a hole in the partitions, she watched for Philip, listening apprehensively for his entry.

He strode boldly in through the front, litter crunching under his boots. "Jurissa!" he called. "I know you're in here."

Guy trembled in her arms and a shiver of dread snaked along her spine. She waited until she was certain which way Philip was headed and picked her way through the rubble in the opposite direction. Though she tried desperately to be quiet, it was almost impossible with the debris on the floor. Guy clung to her fiercely.

"You can't get away, little rabbit," Philip told her as he went from one room to another, driving her ahead of him toward the foyer.

Could she run for the door, reach his horse, mount and gallop away with Guy before he could catch them? Even if he rode her mare bareback, Yvette was old and slow. He couldn't overtake them. But if she did escape, she could think of nowhere they'd be safe.

She'd have to take a stand here. Making up her mind, Jurissa started for the staircase, intent on reaching the cubbyhole where she'd hidden the rapier case. Her foot dislodged a piece of brick that had been supporting a pile of rubble, and it all came rattling down.

She heard Philip's shout of triumph and dashed

for the staircase. By the time she realized he'd doubled back rather than coming up behind her, it was too late. She couldn't reach the rapier without him seeing her. She stopped abruptly and set Guy down.

"Run for the back door," she ordered in a whisper. "Head for the swamp and hide there. Hurry." She gave him a push and, after one frightened look at her, he obeyed.

If Lono had heard the whistle, he'd find Guy. He'd keep him from harm in the swamp. It was a slim hope, but the only one she had for Guy's safety. There was no hope for her.

Philip rounded the turn by the staircase and caught sight of her. She made no attempt to run and faced him as bravely as she could. Philip strode to her and grasped her arm.

"Where's the brat?" he demanded.

"I didn't bring him here," she said.

Philip slapped her. "I heard the whistle."

"I blew the whistle. Someone will come."

He laughed. "With DuBois on a ship headed east and du Motier standing vigil at his sick wife's bedside, I doubt that. Unless, of course, you have admirers I haven't yet met."

He dragged her into what had once been the sitting room and looked around. "Not milady's choice of boudoir, perhaps, but we'll have to make do." He kicked aside broken bricks and chunks of plaster to clear a space on the soiled carpet. Belatedly realizing what he meant to do, she tried to pull away.

He tightened his grip. "There's no place to run, little rabbit. I intend to claim my right as your husband here and now. I find it amusing to take you amidst the ruin of your lover's plantation house."

Thrusting his leg behind her, he pushed her backward. Unbalanced, she fell to the floor. A cloud of dust rose from the carpet, choking her. Before she could move, he was on her, yanking her skirts up and over her head. As she fought to push the cloth away from her face, he jammed his knee between her thighs.

Jurissa struck at him wildly. He grabbed her hands, brought her wrists together and pinned them above her head with one of his hands. She tried to writhe away from him, but his weight prevented her from squirming loose. She continued to struggle, detesting his touch, determined to fight until he knocked her senseless.

Intent on the struggle, she heard nothing except Philip's harsh breathing and was taken unawares when he suddenly let her go, sprang to his feet and whirled around. She sat up hastily, pulling down her skirts.

Lono, a long pole gripped in his hands, stood facing Philip, his wrinkled face grim. So quick she could hardly follow the movement, Lono twirled the pole, aiming at Philip. He jumped to the side but the end of the pole caught him, causing him to grunt.

Jurissa edged away from them and stood up. If she could get to the staircase she could arm herself with a rapier. Between her and Lono, they might best Philip. Lono swung at him again but this time Philip was ready and leaped clear. He bent down to pull something from his boot. Not waiting to see any more, Jurissa made a break for the staircase. As she reached the cubbyhole and pulled out the black case, she heard a cry of pain. Flipping open the lid, she grabbed the hilt of one of the rapiers and lifted it free. She turned back toward the sitting room and gasped. She'd forgotten Philip carried knives in his boots.

Lono was sprawled on the floor, his hand on the knife hilt protruding from his chest. Philip stood over him.

"Snakes, hear me," Lono gasped. "Strike this man dead." Blood gushed from his mouth and he twitched and lay still.

Philip swung toward her, then froze when he saw what she held.

"Stay away from me," she warned.

"You don't know how to use it," he countered, advancing slowly.

"I may not be an expert but I'll do my best to kill you." Hatred throbbed in her every word.

Philip's eyes searched past her as she raised the rapier until the point was aimed at his heart. She expected him to try to rush her and take the sword away so she tightened her grip on the hilt. He took a quick step to her right, and she shifted to keep the point toward him.

Before she knew what was happening, he'd darted to her left and around her. She whirled but he wasn't rushing at her. Instead, he pounced on the black case and yanked out the other rapier.

"Now I'll have the chance to test your ability, little rabbit," he said, smiling as he swished his blade through the air between them.

Jurissa gave way as the point of his rapier flicked at her. She knew nothing about fencing. She had no idea how to defend herself, but she refused to drop her weapon. Edging away from him, she found her back against the wall near the gap where the front door once hung. Philip's rapier danced and twirled in front of her, clanging against her blade time and again as he mocked her with his swordplay. Her hand aching, she hung on grimly.

His point touched her gown between her breasts and ripped along the material. She felt its prick against her skin. He drew it back, grinning, and she took advantage of his momentary inattentiveness to slide over into the opening.

Without warning she was pulled backward so abruptly she lost her breath. The sword was jerked from her hand and she was set aside. She stared in disbelief. Leon!

He drove in at Philip, their rapiers flicking at one another like gigantic snake tongues. Jurissa, hands clenched together, watched in dread fascination as the deadly game of feint, thrust, parry, thrust, and circle played itself out in front of her. When Leon forced Philip to the staircase, she crept inside the foyer, her eyes never leaving the two men.

Philip lunged, Leon sidestepped and broke away, coming back to feint, changing ground, pressing Philip. The swords clanged together, separated, met again. Philip thrust and the tip of his rapier scraped along Leon's cheek, drawing blood as he leaped sideways. Jurissa held her breath until she realized Leon was in control, feinting, then thrusting at Philip until he drove him up several steps of the staircase.

As she watched, it became clear to Jurissa that Philip meant to kill Leon, while Leon was doing his utmost to disarm or disable Philip. She fought the urge to shout at Leon to run Philip through before Philip succeeded in killing him. If she spoke she might distract Leon and that could be fatal. Though she fretted over Guy's whereabouts, she couldn't tear herself away from this life or death duel.

Suddenly Philip leaped to the side and down the steps, lunging at Leon even as he landed on the foyer floor. Only Leon's quick sidestep saved him.

"I see those years with the pirates weren't entirely wasted," Leon drawled.

"I'm good enough to take you, du Motier," Philip retorted. "You're a dead man. As you once tried to make me by throwing me over the rail."

Leon's reply was a feint and a thrust that raked along Philip's arm, tearing his sleeve. Blood welled in the cut. He circled away from Philip's lunge, then drove Philip toward the sitting room with a series of thrusts, each one drawing blood but not seriously wounding Philip. She began to wonder if

Leon was toying with him. What a dangerous ploy!

"You bastard," Leon muttered at Philip when he caught sight of Lono's body. His rapier flicked so rapidly Jurissa could hardly follow its motions, and Philip retreated from Leon's fury.

Leon pressed him harder and harder until, with one final thrust, he jerked upward and Philip's rapier clanged to the floor. Leon put his boot on it, the tip of his own sword pricking the skin over Philip's heart. The two men stared at one another.

Leon had once said Creoles didn't soil their blades on men like Philip. But she knew, as Leon must, that as long as Philip was alive, he was dangerous.

The thudding of hoofbeats startled her. More than one horse, by the sound. The two men tensed, then Philip took the decision away from Leon by flinging himself backward and rolling away from Leon's downward thrust. Too late, Jurissa saw what Philip meant to do. She cried out in warning but by then Philip had jerked the knife from Lono's chest and flung it at Leon.

The knife struck Leon, staggering him. He sprawled onto the floor but retained his hold on his sword. Keeping her wits about her, Jurissa grabbed Philip's discarded rapier. Philip glanced toward the gaping front doorway, the sound of the hoofbeats coming nearer and nearer, then turned and raced for the back of the house.

About to kneel beside Leon, Jurissa held, hearing a cry that froze her blood.

"*Maman!*" Guy shrieked.

Giving one last agonized glance at Leon, she ran toward the back, toward the sound of Guy's voice. When she came to where the mare had been tethered, she halted in horror. The mare was gone and, through a hole in the wall, she saw that Philip, Guy slung over his shoulder, rode bareback on Yvette, urging her across the fields toward the swamp.

"No!" she screamed, rushing outside.

A gray horse galloped past her. Silas! She stopped, breathless. Philip forced the reluctant mare into the swamp and disappeared. The gray stepped into a hole and stumbled to its knees, catapulting Silas over its head. He climbed to his feet, stood for a moment shaking his head, then, ignoring the limping gray, ran toward the swamp. Jurissa watched until he, too, disappeared. In the swamp, a horse was at a disadvantage to being on foot. Silas would be able to catch up with Philip if he didn't lose sight of him in the dense foliage. But what then? Philip was as deadly a killer as the swamp. She greatly feared she'd never see any of them alive again.

Leon! Nothing in the world but her fear for Guy ever could have made her turn her back on the injured Leon. He might be dying! Jurissa raced back to the house, calling his name.

Leon, no longer on the floor of the sitting room, sat on the stairs. Beside him, Nicolas LeMoine cut away Leon's right trouser leg where the knife hilt protruded from Leon's thigh.

"Leon!" Jurissa cried, dropping to her knees and gazing into his face. "Oh, Leon."

She was vaguely aware that Yubah was descending the stairs carrying bundles, but her attention was focused entirely on Leon.

"As you can see, I'm still alive," he assured her.

Yubah knelt beside Jurissa. Leon grimaced as Nicolas eased the knife from his leg. Yubah stanched the blood with a clean cloth.

"Hold this, Miss Jurissa," she said.

Jurissa pressed the cloth against the wound while Yubah readied one of Tiana's packets. By the time she had it fixed and Jurissa eased the cloth away, blood oozed rather than gushed from the cuts. Another length of cloth bandaged the healing poultice against the stab wound and Yubah stood up.

Nicolas offered his arm to Leon but he shook his head, getting to his feet without help, but favoring the injured right leg. His bad leg.

"Another few centimeters to the right and he'd have missed me entirely," Leon said, smiling onesidedly.

"I feared he might have killed you," Jurissa told him, placing her palm against his chest as though to assure herself he was actually alive.

Leon put his arm around her. "I'm hard to kill."

"Nicolas, seem like you could be toting poor ole Lono out back somewhere," Yubah said. "I got to be fixing the rice."

There were questions to ask Yubah but questions could wait. As Nicolas went one way and Yubah the other, Jurissa leaned her head against Leon and put her arms around him. Without words, they held one another.

"He took Guy," she said at last, her voice trembling. "Into the swamp."

"Silas said you had Yubah's boy with you. I heard him cry out. Why would Winterton—"

"Because he hates you. And Guy isn't Yubah's. Guy is your son. Your son and mine."

Leon held her away from him and stared into her face, his eyes wide with shock.

"I tried to tell you before," she said. "At the lake."

"*Mon Dieu!*" he let go of her and ran a hand through his hair. "We have a child? Why didn't you let me know from the beginning?"

"I was wrong not to," she admitted. "I let Yubah pretend she was the mother and that was wrong, too. Oh, Leon, I've made so many mistakes."

"It seems we've both done nothing but make mistakes ever since the *Yarmouth* anchored off New Orleans." He shook his head. "Louise-Marie is dead of yellow fever, Jurissa."

The tears she'd held back overflowed and ran down her cheeks. "Poor Louise-Marie," she said brokenly. "And we've lost Guy as well."

Leon put an arm around her and she collapsed against him, sobbing.

"Ah, *cherie*, you've had a terrible time of it," he murmured, stroking her back. "Yubah says Silas went into the swamp after Winterton. Both of them will be hopelessly lost by now. But I know that swamp almost as well as Lono did." He put

Jurissa from him. "I'm going after our son."

"Your leg—"

"He's my son!"

"And mine. I haven't been wounded. I can help you."

"No, no, you must stay here. The swamp's no place for a woman."

"I want to help. I must help. How can you ask me to stay here while you go in search of Guy?"

*Cherie*, it's because I want to keep you safe."

"Safe! What do I care about being safe with Guy in danger and you, scarcely able to walk, hobbling after him? What if you collapse in the swamp? Who would know? I'm coming with you—don't try to argue, you'll only waste precious time."

"Jurissa, try to understand."

"We're both going. He's my son as much as he's yours and you need my help." She gestured toward his bloodstained bandage. "Your leg's still bleeding. We both know you favor that leg because of your war wound. This new injury can only aggravate the old wound. You need me to lean on. Admit it."

Leon threw up his hands. "What can I do with such a stubborn woman? Very well, come along." He limped briskly toward the back of the house.

Jurissa hurried after him. Outside, there was no sign of Nicolas but Yubah crouched by a ruined wall, tending a small fire. "We're going after Guy," Jurissa told her.

Yubah reached out a hand as though to catch at her gown but dropped it again, shaking her head.

Jurissa glanced at Leon's set face and bit her lip,

aware he must be denying the pain each step was costing him. How long could he keep up this pace? she wondered as she tried to stay on an even keel with him. His leg had to hurt terribly. Yet he was the only one who knew the swamp. She dared not go into it without him. She remembered how lost she had been when she had escaped the British. Could he last until they found Guy?

They were perhaps a third of the way to the dark line of cypress trees that separated the fields from the swamp when Leon stumbled. As she caught his arm, Jurissa thought for a moment he might have stepped into a shell hole as the gray gelding had done. She realized she was wrong when, leaning heavily on her shoulder, he tried to take another step. His right leg buckled under him, refusing to bear his weight.

Leon clenched his jaw and tried again, staggering forward. Jurissa glanced at the bandage and gasped. It was dripping blood.

"Stop!" she cried. "You'll bleed to death if we go any farther."

He paid her no attention, persisting until finally she couldn't hold him up any longer, and they both sprawled onto the ground.

"I can't bear it if I lose you, too," she said as she helped him sit up.

"We won't lose Guy," Leon told her. "We can't."

"Lono cursed Philip as he died. He told the snakes to find him. I hope they do. But what if the snakes find Silas and Guy as well? Oh, Leon—" She rested her head on his shoulder.

"It's not the snakes—" He stopped and pounded his fist on the ground. "If only I'd run that bastard Winterton through when I had him at my mercy."

Nicolas arrived as she was struggling to get Leon on his feet. "Allow me," Nicolas said, taking her place, and helping Leon to his feet.

"You're going back to the house," she told Leon firmly.

Balancing on one leg with Nicolas's support, he stared toward the cypresses for a long moment, then sighed. "May *le bon Dieu* guide you, Silas," he said quietly.

Back at the house, Leon refused to rest on the bed. Yubah had cleaned the floor of the dining room, and he propped himself against what remained of an inner wall so he could look out toward the swamp through gaps in the outer wall. One of the rapiers rested at his side. Jurissa removed the bloody bandage and rebound his thigh with a clean cloth.

As she finished, he reached over and caressed her hair. "You've been so brave. What other woman would defend herself with a rapier?"

Jurissa sat back on her heels. "I meant to tell you I found the rapiers in a case under the bed in Denis's room. I thought they might have been his."

"Denis's rapiers have been lost for years—to think you found them!" He reached for the one by his side. "No wonder they look and feel familiar— Denis taught me how to fence with them. It's almost as though he knew how desperately we'd need his swords." He tried to sit straighter and winced when he moved his leg. "We'll hang them in a place of honor when the new house is built."

We? Jurissa thought. When I'm still married to Philip? How could it be? She touched Leon's hand. "When I thought Philip had killed you," she said, "I was so afraid."

"I've been in agony for weeks thinking of him touching you, hurting you while I tried to find a way to free you."

"I was fortunate in one way—his *amoureuse* kept him too busy to bother with me."

He took her hand in both of his. "I'll never let you go again. You're mine; you've been mine from the first, not his."

Nicolas came into the room with a tin cup full of water and offered it to Leon. "Miss Tiana, she says if you lose blood, you must drink to make more. All we have is water."

"How did you know where we were, Nicolas?" Jurissa asked.

"My sister sent a message when Yubah arrived at her place with Merlette. I came because I was not going to allow Yubah to return to that prison of a house. I planned to slip away with her and sail to France where that beast Winterton would never find her. But then Silas came to tell us what had happened and so we rode here as fast as we could." He shrugged. "Now—who knows?"

Yubah carried in a pot and set it on the floor. When she lifted the lid, the savory smell of rice and beans filled Jurissa's nostrils. She felt, though, that she wouldn't be able to choke down even one mouthful.

At her insistence, Yubah and Nicolas sat across from her and Leon and shared the meal, eating with spoons Yubah had brought. The rice dish was as good as it smelled, but Nicolas was the only one with any appetite and the only one who tried to make conversation. Later, as they sipped coffee, even he was silent.

Yubah suddenly sprang to her feet. "I got to say it," she cried. "I be knowing all along Silas be the one."

"I don't understand what you mean." Jurissa said, frowning up at her.

"I think I do." Leon set down his cup. "Yubah's talking about the *Yarmouth*. Winterton accused me of tossing him overboard from the ship."

"I knew you hadn't," Jurissa said. "You wouldn't." She shifted her gaze back to Yubah.

"Silas, he never be hurting anything," Yubah said. "He always take care of me best he can; never want nothing bad to happen to me. That night he go crazy when he see Massa Philip come at me. Silas, he pick Massa Philip up and he drop him down in the water. Be thinking for sure he drown. Seem like Massa Philip come back from the dead. Silas be saying he a devil, not a man."

"I sometimes thought he was, too." Jurissa shuddered, remembering Philip's cruelty.

Leon gripped her shoulder. "I'll kill him before I ever let him touch you again."

Leon would keep her safe from Philip but Philip already had Guy. God only knew what he meant to do to her little baby. She prayed Silas would be able to save her son.

But the swamp was as treacherous as Philip.

## Chapter Twenty-six

"I dug a grave," Nicolas said after Yubah had gathered up the dishes and taken them away. "I'll bury Lono if you'd like me to."

"I want to be there." Leon shifted, trying to stand and Nicolas hurried to lend him a hand.

They all gathered by the rough grave while Leon said a prayer for the old man who'd been a friend to the du Motiers for so many years. Afterward, they piled bricks atop the ground to make a protective cairn. Leon's leg refused to support him after he'd placed the first brick, and he leaned against an oak, watching the others.

When they were through, Nicolas lifted the rapier he'd laid beside the grave. "I'll stand watch at the back of the house," he said.

Leon nodded and Nicolas, taking Yubah's arm, walked with her away from the grave.

"Leon, you must rest," Jurissa insisted.

"I keep seeing Guy sitting so proudly on Tigre's back," he said. "How could I not have known he was mine?"

"Please come inside again. We can see the swamp from the dining room."

"I should have realized the boy was mine the first time I set eyes on him. Something about him drew me to him but I was too blind to recognize the blood tie."

Her heart ached for Leon. "He made you his hero," she said, "the mighty *chevalier* who allowed him to ride Tigre."

Leon lifted the rapier he'd placed in the crotch of the oak and swished it through the air. "Damn Winterton!"

"Lean on me," she urged. "We'll go into the house."

When she got him settled on the dining room floor once again, Jurissa sat next to him and laid her head on his shoulder.

"Guy summoned Lono with the whistle," she said. "Lono's coming saved me; he died for me. I pray Lono's curse against Philip comes true."

"Lono was a *candio*, a chief, in Africa," Leon said. "The du Motiers respected him. After he was freed, he watched over us. I have a feeling, when he saw Guy, he knew it was a du Motier who called him for the last time."

A lump rose in Jurissa's throat. Poor little Guy. He was so frightened of Philip and it would be worse at night, in the swamp.

Leon stroked her hair. "I can't blame you for not telling me about our son, *cherie*. I'm equally at fault for what has happened. My heart breaks for our brave little boy. If this damn leg—" His voice broke and, touching his face, she found it wet.

Remembering how he'd come to her the Christmas Guy was born and cried in her arms, tears welled in her own eyes. She should have told him the truth then.

"Guy's alive," she cried. "I know he is. He has to be!" Her voice broke on the last word.

They clung together for comfort while evening shadows darkened the rubble-strewn rooms of Dindon.

"Someone comes!" Nicolas's warning cry brought them both to their feet.

Leon gripped the rapier's hilt in one hand as he limped toward the back, leaning on Jurissa. Before they reached Nicolas, Yubah darted away from the house, running toward the man staggering across the shell-pitted fields toward them.

"Silas!" she cried.

Nicolas hurried after her. Dusk shaded the fields, making it impossible for Jurissa to see if Silas carried Guy. If she ran ahead, she'd leave Leon behind and she refused to do so. Whatever happened, they'd face it together. Love was more than Arabel had taught her, more than sweet kisses and passionate caresses. Love was also standing together in the face of adversity. She held tightly to Leon's arm as she watched Silas's faltering approach.

Nicolas caught up to Yubah and they reached Silas at the same time. Nicolas took something from Silas and handed it to Yubah. Guy? It must be! But was he alive? Jurissa held her breath.

Yubah hurried ahead of the two men as Nicolas supported Silas toward the house. Unable to wait any longer, Jurissa pulled at Leon's arm and slowly they headed into the field to meet Yubah.

"Guy, he be fine!" Yubah called.

Jurissa blinked back her tears as, under her breath, she thanked God. Seeing Leon's lips move, she knew he was doing the same.

"*Maman,*" Guy whimpered when Yubah transferred him into Jurissa's arms. He appeared dazed but unhurt.

Leon bent over his son. "My brave boy," he murmured, ruffling Guy's hair. "My little *chevalier.*"

Yubah rushed back to Silas. With Yubah on one side and Nicolas on the other, Silas stumbled forward until he reached Jurissa. She gasped in horror when she saw the knife embedded in Silas's chest. Philip must have had a knife in each boot.

"Can't you help him?" she asked Nicolas.

He shook his head. "If I pull out the knife, he will die."

"Be dying anyhow." Silas pushed the words out with effort. "Seeing dream show me how that devil-man, he gonna kill me. Ole snake get him first afore I break his neck. He be dead for sure." He looked into Jurissa's eyes. "He ain't never gonna come back this time. You and Yubah and the bitty boy, you all be safe."

"Silas," she said, placing a hand on his arm. "Please don't die."

"I be knowing you help Yubah," he said to her. His knees buckled, and the combined efforts of Yubah and Nicolas couldn't support him. Silas crumpled to the ground.

Yubah threw herself to her knees beside him.

Silas gasped out a few words to his sister, so garbled Jurissa couldn't make them out. His eyes rolled up; his body lurched convulsively and went limp. Yubah hugged him, weeping.

Nicolas knelt next to her, easing her away from Silas's body and into his arms. "He saved us all, your brother," Nicolas said. "A brave man; remember him that way."

Yubah gazed at Jurissa, her eyes swimming with tears. "Silas, he tell me, 'Name be Lono.' Don't be knowing what he mean."

Jurissa shook her head. The words made no sense to her, either. "I don't understand what he meant. I know what I intend to do, though. I'm going to give Silas's name to Guy for his second name so he'll carry the memory of your brother all his life." She turned to Leon and he nodded his approval.

"Yubah," he said, "as soon as your mistress and I can arrange it, you will be a free woman." He clapped Nicolas on the shoulder. "Take her to France if you must, but I hope you'll decide to stay on in New Orleans."

It being May and hot, Silas's funeral had to be hastily arranged. He was buried in the du Motier family plot at St. Louis Cemetery. A week later, searchers found Philip Winterton's decomposing body in the depths of the swamp behind Dindon.

"They informed me he was bitten by a snake, just as Silas said," Leon told Jurissa, who was staying in her old apartment at Tiana's. "Old

Lono's curse brought down his killer."

"It may be sinful to feel such relief he's dead," she replied, "but I can't help it. Philip brought misery to so many people."

"I've other news. *Cousine* Anton's assistant has assured me Winterton's estate will be quickly settled. Before he sailed, Anton had written to a Virginia attorney he met while in Washington and that attorney has sent papers that prove without a doubt the Virginia claimant has no rights. Yubah's manumission papers have already been started. As soon as the estate is settled, you can sign them and she'll be free. By July, I'd say."

"Wonderful! Yubah insisted on being a free woman when she married. Now she and the very impatient Nicolas can plan a July wedding. I'm so happy they decided not to leave the city."

Leon pulled her into his arms. "Nicolas isn't the only impatient man around. There's no need for us to wait until July. I can't bear being apart from you. I know the cottage is no mansion but I want you there with me. You and Tanguay Silas du Motier. I've officially registered him as my son and so he ought to be with me. The three of us should be together."

"Your friends will be shocked at you marrying again so soon," she murmured, winding a curl of Leon's hair over her finger.

"True friends will understand. The others—" He shrugged, dismissing them.

"I think Louise-Marie would understand," Jurissa said. "I sometimes thought she suspected we loved one another but she liked me in spite of it. She was a good and honest woman."

"I know. She tried to be everything a wife should be. It wasn't her fault she couldn't be you."

"I'd like to name our daughter after her."

Leon stared at her, his expression so shocked that Jurissa laughed. "When we have one, I mean."

"For a moment I thought this was an announcement." He bent his head and kissed her and, at the touch of his lips, Jurissa forgot everything except Leon.

His kiss sent the deliciously urgent message she knew so well and had missed so long. How many times had she'd dreamed of being in Leon's arms once again, of answering his kisses. She could hardly believe he was really here with her. Before her senses were completely overwhelmed, she drew back enough to whisper, "What if Guy—"

"I promised him a ride on Tigre if he was a good boy and stayed with Yubah until I came back downstairs. Besides, I locked the door." The tickle of his mustache against her ear sent frissons of delight along her spine.

He lifted her, carrying her into the bedroom. He eased onto the bed beside her and crushed her against him. The ever-new thrill of his lips and his caressing fingers made her long for more. Her arms wound around him, holding him tightly. The feel of his need ignited a quivering warmth deep within her.

*"Dieu,* how I've missed holding you," he murmured. "Even a lifetime will never be enough. You're the most beautiful woman in the world."

"As I recall, you also think I'm the most infuriating."

"I wouldn't want you any other way. Or perhaps I should say I want you any way at all. Every way."

She laughed deep in her throat. For the moment nothing existed except Leon and their love for one another. She reached for the button at the neck of his shirt and unfastened it.

"You always were impatient," he said huskily, pulling off the shirt before setting his lips to her throat. "One of your more desirable qualities."

Slowly he undressed her. His hands, then his lips caressed her breasts until she arched to him, moaning. He touched her, kissed her everywhere, driving her frantic with desire. He quickly shed the rest of his clothes. As she reached for him, her fingers brushed the bandage on his thigh.

Jurissa drew her hand away. "I keep forgetting your leg's not healed yet."

"Never mind my leg," he told her, his voice husky. "Don't stop now."

She nestled against him again, and when she touched him he groaned and raised himself over her. She cried out in joyous pleasure as they became one.

"Only you, *cherie*. You've always been my only love." The words, whispered in her ear, lodged in her heart.

"Leon," she breathed. "My love, my love."

Then words became impossible. Unnecessary. Caught in the magic rhythm of life, Jurissa experienced anew the wonder and the rapture of being joined with Leon in love.

He held her afterward, stroking her hair. "We will always have each other," he said tenderly. "You will always be my beloved wife."

Leon, Jurissa, and Guy were established in the new house at Frere by March. Guy accepted with equanimity the announcement that Jurissa was his mother and Leon his father, behaving as though he'd known it all along. The elder Madame du Motier was delighted with her grandson and also pleased about the marriage. But she declined to join them at Frere.

"*Docteur* Marchand has convinced me I should remain at Joyau," she said, "by asking me to marry him. Now that I'm certain Leon has his heart's desire, I'm relieved of my responsibility to see him settled and I've decided to accept the *docteur's* proposal. After all, we're old friends."

"Old friends!" Leon said to Jurissa later, in private. "Her blush gave her away. *Maman* won't admit it but she's very taken with the good *docteur*. As for him, he's always admired her. This is a love match, you may be sure. I couldn't be happier for them."

At first Jurissa had some difficulty adjusting to the du Motier servants after her more familiar, friendly relationship with Yubah and Silas. While she could never accept slavery in her heart, as Leon's wife she was a du Motier and knew she must make compromises. That didn't mean she couldn't try to change the existing order and, as a beginning, she set up a school for the slave children, as well as for the adults who chose to come.

Yubah, who was now Tiana's partner in the bakery, traveled out to Frere often. When, on the fifteenth of March, Jurissa saw the LeMoine cabriolet pull up in the drive, she smiled in happy anticipation of Yubah's visit. With pride, she watched Yubah march up the steps to the front door, for that had been the first battle she'd won: convincing Yubah she had the right to come to the front door of any house where Jurissa lived.

Jurissa's smile faded as she saw what Yubah carried. Surely that was a baby, yet it couldn't be Yubah's. Her child wouldn't be born until late summer.

"I never be so surprised in my life," Yubah said as she settled herself on the loveseat in the sitting room beside Jurissa and laid the bundled-up baby on her knees. She unfolded the blanket that protected the baby from the chill March wind, and black eyes in a dark brown face stared solemnly up at Jurissa.

"A boy?" Jurissa asked.

Yubah nodded. "Miss Merlette, she don't be telling me where she been all this time; she hardly say anything 'cept about the baby. 'My new *amoureux* won't let me keep him,' she tell me. " 'Anyway, I promise Silas to bring him to Miss Jurissa. You take him to her.' She don't say please. She don't wait to see if I gonna do it. She just sashay out of there and leave me with this boy."

Jurissa, bending over and cooing to the baby, was rewarded with a wide, toothless smile.

"Be Silas's, I can tell," Yubah went on, pride in

her voice. "He already awful heavy to carry. Gonna be a big man, this Lono."

Jurissa blinked at the sound of Lono's name, remembering Silas's dying words. So this is what he meant. How could he be so sure Merlette was carrying his child? How could he know the child would be a boy? The same way he foresaw the manner of his death? It was a mystery she realized would never be solved.

Guy came running into the sitting room, as he did every time Yubah visited. His eyes widened when he saw the baby on Yubah's knees, then he smiled. "I thought Silas forgot," he said, gazing down at the baby.

Both women stared at him. "What do you mean you thought Silas forgot?" Jurissa demanded.

"Silas promised me. He said he was sorry he took my Belle away but he'd send me a baby boy to play with. I waited and I waited." Guy touched the baby's cheek with a tentative forefinger.

Lono's hand closed around Guy's finger. Guy grinned and turned to his mother. "He knows me. He likes me."

Jurissa could hardly see her son for the tears in her eyes. She heard boots in the foyer, and Leon strode into the room.

"There you are, son. Have you forgotten our riding lesson?"

"No, Papa. But come, look. Silas sent me my baby." He ran to his father and grasped his hand. "Can I keep him? We can teach him to ride when he gets big enough."

Leon caught Guy up into his arms and walked

over to peer down at little Lono. He glanced from Yubah to Jurissa. She nodded and he raised his eyebrows. "You can explain later," he told her.

Hugging Guy to him, he ran a caressing hand over Jurissa's hair and let it drift to rest on her shoulder. "Silas had already given me more than any man could ask for," Leon said. "How could I know he had another wonderful gift in store? We'll not only keep his son, we'll love him as our own, forever."

# Now you can get more of HEARTFIRE right at home and $ave.

## Preview Four Brand New ZEBRA *Heartfire* Romance Novels...

## FREE for 10 days.

## No Obligation and No Strings Attached!

♥

*Enjoy all of the passion and fiery romance as you soar back through history, right in the comfort of your own home.*

Now that you have read a Zebra HEARTFIRE Romance novel, we're sure you'll agree that HEARTFIRE sets new standards of excellence for historical romantic fiction. Each Zebra HEARTFIRE novel is the ultimate blend of intimate romance and grand adventure and each takes place in the kinds of historical settings you want most...the American Revolution, the Old West, Civil War and more.

# **FREE** Preview Each Month and $ave

Zebra has made arrangements for you to preview 4 brand new HEARTFIRE novels each month...FREE for 10 days. You'll get them as soon as they are published. If you are not delighted with any of them, just return them with no questions asked. But if you decide these are everything we said they are, you'll pay just $3.25 each—a total of $13.00 (a $15.00 value). **That's a $2.00 saving each month off the regular price.** Plus there is NO shipping or handling charge. These are delivered right to your door absolutely free! There is no obligation and there is no minimum number of books to buy.

---

## *TO GET YOUR FIRST MONTH'S PREVIEW... Mail the Coupon Below!*

Mail to:

HEARTFIRE Home Subscription Service, Inc.
120 Brighton Road
P.O. Box 5214
Clifton, NJ 07015-5214

**YES!** I want to subscribe to Zebra's HEARTFIRE Home Subscription Service. Please send me my first month's books to preview free for ten days. I understand that if I am not pleased I may return them and owe nothing, but if I keep them I will pay just $3.25 each; a total of $13.00. That is a savings of $2.00 each month off the cover price. There are no shipping, handling or other hidden charges and there is no minimum number of books I must buy. I can cancel this subscription at any time with no questions asked.

NAME

ADDRESS                                                                APT. NO.

CITY                                    STATE                ZIP

SIGNATURE   (if under 18, parent or guardian must sign)
Terms and prices are subject to change.                                 2466

# SURRENDER TO THE
# PASSION OF RENÉ J. GARROD!

**WILD CONQUEST** (2132, $3.75)
Lovely Rausey Bauer never expected her first trip to the big city to include being kidnapped by a handsome stranger claiming to be her husband. But one look at her abductor and Rausey's heart began to beat faster. And soon she found herself desiring nothing more than to feel the touch of his lips on her own.

**ECSTASY'S BRIDE** (2082, $3.75)
Irate Elizabeth Dickerson wasn't about to let Seth Branting wriggle out of his promise to marry her. Though she despised the handsome Wyoming rancher, Elizabeth would not go home to St. Louis without teaching Seth a lesson about toying with a young lady's affections—a lesson in love he would never forget!

# AND DON'T MISS OUT ON THIS OTHER
# HEARTFIRE SIZZLERS FROM ZEBRA BOOKS!

**LOVING CHALLENGE** (2243, $3.75)
by Carol King
When the notorious Captain Dominic Warbrooke burst into Laurette's Harker's eighteenth birthday ball, the accomplished beauty challenged the arrogant scoundrel to a duel. But when the captain named her innocence as his stakes, Laurette was terrified she'd not only lose the fight, but her heart as well!

*Available wherever paperbacks are sold, or order direct from the Publisher. Send cover price plus 50¢ per copy for mailing and handling to Zebra Books, Dept. 2466, 475 Park Avenue South, New York, N.Y. 10016. Residents of New York, New Jersey and Pennsylvania must include sales tax. DO NOT SEND CASH.*